THE CROWN OF STONES

Magic-Price

Dear Tabetha,

May your life be as magical as the books that line your shelves!

C. L. Schneider

C. L. SCHNEIDER

ISBN: 1492829064
ISBN 13: 9781492829065
Library of Congress Control Number: 2013919478
CreateSpace Independent Publishing Platform
North Charleston, South Carolina

To my dad
Thanks for buying a young girl an old typewriter.

ACKNOWLEDGEMENTS

Above all, I want to thank my husband Bryan, who somehow kept finding the patience to share me (day and night) with a computer. It wouldn't have been possible without you.

To Dawn, for diligently reading and listening, and reading and listening, and reading, and reading—and reading. But mostly, for always believing. Thanks for driving off the cliff with me!

To my friends and family; the best cheerleaders I could ever ask for.

Special thanks to Alan Dingman, for taking the image in my head and transforming it into an amazing cover. And to Marco Palmieri at Otherworld Editorial; your excellent, professional advice was like finding the missing piece of a puzzle.

MIRRA'KELAN
(THE RESTLESS LAND)

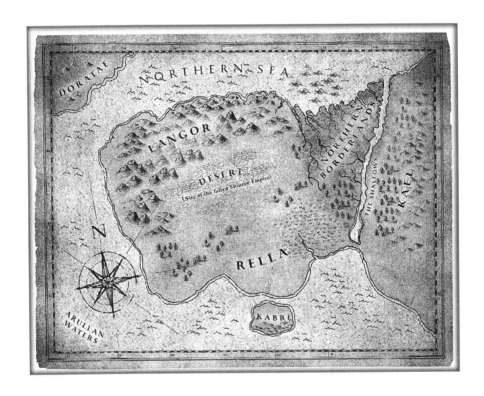

PROLOGUE

Bodies pressed in on me on all sides. More were piled up beneath my feet. The grass, gorged with assorted fluids and trampled remains, squished under my boots as I carved open my opponent's chest, pushed him aside, and moved onto the next.

There was always a next. The Langorians were a swarm…an inexhaustible, savage, mindless swarm. And we had no choice but to become like them to survive. To become animals, going at each other, mechanically pushing against the tide, battering whatever stood in our way with whatever we had; clubs, axes, swords, knives—our bruised, bleeding bare hands. Fighting for days, months, years, striving to hold out against an enemy that knew nothing of mercy, an enemy stronger, and far more brutal than us, we'd become something less than we were.

And we were still losing.

I grabbed the Queen's arm and steered her out of the fray. "We can't take much more of this." Needing to be heard, I drew her close. "We should pull back."

"Pull back?" Queen Aylagar Arcana yanked herself free. She gave me a wild, defiant look. Full of passion and reckless resolve, it made her exotic features come alive. "My order stands. We press on, Troy. As always."

I shook my head. "Our numbers are dwindling too fast. We can't win this."

"We can and we will." Aylagar raised a hand. She touched my face, and the sound of metal clashing and men screaming seemed to fade away. Brushing back the blood-splattered white strands that had come loose from my braid, she ran a finger down the strong line of my jaw. "Trust me, Love. The Langorians will not have Rella."

"How can you still believe that?"

"Because I must. Because I have faith."

"Ayla…" I hesitated. But it had to be said. "I saw the messenger arrive from Kabri. I know he carried orders from the King. You can't keep ignoring them."

She dropped her hand and backed up. "My husband is a fool. I don't care how many messengers he dispatches from his throne, he is not out here. The blood of these men bathes *my* skin, not his. This is my war, Troy. Mine!" she cried. "We fight. We die. We go on until we prevail—by my command. I will not surrender. That is the way of it. That is the only way."

My throat went dry at the fire in her. The way she stood, outlined by the backdrop of chaos, flanked by the crackling flames that consumed our camp, with sweat beading on her dark skin and battle-lust glazing her stare, I wanted to pull her into my arms. I wanted to go back to this morning, on the furs of her tent, when Aylagar's flawless ebony skin was on me. Where status and race didn't matter and death felt far away. Mostly, I wanted to believe her as I had so many times, that every battle brought us closer to victory. That persistence was our greatest strength, and it would carry us through.

But this was it. King Draken of Langor was throwing everything he had at us, making one final push to wipe us all out. To once and for all lay claim to the land his forefathers had sought, and failed, to conquer. Surrendering was unacceptable; she was right in that. Yet, Aylagar had lost her way. Somewhere along the line, the outcome had stopped mattering to her as much as the fight, and my affection, my awe of her, had blinded me for far too long.

"Give me the order," I demanded. "Let me shift the odds."

Her dismissal was quick. "No."

"We can't keep going like this, sword for sword, day after day, until there's none of us left. Let me cast hell down on these black-hearted bastards."

"I have given you my answer. And it is no different than the last hundred times."

I moved closer. "You know what I can do. My magic can give us an advantage the Langorians can't match. We can stop this fucking, never-ending war, Ayla. We can stop it together, with steel *and* magic. If you'll just—"

"You are Shinree," she hissed. "Your kind are meant to do as they are told. Yet, after six years in the ranks you still push for something that I will never bend to."

"Then you're as big a fool as the King."

Her hand, that only a moment ago had caressed me, struck my face. "My husband forced your service in this army upon us both. And from day one, when you stood in my tent, a young man, eager to please, drooling with the urge to cast, I made it plain that this conflict would not be solved with magic. It's dishonorable. I don't trust it. I forbid it. You are my best soldier, Troy. I have given you free reign in my bed, but not out here. Not in battle. Ever. Is that clear?"

Staring at her, my heart went cold. "I don't think I can do this anymore. Fighting as half a man. Ashamed of what I am because you don't approve. I'm not just a soldier." I held up the sword in my hand. I called to the stones embedded in the leather-wrapped handle and they began to glow. Their vibrations pressed in through my skin, down into my veins, and the uncertainty washed away. "I'm a Shinree soldier."

"Put that magic away," she scolded. "Do you want to kill us all?"

"I can control it."

"Can you?" Her eyes were harsh. "Can you promise that when your spell steals the strength it needs to be born, that it won't steal from my men? That it won't steal from me? Your magic is a disease, Ian. Your need for it, your addiction, clouds your judgment. It threatens us all and undermines my orders."

"Your orders contradict my duty to keep Rella safe. I've tried to pretend they didn't. I've tried to be what you wanted. But I can't. I'm Shinree, Ayla. I *am* magic. And if you don't untie my hands, we will all die here today."

Stunned, Aylagar gaped at me. For a moment, there was a rare vulnerability in her eyes, a kind of resigned sadness. Then she raised her sword, turned, and re-joined the battle. She left me standing alone on the rim of the conflict, watching with a crushing sense of finality as the men I'd fought beside for years were being slaughtered.

I can save them, I thought, though they wouldn't do the same for me. A magic user, granted exemption from the slavery that kept my kind in check; I was tolerated at best. Lately, though, I'd seen it in their eyes, next to the pain, the hunger, and exhaustion. They no longer hated me because I might use magic and bring them harm. They hated me for not using it, for continuing to let them die.

Frustration pushed a scream from my lungs. A pang of rage and resentment sped through me. I pulled my second sword, dove into the mayhem, and started swinging. I sliced through bodies one after the other, trying to lose myself in the rhythm. I pressed forward, deeper into the madness; wrath blazing in my white eyes as I strived for an answer to the conflict burning inside me.

My magic knew nothing of sides. My spells fed without discrimination. They were selfish, heartless. They didn't care who was right or wrong, who was strong or weak. To create themselves they would drain friend as easily as foe.

In the villages they called me a champion, but I wasn't. I was a weapon. Somehow, I'd forgotten that.

I looked around me, at the dogged Rellan soldiers fighting for their realm, at the spirited Arullan warriors of Aylagar's homeland, and I made my decision.

I sent the magic back into the stones on my sword. *Not here*, I thought. *The cost is too great.* I had to get out in the open. Going against Aylagar's wishes was bad enough. I couldn't risk catching her army in the crossfire.

Spying an opening, I moved to make my way off the field, and the ground began to shake. In seconds, it was undulating with such force that none of us could stand.

It was inconvenient, but it was no surprise. *Mirra'kelan* was a fidgety continent that didn't stand still for long. And having fought for years in the worst of it (the disputed, quake-plagued region between Rella and Langor) we understood the land would quiver when it pleased. After, we'd all get up and resume the battle.

But today, something was different. The trembling wasn't stopping. The ground wasn't just cracking. It was rupturing. Not in slender, minute fractures as in times past, but in long jagged canyons that ripped across the field, dissecting the valley. In deep chasms that opened without warning, swallowing fifteen men at a time and spewing plumes of ancient dust high into the air. Hillsides were sliding away. Overhanging cliffs broke off and tumbled down. The entire landscape was being violently rearranged, as I lay watching, prone on the heaving, blood-soaked ground.

Coughing out the debris in my lungs, as panic broke out on both sides, I thought, *I should get up.*

I still had a sword in each hand. Enemies were all around me.

I should attack, now, while the ground is still shaking. Before they recover.

But as the land continued to buckle and roll, my attention shifted away from the quake and the battle, to the crooked crevice opening up alongside me, and the object buried within it.

Halfway down one wall, partially obscured by a layer of dirt, was a curved row of fused colored stones. Glowing softly in an array of shades, the stones—sapphire, spinel, diamond, ruby, obsidian—were pulsing, emanating a vibration that was definitely magic. Yet, its tone was unfamiliar. It was pungent. So sweet and alluring, I couldn't look away.

Sliding a sword into the sheath on my back, I scooted closer. The edge of the rift crumbled some at my weight, but I didn't waver. Buried in this very spot was the once sprawling empire of my Shinree ancestors, a fallen realm, lost and unseen by the world for over five hundred years. Whatever artifact the quake had uncovered was worth the risk.

I reached inside the hole. My fingers brushed the rounded lip, and an immediate intense current of energy licked my skin. It ran through me, and I let out a yelp. Not from pain, though. The jolt was one of pure pleasure. It was raw and acute, and I quickly wrapped my entire hand around the thing and held on.

Nine distinct, magical vibrations were alive inside it. I could feel them all, swirling and overlapping. Each had their own well of energy, but together they formed a compilation of searing, pulsing power that was vast beyond any magic I had ever experienced before. It was massive, concentrated.

Enthralled, I abandoned my other sword and started digging. Loosening the soil, I tugged on the artifact. It didn't take long for the dirt wall to collapse and my prize to come free. As I lifted it out of the hole, I shook it clean.

Fashioned like a King's crown, the circlet was pure perfection.

The others, the soldiers around me, wouldn't see it that way. They couldn't feel its magic, couldn't taste it. They had no idea the pleasure it could offer. Yet, simply looking at the stone crown opened a familiar sinking, wrenching pit of need in my gut.

Sweat beaded then poured off my skin. Tremors erupted deep inside me, rivaling those that split the valley floor. I was suddenly so empty, so hungry.

"Troy!"

I heard my name, but I didn't turn. It was Aylagar. I didn't want her to see me like this.

"Troy!" she shouted again.

The urgency in her voice tore at me. Aylagar was Queen. She was my commander and my lover. The ground had settled all across the field. Weary bodies were rising up, raising their weapons to resume the killing. She could be in trouble.

But as I stared at the ring of vibrating, colored stones in my grip, I knew what I had. And I realized I had no choice but to betray her.

The answer is here. It's in my hand...in this crown of stones.

It's always been in me. She was just too headstrong to see it.

Once more, Aylagar called me. This time, I pulled my eyes away and found her.

She was close and fighting her way closer. Trails of blood streaked her skin and clothes. But from the way she was moving, none of it was hers.

I can't let this go on. Good men are dying for her stubbornness.

I have to make her understand, convince her that I can end this. Make her see how we're fighting on borrowed time. That if it wasn't for me we would have been dead a long time ago.

She'll be furious, I thought. If I admitted that my spells had been sustaining the men, bolstering their endurance, tightening their aim and heightening their senses—so long they had no idea their own limits anymore. She would never forgive me.

But there are so few of us left now. She has to realize that magic is the only way.

Aylagar spun to block an attack from the rear. Pushing the man away, she caught sight of me. She gave me a brief smile. Her eyes were fierce and confident. For just a moment, I felt better.

Then a sword point burst through her left shoulder. Another pierced her chest. Aylagar went down and anguish consumed the last of my doubt. Pain obliterated the hope she'd given me. Consequence and reason bowed in the face of so much fury.

As I looked down at the stone crown in my hand, I had one coherent, desperate thought. *This ends now.*

ONE

S quatting down in the wet sand, I slid my knife in between her legs. "Hold still."

"Wait," she gasped.

I lowered the blade. "I won't hurt you. But I don't have time to wait." With a yank, I cut the rope around her ankles. "The bandit that jumped you, was it a man or a woman?" I freed her hands and then did the same for the old man beside her. There were no ropes on his ankles, as he only had one. His left leg was gone from the knee down. "Man or woman?" I said again, more insistent this time.

"Woman," the old man grunted. "And she was one wily bitch."

Anticipation tightened my grip on the knife. "Are you sure?"

Thin and raggedy, he squinted at me like I was a hundred miles away. "You saying I don't know a female when I see one?"

"Not at all."

"You think these wrinkles make me daft?"

"That's not…" I ran an exasperated hand over my face.

"Then maybe you're thinking I'm one of them damn eunuchs," he went on. "That just 'cause I'm a gimp I don't have a good working set of—"

"Father, please," the girl scolded. Shoving a curtain of frizzy brown hair out of her face, she shifted in the dirt to face him. "This man stopped to help us and…you're angering him," she whispered.

"I'm not angry," I assured her. "I just need to know."

"He ain't talking to you anyhow, girl," her father snapped. "Now, fetch me my crutch. It's in the wagon."

I offered his daughter a hand up. She gave me a hesitant look. I made the choice for her, gripped her arm, and pulled her to her feet. "I don't bite."

"Of course not," she said shyly.

I took my hand away. As she hurried the short distance down the road, her father's squint transferred back to me. "Just so we're clear…that was no man's ass bouncin' on my horse as it rode away. My *stolen* horse," he groused. "Damn filthy brigands, taking what they please, leaving nothing for the rest of us." Petulance made his long face even longer. "They make it so a man can't travel in peace anymore."

I glanced around at the flat open grassland and the sandy, barren road that seemed to go on forever. "You shouldn't be out here. Remote places like this are a haven for things a lot worse than thieves."

"Like you?" A knowing gleam twinkled in his eye. "You're that Shinree, fella. The one with the white hair and the eyes and the magic."

"We all have white hair and eyes, old man. And magic."

"Ha!" He wagged a bowed, shaky finger at me. "But they ain't all like you."

"I tell him every day that we should move," his daughter said, returning with a wooden crutch as worn and craggy as the man who used it. "It isn't safe, being on our own with no neighbors to speak of."

"She's got a point," I said, putting my knife away. Bending, I bore the man's slight weight and helped him stand. "King Raynan's law doesn't reach these outer regions. And Langor's border is no more than a day's ride."

"A point," he grumbled. "Rosalyn's always got a point. But that border's been nothing but a crooked line on a map for years. The Langorians don't cross it to bother us. They don't bother nobody. Not since the war. And you know that," he said to me, as I took the crutch from Rosalyn and positioned it under his arm. "You *saw* to that."

Rosalyn shushed him. She turned to me. "I'm sorry. He's always going on."

"It's fine." I stepped away to my horse. Having wandered off the road, the mare was uprooting great clumps of grass from the pasture and swallowing like she knew it wouldn't last. "I don't have much food," I called back to them. "I haven't seen a village for a while. I've been hunting on the road for weeks. But I'll give you what I can."

"That's kind of you," Rosalyn said, coming over. "But unnecessary." She lowered her voice. "My father doesn't mean any harm. You seem to be in a hurry, and…we don't want any trouble."

"Your father is trouble," I grinned.

Rosalyn hid a giggle behind her hand. "I know. I'm sorry."

"Your attacker, did she leave you anything?"

"Just the one horse. And the wagon. Really though, we're all right. I appreciate your charity, but we don't have far to go."

"It's not charity." I pulled out a flask and put it in her hand. "It's water."

Rosalyn offered me a grateful smile. Her close-set eyes were ringed and tired, but I saw strength in them, and outright unremitting endurance. It was a trait I was familiar with. And added to her brown hair and eyes, and her normal every-day features, I was able to say with confidence, "You're Rellan."

Her stare flitted to my hair. "And you're Shinree."

There was something in her voice. "You can't decide if that should worry you."

Rosalyn shrugged. "Our village is small. We don't go into the towns much, so…"

"Am I the first you've seen?"

"No, but you're not like them. You're not like the slaves."

"Because he's not one." Hobbling closer, her father wormed in between us. He leaned toward me so far I thought he would fall off his crutch. "Got business out here, do you? Planning on sneaking over and dealing those Langorian fuckers another round? Maybe you oughtta shove one of them spells of yours right up Draken's ass while you're at it. I'm all for that," he chuckled slyly, like we were in on some great conspiracy together.

"Sorry," I said. "I'm just passing through."

"Are you now?" He let out a snort. "Like they just let you Shinree folk run around all wild and free like you please. Only them healers get to do that, or one of them showy oracle types. And since every oracle I've ever met was looser than a bow-legged whore, I'm guessing you're not that."

Rosalyn gasped in horror. "Father! How can you say such a thing?"

3

"It's okay," I told her. "He's right. I'm not an oracle, or a healer." I glanced at her as I tied my bag shut. "And I'm not bow-legged," I said, making her blush.

Muttering to himself, her father backed up a step and made no attempt to hide his in-depth study of me. Boldly, he peered at my swords, my boots, the braces on my arms, even my dusty leather coat, like they told him everything he needed to know. "Yep," he said, decisively, "you're him. You're that soldier. That, Troy fella, who fought in the war."

"The war's been over ten years, old man."

"You think I don't know that?" Gravity deepened his tone. "I know what you did."

My jaw clenched. I looked past him to Rosalyn. Fear tainted her gaze now, but it couldn't be helped. "Which way did she go?"

"In there." Rosalyn gave a jerk of her head. I followed it to the large expanse of swamp to the east. Bordering all three kingdoms of Rella, Kael, and Langor, as well as the outskirts of the uninhabited wasteland where the Shinree Empire once stood, the broad swathe of marshland had been aptly (and unimaginably) named the Northern Borderlands. Encasing near the entire northeast and part of the south, the thick, dark, vast wall of vegetation was topped with an even thicker, darker roof of swollen clouds.

Where the swamp's edge bled out into the meadow was a good mile away. Yet distance wasn't doing a damn thing to blunt the sweet fragrance of rot on the wind.

"I hear the place is more foul than Langor," Rosalyn said nervously.

"Nothing's more foul than Langor." I studied the shadowy clouds gathering over the dense wetlands. "But I'm guessing it'll be a close second."

Her father tapped my leg with his crutch. "So what are you now? Ain't ever easy puttin' down the sword, so I'm guessing…mercenary? Bounty hunter? Or did she just piss you off?"

"I've done both. Mostly bounties for the last couple years. But, pissed off works too." Taking the reins in my hands, I stared back into the twisted mess of overgrowth and fog. Tracking through it would be difficult. *Not with magic*, I thought, knowing it wouldn't take much. *A simple tracking spell and I'd have her by nightfall.*

The stone on the cord around my neck warmed. My pulse jumped.

Tightening the reins in my hands, I shook off the urge. "When did she leave?"

Rosalyn scanned the sky. "Two or three hours ago?" Her gaze met mine. "So who wants her, your lady outlaw?"

"She escaped from the city prison in Kael a couple months back. But from the amount of bodies under her belt, I imagine a lot of people."

"Well, she's met her match now," the old man chuckled. "No way some girly with a sword is more dangerous than you, a Shinree soldier. I know what you did," he said again.

I nodded. "Do we have a problem?"

"I was an army man," he said, disregarding my question. "First Lieutenant. King's Regiment. In fact, the last time I had two good feet under me, I was standing guard at the castle gates. That was…" his eyes wandered, "must be twenty-five, twenty-six years ago. But you were probably too young to remember."

"Remember what?"

"How it smelled the day King Draken burned Rella's greatest city to the ground."

"Kabri," I said. "I was six. I remember well enough."

"Things turned straight to shit after that. Rella issued a formal declaration of war on Langor, and I sat around with this one leg," he slapped it angrily, "growing old and useless while everyone else went off and died defending my home."

Rosalyn put a hand on his arm. "Father, don't."

"Hush, girl." Craning his neck, he looked around me to the packs on my saddle. "So where is it then, that filthy piece of magic? I'm guessing there's no way King Raynan let you keep it."

I pictured the Crown of Stones where I'd left it ten years ago, in Rella's capital, on the island city of Kabri, nestled in the folds of Aylagar's burial robes. "It's safe."

He watched me a moment. "I get what it was like. I did my time on the line. Reports would trickle in…the massacres in the villages, the kidnappings. I can imagine the things you saw, how desperate it was at the end. The bastards were whipping us pretty good those last few months, but…damn, son…there had to be another way."

"Another way?" My anger flared. The expectance in his voice—it was like I owed him an explanation. Like he wanted me to swear that I'd tried everything else first. That I'd done everything I could to find a peaceful solution. It was what they all wanted.

But I hadn't. And I had to live with that truth every single day.

I said again, "Do we have a problem?"

Tilting his head, he held my stare pretty steady for his age. "Stories say Ian Troy could fell a man in less than a minute. Course, you were younger then. Probably take you at least two, now, eh?" Grinning slightly, he shrugged. "Nah, you best be on your way. I'm too old for problems."

"Good." I put a boot in the stirrup and climbed up into the saddle.

"And you got some chasing ahead of you, anyway," he added. "Chasing..." he gave me a measured, weighty glance, "and I'm thinking maybe some running too."

TWO

I landed flat on my back in the marsh. Cushioning my fall, the soggy ground swallowed me on impact then spit me back out. Thick, wet chunks of mud flew up, and the assassin was on me before they ever came back down.

"Now, let's have a little chat." Straddling me, pressing a thin knife against my throat, Taren Roe leaned in close. Her weight pushed me down. Silt gurgled into my ears. It sloshed up over my arms and legs, flowed thick and cold over my stomach and shoulders.

"We can talk all you want," I said. "But do you mind if I get up first?"

"Actually, I do." Her leather tunic creaked as she wriggled a bit to make herself comfortable. "I like it here."

"Glad you're happy," I said sourly, mourning the loss of my dignity and my sword. "But you're not the one sinking."

Tossing a chunk of muddy yellow hair out of her lean face, Taren's lips curved into a suggestive smile. "Don't you like me on top?"

"You're only up there because you didn't play fair. You distracted me," I said, eyeing the cord holding the front of her shirt together. It was dangling in my face. I could almost catch it in my teeth. *One, little tug*, I thought. That's all it would take to release the generous amount of pale flesh bursting out. *I don't even need my hands.*

"Well. Look at that." Snickering, Taren raised her body up slightly off mine. She looked down between her legs to where our breeches met. "I would never have thought, Ian Troy," pausing, she threw a measure of drama into her words, "notorious sword for hire and ruthless hunter of bandits and brigands, would ever sink so low as to be aroused by one of his own prey. But…there it is." She glanced back up at me. "Like it rough, do you? Or maybe it's just been a while."

"Maybe," I said, edging my fingers through the muck, searching for my sword, "you're just the most attractive bloodthirsty criminal that's sat on me in a long time."

"Is that why I'm still alive? You were hoping I might grant you a tumble before you kill me?"

"You're alive, Taren, because in the last three months you haven't slowed down long enough for me to catch you. Now that you have, I'd like to know why."

"Isn't it obvious?" She pushed the tip of the knife into my skin. "I'm surrendering."

I grunted a laugh. "You killed six guards in your escape from the city prison. You've ridden horses to death, one after another, barely stopping to eat or rest. You've led me through the mountains of Kael, clear across Rella to the edge of Langorian territory, and back again. And now you stop *here*." Mindful of the knife, I glanced around. "I could have gone my whole life without stepping foot in this fetid hole, and you've got us in so deep it's going to take weeks to get out."

"Sorry," she shrugged.

"What are you doing here, Taren? Why did you stop?"

"That poor excuse for a horse I was riding got stuck in a bog. I tried to get him out, but the lazy bastard just stood there."

"That's because he was stuck." I risked a slight, annoyed shake of my head. When she didn't object, I shifted my shoulders some, fidgeting to camouflage my continued hunt for a weapon. "I'm not buying your bullshit, Taren. You're an assassin. You hide in the shadows. Slit the throats of defenseless people for money. Put off a kill for days to avoid confrontation. Apparently, you steal horses from defenseless old men as well. But you don't sit and wait for me to show up so we can fight head on. And you don't surrender." I held her cold dark eyes with my pale ones. "You're up to something."

Taren leaned down. She put her grimy face in mine and pressed her leather-clad breasts against my chest. "Maybe, I let you catch me."

8

I laughed. "Who's looking for a tumble, now?"

"I admit I was curious to see if you were as pretty up close as you were from far away. After all, with the amount of dust I was kicking up in your face, it was hard to get a good look at those fabled Shinree features of yours. Now that I have," Taren ran a slow finger down the sharp slope of my nose, "it was so worth it." Her caress meandered over the well-defined bones in my face, then across my mouth and jawline. "I find most of your kind uninteresting to look at. They all seem so watered down."

"That's what happens after five hundred years of crossbreeding."

"But not you. You're different," she said thoughtfully, continuing to scrutinize me. "They really should make more like you."

"No, they shouldn't."

Fingers still wandering, Taren bit her lip. "Gods, but you are a tasty one."

"You can stop now."

"Why? Did I embarrass you? Don't you like standing out?" She read the answer on me and laughed. "Gods, Troy, get over it. You're a throwback. A relic. You don't blend with anyone, not even your own kind."

I didn't bother replying. Taren's amusement evolved into a peal of taunting laughter, and I knew, not only would she dismiss anything I said, she was right. Having been deliberately bred from two full-blooded Shinree, I was one of the few of my race alive to descend directly from an untainted line. That made my appearance literally straight out of history.

The old records describe my ancestors as tall with a build that's naturally strong and lean. The sketches show their keenly sharp features and tanned skin, their distinctive pure white hair and matching eyes. And I wear their stamp, blatantly. Not just physically, either. I could draw the energy out of any stone pulled from the Shinree mines, shape it and bend it to my will, quicker and better than most.

From the perspective of any breeder, I was the perfect Shinree specimen. From the perspective of the common man, I was an oddity, a curiosity, a danger. And they weren't far off the mark. If you combine my conspicuous appearance with the brutal history of the Shinree, as well as my own grave personal transgressions, the air tends to get real uncomfortable when I walk in a room.

Taren, however, looked a little too comfortable.

"What do you want?" I asked her, shifting in the mud.

"This." She lowered her knife inside the collar of my shirt and slid it under the thin strip of leather tied around my neck. Lifting the cord with the blade, she exposed the slender shard of obsidian fastened at the end. "I want this."

"The stone?" I hesitated. "Why?"

"It's pretty."

"It's a black rock. A poorly cut one at that."

"You're just being modest. We both know the energy it holds." She stared lovingly at the shard. "The wonderful dark power."

"There's no power, Taren. I picked it up on the road a while back."

"And you kept it, why? Because it matched your coat?" She laughed at me. The sound cut out abruptly. "It's been trapped for so long. Waiting," she said, in a dreamy, tender tone. "Waiting for you to feel it, to wake it up...to embrace it." Taren's eyes snapped to mine. "It calls to you."

"You're wrong."

"And you lie. I know what the stone is. Where it's from. What it can do."

"Drop the act, Taren," I said, faking disinterest even as my unease grew. "Whatever con you're playing, it won't work. You're Kaelish, not Shinree. Your kind can't use magic or sense it, which makes this stone nothing more than a chunk of black rock to you. So what do you want with it?"

"I could ask you the same. You gave up channeling magic a long time ago. Yet, you keep a piece of temptation on a string around your neck. So, what do *you* want with it?"

"I want you to get your filthy hands off it."

Taren lowered the knife to my chest and the obsidian went with it. Smirking, she asked, "What's it been, Troy? Ten years since you last cast a spell?"

"Something like that." Groping in the sludge, I stretched my arm out further. Finally, I felt steel at the end of my reach. I tugged it closer.

"Are we pretending to forget? Or wasn't your reason for quitting memorable enough?" Taren's eyes tightened. Her emerging grin was a cruel, devious expression that went well with her next words. "Slaughtering all those men. Killing your own commander. What was her name again, Rella's whore of a Queen?" Taren tilted her head pensively. "Oh, yes...Aylagar."

My temper spiked. "That's enough."

"Personally, I don't understand what you saw in the little dark savage, but I do like the way you repaid her attentions. A Queen shares her bed with you, a lowly Shinree, and you drain the life out of her with magic…along with several thousand of her soldiers." Taren's grin morphed into a proud smile. "It really was a brilliant strategy. Wipe out all the fighters on both sides so there's no one left to fight. I love it."

"That wasn't what I wanted. I didn't mean for it to happen that way."

"You should have. Rella and Langor had been at each other's throats for so long, the only way to bring the dogs to heel was to slaughter them."

I shook my head at her flippancy. "Guess you're not the sentimental sort."

"I can see you are. It's kind of cute, really. But," she bent and brushed my lips with hers, "how about I take your mind off all this unpleasantness for a while? And in return," slowly and meaningfully, she ground her body against mine, "you overlook that little bounty King Sarin placed on my head back in Kael."

"Which one?"

"All of them."

"Am I supposed to forget the family you murdered as well?"

She flashed a wicked grinned. "Which one?"

"I'm not bargaining with you, Taren." Beneath the bog, I tightened my grip the sword. "You're going back to Kael, one way or another."

"Come on, Troy," she whined. "It's a fair deal. It's been a long, lonely three months with nothing between my legs but the back of a filthy horse. And don't tell me you aren't interested," she snaked a hand down the front of me, "because I can feel otherwise."

"I'll live. In fact, I'll probably live a lot longer." I moved my weapon toward the surface. "Now, use the knife, bitch. Or get off me."

Taren frowned. "Here I thought you'd be charming, being a war hero and all."

"I'm not a hero. I never was."

I expected another crude quip, which would be her last; my sword was ready, just below the top watery layer of the marsh. But instead of more sarcasm or another bribe, Taren's expression went strangely blank. Her voice took on an odd husky, almost mannish, tone as she said, "I'm glad you understand that. A magic user is far too selfish a creature to ever be a hero."

Her body was completely still. She wasn't even blinking. "Taren?" She didn't answer, and a tingle of warning streaked across my shoulder blades. "Taren?"

She flinched. The knife in her hand jumped against my throat, nicking my skin. I barely noticed. I was too startled by the creepy way her eyes were rolling back in her head and the rapt, sightless stare she was training on me.

"The stone," Taren whispered, in the same, odd voice. "What do you want for it?"

Unnerved, I said, "It's not for sale."

"You answer so quickly. Can't we bargain?"

"Sure. We can bargain. Here's my counter offer." I hoisted my sword up out of the bog and slammed the muddy hilt into the side of her head.

THREE

"Damn it, Troy," Taren hissed, as I pressed a cloth against the gash on her head. "Give me that." Wrists bound, she yanked the rag out of my hand. She struggled to get up, but her ankles were tied too, and the slippery mud was unforgiving. "I'm starting to dislike you," Taren groaned, settling back down.

"Feeling's mutual." I gestured at her wound. "Tighter. You're getting blood on my rope."

She responded with a rude gesture. I ignored it and squatted down in front of her. Pushing a cascade of mud matted hair back from Taren's eyes, to ensure she saw mine, I said, "I need something from you."

"Really?" Taren bit her lip. "All you had to do was ask."

"Not that." I sat back on my heels. Reaching into my shirt, I pulled out the shard of obsidian. "Tell me why you want this."

That abnormal, unwavering glare she had before resurfaced. "To fix the circle."

"What circle?"

Almost like a song, she replied, "A beautiful circle buried in the sand, seamless and whole…until you found it." Her expression tightened. Her voice followed. "The piece wasn't yours to take. An ancient artifact, fashioned into the shape of a King's circlet, containing a bottomless well of magic…the Crown of Stones is the most remarkable and important piece of Shinree history ever recovered. And you broke it."

13

My entire body stiffened. *How can she know?*

I dropped my hand from the shard and stood up. Dozens of questions were spinning in my mind. All I could get out was, "I didn't break it."

Taren gave me a bored yawn. "A little over ten years ago, you brought King Raynan Arcana the Crown of Stones, along with the body of his dead wife. He buried Aylagar. You hid the crown—not very well, I might add. But before that, he broke off a part and gave it to you. You put it around your neck and haven't taken it off since."

Swallowing my unease, I said nothing for long while. I went from being shocked to thinking about denying it. To deciding there was no point. "You're right. Everything you said is true. But there were only two people in the room that day, and I've never spoken of it to anyone. Neither would he."

"Not willingly."

"Fuck you, Taren. You couldn't get within spitting distance to Rella's king."

She gave me a long malevolent stare. "You can't keep it. Though, I can see where you might imagine you have a right to it. Before you, the crown was nothing but legend. You made it famous. Or is that infamous?" she grinned. "But you have it backwards, Troy. It's the crown that has a right to you. It staked its claim the day you wore it." Inquisitively, her gaze wandered over me. "Odd, isn't it? Shinree have been wearing stones without incident for centuries…until your little episode with the crown." Her eyes settled on their target and she asked coyly, "Did it hurt?"

At first, I thought she was talking about the set of small scars concealed beneath the fall of hair across my forehead. Likely, in our tussle, Taren had seen them. But she wasn't referring to the faintly colored impressions left behind where the crown had touched my skin. She was speaking of a more visible branding.

On the left side of my head, no more than two finger widths wide, was a mark. By ordinary human standards, it was far from disfigurement. But I'm not ordinary. And magic doesn't wound the same as a sword. It doesn't mar the skin or inflict lingering pain. It simply left me with a bit of color where there should be none. A splash of inky darkness set against the light. It was a stain that would likely go unnoticed on anyone else. Yet on one like me, a full-blooded Shinree whose heredity demanded their hair lack all color, a band of pitch-black streaking through the white was stark and undeniable. It was blatant proof of the darkness in me. It was my punishment for taking in more power than I had a right to. And it was there forever, for all to see.

"If you kept that piece of the crown out of some twisted homage to the lives you took—to her life," Taren added loudly, "I think you can give it up now. Your precious Queen Aylagar has been warming Death's bed for a long time. She doesn't give a damn how many ways you bleed for her."

Rage roared out of my throat. "I could end you right now, Taren! One spell…and I could end you."

"Then do it. Cast on me." At the horror on my face, she smiled. "You know how good it would feel. The heat. The swell. The release. It's been so long since you pulled it inside. One time won't hurt. And I promise I won't tell."

"You won't tell because you'll be dead. That's how it works. I cast. People die."

Taren leaned forward. "Show me the violence in you. The power."

"You're crazy."

"I can hear your heart beating faster. See the heat building on your skin."

"Stop it."

"Need," she gasped, her breath quickening, "it burns in your eyes. It pounds in your head." Taren's mad gaze tightened. Her voice dropped an octave. "It twists in your stomach."

"Stop!" I shouted. Because the more Taren spoke, the more my head began to hurt. Knots were forming deep in my gut. My nerves were pulsing, crawling like a mass moving underneath my skin. On nothing more than Taren's words, the abrupt urge to channel magic was on me, stronger and faster than it had been in a very long time.

I took a breath, trying to rein myself in.

"Just look at you. Afraid to move, to think. Like the slightest thing might drop you over the edge." A corner of Taren's mouth lifted in amusement. "I know what kind of Shinree you are. Battle skills, soldiery, and all that comes with it, is the sole line of magic in your blood. You were born to do harm. So go on. *Do it.*"

"I told you. I don't use magic anymore." But even saying it, I could feel something shift inside me. The ever-present thought of letting go, of releasing what I kept locked inside, was moving from the back of my mind right up to the front.

Temptation was stirring.

One spell. Just one and she'll be dead. The months of chasing will be over. I can return to the city of Kael, collect my pay, and move on. Except…

I'll be moving on as a magic user.

The thought left me cold.

I can't. I've worked too hard to give in now.

Swamp trailed off my legs as I stepped away. I wanted a moment to clear my head. Yet, as I put distance between us, my thirst for magic waned.

A few more steps and it disappeared completely.

Seeing my confusion, Taren grunted. "There's a reason your people are enslaved, Troy. A reason the Shinree have been kept drugged and stupid for the last five hundred years. Do you know what it is?"

"We're dangerous."

"You're pathetic."

"You're not looking so great yourself."

"Is that how you cope, with quips and jokes? By acting like channeling magic doesn't get you hard?" Bits of the ground flew off the ends of her hair as Taren shook her head. "You can't deceive me. I know what desire looks like. I've seen the faces of the Shinree healers when they cast, the pleasure that runs through them…the helpless need that brings the poor bastards to their knees." Her eyes raked over me. "I want to see you that way, *witch*."

"Why? So you can kill me when I pass out after?"

"There is that," she conceded, with a knowing, provocative smile. "But I've always wanted to know how it felt to pull power into your veins, to command it…to let it fill you. It must be wonderful."

"It is."

"Then how can you possibly control it? Feeling the aura in a stone is inborn for a Shinree. Yet only you, Troy, seem capable of resisting its call. Why is that?"

"I don't know. I guess most aren't willing to try."

"Most don't have a choice." When I didn't reply, her head cocked to the side. "You aren't troubled by that? You accept the slave laws that regulate your people?"

"I accept that the alternative is too risky. Allowing my entire race to be free, to cast magic at will…countless would die every day to feed our spells."

"So, you believe the Shinree should be condemned to live forever in captivity? Forced to serve, being bred and educated on the whims of their masters?"

Annoyed at her as much as I was at myself for indulging her, my voice sprung up, "What the fuck do you want me to say, Taren?"

"I want you to say that drugging them is wrong. That the *Kayn'l* elixir given to the slaves doesn't just stop their magic, it numbs their senses. It steals their memory."

"*Kayn'l* takes away their ability to do harm, intentional or otherwise."

"It makes them mindless."

"What if it does? At least they're incapable of the things I've done."

Taren froze. "You envy them. How interesting."

"It's not envy. It's…." Unable to stop myself, the words poured out. "I'm not like them, Taren. I wasn't born in some labor camp. I wasn't bred to sweep floors or plow fields. I was made as a weapon, a means for Rella's King to protect his land. And because of a deal Raynan Arcana made with my mother, I'm locked on that course by a spell until the day I die. If Rella calls me to defend her, I go. I have no hope of living any other life. No choice but to do what I was made for. That's the cost of *my* freedom, Taren. I know it. I live it. But some days…it's just real hard to pay."

I walked away. Taren called after me, but I was done with her incessant questions. I was ankle-deep in swamp to do justice in the name of Kael's king, not to waste ten years of abstinence on one mouthy criminal. "Should have gagged her," I mused aloud.

It was an offhand remark, but the idea stuck, and I found myself heading in the direction of my horse to find something to stuff in Taren's mouth. It wasn't far. Unfortunately, there were no straight lines in the swamp and even less solid ground. As a result, what looked like a quick trek wasn't. Hopping from one scattering of rock to another, clinging to patches of vine-choked trees; as I slogged through the endless gooey mire, I did my best to avoid the slender stagnant streams that dissected the spongy ground like outstretched fingers. I wasn't sure what kind of creatures called the coiling waterways home, but I'd seen their dark shapes darting below the cloudy surface. I'd also seen the regurgitated remains of their dinner on the banks, and I wasn't interested in adding my bones to the pile.

At last reaching my dozing brown mare, I ran a gentle hand over her back. "It's all right, girl," I said softly. "We'll be leaving soon."

Kya opened her eyes. Her response was a curt blow of air through her nose and a head toss that was clear petulance. I didn't mind the attitude, though. Kya was one of the few constants in my life. She was the only company I could tolerate for long, even if too many years with me had made her moody.

Picking clumps of mud from her mane, I yelled back at Taren. "Where did you leave your mount? If the poor beast is still alive, I'll make sure he gets back to his owner. That was pretty low, by the way," I added, "jumping a one-legged, old man."

Taren didn't answer. After a minute or two, I glanced over my shoulder. I figured she was unconsciousness or sulking. I was wrong on both counts.

Sloshing eagerly though a stream so deep it swallowed her thigh-high boots clear to the cuff; Taren was free of her ropes and coming toward me.

"That was fast," I said warily. "How'd you manage it?"

Taren stopped. She raised her right hand, displaying a ring on her second finger. The stone was large and red, and radiating a gleam that was far too brilliant to be natural.

"Magic?" I heaved a sigh. "That's how you stayed ahead of me all those months? That's what's been going on with your eyes and your voice?" I ran a hand over my face, nodding at what perfect sense it made. "There's been a spell on me this whole time? Making me follow you, making me—"

"Passive? Compliant? Chatty, even?" She nodded. "Now you get it."

My teeth ground in anger. My hand went to the sword at my hip. I came close to drawing the one at my back, but I wanted a hand free to wring her neck. "Who gave you the ring?"

The stone she wore pulsed. Taren opened her mouth. She worked her jaw back and forth a few times, as if she'd forgotten how it worked. Then a low, dark, decidedly masculine voice overrode hers. "I will see it now."

Shit. I tightened my grip on the sword. "See what?"

Swirls of red crept across the brown in Taren's eyes. "I will see you on your knees." Her ringed finger pointed at me. A wisp of something sharp crackled in the air.

"Wait…" I said.

Energy surged across the small space between us.

"Taren—stop!" I cried, as a swell of pure power smacked into me. I was suddenly on the ground, on all fours, with icy hot tendrils streaming out of the obsidian shard.

The tendrils sunk down, slithering into me.

I looked up at Taren. "What have you done?"

FOUR

"Well?" The man speaking through Taren Roe sounded pleased. "How does it feel to be free?"

Vibrations filled my veins, painful and invigorating. Energy stroked my nerves. I could barely answer. "Free…?" I shuddered.

"Using shame to suppress your magic, shackling your body with grief… Your condition, Troy, your years of self-inflicted slavery, they're over. I've broken your bonds and set you free."

"No… This can't be." My breath was ragged, my mouth dry with fear. "I didn't call to the stone. I didn't pull it in." Frantically, I dug my hands in the sludge, clenching my fists, trying in vain to stop shaking. "You're…not Taren. You're Shinree."

"Obviously." Taren's long legs lifted high up out of the water, and she came closer. "It's a little more challenging to be attacked by one of your own kind, isn't it?"

"Glamour spell," I wheezed out. "You're using glamour to wear her body."

"Close. But I'm not wearing it. I'm controlling it. Though, controlling you is far more amusing." Taren pointed at me with the ring again, and another surge of throbbing heat sped through me.

"Gods…" Wincing, struggling not to like it, I shook my head. "You can't do this. You can't make me cast."

"I'm pushing magic into you. Is it so hard to believe I can pull it back out?"

"Don't. *Please*," I begged. "You have to stop."

"I've found the perfect weapon to use against you, Troy. Why would I stop? Forcing you to channel magic when you have struggled to stay clean of it every day for ten years...it's foolproof. It's far more lasting than wounding you with a sword. And I need only strike once. One hit, one spell, is all I need to break you."

I pulled my hands in closer. Thick black strings of mire clung to me as I pressed my palms down, gritted my teeth, and forced myself up. "Why are you doing this? I have no quarrel with any of our kind."

"Quarrel? I'm not your enemy. I'm your savior. I'm here to show you that magic isn't a flaw to be hidden. It's a gift."

"It's a fucking curse!" I cried out, so forcefully I almost fell over again. "When I use magic, people die."

"I'm counting on it."

"No." Adamant, I shook my head. "I won't do this."

"You have no say. Magic is not a choice."

"It is for me."

"Are you that dim? Do you think yourself cured? Or do you truly not remember what's it like to go without, to suffer through that interminable space between the last time you cast and the next?" Anticipation bringing him closer, heavy wet drops kicked out as Taren moved swiftly through the stream. "The hunger, the emptiness...how it burns inside you, growing, twisting, shredding wits and reason until you're absolutely sure something is eating you from the inside out. And when you can't bear it anymore, you cast to make it go away. Then a little later...it starts all over." Coming to a halt just out of reach, Taren crouched down on a narrow stretch of grass to gaze at me. "I'm sorry, Troy, but it's time to pull your fucking head out of your ass and accept the truth. *This* is what it means to be Shinree."

He whispered a single word through Taren's mouth, and the sensations on me multiplied. Spasms of pulsing pleasure licked at my nerves. Vigor pumped through my veins. Wave after wave of stone magic broke over me, saturating my insides with an explosion of power so great, I thought my skin would rip apart.

It was outright euphoria. My swagger, my claims and convictions, couldn't hold up to its might. They crumbled and got swept away, and in their absence, was something I'd never thought to feel again: complete satisfaction. I was sated. Magic was filling a void in me that I hadn't even known existed.

Gods, help me. I've missed this.

"I pity you." The man shaped a disconcerting look of sympathy onto Taren's face. "All that time you wasted, wrapping yourself in denial, fighting to strip away every morsel of your heritage. Falsely believing you could alter your very being. And for what? You've overcome nothing, changed nothing. It's quite sad, really."

Trembling, I panted at him. "I...am going...to kill you."

"No, you're going to cast for me as many times as I require until I'm done with you. And, as far as your instinct to do me harm...it's understandable. But I don't recommend you try."

"You can't hurt me. You don't have the blood for it. If you did, you wouldn't need to hijack *my* spells. And a soldier can't dominate a body anything close to what you're doing. You're..." I couldn't think. "You're something else."

"What I am is more powerful than you."

I flashed him an impudent, unsteady grin. "Yet, you hide inside a woman?"

Taren's nostrils flared. Words escaped her gritted teeth. They were no more than faint mutterings, but I knew the cadence and the inflection, and I braced myself.

It did no good.

The air changed. The spell formed, and a barrage of white-hot points of power blasted into me. I toppled over as they penetrated my skin, searing like blades heated over a fire. Stabbing shoulders, limbs, chest, and head; the unseen arrows plunged in, tore back out, then drilled in again. Their relentless attack repeated, over and over. Helpless, writhing on the ground, cool mud coated my skin. All I could feel was fire and agony.

I let loose a desperate, gut-wrenching cry, and the spell ended. The pain left a moment later, as if all that had been required to make it stop was an admission of weakness.

Trembling, I lifted up onto my elbows. Spitting gritty lumps of swamp from of my mouth, I shook a mass of sopping hair from my eyes and growled at him, "Where the hell did you learn a spell like that?"

His reply was a low, eloquent laugh. It went on so long I had visions of separating his head from his body with my bare hands just to make it stop. But his body wasn't here.

The man's laughter faded. With it went the unnatural color tainting Taren's eyes, and it was suddenly just her standing above me; staring down with an expression that was almost apologetic. I wanted to hate her it for it, but I had no time.

Taren walked away, and the magic left me. A departure made worse by my years of temperance, it was abrupt and excruciating. Like a hand reaching down inside and ripping a part of me out. Pleasure came next, penetrating the pain, fusing with it until I couldn't tell one from the other. Together, they overran my nerves, sweeping over me and through me, stroking and stimulating the smallest, darkest parts of my soul.

Deprived of breath and awareness, I lay trembling in the mire, as my body became a furious cyclone of energy. It was unbearable, yet, I was smiling. I'd surrendered myself into the grip of a well-trained whore, and I was reveling in her touch, letting her do as she willed to me without regret.

Regret would come later, without fail. Now, I was magic-blind. Caught in a phase that amounted to no more than a hairsbreadth of climax, an instant where it was virtually impossible to give a damn about anything.

I drifted in it happily.

Too long, I thought, savoring the moment. *It's been far too long.*

Distressingly quick, it began to dwindle. And with pleasure's departure, the black aura of the obsidian rose up out of my body. It lingered in my eyes, lending them color. The hue's presence diminished my ability to see, which made the tail-end of being magic-blind not just an arbitrary term.

Thankfully, my interval of sightlessness was brief, and I spent it as I always had: cold, weak, and vulnerable; unnerved by the frailty and nakedness of the moment, and trying to pretend that my utter defenselessness wasn't near as long as it felt.

I let out a quivering breath of relief as my vision returned. I refused to think about where my spell was headed, or who it was aimed at. That damage was already done. Instead, I sat and shivered, wishing I were blind again so I couldn't see the swamp going black and withering around me.

Harvesting without discrimination, my magic would steal from the birds, the lizards, and the plants—Taren. Everything within range would die, except me. As a Shinree, my donation was far less. It would weaken me, likely to the point of unconsciousness. But I would live. I would wake up to the damage I'd done and the lives I never meant to take.

I gasped as the spell glided near me. Its touch was cold and fierce. It robbed my breath like a gust of winter wind. Then it swept through me, and stole what meager bits of strength I had left on its way out.

FIVE

B lurry-eyed, I lifted my aching head. I started to get up, but my legs were too floppy. My fingers were numb from how tightly my hands were bound behind me. Groggy, my throat dry, I groaned, "Where am I?"

"Where do you think?"

"Who...?" It took me a moment. "Taren?"

"We're in the palace of the Duke of Doratae. His giant, golden hawk came and flew us over the sea while you were sleeping. Dinner is about to be served but..." reproach entered Taren's voice, "I'm not sure you're dressed for it."

Blinking, my vision clearing, I glanced around. Above me was overgrowth and clouds. At my back was a moldy tree trunk, one of many, as I sat in a pool of thick, black marshy water that reached nearly up to my waist. "Fuck you," I said.

"I tried, but you weren't interested."

My head started clearing. Clarity returned in a sudden rush, and I remembered the Shinree man that spelled her and what he did to me. My pulse spiked. "No..." Dread sunk deep inside. Nausea climbed up my throat, stealing my breath. I could barely speak to curse her. "You...bitch," I sputtered out, glaring up at Taren.

She glared back with this faint, amused, almost aroused expression.

I wanted to rip her apart. I yearned to make her bleed—but not with steel, with magic. And it wasn't just a passing thought. The idea of casting on Taren, of relishing in the power coursing through my veins while she suffered, was so prevalent. It was instinct. I could feel it, tunneling in and spreading out. Urge and temptation were invading together, searching for the weak spots, striving to take root. Promise wrapped around my anger, bolstering it with a guarantee of pleasure that even now, as I fought against it, was chipping away at the scraps of resolve I had left.

It was just like the man inside Taren had said—foolproof. He'd set out to undo me with a single spell, and he nearly had. But I'd had years to build up my defenses against magic's call. As good as it felt, I could hold out a little longer. I had to, especially against Taren. She wasn't worth it.

And with that notion in my head, I shoved it all away; the fear of becoming what I hated, the panic. Like every time before I'd walked out onto a battlefield, I buried the impulse and the fury coursing through me. Indulging it was too risky. Giving attention to the cravings was equally dangerous. Ultimately, it would reach a point when I couldn't ignore them any longer. But for now, I had some restraint. I could keep my head about me and focus on what was important. At the moment, that was finding out what Taren knew.

I gave her a once over. "You look better."

"Why, thank you." Taren shook out her freshly washed hair. "It took most of the water you had left, I'm afraid, but," she ran a leisurely hand down the front of her mud-free tunic, "it's very sweet of you to notice."

"I was talking about your eyes. That evil red glow?"

"Oh, that." She shrugged it off and took a drink from the flask in her hand. "I'm glad you're finally away. I was getting bored out here all alone."

"I'm surprised I am awake at all," I said, wincing at the kinks in my back. I stretched and moved my fingers, trying to wake them up. "You wasted a perfectly good opportunity to stick a knife in me."

"Are you complaining?"

"It wasn't what I would have done."

"And it wasn't my idea." Taren spun around. She walked away, and I immediately started working on the ropes. I kept my eyes on her, though, and I couldn't deny I got a sick sort of enjoyment out of watching her try to stay clean. Jumping gracefully over fallen trees, tiptoeing across thick patches of muck like it might actually keep her from sinking, all the while, mud splashed up the sides of her long legs.

By the time Taren came to a stop next to my horse, she was as grubby as the mare—and in just as bad a mood. Hair matted, reins dragging, hooves lost beneath water dark as dusk, Kya did not look happy. As Taren made a play for her snarled mane, I wasn't surprised when she bared her teeth and backed up.

Taren hissed. "Your horse doesn't like me."

"Don't take it personal. Kya doesn't trust anything on two legs."

"Can't imagine where she got that from." Grabbing hold of Kya's bridle, Taren yanked her closer. "It's remarkable how the beast went untouched by that spell you let off. Care to tell me how the horse survived when the trees died clear to the roots? Did you witch her?"

"Once. It was a long time ago."

Taren gave Kya a quick inspection. "She looks normal."

"So do you. And you survived the spell."

"Guess someone wants me alive."

Taren shoved the flask into one of the packs on my saddle. After fastening the bag shut, she secured the others. Both my swords were shoved into the girth on Kya's right side, and she checked them as well. Smartly maintaining a firm grip on the bridle, Taren bent down and plucked the ends of the reins out of the water.

Straightening, she tilted her head back and stared at the sky. "Damn. It's getting dark already."

I followed her gaze. Only a few streaks of low hanging sun poked through the thick overgrowth of green and brown. "Going somewhere?" I asked.

"Thought I was." Taren wrapped Kya's reins around a cluster of vines and trudged back to me. "Now it looks like I'm sleeping here...with you." Her expression changed. Her brown eyes fixed on mine. I could see her thinking, but I wasn't sure about what. Slinking across the swamp, giving me a determined, suggestive smile, I couldn't tell if it was murder or sex on Taren's mind. As she straddled my lap, wound her arms around my neck, and kissed me, even then I wasn't sure.

Pulling back, she ran her tongue over her lips. "Mmmm...so that's what Shinree tastes like."

She moved in to kiss me again, and I turned my head. "Who gave you the ring?"

"Silly question." Her mouth hovered over mine. "One of you, of course."

"He hired you to kill me?"

"Not kill you. Just get you away…far, far, away." She sat back and slid her fingers into my hair. Raking them down, forcing her way through the clumps of dried mud and tangles, she grabbed onto the black ends resting against my jaw and tugged. "I still don't understand this. I thought you people only gained color when you cast a spell."

"That's our eyes," I said, impatiently. "Tell me about the Shinree who hired you. Casting through someone, forcing another to use magic; those aren't things easily done."

Taren yawned. "I wouldn't know."

"Healers mainly influence the body. Oracles command spells that manipulate the mind. Most of us can use glamour in one form or another, but I've never heard of anyone that could take someone over from a distance. And that attack he threw at me was classic soldiery. His skills just don't mesh."

"Sounds like you have a mystery on your hands."

I tried to catch her eyes. "One you can help me solve."

"Sorry." She ran a few kisses down the side of my face. "I'm busy."

"He's using you, Taren. What do you think will happen to you when he's done?"

Blowing out a breath, Taren straightened and drew her legs up. She propped her elbows on her knees, rested her dimpled chin in her hands and looked at me. "You have a woman sitting on you and all you want to do is talk about another man?"

"If you answer my questions, I'd be happy to move on."

"I say we move on now." Taren pulled a dagger from her right boot. She lifted off me some and kicked my legs apart. Kneeling between them, she lowered the point of her dagger until it touched the waistline of my breeches.

"Careful with that," I said.

Smiling, she slid the blade under my shirt and poked it up through the material. Slitting the fabric open all the way to the neck, she separated the two halves, one at a time, with the point of her knife. "Very nice," she murmured, tracing the muscles on my stomach with her free hand. "In fact…" Shoving the torn cloth back off my shoulders and arms, all the way down to the ropes around my wrists, she poked a finger into my chest and smiled. "No more shirts for you."

I struggled not to look cross. "Give me his name, Taren. Tell me where he hired you. You aren't stupid enough to take a job without meeting the man who's paying you."

"That was almost a compliment."

"I'll give you more than compliments if you tell me what I want to know."

"Fine," she sighed. "He approached me in a tavern on the west side of Kael. A dismal little place called the Wounded Owl."

"I know it. Describe him."

"He kept to the shadows. Wore a cloak. He was tall."

"Anything else?" I gave her a hard look. "Anything useful?"

"He's Shinree," she said, her exasperation matching mine. "White eyes, white hair…like you. Minus the lovely black stripes, of course."

"Yeah, those are all mine. Was he alone?"

"I think so." Lazily, her fingers traveled up to my shoulder. "He didn't seem to be owned. He certainly wasn't on *Kayn'l*."

"He must have been off it a long time. You don't get that good without tutelage and practice. And slaves don't get either."

Pursing her lips, Taren gave me a leisurely once over. "I expected more scars. Did you actually fight in that war you were in?"

"Six years."

"Sounds tedious."

"Not at all. There was lots of blood, lots of pain. You would have liked it."

She let out a long exhale of disappointment. "Don't you have an old arrow wound, or anything?"

"Sorry. Aylagar's healers were well trained."

"Shinree healers?" She laughed. "So, Rella's Queen was a hypocrite as well as a whore?" At the blankness on my face she let out a snappy, "Please, Troy. Everyone knows that bitch's distrust of magic is why the war lasted as long as it did. She kept you strapped to her side, all roped and hungry, saddled so she could ride you whenever the mood struck." Taren gave me a wink. "I can totally see why, of course. Yet, apparently, while the Queen tied a noose around your balls, she put no restrictions on the magic her healers used." Taren snorted out an abrupt, unbecoming cackle. "After being caged for all those years, it's no fucking wonder you decimated them all."

"You goddamn—"

Her kiss cut off my words. I had a quick thought of pulling away. Then another of sinking my teeth through her bottom lip and ripping it off. But she still had the knife, and I'd just found a rock under the mud. To keep her from noticing my movements as I sawed at the rope, I had to kiss her back. I pulled eagerly at her tongue, and her rough response was more than enthusiastic.

Taren's breath sped up. Her mouth moved faster to keep up with mine.

Moaning, she dropped the dagger and grabbed both my arms. Taren was strong, eager. I couldn't deny her clutching and kneading felt good. Her mouth didn't feel half bad either, and for a moment, I put off my attempt at escape and enjoyed the feel of her.

When I regained my senses, I drew my knees up slowly out of the gluey water. I pressed them in close, one on either side of her body. I held her that way a while, taking my time, letting the kiss deepen. Even after I cut through the rope, I kept it up, until the tension in her eased and her eyes fell closed.

Her muscles loosened. Taren melted against me. That's when I knew I had her.

With slow, subtle movements, I slipped my hands out of the ropes. I shed the pieces of my torn shirt and leaned toward her, positioning myself better so I could clutch her tighter with my legs. I let her get comfortable. Then, drawing her tongue far into my mouth, I pulled my arms out from behind my back and gripped her face.

Taren sighed. Her nails pressed into my chest. She was ready to go— right up until the moment she realized I was free.

Stiffening, Taren's eyes flew open. She tried to pull back, but I held on, pressing my knees in tighter, my fingers in harder, my mouth more firmly against hers. She pushed at me, crying out a garbled objection against my lips that I paid absolutely no mind to.

When I was done, I pulled back and smiled. "So that's what *fool* tastes like." Twisting my lower body, I threw her off me; face first into the muck.

Floundering, Taren lifted her head.

I shoved it back down. "What's it going to be?" Leaning over, I fished around for her dagger. "Are you going to give me that ring, or do I have to cut off your finger?"

I let her up. Mud sputtered from her lips. "I'm going to fucking cut off your—"

"Wrong answer." I started to push her under again, and Taren swung her legs into mine. The strike, on solid ground, would have gotten her nowhere. But she unbalanced me just enough. One of my boots slid into a hole the size of my horse, and I was suddenly splashing into the soggy ground next to her.

Climbing on me, putting all her weight forward, Taren shoved my head under the bog and punched it. I reached a blind hand up and locked it about her throat, but she was unrelenting. Her ring tore into my scalp. Bits of leaves, chunks of mud and other vile things filled my mouth and nose. Swamp slid down my throat, foul and thick as she held my head under.

As the air stopped reaching my lungs, I released her throat and groped at her legs. Going on the fact that I'd never met an assassin that wasn't prepared, I slid my hands down her thighs and into the cuffs of her boots, looking for a second dagger.

When I found it, I pulled it out and jammed the blade into her thigh.

Screaming, Taren lost her grip. Throwing her off me, I hauled my head up out of the swamp with a gasping roar and a rain of wet earth. Sludge dripped from my clothes as I got up. More spewed from my mouth as I tried to breathe. Spitting it out, gagging at the taste, I wiped the slime and silt from my face. It was in my coat, in my nose, down my pants. It stunk, and so did I.

Shoving my dripping hair back off my face, I staggered over to where Taren had landed. A steady stream of blood was burbling out from around the blade in her leg. Without any preamble whatsoever, I bent down and yanked the dagger out.

Her responding shriek bounced against the insides of my aching skull.

"Shut up!" I kicked her other leg until she fell quiet. Sliding Taren's dagger into my belt, I crouched down and lifted her right hand out of the water. It was slathered in mud. Her skin was barely visible. The red crystal, however, was glowing brightly.

"He lied," Taren groaned. "He promised it would keep me going. Said I wouldn't have to eat or sleep for days. He told me you couldn't catch me, couldn't hurt me." She tilted her head back and yelled at no one. "Damn, filthy, lying prick! It doesn't work!"

I pulled the ring off her finger. A hot tingle ran across my skin. "The stone works. It's the spell that's expired." I glanced at her. "Guess he doesn't care about keeping you alive after all." Straightening, I stared at the ring. "It takes guidance to learn how to spell an object like this." I frowned, thinking. "There was that group of runaways that use to stir up trouble a while back. It could be he's one of their descendants, raised free like me."

"Are you talking about the rebel cast-offs?" Taren let out a stilted, breathy laugh. "You must be desperate, Troy, if you're laying blame on a bunch of magically impotent half-breeds. They're so powerless no one even bothers rounding them up anymore."

"You're right. The spells your employer is pulling off are too complex. He couldn't have mastered them without training. And overlapping them the way he is, I don't know who could do that, short of an erudite."

"Never heard of it," she said casually, busy inspecting the wound in her leg.

"Erudite isn't an 'it', Taren. It's a title. One that doesn't exist anymore."

"So now your suspect doesn't exist? I must have hit you real hard."

"Erudite were the best of us, an elite bloodline, more wise and powerful than all the rest. Back when the Shinree Empire was strong, they were our teachers, our leaders."

"Gods, there are more types of you people than there are notches on my bedpost."

"I doubt that. Doesn't matter though," I said, paying no attention to the face she was giving me. "There hasn't been an erudite alive in hundreds of years."

"Like I said…it's a mystery."

I stared hard into her eyes, trying to find an answer that wasn't there. "Who is he, Taren? Why is he interested in me? What is he doing while you keep me here?"

"I don't know," she said, and I almost believed her. "But he's a filthy liar."

"You didn't have to take the job."

"Don't pretend you haven't been desperate, Troy. That there weren't times you would have killed your own mother for enough coin."

"I did kill her."

"Really?" Delight infected Taren's shocked laugh.

"But it had nothing to do with money." *It was magic*, I thought; always believing it was my fault, my stray child's wish that ended her days. I'd never truly known, though. I just woke up one morning and she didn't.

My first victim…

Sighing, I rubbed at the incessant throbbing in my head. My palm burned where I held the ring, but it felt good compared to the rest of me. It felt so good, the notion hit me that I should throw it away. I knew better than to touch any stone taken from the western mines. Why then was I recklessly and deliberately resting one against my skin? Why was I allowing the garnet's pulsing energy to dance across my nerves?

It was just plain stupid.

But I didn't care. I had no desire to squash the shiver of anticipation growing inside me. There was a particular kind of pleasure that came from letting it build, to teetering so close to satisfaction you could taste it.

What's one more spell? The damage is already done.

My hands started shaking at the thought. My pulse quickened. Knots of anticipation formed in my stomach. They burrowed in, and the urgency grew.

It can't hurt anything. There's no one out here.

I stopped before. I can stop again.

I can handle it.

Just one more…

I closed my eyes and let go. Power fell into me, sweeping hot beneath my skin. It soared through my body, and the pain in my head disappeared. The weariness faded. I wasn't hungry or thirsty. I wasn't angry. Even the rancid taste of swamp was gone from my mouth. Magic ran with the blood in my veins. I felt wonderful.

I smiled and breathed deep, savoring the sensations. I opened my eyes and lost the smile. Shimmering dark and red; the garnet was undulating as if it were fluid.

The stone looked like blood.

Disgusted, I closed my hand over the ring. I squeezed until the metal prongs dug in. I watched the blood drip out from between my fingers and thought, *Aylagar.*

That's all it took. That's all it ever took to make her face emerge like a ghost in my mind, dark, beautiful, and fierce. Next, was the sting of how she trusted me, and I betrayed her. I topped that off with the feel of her dead body in my arms, withered, gray and unbelievably cold. The entire battlefield was dead and cold. The only warmth to be had was emanating from the pulsing stones of the crown.

I hated remembering it. But guilt and pain were the only effective ways to suffocate the cravings. And when the guilt became too much, I suffocated that with wine.

At least I used to. I had the sinking feeling that, soon, neither would be enough.

"What's wrong, witch?" Taren's question startled me. "Feeling poorly?"

I tossed the ring on the ground. Slogging through the muck, in four strides I was standing over her, bending down, grabbing a handful of her shirt and drawing back my fist. The urge to cast pain on Taren Roe like she'd never felt before—to make her spit out the truth until she begged to die—was overwhelming.

But her eyes were red again. And the man's voice was in her, saying, "Tell me. Tell me how it feels to kill your Queen…your lover," with so much persuasion, that I hesitated. My arm dropped. My grip eased on her shirt. Out of nowhere my anger faded. "Tell me," he said again.

And I understood. "You have another stone."

Satisfaction slithered across Taren's muddy face. "There's no point in resisting. The more I speak, the more compelled you are to answer."

"Where is it?" I started searching her pockets. "Where's the stone?"

"Inside her," he whispered. "Would you like to know how much coin it takes for a Kaelish tramp to let you cut into her skin?"

Revolted, I shoved Taren's body away. "What do you want from me?"

"At the moment? Conversation."

"Buy me a mug of ale the next time you're at the Wounded Owl, and we'll talk."

"Did you really think using the Crown of Stones would bring peace of any kind?"

"Go to hell."

"How did it feel to be the sole survivor on a field of thousands, surrounded by all those sightless, staring eyes, all those rigid, soulless bodies?"

His spell pulled at me to answer. "They…" I tried to resist. It pried into me, dragging the words out. "They were…they were everywhere. Their skin was pale and gray. Thin—like parchment. Their bodies were caved and sunken. Everything inside of them had dried up. The grass was dead. The trees were dust. The smell was…" I drew a breath and shook my head, "indescribable."

"I have no doubt. Your attack on King Draken was most impressive, as well. Infiltrating the mind of your enemy's ruler and condemning him to a life of madness. I imagine making the catalyst of Rella's suffering endure such torment was incredibly gratifying."

"It was."

"Any Shinree capable of such power as you should be King."

"King? Why the hell would I want that?"

"It might have made your mother proud."

The mud-dried hairs on the back of my neck stood on end. "My mother died a long time ago."

"Apparently, she died without instructing you how emotion can pervert the outcome of your spell. That the larger and darker the working the more energy it needs. The more life it takes." A sudden spout of anger tightened his voice. "Did she prepare you at all? Or was your mother remiss in teaching you the very basic rules of magic?"

"My mother was remiss in a lot of things."

"Have you no respect for the woman who gave you life? V'loria Troy was a gifted healer. She held an esteemed title."

"V'loria Troy cast on King Raynan's whim. Taking life from one man and using it to heal another that the *he* deemed more deserving. How can I respect that?"

"She was a King's Healer."

"She was a King's whore."

Taren stood. She came at me through the muddy water with strides too quick and sure for someone with a hole in her leg. "Did you love her?"

"Who? My mother?"

He grunted like I was stupid. "Aylagar."

I clamped my mouth shut and ground my teeth on the answer. I wasn't about to let him pull the past out of me like it meant nothing, like I hadn't spent years trying to hold it in.

"Well?" he goaded me.

"Why are you doing this?"

"To find out what kind of man you are."

"I'm going to smile when I cut you. Does that tell you anything?"

He heaved Taren's body in a great sigh. "I need to know if you're capable of crawling out from inside that grave of self-inflicted pity you've buried yourself in long enough to be useful. Or are you nothing more than a disgraceful waste of my time?" He gave me no chance to reply. "You've lied to yourself so long, Troy, you've forgotten the truth. You didn't care about her. You were last in a long line of playthings for a privileged, lonely Queen. You knew that. And that's why you drained the life out of her body and never looked back. Because she was nothing more than a soft, warm place for you to—"

"Yes," I growled, cutting him off. "Yes, I loved her...you fucking bastard."

"Nice," he purred. "You loved her and you killed her anyway."

I closed my eyes against the look on Taren's face. But I couldn't block out the slow, satisfied laugh the man was pushing out of her throat. The sound was an unmistakable show of approval, a genuine release of pleasure at my expense. It felt like the point of a sword pushing into my skin. And the harder the laugh came, the further the sword pushed in; twisting and turning, digging at old wounds and making them new, stripping away the layers and leaving me with only the raw, ugly memories.

His cruel amusement did something else as well. It kindled an unintentional fire deep within me. The flames burned hot and fast. They ignited the very things his spell had worked so hard to dampen, and wrath came around again. Aggression was set loose.

I felt a *crack* as his spell on me shattered.

No longer restrained, emotion and intent moved through me like blood flowing to a sleeping limb, and I launched myself forward. Striking Taren hard across the jaw, I hit her twice more, driving her down into the mire.

"How many pieces do I have to cut her in before you shut up? How many?" I yanked her up.

Taren's head whipped around. She licked her torn lip, and her red eyes glowed. "Kill the bitch if you like. But it changes nothing—nothing!" he cried out. "You *will* turn the ground red with blood again, Troy. I promise you. It's what we are."

Taking the dagger from my belt, I grabbed a handful of Taren's muddy hair. I shoved the blade under her chin and ripped it across her throat. "It's not what I am."

SIX

The grass crunched with my every step. It was an odd noise, out of place. It wouldn't be in another month. Cold came early to the mountains. Yet the black dry condition of the woods had nothing to do with winter or the rapidly approaching night. The bare, lifeless branches, the curled brittle underbrush and numerous carcasses of birds and other small creatures littering the forest floor weren't made by natural means. They were dead because of me.

I wasn't shocked. Losing his vessel in Taren's death had done nothing to hold my Shinree enemy at bay. He'd seized my magic three more times before I'd found my way out of the swamps, and again shortly after I'd crossed over into Kael. Since then, as I'd traveled the mountain paths and moved deeper into the kingdom, his intrusions had grown farther apart.

I would have been grateful for that. Except, as the time between spells lengthened, the faster my appetite for them grew. I'd been able to resist casting on my own, so far. But fighting the urge was getting painfully hard. When it became impossible, and I couldn't hold out anymore, I wouldn't be able to shift the blame to my enemy. Whatever was drained, whatever died when I cast, it would be entirely on my shoulders.

It is now, I thought soberly, looking at the death and desolation surrounding me. The spell may not have been my doing, but it was mine. I was the reason that Kya was the only other living thing in the woods besides me.

It was my fault she was wandering alongside the trail, nose to the ground, searching for something edible that wasn't here.

I'd killed breakfast. Again.

It was her only concern, the lack of green vegetation, and I wished I could be more like her. I wished that the forest, giving its life to feed my spell, meant nothing. That my stomach didn't turn at the sight of so many tiny desiccated bodies at my feet, at the hordes of industrious insects and worms feasting on their shriveled remains. It would be easier if I didn't care about the village nearby, simpler if I could ride on without remorse.

But riding on meant finding out what I might have done to them.

There are children there, I thought, imagining their little forms bent and shrunken, their skin thinned and wrinkled like fruit left too long in the sun.

If I'd killed children I didn't want to know. I couldn't live with not know-ing, either. I certainly couldn't go on like I was, leaving a trail of death behind me while some rampant Shinree helped himself to my magic. I had to stop him.

How exactly, I wasn't sure. I had nothing to go on but a vague descrip-tion and a voice I didn't know. Neither would get me even a halfway decent tracking spell. The only workable lead I had was the tavern where Taren was hired. I knew the place. I knew the kind that went there. They responded to money and fists, and I was glad to give them both if it got me answers. It wasn't without risk though. The Wounded Owl was in a city of thousands. If I was forced to let loose a spell while I was there, the worms would be gorg-ing on much larger meals than squirrels and mice.

The only way to pull it off safely was to get in and out quick, between spells. Yet betting lives on my enemy sticking to his recent pattern didn't sit well. Being able to resist him, or even put him off for a while, would make entering the city a little less hazardous. But despite burning with the urge to defy him each time he made me cast, I hadn't. I hadn't managed to deflect him in the slightest—not once. It was a failure that had led me to a painful conclusion: I didn't really want to stop. Having magic in me again felt too damn good.

Ashamed, I started revisiting the few options I had for fighting back.

I wasn't fond of any of them.

Ingesting *Kayn'l* was the most obvious. It would completely impede my ability to cast (unwillingly or otherwise), yet I couldn't afford the side effects. If I wanted to actually find and stop my attacker, I needed to be coherent. Regularly channeling the obsidian on my own would keep the stone depleted and lower his opportunity to use it. Keeping the workings small would lessen the harm to others, too. But the harm caused to me, by indulging so frequently, would be immeasurable. I was already sinking into a hole I might never get out of again. Deliberately throwing myself in deeper wasn't smart.

Disposing of the shard would work. With no stones in my possession my enemy would be cut off from my magic. Unfortunately, though, so would I. And I'd be defenseless when I found him.

That left figuring out a way to counter his spell, or keep him out entirely. But he was too cunning not to be ready for me to craft a barricade or shield spell of some sort. Depending on what stone he was using, whether I could offset it or not would be hit or miss, anyway. To keep him busy I would need more than one spell. *Wait…*

More than one…

An idea forming, I started pacing.

Accessing my abilities, forcing the magic in, shaping it…

That's three different types of persuasion, three different spells.

He'd have to cast them separately, in stages. Which means—

I stopped moving. "A lag."

It would be brief. I'd have less than a handful of moments, the time it would take for him to make clear his intent for one spell and speak the words for the next. But if I could do it, if I could regain control of the aura right after he pushed it into me, I could pull the whole damn thing out from under him.

I could limit the loss of life. Show him I'm not as easy to handle as he thought.

Brazenly opposing the man's plans might also make him angry enough to force a show down. *And if I can bring him out of hiding, I can kill him.*

Just like that I had a plan. And the first shred of confidence I'd felt in a while.

It put a bit of pep in my step as I whistled for Kya. "Let's go!" I hollered.

Kya gave me a brief, terse glance, and then went back to sniffing the dead woods.

"We don't have time for this." I lapsed into Shinree and barked firmly at her. "Intae'a!" The old language wasn't spoken much, having died long before I learned it. Yet there were one or two words that just felt right saying. Like the term of affection I often used with Kya. Even spoken harshly, something about the sound guaranteed me attention. And not just with horses.

Sauntering obediently in my direction now, I met the mare halfway. As I swung up into the saddle, I caught a glimpse of the small dark crystal peeking out from the neckline of my shirt. Cold and harmless, rundown from whatever spell I'd just cast, the shard looked nothing at all like a fragment from the deadliest weapon in Shinree history. For that matter, outwardly, the crown itself betrayed nothing of its true nature. Yet, it had crowded my veins with what felt like endless magic, granting me a range of power and abilities far beyond what I was born with, far more than I knew what to do with too, or how to control.

With a single use of the Crown of Stones, I'd changed the world.

Only one thing had gone in my favor that day: the crown fell into my hands and not the Langorians. If they'd gained access to all that magic, they would have painfully persuaded a Shinree to work it for them, and the resulting damage would have been infinitely more wide spread. With the crown in their possession, no army could have stopped Langor from dominating Rella and every other land within reach.

Anyone who wielded it could make themselves King.

A chill took me at the thought.

Another ran up my spine me as I quoted my new enemy. "Anyone with such power as you should be King."

I thought of Taren then, talking about the circle being broken. How she'd hinted at wanting the obsidian shard to fix it. Still, if her mission had been to retrieve the shard, I'd given her multiple opportunities. Instead, her employer had interrogated me. He'd mocked me, plagued me with questions. He'd asked about the war, about Aylagar, about the Crown of Stones. *He said I didn't hide it very well.*

Struggling, I tried to recall every word of our conversation. I didn't remember saying anything that would reveal the location of the crown. But the man hadn't asked, either. He'd focused on getting me to reveal deeper things. Things like what I feared and what I loved. Like where my mind and heart were before, and after, I channeled the crown. He'd wanted in my head, and he'd gotten there.

If he was truly after the artifact, I'd given him a good place to start looking.

Not only that, I was too far away now to stop him.

Far, far away. Just like Taren said.

I crushed the reins in my hands. *I have to go back.*

I had no choice but to make sure the crown was still where I left it.

Only what if I was wrong? *What if I lead him straight to it?*

Going back to Kabri might be exactly what he wanted. It certainly wasn't what I wanted. Ten years had done nothing to diminish the reasons I left.

Situated just off the southern mainland of Rella, the island city of Kabri was the seat of power for the entire realm. It was where I was born and lived as a child. It was where my mother died and where I caught my first real glimpse of the large scale brutality the Langorians were capable of. It was where I surrendered Aylagar's body to her husband, King Raynan Arcana, and where I hid the Crown of Stones.

I should have left it where I found it.

I should have never brought it back.

I'd thought that many times. How I should have buried the accursed thing in the sand and let it return to whatever hell it came from. But I'd needed a way to explain, and to cement my grounds for punishment. Torture, exile, slavery, even execution would have been fair. Instead, I got the King staring at me like he wasn't surprised, as though he'd always known that one day I would slip and rain destruction down on everyone.

After relieving me of duty, he'd firmly suggested I leave the city. Tensions among the citizens were high. King Raynan claimed he was worried I might be strung up by the families of the men that didn't come home. But his protection of me had always been a purely selfish concern. If I died, Rella would be without the defense of the magic user he'd had worked so hard to groom.

King Raynan's last order was that I put the artifact somewhere safe. I'd argued for destroying it, throwing it in the ocean—anything. But he'd wanted it available should its power ever be needed again, and I'd been in no position to make demands.

Thinking on it now, I'd probably misinterpreted his words. He likely hadn't meant for me to leave the Crown of Stones in the catacombs under his castle, inside Aylagar's tomb. But at the time, I was the one person the crown needed to be safe from.

I found it. I used it. I alone knew the wonders and the dangers, and that was the sole reason I chose the hiding place I did. Because if I were ever tempted to claim the crown's magic for myself, if I ever thought to use its power again, I would have to go back there, open Aylagar's crypt and reach my hand in. I would have to touch her dead body, face her and what I did, and no amount of magic was worth that. Not to me anyway.

But to another, lured by the promise of supreme power, it would be a small thing to defile the tomb of a dead, forgotten Queen.

I gave Kya a kick and started her forward. If I was right, and the crown was in danger, forward was the wrong direction. But the kingdom of Rella was weeks away, and I was too close to Kael to turn around without checking the Wounded Owl first. It was the last place my Shinree enemy was seen. Someone there might know his identity or his whereabouts.

Pushing the mare, the ground sped by in a blur of stripped spindly thickets and scattered piles of dead wildlife. Leafless branches hung down over the path as it dipped into little hollows and rose up over gentle sloping mounds of parched black grass. As the sun set deeper, the path flattened out. As it widened into a genuine road, I hit a straight patch. Dust gathered in the waning light up ahead. In its center was the dark shape of a single horseman.

I came to a halt and drew a sword. After Taren, I wasn't taking any chances.

The man pushed through the cloud. His approach was fast.

Sword ready, I held position. I assumed the rider would swerve off when he caught sight of me. Instead, he released a high-pitched cry of panic and jerked like mad on the reins. Bringing his mount to a loud, skidding stop less than a hands length away from Kya's right flank, a spray of dead leaves shot up as high as my knee. The dust rose higher.

Coughing on it, I backed up and prepared to lecture the man about looking where he was going, violently. I held off when I saw how badly he was shaking.

Hunched inside a hooded brown traveling cloak, his white-knuckle grip on the reins began to loosen. His slight form uncurled, and the edges of his cloak fell away. The hood slipped off then, and revealed beneath it, not a man, but a boy. No more than fifteen or sixteen years, dressed in garments dyed the colors of my current employer, King Sarin of Kael, his fresh, round (and unmistakably pale) face was not quite old enough to have seen a single shave.

I grunted in surprise. "You're from the King's court. What are you doing out here?"

Forcing away his anxiety, the boy squared his jaw. "Good day to you, My Lord." He gave me a quick nod, and the careless mop of sandy hair on top of his head bounced down over his face. He tossed it back. "I have been sent to escort you to the home of King Sarin."

"Did you come through the village?"

"Yes, My Lord."

"Was it intact?" Watching him closely, I swallowed, waiting for his response.

Bewilderment tightened his gaze. "My Lord...?"

"Stop calling me that."

"Yes, My Lord. Forgive me."

Licking dry lips, I blew out a breath, and tried again. "Did the village look like it does here?"

Lowering his eyes, the boy shook his head in confusion, and the shock of hair fell across his face again. For a moment, I was tempted to pull out a knife and cut it for him. "Look around you, boy," I said, close to yelling now. "Did the village look like this?"

"I don't know what you're asking." Noticing my sword, he recoiled. "Please..."

I lowered the weapon. "Calm down. Take a look around and answer me."

The young Kaelishman's nervous gaze moved off mine. Leather creaking, he turned in the saddle, right then left. He stared at the lifeless woods, at the ruined ground and the rotting animals, and revulsion turned his face an unbecoming shade of green. "You did this," he whispered. Horror strained his voice. "You did this with magic."

His tone stung. "Yes, I did. But are they safe in the village?"

"You killed it all," he muttered. "You killed everything."

The air went out of me. My eyes fell closed. "Then...they're all dead?"

"Oh—no, My Lord, that's not...they aren't..."

My eyes snapped open. "Which is it?"

"I'm sorry. I didn't mean..." His flustered stare grew huge with embarrassment. "The village is fine. There's grass," he glanced over his shoulder. "It's just a ways back. I can show you."

"No. No, it's all right." Running a hand over my face, I wiped the emotion from it. "I believe you."

"Good. Then, may we go now?"

I squinted at him in the growing dark. Clearly, the boy had no grasp of the utter panic that had been moving through me only seconds before. Or what it took to put it away. He'd probably never felt anything like it. "I've seen you before," I said. "You're not King Sarin's page. You belong to his son, Guidon."

His whole body stiffened. "It is my honor to attend Kael's heir."

"Is it?" My mood broke some at his well-practiced lie. "What's your name, boy?"

"Liel," he said, tentatively.

"Well, Liel, forgive me for being cautious, but I've been tasked with hunting Kael's outlaws for two years now. And not once has Sarin sent someone to fetch me."

"Escort you, My Lord. I'm an escort, not a...a dog." I laughed at that, and he panicked. "Please, forgive me, My Lord." Liel bent his head. Not even his mountain of hair could hide the redness creeping up his cheeks. "I should be punished for speaking so."

"Speak how you like. Just tell me one thing." I slid my sword away. "How did Prince Guidon know I'd be on this trail, today, right now? Did he pay for a spell to track me?"

"I wouldn't know, My Lord. I was told only that my duty was to bring you."

"Then your duty has to wait."

Getting bold now, Liel lifted his chin. "I'm sorry, but I must insist."

"And I insist you go back without me. I have business in the city. I'll come by the castle after, but have my pay ready. It's best if I don't stick around."

He relented. "Yes, My Lord." But I could almost see the risk of Prince Guidon's displeasure hanging like a shadow over his head.

"Wait." Twisting around behind me, I took hold of the leather bag tied to my saddle. "Take this." I pulled a knife and severed the line.

Liel stood in his stirrups, straining to see. "What is it?"

"Something I hope might keep you from getting into too much trouble." As I turned back around and opened the flap, Liel threw a hand over his mouth. "Use it," I told him.

"As what?" he balked.

"Proof you found me." I closed the flap and tossed him Taren's head.

SEVEN

I flipped a handful of coins on the counter. "Another."

The gangly Kaelishman behind the bar pushed the dirty-water-colored hair out of his eyes and tallied the coins with a sour expression. Slowly, his disagreeable stare lifted. "We don't serve your kind in here," he said, taking the coins and slipping them into his pocket.

"Your girls have no trouble serving me," I reminded him.

"My girls have no wits."

"I've been here before. I've had your ale. And your girls."

"I remember." His pointed, scruffy jaw went tight. "And I remember how my place looked after you left."

"Your place is a shithole," I said, kicking at the dirt floor. "But I paid for those damages. Both times."

"I'm thinking, this time, you should pay in advance."

My hand twitched. I'd been trying all night not to give into my temper. Anger was too closely linked to casting for a Shinree soldier, and I was barely ignoring the urge as it was. Even so, I almost hit him and got it over with. But I lost interest as a woman's arm came around the barkeep's bony shoulder.

Moving out from behind him, the winegirl shamelessly draped her body over his. She snuggled against his cheek and whispered in his ear. "I'll take care of this one."

He gave no argument. The barkeep slipped quietly away into the kitchen with an almost blank expression, leaving the woman to size me up with her pretty blue eyes. They were pale and bottomless, and gave her square face a pleasing, sultry quality.

"What are you drinking, Shinree?" she asked.

The answer was easy. "Whatever you're pouring."

"In that case…" Giving me a quick frisky smile, the winegirl turned to the rows of shelves on the wall behind her. She reached up high for a lone black jug sitting at the top. "Ever heard of the Wandering Isles?"

"Don't think so," I said, enjoying watching her move. Her hair was an avalanche of wide autumn curls. Her body was healthy, scantily dressed and full of curves, and I liked the way her skirt lifted as she stretched.

"It's a little group of islands just off the coast of Doratae." She glanced back. "They say their spirits were the best ever made."

"Were?"

"Not much trade comes out of the islands anymore. But this little treasure has been here a long while." Making contact with the jug, she pulled it down, parted a set of lips that were perfect for kissing, and blew the dust off the label. "What do you say, Shinree?" Grinning, she sat the jug down in front of me. The label was cracked and faded. The dark glass was ancient. I wasn't sure how it was still in one piece. "Are you brave enough to find out if the stories are true?"

"Only if you're brave enough to join me."

In reply, she popped the cork, and the man at the bar beside me slurred in a deep voice, "Your presence brings with it a foul odor, witch."

I turned slightly toward him. He was big for a Kaelishman. He was also considerably drunker than I was. But that didn't make him wrong. "I bet it does," I said, sniffing at the remnants of swamp on my coat.

"Maybe I wasn't clear," he said. "You stink." Teetering, the brute edged closer. The layer of ash caked on his hair and skin was thicker than the coating of grime on the tavern windows. *Blacksmith*, I thought as he leaned in close. "You don't belong here."

"You're right in that," I agreed, surveying the room full of shadowy figures hunched over their mugs. Since none of them had given me anything on my elusive, Shinree enemy, I should have left hours ago. Instead, feeling sorry for myself, I'd stayed and hit the wine. I'd thought a mug or two might help. Now, after a few more than two, I could comfortably say that I felt far worse than when I walked in. A cold sweat had my shirt clinging to my skin. Small earthquakes were traveling the length of my insides. My head was pounding.

The only thing I'd found worthy of distracting me from my craving for magic was the girl behind the bar. So I put my back to the unpleasant blacksmith, smiled at her, and nodded at the jug. "Shall we?"

She sat two cups down on the counter and began filling them. The liquid, as it fled the bottle, was dark with a pungent, spicy smell.

I eyed it warily. "What's your name, girl?"

Her reply was an ornery grin. Selecting one of the cups, she saluted me and drained it—and her face immediately contorted in pain. She was coughing and laughing so hard, I could barely understand when she wheezed out, "Imma."

I wasn't sure yet about the drink, but I liked her.

I dug in my pocket and put a few more coins on the counter. "You get many Shinree in here, Imma?"

Still wincing, she cleared her throat. "Sometimes the nobles come in with their slaves looking for a discreet place to get their money's worth. If you know what I mean."

"Not a slave. I'm looking for someone off *Kayn'l*. A man."

"That's funny," she grinned. "I'm looking for a man too." Imma leaned toward me over the bar. "And I think you'll do just fine." She inclined her body further in my direction. The rounded collar of her bodice gaped invitingly, and I caught the faint scent of lavender that clung to her red-brown hair. Plucking my untouched drink off the counter, she held up it to my lips. "I hope you like it hot."

With difficulty, I raised my gaze from her overflowing breasts to her sensual eyes. I took the cup from her hand, and a sudden involuntary shudder of craving raced up my arm. "He's tall," I said, tightening my grip. "He was wearing a cloak. I know that doesn't help much, but he came in a while back looking to hire. Met with a woman. Name of Roe."

Imma scooted back off the counter to her side of the bar. With that slight distance, the scent of her vanished. Strangely, I found myself missing it.

"Roe's been here before," she replied, "but not for some time. As far as your Shinree goes…healers don't come unless enough blood spills to get the magistrate involved. And oracles don't come unless you pay them—which we don't. To cite our great and wise owner," Imma deepened her voice and slowed it to a coarse drawl, "why in hell's name would I pay for some friggin' lout to learn his future when he'll be too drunk to remember it come morning?" Slapping a hand on the jug between us, she lifted it high. "This is all the entertainment these good-for-nothing, tightfisted, lousy pricks need." Putting the bottle down, Imma ended her impression with a laugh. "You're in the Wounded Owl, handsome. If you want oracles, you need to go uptown a bit."

"Nah, I think I'm good here." I tossed back the drink in my hand. It was like liquid fire. I was still trying to breathe when the blacksmith stumbled into me.

"I heard about you," he said.

I didn't even glance at him. "Don't suppose any of it was good?"

"It was shit. Must be shit," he said, his words running over each other. "Since you look like just any another ugly, spooky-eyed witch to me. Cowardly and cock-lovin' too, I bet." He shoved his shoulder into mine. "Prove me wrong."

"You really don't want me to do that," I told him.

"Let's say I do. Let's say I grab your head and slam it," he smacked his hand on the bar for effect, "until it cracks. What would you do then?"

"Something you wouldn't like. Now, if you don't mind?" I held my cup out to Imma. She re-filled it, but her posture had changed. The lighthearted casualness of before was gone. She looked angry.

Then she looked scared as the blacksmith shoved me again. His push was harder this time. I fell forward across the bar, bumped into Imma, dropped my cup, and spilled my drink on us both. She lost her balance, and I had to grab her with one hand to keep her from falling, while my other gripped the edge of the counter; fingers digging into the wood as I furiously struggled to re-route my anger.

"You okay?" I said.

She nodded, and I let her go. Releasing my grip on the bar, I shook the wet off my hand. I turned around, hoping to find a way to get rid of the blacksmith without it turning violent—and he hit me.

Knocked once more into the bar, I rubbed my jaw as I righted myself. I spit a generous amount of blood on the floor, and the bastard scowled at it as if it wasn't enough. As if I should have been flat on my back, out cold with one hit.

"Are you Ian Troy?" he said then.

I had to spit again before I could answer. "Maybe you should have asked that before you hit me?"

The brute grunted, possibly in agreement, but he was too busy trying to stare me down to elaborate. He couldn't manage it, of course. My reputation regularly drew in aspiring challengers like flies, and I'd spent years perfecting the right amount of unshakable belligerence it took to warn them off with a glance. Not to mention that too much ale swam in this one's veins for him to see straight.

Still, I let him win. I had to. My nerves were jumping like hot embers from a fire. The effort it was taking to *not* put the bastard down had spasms running through me, so intense, I didn't bother with my cup. I picked up the jug and took a long, desperate swig.

Imma frowned at me. "You don't look so good."

The jug wobbled in my grip as I lowered it. "It's nothing."

"Really?" She put her hand on mine to stop it from shaking. "You should get out of here. Before someone catches what you have."

"They can't." But she was right. I couldn't stay. The sickness and disorientation had finally reached that critical point. I had two choices now. Continue to deny my body what it yearned for. Or give in.

I didn't want to even consider the latter. But as long as another was in charge of my spells, it was futile to suffer through the pain of abstinence. Whatever gains I might make would be undone at his whim. Not to mention, I'd be a vulnerable mess. From here on, there was only one way to stay sharp: to alleviate my symptoms as they came on. I had to cast regularly and willingly, and I had to live with it. I had to let go of the years I'd spent honing my self-control and fall back into old patterns; using secluded places to gorge myself; learning to get by on small bursts to avoid draining innocents. I had to accept that once more my life would be measured by how long I could last between spells.

I hated being that weak. Yet I saw no way around it.

"Fucking, witch," the blacksmith slurred, breathing his hot stale-wine breath in my face. "Your kind drinks from the trough outside. Let me show you." He put a hand on my arm.

Imma gave me a grim look, like she knew I was on the verge of doing very nasty things to him. "Go," she urged me. But I didn't want to anymore. Just the idea of relief being a wish away had my heart racing and my mind shuffling through potential spells.

If I can lure him outside, some place deserted, no one else has to get hurt.

Something fast and easy…

I just need a little.

No one would miss him, at least not until morning, and I'll be gone by then.

Spittle hit my face as the man thundered, "The trough witch! NOW!"

And with that, my patience was done. Suddenly, my urges felt justified. The path ahead of me was clear. As I threw off his hold, spun, and faced my tormenter full on, I was fully prepared to cast. More so, as I glared deep into his soot-ringed eyes and found them narrow and hard, full of an ignorant all-consuming pride that sickened me. They were alive with nothing but hatred and cruelty.

But they were still alive.

When I was done, they would be glazed, empty and accusing. His corpse would be curled up on the filthy cobblestones, gray and parched, dinner for the rats and the crows. Empty. Dead.

Like Aylagar.

I tried to let it go, to shake off the memories. I tried not to see the countless bodies reflected in the blacksmith's harsh stare. Or Rella's former Queen splayed out on the barren ground. But they wouldn't go away. She wouldn't go away. And the weight of what I was about to do—choosing a sacrifice, willfully planning a murder—nearly toppled me to the floor. *Gods, what's happening to me?*

Imma ran her hand up my arm. Startled, I realized she was standing next to me.

I'd been so self-absorbed. I hadn't even seen her come out from behind the bar.

Her touch moved to my face. She mouthed one word, "Come." And I wanted to, badly. Her stare was chocked full of desire. It promised the kind of night I hadn't seen in a long time. "This way," she urged, stepping toward the door. The coaxing in her stare deepened, and I felt a pull. I wanted to follow her. When I didn't, Imma extended a hand to beckon me, and an uncomfortable tightness pinched my chest.

The longer I hesitated, the worse it got.

In no way, was it natural.

Damn. I'd been cast on. Or, she had. Either way, magic was inclining me toward the pretty barmaid. The question was why?

What was my new friend from the swamps up to now?

Disappointed, I almost went with her anyway, to see where she might take me. But the blacksmith shuffled in between us. "Move, girl," he grunted. "You soil yourself standing so close to the garbage."

I cringed as Imma laughed. "Am I supposed to soil myself with you instead? Let you stick your fat, grungy, soot-infested cock inside me? I don't think so."

Jaw hard, the man raked his eyes over her. "Rumor says that Prince Guidon has the teeth pulled from the mouths of all his whores. I wonder what he'd pay if I did the job for him? And maybe remove that wicked tongue of yours too, eh?" He reached for her.

I clamped a restraining hand on his arm. "I'm giving you one chance to leave. I suggest you take it."

His sluggish drink-addled gaze slid to mine. "I'm going to paint the walls with your blood, Shinree. And when I'm done, I'm going to teach her the difference between a man and a witch. Might take a while, though. Hours," he smirked. "Days even."

Balling his stained shirt in my hands, I jerked the man closer. "I tried hard not to kill you. I really did." I gave him a shove. He tumbled backwards and his considerable weight pulled him down fast, along with a few chairs. I tossed one out of my way and straddled his chest. "You're right," I said, pressing a knee under his chin. "Teaching the difference between us could take a while." I drew back and punched him in the mouth. "Days, even." I punched him again.

"Goddamn witch!" he howled, spattering blood across my chest. "I'll lock those fucking chains around your neck myself!"

"You better make peace with whatever gods you worship first, asshole, because if I don't kill you, Raynan Arcana will have your head on a pike."

A muted smile curled his ruptured bloody lips. His voice dropped to a taunting whisper. "What do I care of a dead, Rellan King?"

"Dead?"

"That's right. You can't hide behind King Raynan's protection anymore. It died with him."

My heart sped up a little. "I don't believe you."

"Oh, he's dead all right, Shinree. He's dead...like you." Laughing, the blacksmith's eyes flicked off mine. His head tilted forward in the barest traces of a nod.

I had enough time to think, *ambush*, before a chorus of ringing metal erupted behind me.

EIGHT

The Wounded Owl had seen its share of scuffles. Typically, the patrons offered a disinterested glance to the parties involved and took their drinks to the other side of the room. Today, the hush that fell over the tavern was impressive. It meant I was in real trouble.

Heavy footsteps came at me from the rear. Getting rid of one problem, I snapped the blacksmith's neck and shoved to my feet. I stepped away from the body, and a long, wide shadow stretched over mine. It shifted, circling me.

An anxious, wet breath wheezed out of the man it belonged to. "Ian Troy?"

His heavy, distinctive accent startled me. As he came to a stop, I looked up past his substantial girth to his scraggly bearded face. The nostrils of his bulbous nose flared at my inspection. His deep-set gaze narrowed. But I kept going, all the way up to his head of long unkempt hair. Wild, wavy, and matted, the thick shoulder-length strands weren't brown or black, or even something in between. They were profoundly dark. Like a bottomless pit or a fetid cell when the lights were turned out. They were dark like the color of Death himself.

During the war we called it Langorian Black, and I had seen the shade up close so often there was no mistaking it. But I hadn't seen it for a long while. After I used the Crown of Stones to slaughter an entire army of the black-haired fiends, the whole of the realm shut itself off. It was rare when one

59

even crossed the border, and none had been spotted this side of the Kaelish Mountains in years.

Behind him was an armed mob of about twenty Kaelishmen. A few were big and rough looking. The rest were your basic desperate city-dwellers out to earn a fat purse. Some were taking their job seriously, positioning themselves at the door and the stairs. Six of them were really ambitious. They ripped hostages from the crowd, leaving the remaining customers and tavern workers to huddle together in a corner whimpering and praying for their lives. Imma wasn't among them.

As I turned to look for her, a bottle hit me in the side of the head. Glass and pain exploded across my vision. I spun around and caught another in the chest. A third bottle smashed into my right shoulder. "Son of a bitch!"

I pulled the sword off my back. Rivulets of blood and wine streaked down out of my hair. More streamed off my forehead and slid inside the collar of my shirt. By the time I'd wiped the stinging liquid from my eyes, one of the hostages was dead on the floor.

"Toss it," the Langorian ordered. "Both of them. Or…" pausing, he made a show of adjusting his grip on the axe in his hand. Its long, sharp head was substantially bigger than the one on his shoulders. "You can watch them all die."

I gave up both my weapons and slid them across the floor.

The Langorian shifted the axe to his other shoulder. "Answer the question, worm. Are you Ian Troy?"

Dabbing at the cuts on my head, I snarled at him. "You know exactly who I am."

"I want you to say it. Say what you are. Murderer. Butcher. Slayer of Kings." His meaty cheeks puffed with a smile. "War criminal."

I froze. "Did you just say…?" He nodded, and everything in me constricted. "You can't be serious."

"Your crimes against my kind are well known, Shinree."

"*My* crimes? Your fucking kinsmen were a plague on the land for years. They were a disease, an infestation that deserved to be wiped out." Temper overriding caution, my voice spiked. "The torture. The rape. The beheadings. Entire villages burned to the ground. Children gutted. I should have ripped your people's goddamn insides out one piece at a time."

"Careful, you might give me ideas." His fleshy lips curved upward. "My name is Danyon. Remember it when you beg for your life."

Astonishment added to my anger, and I laughed. "Gods, you fucking Langorians are all the same, with your balls bigger than your brains. Tell me, Danyon, how did you manage to make so many friends?" I nodded at his henchmen. "You've got about as much personality as the mud on the bottom of my boots. And let's face it…there's no love between the Langorian and the Kaelish."

"There's love between the Kaelish and their coin. And it didn't take much to sway them to the truth."

"Which is?"

"That you are evil and they are trespassers."

"Trespassers?"

"Are my words not plain, witch? Kael's claim to this region is unjust. A thousand years ago all of this," he opened his plump arms wide, "Kael, Rella, everything from sea to sea, all the Restless Lands, belonged to us."

"Guess you should have done a better job claiming it then, asshole, because *Mirra'kelan* is an ancient Shinree word, not Langorian. Besides, don't you think a thousand years is a little long to hold a grudge?"

"We were a peaceful people, simple farmers and hunters. The Shinree were the disease, emerging like insects from their mines below the ground, crawling out of the mountains, spreading from shore to shore, overrunning us, conquering us, forcing us into the mines—enslaving us with magic." Danyon's ample jowls tightened. "We lived like *animals*. We lost our history, our identity." He looked at me long and hard. Air rattled in his throat as his breath picked up speed. "Do you dare deny that?"

"You know I can't. But that way of life, what my ancestors did to create and sustain their empire…they paid for it."

"Yes. The gods saw the wickedness of your kind. They saw our persecution. They reached down, grabbed the land of the Shinree and shook it. They opened the mountains and pulled your entire domain down under the ground where it belonged. You fell. And we rose!" he exclaimed, thumping a hand to his chest. "We survived. We grew strong while the Shinree, without their precious rocks, became weak, slobbering fools. They became the slaves." He shifted his axe again. "Kael has not yet paid. Rella has not yet paid."

61

"And what exactly do they owe you?"

"The ground they live on. We want it back."

The depth of his stupidity made me smile. "You're a fool, Danyon. The centuries of fighting between Rella and Langor, the war, was never about land. The original treaty that was signed—signed and then broken by Draken's father, King Taiven—had nothing to do with territory. It was broken over a woman."

"King Taiven made a legitimate offer of marriage to that Rellan wench. What happened when she turned it down was her doing."

"That Rellan *Princess*," I said, emphasizing her title, "was already betrothed. Your King should have respected that. Instead, he sent men into Rella to drag her to Langor. Then he wasn't even man enough to marry her. He threw her into his dungeon and let her starve to death." Brazenly, I stepped forward. "The only property that Rella and Langor fought over for twenty-five years was the battered body of a dead Princess."

He sniffed. "You know nothing, Shinree."

"I know I didn't slay your damn King. Either of them. Some other fortunate soul ran Taiven through long before I saw my first battle. And his son, Draken, he was certainly worthy of a painful end, but we both know I didn't give him one."

"No, you did far worse. King Draken was a good man before your magic fouled him. He was noble. Decent."

"Draken? Decent?" I rushed closer. Nose to nose, I snarled at him, "What decent man orders a child stolen from her bed?"

"Elayna Arcana was old enough to be Draken's Queen…if she had survived."

"But she didn't. Did she? Draken only fancied a Rellan bride because he wanted to succeed where his father failed. But ordering that poor girl brought across the Langorian Mountains in the middle of winter…your noble King might as well have murdered Aylagar's daughter with his bare hands."

"She had another. The bitch should have been grateful we didn't take them both."

Rage sped through me as I remembered all too well the day Aylagar learned of her eldest daughter's death. It was the only time I'd ever seen her cry.

"How the hell are you even alive?" I asked him. "You weren't on the bat-tlefield that day or you'd be dead. Were you a deserter? Is that it? Where've you been for the last ten years, Danyon? Sitting around some stinking Langorian drink-house, working up your courage and saving your coin so you could recruit enough village idiots to come against me?"

"You will regret that."

"I regret a lot of things."

Another man's voice filtered down from upstairs. "That is good to know. I would be displeased to learn that you live without shame."

Alarms went off in my head. I turned to look, but I didn't need to. Like Danyon, I knew the accent coming out of the man. It wasn't Langorian. though. It was measured and exotic. It was Aylagar's.

"You're a long way from home, Arullan," I said, watching the man descend the stairs.

"Six months by ship," he confirmed. "But you are worth it."

"I'm flattered."

His boots hit the first floor and he paused. "Don't be."

Crossing the tavern, the Arullan halted in front of me, and I was sud-denly all out of glib comments. Because the man didn't just share a homeland with Aylagar, he shared her blood. There was no mistaking it. Set within a masculine face that was all angles and lines, were her crescent eyes and expressive mouth. On a taller, wider frame was her perfect symmetry of elegance and lean muscle. He had Aylagar's skin, dark as midnight and flaw-less. His hair was the same jet-black strands that hung twisted and gnarled all the way to the small of his back. *Just like her.*

I cleared the shock from my throat. "You're a warrior in the Arullan Guard," I said, gesturing at his breeches and sleeveless shirt. They bore no markings of rank, but the supple material was crafted with an intricate, symbolic stitching I recognized. "Your countrymen aided Rella in the fight against Langor. They were brave beyond words."

"It is our nature. Your nature however..." Smiling slightly, the Arullan's somber, brown eyes searched mine. "My people say there is little that sepa-rates bravery from insanity. Even less lies between penance and acceptance." His smile thinned. "I believe you, Shinree, live somewhere in between."

"It's been a long day, Arullan. Why don't we just stick with who you are and what you want?"

"My name is Lareth." He bowed slightly. "What I want is your head."

I blew out a breath. "Is that all?"

Beside him, Danyon laughed. "Polite, Arullan. Why ask when you can take?"

Lareth didn't even look at him. "Your opinion means less to me than his, Langorian. I suggest you don't offer it again."

As Danyon sulked away, I nodded after him. "You two make an unusual couple."

"Not for much longer." Lareth smiled again. The expression came nowhere near reaching his eyes. I didn't trust it one bit. "I have no wish to hurt you, Shinree. Submit yourself for execution and you will feel no pain."

"You do this now? After ten years?"

"Grief is patient. It waits for justice…while governments change and kings fall."

"I fought alongside your people, Lareth. I watched them die defending a realm that wasn't even theirs. I bled with them, befriended them."

"Killed them?" His perfect jaw twitched. "Aylagar was my cousin."

"She was my commander. I felt her loss, too."

"She was a Princess of Arulla. A daughter of my King's house."

"And I honored her for that."

"You defiled her. Murdered her."

"I didn't—"

"Yes," he broke in. "You did."

Nodding, I ran a shaky hand over my face. "I never meant to hurt her. I never meant to hurt any of your kind."

"Perhaps not. But the mind cannot always know what the soul intends." He went still a moment. "I sense honor in you, Shinree. You would prefer no one see it. You want us all to revile you, to hate you, as that gives you leave to hate yourself. But I am not here out of loathing. I feel no more animosity toward you than I would a starving wolf caught consuming my flock for sustenance. You are what you are, just as the wolf is. But when the beast can no longer be trusted to curb his hunger, when he crosses the line, he must be destroyed."

I held his gaze. "If it would bring her back, I would give you what you ask, without question. I swear it."

"I believe you." But I could tell by the look in his eyes that it wasn't enough.

Danyon moved forward. He bellowed at his mob, "Rip the witch to pieces! An extra bag of coin goes to the one that gets that rock off his neck!"

The Kaelish tossed their hostages to the floor and formed a line in front of me. Shouting obscenities and brandishing weapons, as they worked themselves into a nice frenzy, I pulled the two small throwing knives hidden in the braces on my forearms. Then I immediately beckoned to the obsidian shard at my throat. I didn't think. I didn't agonize over how I was willingly channeling magic again, or risking lives.

After all, the Wounded Owl was a den for outlaws and thieves. If King Raynan Arcana truly was dead, and the Crown of Stones was compromised, there was a lot more at risk than a few delinquent tavern-dwellers.

I have to protect Rella. I can't die here.

I opened myself up to the stone's aura. I swallowed everything it had, and a wave of heat layered my skin. A stream of piercing cold pumped through my veins. Vibrations stroked my nerves. Choosing a spell that wouldn't sap me too much, I uttered the words and hurled the power out.

Born out of necessity, urgency, and desperation, casting battle spells was a naturally swift process. More so than any other kind of Shinree magic. Even so, it had been a long time since I'd used magic in a fight. And as euphoria masked the remaining pain of my injuries, the stone's aura blinded me and my energy level dipped—all blindingly fast— the sudden barrage of overlapping sensations left me teetering.

A breath later, as my spell sought out the strength it needed to be born, bodies starting falling. I heard them, but as my vision cleared, I didn't look to see who or how many. I didn't check to see if they were dead or only unconscious. I'd cast on myself to keep the cost to others low. It was all I could do.

My mood lifted some at watching the gang of men waiver at the sight of me. Unabashed fear gripped the faces of more than a few. "Sorry, boys. Guess this is a little more than you signed up for."

"You won't cast here," Danyon blustered with confidence. "What the Arullan said is true. You consider yourself an honorable witch."

"Maybe. But right now I'm an angry one."

"Angry enough to kill all these people to save yourself?"

"You involved them, not me. Tell you what, though, Danyon. You clear the place out, and I'll put the spell away. You and I can go blade to blade. It's what you really want anyway. Just let everyone go. We..." the words jammed in my throat. I couldn't catch my breath. I couldn't move. Out of nowhere, a fresh violent wave of magic was rushing into me. Caressing my nerves, blindingly fast and hot enough to make me flinch; at first, I thought my friend from the swamps was at it again. The feel was definitely obsidian in nature, but the shard around my neck was a dry, vacant husk. I'd already taken everything it had.

There was a slight variation in the stream. Almost like the power wasn't originating *in* the shard, but flowing through it.

The spill quickened. The vibrations magnified. They turned fierce and forceful, and a stampede of blended auras piled in. The painful pressure in my veins, the provocative throb of one current riding atop the other, brought such sweet agony. It was almost too much to comprehend. The sensations, the power moving through me, accelerating and intensifying; I was a barely contained explosion.

My body wanted to celebrate, to revel in the moment. But I'd encountered such terrifying splendor only once before in my life. It was an experience in pleasure and pain that I would never forget. "No," I gasped. "It can't be."

It's hundreds of miles away. This isn't possible.

How is it in me?

But how didn't really matter. The power of the Crown of Stones was surging through my body, and there was no way it was coincidence. Being Shinree, I didn't believe in such things. I put no faith in luck, good or bad. Fate had his dirty little hands in everything. So there had to be a reason that this, the first time I'd willingly channeled the shard in years, I'd gotten the crown too. Unfortunately, there was only one reason that made sense: the crown and the shard were connected.

If that were true, then when King Raynan chipped the slender piece of obsidian off the Crown of Stones, he'd broken the piece from the whole physically, but not magically. Whatever held the crown together, whatever formed the artifact in the first place was a link too strong to be broken by crude tools, or apparently, separated by kingdoms.

All this time…all these years…

I'd worn the shard every day. I'd considered it a symbol for the embodiment of all that was wrong with my people. I'd seen the stone as a temptation to overcome. Evidently, it was much more. And I was betting my Shinree enemy from the swamps knew it, too. He knew pushing the magic into me wouldn't be enough to reach the crown. So he'd ignited my addiction, then sat back & waited until I had enough motivation to cast on my own—with the only stone in my possession.

By channeling the shard, I'd inadvertently reestablished its connection to the crown. A connection he could access through me.

I should have known. I should have at least considered the possibility of a link.

I'd been a shortsighted fool, and I was paying for it. The crown's magic was burrowing straight to the very heart of me. I could feel it, just like last time, heightening my aggression, toying with my anger, accentuating my hostility. Soon, nothing would be in me but the need to do violence and the desire to remind the world what I was capable of. Already, the thoughts were churning. The notion of what I could do with so much magic at my fingertips.

I can wipe out the Arullan and the Langorian, the entire tavern—the whole of Sarin's kingdom.

All I had to do was let go.

I can't. Not here. Not again.

Grinding my teeth on a scream, I fought like hell. I pushed against the overwhelming power amassing inside me.

It was like holding back a raging river with my bare hands.

The combined auras of the crown were too ferocious, too willful. They didn't want to go. They liked it inside me. They promised to make me great, to quench my thirst—if I would just give in.

What does it matter? I thought. *Why shouldn't I kill them? They're all fools. They have no idea how powerful I am. They trifle with me, taunt me.*

No one here cares if I live. Why should I spare them?

I envisioned the city afterwards, how it would look; brittle bodies strewn, ash blowing over the silent, empty streets. I imagined the stink of thousands of moldy corpses roasting in the late summer sun, and the idea excited me. It filled me with such a rush of eager satisfaction, such sick exhilaration. Then the battlefield flashed across my mind. I saw the land I turned to desert, the soldiers I turned to bones and dust, both besieged by hungry crows and soured by the air.

And all those drinks I'd so hastily consumed, nearly came back up.

Digging deeper, repulsed by my own desires, I resisted the crown's lure with everything I had. I clung to the disgust, to the fear that I wasn't strong enough—that I didn't want to be. I shoved, pushing at the excess magic, forcing it out, forcing myself to be stronger, to be braver. Until at last, the crown's hold gave way and its magic began to recede. As it left, awareness returned. I became conscious of myself again and realized I was on the floor, on my back, with Danyon's boot ramming into me.

I had no idea how long I'd been indisposed, struggling against the crown, but every part of me hurt, and his axe was raised high above my head for a killing blow.

"Your time is at an end Shinree," he grinned. "This is the Age of Langor." His weapon came down. I rolled to the side, and steel bit into the floor less than an inch from my head. Noticing the throwing knives still in my grip, as Danyon yanked his axe free, I lifted up and thrust my slender blades into his gut. With a howl, he dropped to one knee beside me. His grip on the axe loosened slightly. I grabbed the shaft with both hands and jabbed the butt end up into his face.

From my position, the blow lacked force. Yet it startled him. Enough, that as he wobbled, I reached for a broken chair leg off the floor, leaned up, and bash him across the jaw with it.

Danyon collapsed. I felt like joining him. But a dozen men still blocked the front door and Lareth was advancing. With the spell I'd conjured still active inside me, I faced him. I held up my right hand. The air in front of it shifted.

One last time, I tried. "Don't make me do this."

"Do what you must, Shinree," Lareth said bravely. "If I die, I die for her."

"I've been dying for Aylagar for ten years. It isn't that great."

"Then let me end your pain." Lareth drew his sword. He ran at me like a charging bull, and I released the magic. Rippling out from the center of my palm, translucent waves, pulsing black from the obsidian, spread out between us.

Lareth didn't even blink. He met them at full speed, and the impact shot him backwards. His body hit the far wall, then the floor.

I spun to find Danyon. Expecting the hulking Langorian to be on his feet by now and preparing to attack, I was poised to send the same surge of power in his direction. But he wasn't attacking or even standing. Danyon was face down on the dirt floor. His giant axe was beside him. The blade of a fancy Kaelish long-knife was buried in the center of his back.

Frowning, wondering who the weapon belonged to, I lifted my hand to aim the magic at Danyon's men, and suddenly it all caught up to me: the beating, the drink, the energy I'd given to make the spell. I couldn't focus. Their faces blurred. The tavern revolved. It started spinning around me. When a pair of polished, black Rellan riding boots moved in to straddle Danyon's body, I thought I was hallucinating.

The owner of the boots bent down to retrieve his knife from Danyon's back. Straightening, he stared at me. I got a good, long look at him. And then I was absolutely certain something vital had been knocked loose in my head.

NINE

I blinked a few times, but the face didn't change. The man was still Langorian, and he was still alive when he shouldn't be.

Like Danyon, he was of the right age to be dead. Considering that during the war Draken had ordered all able-bodied men conscripted into his army. There had been no exceptions to his decree and no escape from my spell. Or, so I'd believed. Yet here they were; two able-bodied exceptions in a run-down tavern on the edge of Kael.

Exactly why they were here, I was a little fuzzy on. But one thing was clear. Whatever hole the two of them had crawled out of, they didn't crawl out of it together.

Danyon, as most of his ilk, was massive and ogre-like, keen for little more than food, women, wine, and a good dose of carnage. In contrast, Danyon's killer belonged to a more atypical class of Langorians, a caste whose education, form, and behavior set them apart from the common stock. They were the decision makers, the privileged, and the rich. They were the minority in the realm, yet they still managed to hold all the power.

Draken was one of them. If I didn't know that pure evil wafted off the man, by sight alone I would label him refined and debonair. He was the only person I'd ever seen who could wade across a battlefield knee-deep in bodies and still look striking and cultured by the time he reached the other side—until now.

Exuding that same highborn quality, the man in front of me, had eliminated Danyon as smoothly and effortlessly as he likely did everything else. He wasn't a killer by trade, though, or even a soldier. There was nothing cold or cautious in the way he carried himself. I didn't detect a whiff of the customary condescension or cruelty that clung to his kind. To the contrary, as the man swaggered in my direction, his movements were neither heartless nor arrogant. They were pure confidence, in a fluid, careless way that was very un-Langorian like.

His features were equally out of the ordinary. Though possessing the deep-set eyes, sharp nose, and large build common for his kind, he wore them better than any man of Langor I had ever seen. *Because he isn't one,* I thought, *at least not entirely.*

He was a half-breed, but the man was no mutt. He was a distinct blend of superior blood, with notable diverse influences. Instead of the classic Langorian girth, he was tall and unmistakably muscular beneath fine Kaelish garb. His dark gray breeches and carefully matched tunic were cut from expensive cloth. The fabric didn't billow or crinkle in the least as he walked. It fit over his form like a second skin, which was a noticeably lighter shade than the usual Langorian dusky brown. His eyes, as he trained them on me, were a conspicuous granite color. His hair was dark, but it lacked the extra intensity I despised. Even more remarkable, he wore it cut high in a straight, distinguished style that most Langorians would never care to maintain.

The man paused in his approach. Reaching inside his leather cloak, he pulled out a small cloth and started wiping down his knife. He didn't miss a spot. Not seeming to notice or care that the entire tavern was watching, he went on, meticulously tending his weapon for so long, I didn't know whether to be angry or amused. Such blatant, self-absorption was a clear act of cold, arrogant pretense. Yet, somehow, he came across as regal and intelligent as he cleaned Danyon's insides off his blade.

Finally returning the knife to an embroidered sheath fastened to the outside of his leg, the man flashed me a roguishly charming smile. "Sorry I'm late," he said in a fine, Kaelish lilt—the absolute last thing I expected to hear. "I see you started without me." He tossed the bloody rag at Danyon's back. "I'm Malaq." He was poised to say more, but I interrupted.

"Call off your friends."

"Friends?" Malaq raised a single tidy, dark eyebrow. As if mulling over the meaning of the word, he scanned the room. Taking in the details of the ambush as methodically as he cleaned his knife, Malaq looked at each of Danyon's men in turn, then made note of the patrons and tavern workers. It was apparent that he was in no hurry. And while I was itching to interrupt his painstaking inspection, I kept my mouth shut. Because whatever Malaq was doing, measuring the odds, sizing up weapons, ogling the barmaids, it was working. As wherever his gaze fell in the Wounded Owl, movement stopped.

At last he looked back at me. A slow grin emerged from beneath his barely-there mustache. "I usually drink with a man before I call him friend. And I don't recall drinking with any of these...gentlemen," he said kindly. "I could be wrong, of course. But that doesn't happen often." His gray eyes slid to the side. "Behind you," he said, so careless and calm, I didn't even catch his meaning until I felt the blade against my back.

"Langorian," Lareth snarled, his spit hitting the nape of my neck. "Identify yourself."

"My apologies," Malaq responded, voice and eyes equally impassive. "I did attempt introductions, but the Shinree wasn't interested. Not that I'm surprised." Malaq waved a dismissive hand in my direction. Nonchalantly brushing his cloak back, he rested a hand on the hilt of the sword belted on his left hip. "I believe we came here for the same reason, Arullan. Shall we get on with it?"

Lareth hesitated. "You're here for the witch as well?"

Malaq pulled his sword. The scabbard was elaborately etched. The blade was incredibly shiny and elegant, but it was far from flimsy. I could see exactly how strong the steel was as he pointed it at my face. "I certainly didn't come for the food."

"Fine," Lareth grumbled, "I will allow you the kill. But the body is mine."

Malaq's Kaelish lilt turned serious. "My kill, my body."

"All but the head," Lareth countered. "I came a long way for it."

"I don't know," Malaq grimaced. "Why not take the heart instead? That's always a bold statement."

Stuck between them and their swords, as they argued over who got which pieces of me, my muscles were twitching. I couldn't see Lareth, but Malaq's sword arm wasn't wavering in the least. There was zero tension in him. His face betrayed nothing of what he intended. He had yet to give me any clear signal to indicate if we were even on the same side, or if he cared in the least whether I lived or died.

Still, I wasn't worried. I couldn't put my finger on it, but Malaq had an undefined way about him that wanted me at ease. Maybe it was the lack of malice or threat coming off him. More likely, it was how dangerously close I was standing to the end of his sword. It gave me a vantage point Lareth didn't have. One that I hoped explained exactly what Malaq was up to.

"Nice weapon," I said, disrupting their exchange. "Very fancy."

Malaq's sharp eyes snapped to mine. "Yes, it is."

"Custom made?"

"My own design."

"It's very..." I gave him a deliberate look. "Subtle."

Malaq didn't reply. His expression, which was a complete lack of expression, stayed the same. Nevertheless, I sensed he'd understood my meaning, and knew that I'd noticed the secret his sword held; a well-concealed second blade riding discreetly along the underside of the first. Made to rest perfectly in the furrow of the main blade, the slender miniature sword was practically invisible at anything but a fatally close range. It appeared to be activated by a trigger woven into the folds of an elaborate basket hilt, detailed and intricate enough to provide the perfect camouflage.

"Bet it cost you," I said. "Mind if I get a closer look?" Malaq extended the weapon. As the tip nearly touched my left eye, I fought against moving. "Do you know how to use it?"

He chuckled as he lowered the blade to my neck. "I am an expert swordsman."

"Just because you carry a sword, Langorian, doesn't make you an expert."

"Then I suppose I should give you a demonstration."

"Anytime," I said.

With that, Malaq pulled the trigger. He activated the hidden blade, and it popped out with a flash. I barely had time to hit the floor and look up, before steel was penetrating the dark flesh of Lareth's throat. Just as quick, Malaq retracted the weapon. Grasping the hilt in both hands, with a furious swing, he slashed the main blade across Lareth's stomach, splitting the Arullan near in half and sending out a sweeping burst of blood to shower the air. Bits fell like hail. The corpse hit the dirt floor beside me and a warm, wet cloud rose up, covering me in enough dust and gore to change my skin tone.

"What the hell?" I coughed out. "A little warning would have been nice."

"You asked for a demonstration."

I gave Malaq a hostile glare as I wiped the splatter off my face. "I didn't ask you to drop the body on top of me."

"You're welcome." Already cleaning off his blade, he gave me a distracted, cursory glance. "I suppose you are a little gruesome. But it's nothing a bath won't cure."

Wiping my face again, I got to my feet. "All right. Let's do it."

"Do what?" His tone said I'd confused him. The matching expression wasn't on his face though. Nothing was, so I couldn't tell if his uncertainty was real.

"You didn't come here to fight me?"

"Why would I do that? I just went to a lot of trouble to save your life."

I grunted. "I don't have time to pull the truth out of you, Langorian, so do us both a favor and go. Take the stairs. Last room on your right has an exit to the roof. There's a hay cart that comes through most nights about this time. It'll cushion your jump."

Still tending his blade, Malaq's eyebrow lifted again. "While I'd love to hear the, no doubt nefarious, story as to how you know that," he glanced up and smiled thinly, "the front door is really more my style."

"Go right ahead." I motioned to the exit. Danyon's mob looked considerably less organized now that their leaders were dead. But they were still blocking the door. "Maybe they'll step aside if you ask nicely." When Malaq didn't reply, or make like he was leaving, I got blunt. "Having a Langorian at my back in a fight doesn't sit well."

"I see." He gave no outward indication of disapproval, but I could feel it. "Well, if you're planning on using that," his eyes wandered to the obsidian, "you might want to reconsider. Things could get out of hand quickly."

Suspicion sent my hand to the shard. "You know what this is? Where it comes from?" I didn't wait for his answer. "Who the hell are you?"

"Kael's new Peace Envoy." Malaq slid his sword away. He discarded another bloody rag on another body. "Newly appointed by King Sarin not a week past."

"An ambassador," I said, not overly surprised. "So that's what you were doing when you killed Danyon? Promoting peace?"

"I was trying to keep you in one piece. Not that you seemed to appreciate it." Almost imperceptibly, Malaq's eyes tightened. He turned toward the closest window and squinted, straining to see through the dirty glass. "You hear that?"

I listened a moment. The wind was picking up. "It's just a storm." But in the time it took for the words to be said, the wind outside had evolved from a spirited breeze to a persistent violent gust. Increasingly intense, the blast of air roared over the building. Shutters clattered outside, banging open and closed. Debris smacked against the windows. Cracks formed in the panes, crawling like web across the glass, as The Wounded Owl rumbled and shook. Wooden walls bowed. The ceiling shuddered. The door quivered on its hinges. It flung open wide. And every window in the place exploded at the same time with an earsplitting *shatter*. Slivers of propelled glass sliced open my skin. One of Danyon's men took a shard to the throat, another to the stomach. As the raging gale rushed unfettered across the tavern, anything lacking weight went airborne.

Shelves were cleaned of their contents and ripped off the walls. Chairs and tables shot across the floor. Dust swirled up from the ground. Those who weren't already in hiding, hurried to take cover. I fought to stand against the onslaught, to keep track of where my enemies were scurrying off to. But one by one, the candles were going out. Then the fire in the hearth went cold, and the room sunk into blackness.

The door slammed shut, and I jumped. All at once the wind disappeared, the walls stopped quaking, and the wood stopped groaning. Everything that was being tossed fell with a crash. The only sound remaining was the whispered murmurings of fear.

"Troy..." Malaq said cautiously. As I turned toward his voice, peering into the gloom, a glow flared up between us. It took form and grew into a small sphere of yellow light.

Suspended in mid-air, about the size of a wagon wheel, the sphere was hot and hard to look at, but it wasn't anything close to fire. It wasn't solid, either. The edges were running, dripping light like a candle drips wax.

Malaq came around the object to stand next to me. "Tell me this is you."

"Wish I could." I stepped toward the glowing ball. "This is something elemental. Something I've never seen before. Something I definitely can't do."

"It's beautiful."

"Elemental magic usually is. But influencing nature like this can have massive consequences. It's not even supposed to be done without a King's permission."

"I'm betting Sarin didn't order a small sun to be delivered to the Wounded Owl."

I grunted at his jest, and we watched the undulating rays in silence as they swelled and brightened, expanded and intensified. Fiery waves rippled out from the core.

They rushed over us, and Malaq gasped in surprise. "There's no heat."

The blinding surge continued on. It left no one untouched. It chased every shadow from every corner of the room. Then the billowing light passed through the walls and vanished, leaving an abrupt lack of brightness that played with my eyes.

Rubbing them, I heard the fire in the hearth crackle back to life, then movement and voices. The noises devolved instantly into shouts of alarm, followed by multiple thumping sounds I knew all too well were people falling to the floor. As the spots left my eyes, I saw Malaq curled up on the dirt floor. He was wheezing and grabbing his throat. So were a lot of other people.

It wasn't affecting me as severely, but I could feel it. The air in the tavern was thinning. It was getting hot—real hot, real fast.

"Hang on," I told him, "I'll get us out of here." But I wasn't sure how. The front door had been magically fastened shut so tight it was glowing. So were the walls, the space in front of the stairwell, and the empty window frames.

If there was a way out, I couldn't see it.

Danyon's ill-planned ambush had failed, but this one had worked just fine, and I was trapped. I was locked in a room full of so much power I was choking on it. We all were. And we were dying.

TEN

D own on one knee, ripping at the neckline of my linen shirt, I scanned the room. My thought was that after such a glitzy performance, the caster would be vain enough to stick around and admire his work. But my reasoning was flawed, or just plain wrong, because no one was left standing.

Then a voice penetrated the haze in my head. *"You will not find me with your eyes. I speak only in your mind."* The voice was unfamiliar, soft and overtly feminine, and I was shocked. After what happened with Taren Roe, I expected my Shinree enemy to be a man. *"We are not enemies,"* she assured me. *"This spell was not meant for you."*

Her words were gentle, her voice soothing and breathy. I would have enjoyed the sound if I weren't suffocating. "Air," I gasped.

"You're angry with me?"

"Air…?"

"Of course."

Instantly, my lungs filled. The harsh, abrupt sensation knocked me to the floor.

"Better?"

"No," I croaked out.

Through the spell I felt her bristle. *"You're injured. Let me heal you."*

Before I could get a word out, a blanket of healing magic rippled across my skin. It was calming. Soothing, like a warm woolen blanket. Badly, it wanted to lull me to sleep. Her voice willed me to close my eyes, promising the pain would be gone when I woke.

But when I woke, Malaq and everyone else would be dead.

"Stop," I said, fighting the grogginess. "Him first." I tossed my aching head in Malaq's direction.

"He's Langorian."

"I know what he is. And I want him alive. I want them all alive."

"You would save those that try to kill you?"

"Not all of these people were a part of that."

"Those without weapons would have stood by and watched you die without a moment's guilt. I see no difference."

"I do."

After a small delay her healing spell lifted, and I immediately felt like shit. Crawling the short distance to Malaq's side, I struggled to pull him onto my lap. Weak, strangled sounds were coming out of him. Very little air was going in.

"What are you waiting for?" I shouted at her. "I swear woman, if he dies, you die. Make your choice."

There was no response. I was hoping the silence didn't mean she planned on calling my bluff. Unmistakably, the woman owned a magical stamina that far surpassed mine. If I went after her with a spell and failed, I'd be at her mercy. If I went after her with my new-found access to the Crown of Stones I wouldn't fail. But my conscious was full enough without adding a tavern full of deaths to the tally.

There was only one other way I could think of to handle her. It was desperate and foolish. It was something I shouldn't even consider.

Carefully, I slid Malaq to the floor. I stood up and addressed the woman in Shinree. *"Kay'ta Roona, areen'a.* Do you hear me? *Kay'ta Roona!"* I took a deep breath. "An oath for a life," I said, translating the words into Rellan to remind myself what a completely horrible idea it was. "Grant my request. Save these people, and I offer you gratitude. Two fold," I threw in.

"As in the ways of the old Empire?" Her shock evident. *"For their lives you would bind yourself to me in such a manner? Why?"*

"My own reasons."

80

"And you will do for me without question?" Anticipation overrode the sensual nature of her voice. *"Twice?"*

I didn't like how happy she was at the prospect, but Malaq was turning blue. "Yes," I vowed. "Two debts to repay as you see fit."

"An oath made in the old ways is governed by them as well. If I come to you, and you deny me, I have the right to compensation. Your life could be forfeit, if I so choose."

"I understand how the oath works. I won't refuse you."

"You cannot refuse me."

"I cannot," I echoed, and the words left a cold chill on my skin. I wished for a way to take them back. My pledge to her was irrational and thoughtless. It was a mistake that I had no doubt would hunt me down and bleed me later on. But it was done. Malaq and the others were already sucking in great gulps of air, and I couldn't sense the woman's presence anymore. She'd taken my offer and ran.

I looked down at Malaq. "You better be worth it."

Coming around, he groaned some unintelligible response. I didn't bother asking him to repeat it. I was so exhausted and sore I just fell down where I was and went to work adding up the bodies I'd been too late to save. I felt a little better watching the ones that made it stumble to their feet. A few stumbled all the way to the bar. Most fled into the growing darkness outside.

The staff, or what remained of it, diligently started the unenviable task of cleaning up. Someone lit the hearth, and I noticed the color creeping back into Malaq's face. He was still drawing in deep fractured breaths and his hands were shaking like it was mid-winter, causing the multiple gold rings on his fingers to clack out a nervous rhythm.

Watching him, I noticed one ring was different from the rest.

A black pearl, cut in half and set in the middle of a plain band of deep blue coral, the ring's design was simple for a nobleman. Understated even, if black and blue weren't the colors of the Rellan flag, and if black pearls (due to their worth and scarcity) weren't a trinket afforded only by members of the Rellan royal family.

My interest in his identity piqued, I was still studying the pearl when Malaq moved his hand up the front of his cloak. His fingers stopped. They closed on the circular pin holding the cloth together at his neck with a kind of desperate relief that seemed out of character. Malaq must have thought it was too, as his regal features held the expression so briefly that by the time he dropped his hand—giving me a clear view of the pin—the outward manifestation of his anxiety was gone. Mine was all over me.

The pin wasn't just a circle. It was a golden serpent swallowing its own tale.

My pulse raced as I stared at the clasp. It was a symbol of royalty, like the pearl ring. But it wasn't Rellan in origin. The serpent was a sign of Langor, and the clasp currently on Malaq's cloak was handed down from father to son. How Malaq got his hands on it, I had no idea. But there was no mistaking it. I'd seen the serpent on King Draken, the morning of our last battle, just hours before I unleashed the magic of the Crown of Stones.

I glanced down at the ring, then up at the serpent again. I looked at Malaq's finely crafted Kaelish sword, his expensive Rellan boots, and half-Rellan features, and wondered, *thief?*

But that didn't sit right.

"Why do they bother with walls if they have no floor?" Malaq grumbled, slapping at the dirt on his cloak as he stood. He reached an absent hand down to help me up, and I sat there, staring at it. When he realized I wasn't taking his offer, he pulled his arm back with a hiss. Yanking the nearest chair upright, Malaq sat down and began furiously dusting the floor from his trousers. "Ungrateful fool," he murmured.

"I'm not ungrateful. I'm skeptical." Wincing, I sat up and leaned against the bench behind me. "I haven't met a Langorian yet that hasn't tried to kill me."

"Perhaps it's because you're always trying to kill them."

His remark pulled a shaky grin out of me. "I'd get it if the Owl was a Rellan tavern, but the Kaelish generally don't give a damn about me. And the Arullans, after all this time, looking for revenge, allying with a Langorian...I don't trust it."

"So you're ill-mannered *and* skittish? Wonderful."

"No offense, *Nef'areen,* but skittish doesn't come close. With your dialect, your clothes, and your face, I have no idea where we stand right now."

Malaq stared down the sharp angle of his nose. "Did you just insult me?"

I recalled my words. "Possibly."

"What is that, then? *Nef'areen?*"

"Don't do that. Don't speak Shinree with a Kaelish accent and shove it out a Langorian mouth. It sounds wrong."

"Remind me why I saved you?"

"I saved *you*. And it isn't an insult. *Nef'areen* is a title, a way of addressing a nobleman, like a lord or a Prince."

Malaq's eyes grabbed mine. "You believe me royalty? Why?"

"That fancy Kaelish sword, for one. King Sarin has a weapon of the same craftsmanship. Though his is without that special, second blade." I glanced at Malaq's hand. "The ring makes you a possible heir to Rella." Then up at his neck. "The snake pinned at your throat says you're currently ruling the fine realm of Langor. Except, Draken's sister, Jillyan, is Queen there. And she has no husband."

"Oh, Jillyan has a husband. She married Prince Guidon Roarke not a week past."

My mouth gaped open. "Guidon? Sarin's son? You're telling me Kael's Prince is married to Langor's Queen?"

"Former Queen. Jillyan gave up her crown in Langor to be Princess of Kael. Of course that means when Sarin dies, and Guidon inherits the throne—"

"Draken's sister will rule Kael at Guidon's side." I really didn't like the sound of that. "How the hell did this happen?"

"Well, there was a wedding," he said dryly. "It was your typical over-the-top, Kaelish affair of lavish debauchery. And that was just the ceremony. The feast afterwards lasted for days. Don't ask me how many because it's all a bit of a blur. In fact, I believe half the kingdom is still hung over."

"I missed something."

"That, my friend, is a very *large* understatement."

I gave him an irritated frown. "Why would Sarin ally himself to Langor?"

"He hasn't. Not officially. Perhaps, Sarin was simply hoping to disguise Guidon's worthlessness with a strong match. A good woman can make all the difference."

"She's Langorian," I said plainly.

Malaq's eyes narrowed. "So?"

"I've seen Langorian women. The only thing good or strong about them is their thighs. So whatever Guidon is up to by taking Jillyan as his bride—there's no way Sarin approved."

"You surprise me, Troy. Being born of a persecuted race I expected you to be a bit more broad-minded. We're not all slobbering brutes, you know."

"You're right, Malaq. You're a fraud. Or, a thief…or, a Prince."

Watching me, he grinned. "My identity troubles you that much?"

"Just the Langorian part."

"I'm half Langorian. And I was raised Kaelish."

"I can hear that. But you're only Kaelish on the outside."

"That's not good enough for you?" I said nothing and a whiff of his temper poked through. "I could have let them kill you."

"And I could have used magic and killed them all. Including you."

"But you didn't."

"No, I didn't." I thought of the Shinree woman in my head and what I'd promised her. "I guess that makes us both fools."

A trace of somberness settled on Malaq's face as he got up from his chair. "What it makes us, my friend, is outcasts." He reached for me again. "If we don't help each other, no one else will."

Relenting, I let him pull me up. "Thanks."

Malaq's response was a satisfied grin that was just begging to be punched.

Curbing the urge, I went in search of my swords. I spotted them against the wall on the far side of the room. Someone had actually collected my weapons into a nice pile instead of stealing them. Today was one surprise after another.

I went to retrieve them, and a woman's hand came over mine. Behind me, her long, delicate fingers trailed over my wrist and up my arm. In the wake of her touch, my skin tingled.

It was impressive, considering a shirt and a leather brace stood between my arm and her fingers. "So you're back," I said, taking a guess. "And in person this time." Eager to see the face of the Shinree woman I indebted myself to for Malaq's life, I started to turn around.

I didn't get so much as a glimpse. Out loud, soft and husky, she said, "Now, I will heal you." And I was unconscious before I even hit the floor.

ELEVEN

Leaning back in his seat, Malaq inclined his mug in my direction. "You're heavier than you look, my friend. And those swords of yours..." he shook his head. "Why would you want to carry around all that steel? Mine weighs half as much and it works just fine."

I persuaded my head up off the table and scowled at him. "I like my swords," I mumbled. Blinking, trying to wake up, I pushed at the tangle of hair in my face and glanced around. "We're still at the Owl?"

"That we are."

"And you're still here?"

"That I am."

"I need a drink."

"You know, I'd be happy to let you give Natalia a try. You can't deny the results."

I thought a moment. "Your sword? You named your sword?"

"Why wouldn't I? She's beautiful. She sleeps beside me every night. Most importantly, Natalia never lets me down." Malaq pointed an accusing finger at me. "It's no different than you naming your horse."

I motioned for his cup. "Everybody names their horse."

"Not true," he argued, sliding his drink in my direction. "To give that beast I ride a name would imply that he was tame—which has been proven impossible. I'd have more luck breaking one of those giant bald creatures that runs around eating goats in the hills of Arulla."

Wrapping my hands around the cup, I took a long swallow and looked at him doubtfully. "A skin bear?"

"That's the one. Were you aware that Langor used to train soldiers by throwing them in a ring with those hairless monsters?"

The image made me grin. "I'd like to see that."

"Actually, so would I, but the practice died out fifty years ago. Someone with a smidge of intelligence finally realized the realm had more lame men than fighting men. Of course, they couldn't have been that smart or they would have shipped the beasts back to Arulla instead of turning them loose in the highlands. They don't breed much, thank the gods, but they eat. There's not a single mountain goat left in the whole of Langor."

Draining the cup, I slammed it down. "Congratulations, Malaq. That was the most pointless conversation I've ever had."

His jaw twitched slightly. "I see you left your manners in the swamp."

"Right next to my patience." I turned in my seat. We were the only customers in the entire tavern. "A little lack of air and everyone goes home."

"Like I always say, the Kaelish have no stamina."

My eyes went to one of the broken windows. "It'll be dawn soon."

"Tell me about it." Malaq picked up his empty mug and tapped it on the table. "Do you realize how many of these I've had to drink waiting for you to wake up? You'd think as much as I've paid the man he could at least bring me something that didn't taste like horse piss."

"You didn't have to stay. Really," I added; spending the night hunched over on a sticky, tavern table, unconscious from a healing I didn't ask for, hadn't left me in the best of moods. Neither had being trounced by two of my own kind in a matter of weeks. I wasn't used to being outmatched. It wasn't doing much for my attitude or my confidence. "But since you are here," I said, "what do you know about Shinree magic?"

"That's a vague question. Why?"

"Because I've been talking to myself for weeks, and it isn't helping."

"Okay…" Malaq said slowly, with a bemused, sideways glance. "Well, Shinree are one race, but your blood defines and divides you. It limits your magical abilities. Which, determine your value, or lack of it. Take you, for instance. Your mother was a gifted healer. But your father's line was stronger so you inherited his magic, his skills as a soldier. That's all you can do. You can't alter time or the weather or conjure a drop of water, unless you can somehow use it as an offense or defense."

He'd given me a lot of details for a vague question, but I let it go. "What about slaves? You clearly have some sort of clout here in Kael. Heard of any unusual lines being bred? Any accidental births?"

"Accidental births aren't possible. The breeders are too well trained, too well versed in which lines are dominant."

"What if one of us couldn't be classified so neatly?" I asked, thinking of the man who'd hired Taren and the woman who'd just invaded my head.

"You're all classified, Troy, by blood, by line, by status. If you were put into one of the camps as you are right now, they'd mark you down as a full pedigree soldier with regulated freedom and no previous owners."

"Damn. You rattled that off quick."

"I don't deal in slaves, Troy. But the world does. It helps to know the language."

"I'm betting you know all the languages."

"I don't understand."

"I think you understand perfectly."

"Does that mean you've finally figured me out?"

"I'm working on it."

"Mind if I hear what you have so far?"

It was a clear challenge. I studied him a moment then took him up on it. "Your basic features are Langorian, but they've been softened by privileged stock and diluted by what I'm thinking is Rellan blood. It's what slims you down and stretches you out. It gives a thinner shape to your nose and a higher brow. Tames your hair too and keeps it from being that foul shade."

"My hair is black."

"Not Langorian Black."

"There's little difference."

"There is to me. There is to a lot of people in Rella."

"We aren't in Rella."

"We aren't in Langor, either. But I suppose that's a good thing because if we were someone might take offence to that royal Arcana ring on your finger and chop it off."

Malaq looked down in silence at the dark pearl.

When he didn't confirm or deny, I went on. "From the elegance in your Kaelish accent, and the obvious price of your clothing and weapons, you're connected to King Sarin's court. Loosely though, or you wouldn't be associating with a pariah like me in public. Now that," I said, pausing to point at the clasp on his cloak. "That confuses me. I can't figure how you got your hands on a pin that's supposed to be worn only by the King of Langor. Unless you stole it."

"Not bad," Malaq nodded thoughtfully. "Your conclusion?"

"Don't have one." Hands on the table I pushed to my feet. "Sorry, Malaq. But it's late, and I have enough riddles to solve without adding you to the stack."

"You're right," he said. "The clasp was stolen. Draken's is a fake."

I sat back down. "I'm listening."

"For generations, the serpent was passed from father to son, from Langorian King to his successor. But all those years ago, the night King Taiven was found dead, the pin disappeared. The heirloom was such a well-known sign of Langor that a replica was crafted and presented to Draken on the day he took the throne. I'm not sure he ever knew it wasn't real. The truth is so well hidden."

"Then how do you know?"

"My mother killed King Taiven and took the serpent off his body."

I laughed. "You really have been at the ale the whole time I was out."

"I have. But that doesn't change the truth. She was held in the dungeon at Keep Darkhorne in the mountains of Langor. It's a particularly unpleasant place, reserved for the King's most prized prisoners."

"I know what it is. But Taiven died in battle. I've heard the tale a dozen times."

"And are all the tales of *your* exploits completely true? I certainly hope not."

I let out a weary sigh. "You have proof?"

Malaq looked away. His stare fixed on the wall next to our table. It was an empty wall. The wood was rotting and dirty. But as he gazed intently at it, I got the feeling he was seeing something far different than the smoke-wrapped walls of a grungy tavern.

"The pin wasn't the only thing my mother brought out of Darkhorne," he said at last. He looked me square in the eyes. "She brought me."

"That's where your Langorian ancestry comes from? She conceived in prison?"

"She was raped in prison."

"Of course. I'm sorry."

"There were rescue parties. But there was no way to breach Taiven's defenses."

Suspicion crept up my spine. "Rescue parties weren't sent that far into Langorian territory for just anyone."

"She wasn't just anyone. Neither was my father. But that didn't stop her from stabbing him in the heart with a table knife."

"Brave woman."

"Desperate woman. She was afraid of what I would become being raised in that place by his side." Malaq drew in a long, slow breath. He let it out like it hurt. "So, you see, Troy, you were right. I am a Prince."

His implication sunk in. "You're saying King Taiven was your father?" He nodded, and my first reaction was to laugh it off. Malaq's claim was outlandish. But looking at him, at his features, how he carried himself, the way the story affected him, it was entirely plausible he was a bastard son of Langor's late king. "And your mother?"

"I'm not sure how she escaped. It's been suggested that Taiven was drunk and she stabbed him in his sleep. But the facts remain unknown. It was pure luck the Rellan soldiers even found her. The winter had turned brutal. They were packing up to leave. From what I understand, they shouldn't have been there at all. Their incursion into Langor hadn't been sanctioned by Rella's King. It was undertaken by a young, idealistic Prince desperate to bring his sister home. And it hadn't gone well. Most of his men were dead. Supplies were near gone. The order had been given to mount up when someone spotted my mother in the snow." Malaq tried to stifle it, but a wave of grief thinned his voice. "She gave birth to me on the frozen ground in the middle of the Langorian Mountains and died an hour later. Without ever knowing how her life would impact the world."

"Hold on." I could feel my headache coming back. "Are you suggesting that the Prince was Raynan Arcana, and that your mother was his sister, Lareece—the Princess that King Taiven kidnapped over thirty years ago? *The Princess whose infamous capture sparked a twenty-five year war between Rella and Langor?*"

"I'm not suggesting."

"So, Raynan Arcana is your uncle and Draken of Langor your brother?"

"Half-brother."

I looked at him a long moment. "That would make you an heir to both thrones, Rella and Langor. And you've been living in Kael all this time, unacknowledged and anonymous? You walk around with that ring and that clasp, looking as you do, and no one questions it? No one challenges it?"

"This is the first time I've worn them in public."

"Yeah, I can see where they might cause a stir." Frustrated, I shook my head. "So why now? Why risk exposing your existence after all this time?"

"Circumstances have made it necessary."

I couldn't help it anymore. I let out a short, skeptical laugh. "I'm sorry, Malaq. King Taiven died on the battlefield, and the woman you claim was your mother, died in prison. Lareece Arcana was never rescued. And she never had a child."

"I'm sitting right here, Troy." Malaq leaned in. "Because of the shame my existence brought to my Rellan grandfather, because of the Langorians need to preserve their king's name, the two realms came together and fabricated the story." He threw himself back in his seat with an exasperated grunt. "And who said Rella and Langor couldn't find common ground?"

"If there was an agreement, then why did the war escalate? Before Taiven died there was talk of a treaty."

"Yes. And even after Draken was crowned, my grandfather tried to end the hostilities. He felt enough blood had been spilled on both sides. Draken felt differently and launched a major strike against Rella."

"You mean the raid that came on the heels of Taiven's death, the one that nearly burned Kabri to the ground—that was in retaliation for what your mother did?"

"It was."

A flash of resentment tore through me. "Do you have any idea how many died in that attack? How many were lost to starvation and disease in the weeks after?"

"It was a terrible tragedy."

"It was a slaughter. I was six years old when the Langorians sent Kabri up in flames. I couldn't stop it. I had no real magic yet. I couldn't do a damn thing." I gripped the table to keep from coming out of my seat. "I watched the people I was born to protect being butchered in the streets. I watched them burn alive."

Quick enough to make me jump, Malaq stood. "And you were responsible for the deaths of how many men during the war? Can you even count that high?"

"I know what I did, Malaq. Believe me. But the repercussions of that woman's actions run just as deep. That attack on Kabri was a turning point in the conflict. If she'd never killed Taiven—"

I may never have gone to war. Never found the Crown of Stones.
Never used it.

"Nine years," Malaq said, slowly sitting back down. "Can you imagine being a prisoner of Langor for nine years? What they would do to you? What lengths you would be driven to? What you would become?" He took a long, deep breath and tried to move on. "A King's Healer was with the rescue party. She delivered me. She kept me warm and nourished. Without her I would have died."

"And whose life did she drain to keep you alive?"

"I'm sorry, what?"

"In the army, our healers used captured Langorian soldiers to feed their spells. Old, young…it didn't matter, as long as Aylagar's troops were restored."

"I should think that would have made you happy."

"It did."

Malaq's lips pursed. "Things happen in times of crisis, yes. But from my experience, most healers keep a good stock of animals. If necessary, they use condemned men. But they're already dead."

"Sorry, *Nef'areen*, but they're very much alive when the spell drains them."

"So you prefer Sarin's way, then? Using Kaelish healers that can't pull out a damn tooth without killing their patients? And mercenaries like you who carry out justice by hunting people like animals?"

"If you act like an animal, you deserve to be hunted like one."

Releasing a perturbed breath, Malaq peeked in his cup like he'd forgotten it was empty. "This particular King's Healer," he said, going back to his story, "carried me all the way to Rella. She presented me to the court where my grandfather declared I was an abomination. After berating his son for even attempting the disastrous rescue, he decreed I be put out and left to die."

"Nice homecoming. What changed his mind?"

"A young, Kaelish Prince by the name of Connell Roarke."

"King Sarin's brother?" Now I was really confused. "Isn't he dead?"

"No. Connell was betrothed to my mother. Out of his love for Lareece, he took me in and named me as his own. And for that kindness he was disowned and exiled. We both were." Malaq gave me a level stare like he was waiting for me to say something. When I didn't, he said tightly, "It was your mother, Ian. V'loria Troy was the King's Healer that saved my life. Did you know?"

Part of it, I did. But saying my mother told me she was there when the Rellans tried to rescue their Princess, and admitting that she deceived me about the outcome, wouldn't change anything. It certainly wouldn't alter the fact that Malaq was staring at me with eyes that resembled Draken's and Raynan Arcana's all at the same time.

So I ditched his question for one of my own. "What are you doing here, Malaq? If you lent me a hand tonight as repayment for what my mother did…consider your debt settled."

Finding a knot on the tabletop, he studied it. "A Royal Messenger is staying at Sarin's castle. He hails from Kabri and carries the Arcana seal. Go see him."

"I don't need to."

"The messenger is here for you, Troy."

"If he's here to tell me that Rella's in danger, I already figured that out."

Malaq's stare lifted. He looked at me. "You should speak with the man."

"I should do a lot of things."

"Does that mean you aren't going back with him?"

92

"Of course I'm going back. I have no choice. Rella calls and I answer."

"And you resent that."

"I'm under a spell that compels me to fight for a realm that's not my own. Some would say it's no different than a chain around my neck."

"A chain that hasn't been pulled in a very long time," he reminded me. "But, I'm sure tramping across the country, stalking Kael's most notorious, is more fulfilling than defending an entire kingdom. It certainly pays well, with all the money you were throwing at the barkeep."

My gaze narrowed. "You were here from the start?"

"I stepped in when things got bad."

"It wasn't bad when Danyon was kicking me?"

"I didn't want to swoop in too soon and damage your pride."

"My pride wasn't what he was damaging."

Malaq frowned at me. "See the messenger, Troy. Then we'll talk."

"We just did." I slid out from the bench and stood up.

"I didn't say you had to talk to him *now*. Sit," he said. "I'll tell you all about growing up in a Kaelish fishing village. It's really far more exciting than it sounds."

Almost, I sat back down. It wouldn't hurt anything to spend a little more time with Malaq and his past. We could trade jests and insults. I could listen to his stories as he spit them out in bits and pieces. I could, maybe, make sense of his motives.

But the ale was gone, and I wasn't sure I could tolerate him without it.

"No thanks," I said. "I came here for answers, Malaq, not a drinking companion, or a bodyguard. I certainly didn't come looking for the exiled, half-breed stepson of a Kaelish Prince."

If Malaq took offense, he didn't show it. "The messenger and I both arrived in Kael about a fortnight ago. Every morning since, he's gone out to the tournament field at some ungodly hour…like this one. Do yourself a favor, though. Don't sneak up on him. He's awfully prickly for a young fellow."

"I'll keep that in mind." I reached into my pocket and dropped the last of my coins on the table in front of him. "Have a round on me, Malaq. For Natalia," I added. "She did good tonight."

TWELVE

Breaking over the top of the rise, sunshine blazed at my back. Long, warm streams stretched across, bringing light to the neighboring summit and the towering forested bluffs that stretched far beyond my range of sight. In the distance, behind me, the echoes of men punctuated the fog as the city woke up and came to life. Closer, at the castle, morning bells rang to mark the guard change at the main gate. My destination was before me, in the sweeping valley below. Flanked by sloping hills on three sides and a dense, dark wall of mountain on the fourth, the basin in the middle (Kael's legendary arena) was still mostly in shadow.

Sizeable enough to accommodate even the largest of tournaments, between contests, Kael's troops made use of the field for practice and training. Typically, a contingent of soldiers could be found in the valley, honing their skills, or at least a few friends locking swords and wagering on each other's talents. Today, however, the arena was all but empty. There were no soldiers, no cheers, or clash of metal. There was only a single man and his bow. So completely focused and absorbed in his art, that he appeared to have no idea I was here.

I watched him a moment before starting Kya down the steep hill.

The grass was lush, slippery, and wet with dew. I kept her at a slow pace and used the time to decide if the man was indeed who Malaq sent me to find.

It was a quick assessment.

Even at a distance, with muted light, I could tell by his brown hair that he wasn't Shinree. Neither was he Kaelish; his weapon was too small. Sarin's archers trained with longbows taller than they were. Any trace of Langorian decent was unlikely too, since the man was at least half of Malaq's build, and his skin was substantially lighter. Another clue was his close-fitting white tunic and blue breeches. Both sported a black trim, which conspicuously gave him all three of the Arcana family colors.

Then there was his age. Malaq mentioned the messenger from Kabri was young. And though he was noticeably older than the page I'd met in the forest, as I drew closer, I gauged him at no more than a smidge or two over twenty. Despite that, and his trim, lithe frame, I wasn't mistaking the young man for weak. He drew the string back like it was made of water and sustained the position effortlessly.

Motionless, he considered his target. Then, swift and deft, he let loose the first arrow and retrieved another from the quiver on his back. More arrows followed in rapid succession. His concentration was solid. His pivots and adjustments as he changed targets were slight. The braid hanging down his back seemed not to move at all.

The quiver emptied quickly. As he notched the last arrow, he whirled around to face me. It was a single, fluid motion, a flawless rotation that brought the point of his weapon around to aim at my chest. He didn't release his weapon. He just stood there, poised to shoot me. His entire body was completely relaxed. I was betting he could hold position, squinting down the length of his arrow at me, for hours.

Slow and careful, I took my hands off the reins and motioned to the purse at his hip. "I think you're looking for me."

There was no reply. Concentration held the messenger's mouth in a grim, hard line. His high brow was scrunched into a low scowl. I imagined, if he relaxed long enough to smile, the girls at court would consider his boyish features attractive. In my position, I found his current expression fairly menacing.

"Think you can point that somewhere else?" I asked him. "I'm not really up for digging an arrow out of my chest."

Without moving an inch, he said flatly, "I was going for your head."

"That does seem to be a popular item lately."

His gaze tightened further. Spinning on his heels, the messenger turned and released the arrow. It sailed toward the last target at the very end of the field—and kept going; narrowly missing its mark and sinking into the ground at the base of the mountain.

"Huh," I said, surprised to see him miss.

As the messenger silently went to retrieve his lost arrow, I slid down from Kya's back. Leaving her at the bottom of the slope, I set off across the open arena.

The field was vast. I felt small as I walked its length, stepping over painted boundary lines for mock combat, passing groupings of tall, willowy trees meant to give shade to the wooden spectator stands. On the sidelines were colored stalls for merchants to hawk their wares and sturdy fences to keep the audience back. Closer in, laid out in a half circle, were large granite benches where participants could await their turn or rest between matches. Tossed across one of the benches was a light traveling cloak.

At the first effigy, I stopped and removed the barb from the man-like figure's straw head. The fletching was the expected black and blue, but the distinctive pattern etched into the plane of the arrowhead threw me. "Kabrinian Archers Guild?"

Intrigued, I moved on. When I had all eleven arrows, I headed to the far end of the field where the dark mass of the mountain forest spilled out to meet the edge of the meadow. I arrived in time to watch the messenger exit a wall of bramble thick enough to dam a river. Burrs were stuck to his hair and tunic, but he'd managed to find his arrow.

"You must have influential friends," I said, approaching him. "Friends that kept you from being forced into soldiery despite your obvious talent."

"Hmmm?" Fretting over the state of his arrow, he ran a slow finger over the length of it.

"How else does a guild member end up as a Royal Messenger? Or for that matter, how does a courier get admitted to the guild?" I glanced down at the arrows in my hand. "Unless you're that good. Good enough they allowed you to choose for yourself."

"My father was with the army," he said, gently blowing debris from the feather. "He never had a choice. He lived and died with a bow in his hand."

"And you?"

"I was luckier." He dropped the quiver and bow off his shoulder. They slid down his arm in a smooth, natural motion and came to rest in his palm. "I've been pulling arrows since I was old enough to know what they were for."

"Then what happened just now?"

He gave a lazy, one-shouldered shrug and extended his hand. "May I?"

I handed over what I'd collected. He added his and slid all twelve arrows carefully down inside the quiver. The rounded vessel, made of the same soft, black leather as his boots, was flaunting a slightly tattered, red silk ribbon. "Someone is missing you in Kabri," I said, gesturing at the ribbon.

"Neela gave it to me the night I left." Realizing how that sounded, he blanched. "We're friends," he said, a little self-conscious. "Old playmates, really."

"Playmates with the Princess of Rella? That's convenient."

The messenger's face froze. He looked at me straight on, and I got my first real good look at his eyes. They were a deep shade of blue and expressive, betraying his embarrassment, and a clear affection for Rella's heir. "My mother was a seamstress in the castle," he explained. "Neela and I are of a similar age, so we played together as kids." He donned a sad smile. "Sometimes, it's hard to remember what she is now."

I left it alone. Considering my involvement with Neela's mother, I certainly couldn't judge. "I'm told you have a message for me?"

"Yes, of course." He shouldered the bow and quiver again. Digging into the leather purse on his hip, he pulled out the message and handed it to me. After watching me uneasily a moment, he walked away, and left me staring at the folded piece of paper in my hand.

I ran my fingers over the imprinted wax a couple of times. It had been many years since I'd seen the Royal Seal of Arcana. But it wasn't a wistful gesture. Knowing what the contents meant for me, it was more like dread.

Carefully, I cracked the seal and unfolded the page. Words immediately jumped out, and my pulse started pounding. I stopped then and went back to the beginning. I read the whole thing through, quickly, and then slower the second time, in case I was wrong. The third time, I couldn't even make it to the end. My eyes were burning, and the words had become too blurry to read.

Taking a handful of breaths, I looked up for the messenger. He was sitting on the bench beside his cloak. He met my eyes and knew exactly what I was thinking: I needed a lot more than Princess Neela Arcana had given me.

Crumbling the message in my fist, I came up on him fast. "How bad is it?"

"Bad."

"Kabri?"

He swallowed, once, twice. Then lowered his eyes and shook his head.

I pushed him. "Casualties?"

"Heavy."

"The Rellan Army?"

"Many are dead. Some were taken prisoner. The rest deserted to search for their families. A number of Shinree got out," he said, though not happily. "Those damn rebels came in right behind the Langorians and raided the slave camps. They didn't help put out the fires, or fight with us. They just took their people and left us to die."

"What about the rest of the realm?"

"I don't know."

"The villages? The Southern Cities?"

"I don't know."

"Kabri's harbor?"

Dropping the bow and quiver off his shoulder, he slammed it down on the bench. "What do you want me to say, Troy? The city is a husk, a black shell. Our enemy was very thorough and those that aren't dead wish they were."

I closed my eyes, briefly. "I don't understand. How could this happen?"

"I was hoping you would know. No one thought he would ever recover from what you did. Now, out of nowhere, he has an army? It doesn't make any sense."

The first line of Neela's message echoed in my head: *Draken has risen.*

The fourth line told of his men storming the castle and defiling the catacombs.

Though Neela made no mention of it, I knew exactly what they were after. "Draken has the Crown of Stones, doesn't he?"

"Yes."

"And a Shinree to use it for him."

"Draken made reference to a magic user, but there was no Shinree with him."

"Trust me. He has one."

"We're still trying to figure out how he learned the crown's location in the first place. Even Neela didn't know it was in the crypt with…" he hesitated. I didn't think he was going to say it. "Aylagar."

It was amazing. After all this time, the sound of her name was still a blow to my chest. It was a penetrating, self-inflicted ache. But it wasn't as bad as the tension in me. That was down deep, stuck in, and buried like a hook. And the knowledge of the massacre in Kabri, of Rella's need, was pulling it taught—pulling me back.

I rubbed at the pain. "I heard Raynan Arcana is dead. Is that true?"

Visibly, the messenger shrunk from my question.

I raised my voice. "Is King Raynan dead?"

His eyes dropped to the ground. Leaning over, elbows on knees, head in his hands, he drew in deep, ragged breaths, as if my question made it hard for him to breathe. "Draken's men," he said, starting slow, "they rounded up everyone in the castle. They put us in the hall and then ransacked the place. They destroyed everything. They forced us to watch as they stripped our King naked. They tied him, whipped him. Beat him until I couldn't recognize his face. Then they dumped him on the floor so he could watch his own people die. The King's personal guards were beheaded. Servants were picked at random and butchered. The women were…" pausing, he tried to smooth the pain from his voice. "They were used badly."

"The Princess, was she injured?"

"No. Draken kept her close. He wouldn't let her look away. Those of us that were left, we tried to fight. I tried to reach her…and the King. But the bastards clubbed any of us that moved. They were so damn strong, and… I tried," he said again, soft and apologetic, as if the entire thing were his fault. "After a while, I just couldn't get up."

"It's best you stayed down. If you'd gotten up they would have killed you, too."

"It wasn't by choice." Dropping his hands, the messenger burrowed his fingers into the edge of the stone bench and glared at me. "I couldn't get up because they broke my fucking legs. I had to lie there and listen to Neela scream while Draken's soldiers gutted King Raynan and pissed in his blood. They cut him open. Defiled him. And we didn't do a damn thing to stop it. We let him die." His blue eyes fixed on me; so full of dark emotion they were hard to look at. "*I* let him die."

I cringed at the anguish in his voice. Listening to the explicit details of Draken's attack was bad enough. Bearing witness to such personal grief over the death of Rella's King was distressing in a far different way. I knew the polite thing to do was voice my sympathies. The messenger needed that. He needed someone to commiserate, to speak kindly of the King and the great loss Rella would suffer in his absence. But I couldn't. Any condolence I might offer in regret of the man's passing would be a lie.

Despite the fact that Raynan Arcana allowed me to be born, that he afforded me no punishment for the loss of his army or his wife, and that it was by his grace alone that I enjoyed freedom, (conditional as it was), I didn't see him as the messenger did—as the esteemed sovereign ruler of Rella. I saw him as I first knew him; as the man who relieved the tensions of his kingship in my mother's bed. His use of her, right up until the day she died, was blatant. As was his obvious neglect of his own wife, Aylagar. He had no regard for either of them. And that alone left me with far less sympathy for the death of King Raynan, someone I'd known all my life, than for the young man I'd just met who watched him die.

"A Shinree healer in the city put my legs back together," the messenger said then. "I'd never had a spell like that done on me before. It was strange. All that pain, and then to wake up and feel good, almost like it never happened. Except…there were piles of bodies. The city stunk. The castle floors were stained in blood. And I've tried, but…I can't forget the King's face." Fingers tapping fitfully on his knees, the muscles in his jaw twitched. "I'd never seen him like that before. He looked at me with these wide eyes full of fear. He looked *right at me*. Like he was trying to tell me something."

"After what they did to him, I doubt the King was even seeing you at all."

Quiet a moment, he shrugged one shoulder and let out a short, dismissive grunt. "Yeah. You're probably right." But the words brought him no comfort. Nothing would for a long while. Deep lines had settled in, aging the messenger's young face. Memory haunted his eyes. Somewhere between

Kabri and Kael—hardened by the horror and shame of being unable to save the person he'd pledged his life to—his pain had become a gnarled nest of bitterness and rage.

It was like looking into a mirror.

"What's your name, kid?" I said.

"Jarryd." He cleared his throat and stood up. "Kane," he added, retrieving his cloak from the bench. As he put it on and fastened it, I noticed the clasp, made of solid sunstone, bore a carved miniature version of the Arcana crest on its face. The same design, made of brass, adorned the flap of his purse.

Likely, if I were to look, I'd find more examples of Jarryd Kane's loyalty on his person or his belongings. His duty to the realm was clearly a source of pride. Now, thanks to Draken, it was a source of pain.

Jarryd picked up his bow. "When I left, Kabri was heavily occupied. We were prisoners in our own home. Three of us snuck out with identical messages. I was the only one to make it off the island. Langorians followed me for a while, but I once I got to high ground I had no trouble picking them off." Taking up his quiver, he looked at me. "King Sarin is going to ask you to stay and protect Kael."

"Is Draken expected to come this far?"

"I don't know." Jarryd started moving. I joined him, and we headed toward the edge of the arena. "But we should leave for Rella as soon as possible."

"Sarin has been good to me. I have to at least hear him out."

We stopped at the base of the slope where Kya was grazing. She gave Jarryd a good sniff. He ran a gentle hand over her mane. "King Sarin is aware of your permanent obligation to Rella. He should know you can't stay."

Jarryd's words irked me. "I didn't realize my 'obligation' was so well known."

"The nature of your service was never the secret the Arcana's wanted it to be. Besides, even if the truth is unknown to Sarin, he's at least heard the rumor."

"What rumor?"

"That your mother's pregnancy was unplanned. That V'loria Troy begged King Raynan for the life of her unborn child, and when that didn't work she threatened to give you over to Langor. The King feared that greatly. He agreed to your birth on the condition that you were made harmless to the realm. V'loria agreed, a Shinree was found to do the binding spell, and you were born compelled to defend Rella from her enemies whenever summoned. To do otherwise would bring you instant death."

"I hadn't heard that one," I said awkwardly; shocked by Jarryd's bluntness.

"It doesn't matter. You'd come back to Kabri even without the spell."

"And why is that?"

"It's the only way you'll find absolution."

I took a step back. "Absolution?"

"For the lives you took to stop the war," he said, still being blunt. "For the husbands and fathers, the sons and brothers that died. If there is any forgiveness to be had for their sacrifice, it would be found on Rella's shores, not here in Kael."

With gritted teeth, I held back the curse on my tongue. I wanted to let it out and drop the young fool for simply having too much nerve. But impudence had nothing to do with Jarryd Kane's words. His tone had been too level, too emotionless for disrespect. His face, even now, was completely without spite or disdain. No judgment shone in his eyes. No contempt or resentment strained his voice. His speech, difficult as it had been to hear, hadn't been about laying blame or condemnation. It hadn't been to accuse me of his father's death, either, and given what I'd just heard of the man's end, my involvement was likely. Jarryd was merely stating the facts as *he* saw them, honestly and brutally.

But, for the life of me, I couldn't understand his views.

His outright acceptance of those facts and his tolerance of my actions—actions even I couldn't tolerate—was baffling, and it drained the anger right out of me.

Unclenching my fists, I pushed the balled up message in my pocket. "Let's go."

I moved around him to grab the reins, and the hairs on my arm stood straight up.

Kya's mane lifted away from her neck.

The air tightened. The grass rippled beneath my boots.

I glanced at Jarryd. "You feel that?"

Another ripple, stronger this time, and the vibrations shot straight up my legs.

"Whoa!" Jarryd cried out.

I shoved Kya's reins in his hand. "Stay here."

Leaving him, I moved back across the field. As I walked, the ground rumbled. I watched it, listening. But I knew it wasn't a quake. I was well aware what a normal shifting of the land felt like, and this wasn't it. The motion was too localized. The leaves on the trees outside the valley were still. The grass on the hillside swayed gently in the breeze. Yet the field was undulating. It wasn't cracking, though. The disturbance was deeper than that. It was as if the surface wasn't even moving. *It's not,* I thought.

Something's moving beneath it.

I sprinted back to Jarryd. "Where's your horse?"

"I walked. Seemed like a nice day."

"Not anymore." The obsidian at my neck began to warm, and I stopped short. "Get to Kya." The shard began to glow. "Go as far and as fast as you can and don't stop."

Jarryd took a step in my direction. "Ian…what's going on?"

Power pushed against my skin. "Go—now! Or I *will* kill you."

THIRTEEN

Sprawled out on the grass, spent like a boy who'd just lifted his first skirt, euphoria wasn't enough to lessen my failure. I'd been so intent on getting Jarryd to safety, that I'd used what little time I had holding back the spell, when I should have been trying to wrestle control of the magic from Draken's pet Shinree.

Now, my need to save a single life was going to cost countless more. Because this time, I wasn't ignorant of what my enemy was doing. I wasn't removed from it. I was smack in the middle of it, watching as countless pairs of long, black claws pushed their way up through the ground. Hands followed. Thick and substantially larger than a man's, the appendages, entirely without skin, were no more than elongated bleached bones. Tearing at the grass, wriggling and clawing, the talon-like hands rapidly turned over the field. Arms pushed up and uncurled. Skinless frames heaved themselves up onto solid ground. Massive hind legs unfurled, and the skeletal creatures stood.

With their backs slightly bowed, and their legs jointed the wrong way at the knees, they seemed incapable of rising to their full height—and I was glad. Most were already a head or two taller than me. A few were twice that.

Arms reaching upward, stretching as if they'd been confined far too long, dirt fell away from their bones and organs began to grow. Two hearts formed side by side and began pumping, shielded beneath a double rib cage. Tissue and muscle developed and extended swiftly, speeding across exposed bone and layering it with slithering, spreading veins filled with dark blood. Eyes swelled to fill their sockets. Gums shaped and sprouted teeth that matured and lengthened in seconds.

Lastly, came a wrapping of tough, black hide and a heavy, dark pelt.

Then: awareness. I saw it settle in. It was obvious by the abrupt change in their posture and the way the multitude of heads all turned as one in my direction. The entire arena full of monstrous towering bulk, wide and tall enough to block out the rising sun behind them, were fixated on me.

I jumped as a unified growl tore from their lungs. The deafening sound vibrated through my bones as I watched their jagged teeth chew at the empty air. Strings of saliva oozed from their spacious mouths, stretching to hang off the ends of black fang-like tusks at least six inches long. Bobbing with each snarl, the tusks extended down, curled sharply back up, and ended in points sharp as daggers.

Already sweating over their size, and how absurdly outnumbered I was, my anxiety doubled as I grasped exactly what was surrounding me. *Eldring.*

For once, I had an opponent with a reputation far worse than mine.

Deadly enough to have once been considered a plague on the Kaelish countryside, and proliferate enough that it took the combined effort of the Rellan and Kaelish armies to wipe them out; eldring were the stuff of childhood tales and nightmares. Driven by bloodlust, they were said to have poured down out of the mountains in packs, consuming herds of sheep and cattle, or anything else foolish enough to be outside after dark. When prey was scarce, livestock became fair game. When starvation set in, so did children.

In reality, the eldring had likely acted no different than any other hungry animal trying to survive. But the loss of life had been great. Entire villages had been forced to pack up and move away. Eventually, Kael's King implored Rella for help, and the beasts were hunted to extinction—over three hundred years ago.

I couldn't have done this, I thought. *I couldn't have brought them back to life.*

I didn't have the slightest idea which type of Shinree magic could resurrect ancient creatures out of dust and bone. Apparently, the man casting through me did, though. He knew a lot of things. Like how to use me as a conduit.

It was the only explanation. I'd been an instrument, a means for the broken piece to work in concert with the whole. Consuming every morsel of power in the shard around my neck, he'd used me to create my own adversaries. And then he'd left me without a drop of magic to fight them with. "Bastard," I muttered.

Keeping my movements careful and deliberate, little by little, I rose up from the ground. My swords made no noise as I emptied both sheaths. I didn't move for a while, then. I held position, and the whole lot of them sat back on their haunches, issuing faint guttural sounds from low in their throats, and drooling at me as if I were a nice, juicy shank of lamb.

Their ears twitched. Mine heard the sound a few seconds later. A few more, and Jarryd Kane came riding down over the hill. He spotted the creatures spread out across the field and slowed Kya to a cautious advance. Stopping just outside the circle of eldring, Jarryd slid down to the ground, drew his bow, and picked a target.

"You all right?" I asked him.

"Fine. Your horse runs fast." He edged closer. His movement drew a snarl or two, but the creatures didn't move. "They don't seem too interested in attacking. What are they waiting for?"

"Let's find out." I crept forward. I made it a couple of feet, and the pack came to life. A line of five slunk around behind me, low to the ground.

"I'm not sure that's a good idea," Jarryd warned.

I took a few more steps. Five more eldring moved up alongside me in a slow, stalking crawl.

"Troy..." Jarryd said, more insistent.

I kept going. All ten beasts quickened their pace. They closed in.

"Stop!" he shouted.

I halted. So did the eldring. "Guess that answers that."

"They don't want you to leave. Why?"

"Good question. If Draken's magic user went to all this trouble to corral me..."

"He's either messing with you, or..."

"There's some place else he doesn't want me to be." I shared a worried glance with Jarryd. "The castle. I need to get out of here."

"Okay. But how exactly are you going to do that?"

I looked at the eldring nearest me. Up close as I was now, I could see just how long and sharp their claws were. How striking and penetrating their stares. Surprisingly animated, their lidless, feral eyes were a strange cloudy blend of orange and yellow, almost the color of a hazy sunset. It was beautiful. Moreover, I didn't see a trace of the blind primal rage I'd expected. Instead, the eldring's eyes reflected a clear, noticeable intelligence.

"They're smart. Especially that one," I said, spotting a male eldring whose gaze was different than the rest. Deeper and more focused, the beast had an almost mesmerizing cleverness that instantly drew me in.

As I stared at his eyes, the orange started bleeding to red.

The red pulled at me. I took a step toward it.

"This isn't normal," Jarryd's said. His voice startled me. "Eldring were nocturnal. Look at the ones behind you, cowering from the sun. They didn't hunt in groups this large either."

Blinking, I focused on him. I pulled my gaze away from the red eyes, and my head felt like it was moving through quicksand. "This isn't a hunt," I said. "They're being controlled."

"All of them, all at once? Can he do that? Is he that good?"

"He's better than me."

"Shit."

"I'll distract them. You make a run for it. It's me they want."

"Yeah," Jarryd grunted. "For dinner."

"Look," I said earnestly, "this could all be nothing but a show, a display of strength. But if Draken is attacking, I need to be there." Allowing Jarryd no chance to argue, I raised both swords, and took two bold steps.

Nothing happened.

I took a third step, and the line of eldring in front of me dropped to all fours. Sunlight streamed over the tops of their heads, glinting bright and blinding off the steel in my hands. The glare bounced. It hit the faces of the eldring standing in the second row, and they started shrieking. Recoiling violently, as their bodies jerked in pain, the creatures toppled over and curled into tight convulsing balls of fur.

Curious, I spun around. The eldring guarding me from the rear were facing the sun. But they were all nearly flat on the ground, with heads low and heavily clawed hands shading their unprotected eyes.

"Change of plan." I turned to Jarryd. "I need that sunstone on your cloak."

"For a spell?" I nodded, and a frown entered his voice. "How do you know it was even taken from a Shinree mine?"

"I can feel it."

"From there?" I nodded again, and the frown hit his face. "It was my father's."

"You'll get it back. Just take it off and throw it to me."

"It's stitched in. I'll have to drop the bow."

"Slowly."

Jarryd lowered his arms. As he went to work on the clasp, I slid a sword into the sheath on my back and checked on the injured creatures. They were still writhing on the ground, still working to keep the light out. The rest of the pack was watching me intently with heads bowed, as if wary of lifting their eyes any higher than my boots.

"How's it coming?" I asked.

"Got it."

Jarryd threw the clasp. I caught it in my free hand. Its edges were smooth. The base was fastened to a thin layer of bronze. Yet the metal did nothing to dampen the potency of the aura inside. "Perfect." Clenching the stone in my fist, I gave Jarryd a stern directive. "You need to go."

"Before you kill me?"

Dry amusement softened his jest. I still winced. "I understand if you want to try something else."

"There is nothing else." Jarryd's hard blue gaze was unwavering. "I'll be fine."

Fool, I thought. *He's not afraid. Not even thinking I might hurt him.*

Why anyone would rely on me with such an outward display of stalwart conviction, I had no idea. It was infuriating.

"Are we doing this?" he said impatiently.

I gripped the stone tighter. "I don't know how far this will reach. You need to ride fast and shut your eyes. Don't open them. Don't look back. Kya will get you to the road."

"What about you?"

"I'll be right behind you."

Jarryd's eyes flashed. He knew I was lying. "I swore to bring you back to Kabri."

"And you will. But even if this works, there's no guarantee I'll get them all. And if you ride back in here after I cast, you won't be able to see."

Confusion replaced his anger as he asked, "It'll be too dark?"

"No. It'll be light."

FOURTEEN

Big, angry magic is never a good thing. Rash, unfamiliar magic was just as bad. Unfortunately, the eldring didn't give a damn that I'd never channeled a sunstone before. They weren't going to grant me time to get used to it or show a drop of sympathy that its vibrations made my blood feel like liquid fire.

This has to work. It should work. My soldier's bloodline granted me complete control over the blade in my hand. Which meant, in theory, I could do what I wished with it—no matter how crazy the wish. All I needed was a succinct, coherent goal, and the ability to forget my limitations (what I wanted from the sunstone wasn't your typical soldier fare). I also needed to let go of another, potential problem: I had no scripted spell and no time to write one.

Without words to center me, I'd have nothing to keep unwanted thoughts and emotions from seeping in and altering the outcome. I'd be totally relying on the idea itself and my desire to make it happen, which was a little worrisome. Yet, at its core, magic was all about belief and intent. If I possessed enough of both, if I believed without question in the outcome of my spell, I shouldn't need any words.

The ancient scrolls called the process 'thought-casting'. According to the writings of my ancestors, the practice wasn't limited to the fabled erudite or even their most accomplished pupils. All full-blooded Shinree were capable of mastering the process. All they needed was a couple years' worth of training.

I had a couple minutes at best. But I also had an advantage.

Twice in my life I'd pulled off something that could be considered thought-casting, and neither instance was due to tutelage or practice. The first time was born out of simple desperation. I'd come upon a pit rigged with Langorian spears, too well concealed and too wide to jump. With no chance to turn and no time to cast, I'd simply wanted my horse to pass over the spears unharmed. And she did.

I must have wanted it real bad, too. Since not only was she unharmed, Kya remained whole and untouched that day—and every day after. She hadn't aged or sickened, or had so much as a single fly bite in fifteen years. My objective, my desire, had been that strong and that perfect. It was just as strong the second time when I unwittingly used the same technique with the Crown of Stones. Only the result was far less perfect.

I glanced at Jarryd. Sitting on Kya's back at the crest of the hill, steady and alert, arrow drawn, gaze fixed, stance perfect. Despite the lack of uniform he looked every bit the Rellan soldier he chose not to be.

I nodded at him. Silently, I vowed he wouldn't die the same way as his father.

He nodded back, turned Kya away, and I started clearing my mind.

Generally, discarding the clutter didn't come easy. I had a lot of it. Nevertheless, I knew so fully what I wanted right now, that my emotions stilled fairly quickly. My thoughts converged even faster. They tapered to a single, solitary pinpoint until there was only the spell. It was in every part of me. Floating in my mind, flowing through my veins, swelling my lungs; I existed for it. I existed because of it. Its outcome was as certain as my next breath.

I let the power go. I raised my sword high and waited.

I caught a glimpse of movement, no more than a blur, before the color of the stone took my vision. Then I couldn't see a thing. Still, I closed my eyes and dug my boots in. I was ready to ride out the normal surge of euphoria. But expelling the sunstone felt like pushing hot needles out of my skin. There was no pleasure in it, only a suffocating swell of prickling heat and the relief that came when it was gone.

A brief bout of weakness followed. Directing the spell onto me, or my belongings, required only a minimal gift of energy. But I'd asked a lot of the sunstone's aura, and it didn't hesitate to reach out and take from the eldring. I heard one or two collapsing on their weakened legs, releasing a weak groan of confusion as my spell sapped their strength. As the sounds faded, I rushed forward into the middle of the pack, and the field exploded in a blinding sea of radiance.

Heat and light were everywhere. Even with my eyes closed, the vivid glow broke through. It was like standing inside an unending bolt of lightning. The extreme warmth touched everything. It didn't matter that I'd focused the spell on the eldring. Its might was too great to be contained, and the overflow was trickling out into the air, the ground—the hilt of my sword. Behind their lids, my eyes hurt. My skin baked. My throat was parched, like I'd been exposed to the high summer sun for days. Yet I was getting off easy compared to the eldring. The sound of their pain, eerie, desolate screeches of agony and fear, reverberated in my bones. The smell of their smoldering hair and melting flesh was rank on my tongue.

Their plight bothered me, though not as much as it should have. I didn't feel any real sympathy for their suffering. I felt pride. It was morbid and disturbing, and unequivocally shameful. But their suffering was my accomplishment.

By amplifying the glare off my blade and stretching it over the entire field, I'd turned the sun into a weapon. It was unlike anything I had ever done before, and I'd done it without an actual spell. It was a moment worth gloating over. *Later.*

I still had to get out of the valley, through a pack of wounded eldring without the use of my eyes. I couldn't risk opening them. Not until the light had dimmed. And since eldring weren't truly the monsters they appeared, but animals (ferocious, ill-made, flesh-eating, nocturnal animals that didn't need eyes to hunt), they could locate their prey by scent alone. Probably, they already had. Probably, the creatures were dragging their hulking, bleeding bodies toward me across the torn grass, angry and hurting and knowing I was the cause. It wasn't a reassuring thought.

Neither was the idea of putting myself in Fate's hands. I didn't want to trust him to guide me across the field. The old bastard was a fickle, unsympathetic god who had proven time and again that he didn't particularly like me.

I was just hoping he was in a good mood.

Okay, I thought. I took a deep, cleansing breath. I let it out. *I can do this.*
I just need to stay calm. It's only a hundred paces.
A hundred paces and I'll clear the valley.
I stuffed the sandstone in my pocket.
It's not that far. I can do this.

Tightening my grip on the gleaming sword, with eyes still shut, I took off.

The cool rush of air felt good on my hot skin. To be doing something instead of waiting to be eaten felt good. But as much as I was trying not to step on any of them, or to smell like anything, or to breathe too loud, I wasn't exactly being stealthy. With the sword slapping against my back, my boots thumping against the churned up ground, and the sweat pouring off me, I was definitely drawing attention.

I felt the ground angle slightly upward. *Almost there.*

At the base of the slope I started up, and a wet snarl hit my ear. Half a breath later, the weight of a small mountain smashed into me, and I was airborne. The gleaming sword flew from my hands. Massive furry arms wrapped around me, and we hit the ground rolling.

Sliding and tumbling, held tight by the creature, its crushing weight drove the air from my lungs. I tasted the mold and dirt on its pelt. Its body stunk of blood and decay. With each rotation, my sword jabbed into my back. A cold, bony tusk scraped the side of my neck. A wet muzzle brushed my ear; filling it with slobbery, anxious growls.

The growls ended in a sharp *yelp,* as we struck something hard. We stopped, and the beast lifted up. It shook like a dog shedding some momentary discomfort, then got up off me with a grunt that was full-out satisfaction. With the pressure abruptly gone from my chest, I sucked in deep wheezing breaths. Every one of them hurt.

Stifling a groan, and ignoring the powerful itch to open my eyes, I rolled onto my stomach. I had no idea which way to go. I picked a direction and started crawling, and claws seized my ankles. The eldring's grip tightened. It started dragging me back.

I fought, clutching at the grass. Knowing my resistance was pointless, I had a brief thought of going for one of the knives tucked in my braces. But that notion, and every other coherent thought vanished as the beast flipped me over onto my back, jumped on my chest, and poked the four bony protrusions of its clawed hand clean through my jacket, into my shirt, and down into the meat of my right shoulder.

Flesh ripped. Muscles tore. Veins opened and began emptying. Blood ran out of me like juice draining from a piece of fruit. And still the eldring burrowed deeper. It pushed; smoothly through layers of sinew and muscle; with effort through cartilage and bone.

The eldring retracted its claws with a quick yank. A strange, brief moment of relief followed. It ended as the knife-like claws raked down the length of my arm. Skin shredded, yet after the initial shock, I scarcely noticed. My nerves couldn't admit to any more pain. My mind shut down, and I faded a moment—then woke to the distant *drip-drip* of saliva on my neck. Eager breath that smelled of festering meat blew across my face. A clawed hand closed over my throat.

Eyes tightly shut, as I waited for the fangs to sink in, I prayed that Death had swift feet and would soon come to claim me. In all the times I'd imagined dying, I'd never considered being eaten alive as a possibility. I wanted no time to ponder it now.

Instead of ripping into me, though, the eldring did something completely unexpected and impossible. It spoke.

The words were Shinree. The voice was masculine. *Familiar.*

The man, who'd spoken through Taren Roe, was now speaking through the eldring. *No,* I thought dimly. *Not speaking. Casting.*

I tried to translate, to focus on the rhythm of the sounds. The same six phrases kept repeating. I just couldn't quit my ragged breathing long enough to hear them clearly.

The chant continued. The eldring let go of my throat and sat back on my legs. It didn't move after that. It no longer seemed interested in restraining me or trying to carve me up. Being inhabited seemed to complete override its animal mind.

But for how long?

Taking the only chance I was going to get, I raised my left arm off the ground. I reached over, across my body, going for the knife hidden in the brace on my right wrist. It was only a slight movement. A brief jostle as I took hold of my injured arm and adjusted the angle. But what remained of the limb was a sopping, twitching mess. and I might as well have been ripping it off.

Gasping and trembling, I fell back to the ground. I blew the air out through my chattering teeth a few times. Then I clenched them and tried again. Fighting pain and the deadweight of my body, as I struggled to lift up, it came to me that the light on the other side of my lids wasn't so bright anymore. My spell was fading.

I risked a peek. Opening my eyes, my vision cleared. My view was filled with the blood, gore, and exposed bone of my arm, and I nearly gagged. The eldring was still sitting on top of me with pieces of my skin stuck to the edges of its claws.

I shut out the sight and focused on my goal.

Sliding two fingers into the brace and down inside the inner sheath, I found the knife and pulled it out. Gripping the handle, I stared into the creature's vacant red gaze and hoped that the magic user on the other side could see me as I let out a rage-filled, triumphant scream—that he could feel me, as I reached up and shoved the entire blade though the side of the eldring's thick furry neck. Swiftly, I ripped the knife out and stuck it in again, and again, and again. I stabbed as fierce and as fast, as many times, and in as many places, as I could. And the eldring didn't even flinch.

At some point the voice ceased. The beast's black pelt tore. Its insides emptied out onto my chest. Dark red blood pumped from severed veins, turning its fur red and encasing my hand and arm like a glove. But I didn't ease up. I kept slashing and hacking. Only when the butchered carcass hunched over and fell off me did I finally let the blade slip from my trembling hand. I attempted to move then, to sit, but too much of me was coloring the ground. It was easier to lie in the wet, warm grass. Night was falling, and it was quiet.

A hazy figure hovered over me. "Ian," it said, and I groped for the knife. "Relax. It's me."

A face came into focus. "Jarryd?" I breathed. "I told you not to come back."

"Good thing I didn't listen." Bending down, he pulled at me. "Come on, get up."

"Can't."

"You have to."

"The eldring…"

"Are all dead. Gods," he groaned. "You're a mess."

"The castle…?"

"Never mind that now. How much of this blood is yours?"

"Too fucking much." For some reason that was funny and I panted my way through a laugh. "Way too fucking much."

"I can see that." Jarryd pulled a dagger from his belt. Taking his tunic off over his head, he cut the material into long, wide strips. "I think you need a new jacket," he said, cutting off the sleeve and tearing my own tattered shirt away from my wounds.

"It's okay. It smelled like swamp anyway."

Jarryd grinned a little, but it was taut and fleeting as he set out on the unenviable task of tending my arm. He tried to be careful. But nervousness and inexperience made his moves clumsy, and it was hard to stay lucid. While he packed cloth on both sides of my shoulder and wrapped my arm clear to the wrist, it was only Jarryd's incessant talking that kept me awake and breathing; an act made acutely difficult by my matching set of broken ribs.

By the time Jarryd was awkwardly maneuvering my arm into a make-shift sling, worry had washed the color from his skin, and I was in agony.

Wiping the sweat from his brow, he blew out an anxious breath. "How's that?"

I glared at him. "I feel like a trussed cow. A half-slaughtered, trussed cow."

"You kind of look like one." More serious, he said, "Can you do this?"

I'm going to lose the arm.

"Ian?" he said. "Can you ride?"

"Just get me to my horse." Jarryd brought Kya around and helped me to my feet. Sweating and wincing with every move, a bout of dizziness hit me, and I fell against her flank. "Looks like I owe Sarin some grass," I said, but my jest only made Jarryd more edgy. "What is it?"

"I met Malaq on the road. He was coming to find you." Jarryd's blue eyes darted away, then back to mine. "I'm sorry, Ian. King Sarin is dead."

A new ache started in my chest. "Eldring?"

"Langorians."

"Damn it. Goddamn it. Goddamn, fucking Langorians!"

"Easy…"

"No—that's twice now. *Twice* I've been pulled away from the real target. First Kabri. And now here."

Like it was obvious, Jarryd said, "You scare him."

"Who? Draken's magic user? The man who just grew eldring out of dirt?" I grunted in angry disagreement. "I'm pretty sure that makes *him* the scary one."

"He kept you here. He kept you back from the real fight because he knows you're the only one capable of stopping him."

Gripping the saddle with my good arm, I looked at Jarryd. "And just how am I supposed to do that?"

His face fell. "I don't know."

"Well, neither do I." Rage sending strength flowing into limbs that a moment before had none, I sunk a boot in the stirrup and hauled myself up onto Kya's back. "And I'm getting damn tired of that."

FIFTEEN

I'm not squeamish or easily shaken, but there were things in my life that I'd hoped to never see again: the inside of a stinking Langorian prison, trees filled with the swinging bodies of dead children, plains of desiccated bodies, piles of severed heads.

Now I had something new to add to the list; the desecration of a King's hall.

Repulsive amounts of blood smeared the floor, walls, and furnishings. There wasn't a single body that hadn't been mutilated in some fashion, most beyond recognition. Jagged wounds and lopped-off scattered parts were widespread. Burned cloth and flesh curled away from the edges of blistered holes. Portions of sagging entrails were seared an ashy black. Charred torsos clung loosely to crushed hips and protruding splintered limbs bones.

Breaking their enemy's legs was a common Langorian tactic. It kept their prisoners from running, kept them helpless to the torture that would follow. Thankfully, Jarryd had been spared such a brutal end during the attack on Kabri. But here, in Sarin's home, Draken's men had shown no clemency and no prejudice. All had been cut down; nobleman, guard, advisor, servant, cook and courtier. *Even a King.*

My eyes drifted to the back of the room where heavy veins of red trailed across the white marble stairs leading up to the dais. On it, Sarin's blood-splattered chair sat empty. I couldn't see his body. A group of mourners were blocking my view. But imagining how it looked drained my wrath-fueled burst of energy right out of me.

"Over here!" Jarryd called. Pushing through the crowd, he rushed up with a weathered grizzly-haired Kaelishman in tow. Wearing a heavy mustached-scowl, the man, whose brown robe was covered in ugly, dark stains, surveyed me with outright disapproval. He grumbled something that sounded like, "despicable," took hold of the sling and yanked it off over my head.

Pain stole my balance. I staggered against the wall, cradling my bandaged arm against my chest. "What the hell...?"

"He's a physician," Jarryd said, pulling me upright. "And the lord he was treating wasn't too happy with me. So let the man do his job before someone comes to retrieve him."

It didn't seem like I had a choice. Without asking, the Kaelishman started undoing the bandages on my arm with far less care than Jarryd had used to put them on. "Gods, man," I griped, flinching. "Can you do this later?"

He dropped the bloody cloth on the floor. "Later you'll be dead." Reaching back, his wrinkled hand grabbed the collar of a fluffy-haired boy and pulled him closer.

"Liel?" I said, recognizing the boy.

"My Lord," the page replied shakily. With a leather bag slung over one shoulder, and a pitcher of water in his hand, he gave me a remorseful, uncertain smile.

The physician glanced at Jarryd. "Hold him." Then to Liel: "Ready?"

The boy nodded, and I understood what they were about to do. "No." I shook my head at the old man. "Not now." I looked at Jarryd. "Not here." I turned to the boy. "Liel—stop."

No one listened.

The physician took hold of my injured arm. Jarryd took the other. Liel poured the pitcher of water over my wounds and, as the cold stream hit the exposed meat of my arm, I went down. Choking on the cry in my throat, bile replaced it. I tried not to throw up as I curled against the stone wall.

Jarryd sat next to me. "I'm sorry, Ian. It couldn't wait."

It would have taken strength to answer. Since I had none, I leaned against him and trembled; watching the colors of the room fade in and out.

"Here, My Lord." Liel pressed a steaming cup in my hand. "This will help." He leaned down over me, and his face disappeared under his hair. "I hear the physician's brews are quite potent."

Jarryd steadied my grip, helping me as I sipped at the steaming sour liquid.

After a few swallows, everything went numb. Breathing no longer brought pain. My racing heart slowed and my thoughts settled. I glanced up to thank Liel, but he was gone. The crabby physician was gone, too. So was what remained of my tattered shirt and coat. My bare chest was wrapped. My arm and shoulder were re-bandaged. I was sitting on the floor, slouched against an overturned table, while servants with ashen faces were scooping up remains and loading them into wooden carts. A row of soldiers that hadn't been there before were standing guard at the door.

Frowning, I wiped at my blurry eyes. "I was out?"

"For a bit," Jarryd said, still beside me. "How do you feel?"

"I'm not sure." The empty cup was on the floor between us. My entire body ached, except my bandaged arm. So little sensation was coming from the limb, I had to look to be sure it was still there. "Did he say anything, the physician?"

"He said to get you to his chamber as soon as you came to. Before you bleed to death, were his actual words. So we should probably go now."

"Ian!" Dodging the maze of people, Malaq hurried over to us. In his right hand was Natalia, still wearing the evidence of her recent work. "I saw him." Pausing, Malaq raised an arm and wiped at the blood streaking his face. "Draken's Shinree was here."

I perked up. "Did you get a look at him?"

Malaq shook his head.

"I don't get it," Jarryd admitted. "Sentries are posted on the road. Guards are all over the courtyard and the castle. There is no way Draken could have gotten into the city, let alone this room, without someone sounding an alarm."

"Unless his Shinree is a door-maker," I said.

"A door-maker?" Jarryd echoed.

"A Shinree that makes doors." At the annoyed look on his face, I went on. "You step through in one place and come out somewhere else. There was a rumor during the war that Draken had one, but…"

121

Malaq was nodding. "That could explain why there's no evidence of them breeching the outer wall or infiltrating the castle. They were just suddenly here." Putting his sword away, he looked out at the chaos of overturned tables and strewn bodies. Then he looked at me as if I should have seen this coming.

"It's very rare," I said in defense. "No King wanted their enemy to have access to such a spell, so they tightened the laws on their breeding until the line eventually died out. A Shinree that can open doors hasn't been born in hundreds of years. But that's what I thought about the erudite."

Pointedly, Malaq asked me, "So is he an erudite then, or a door-maker?"

"Erudite are door-makers. And elementals, and soldiers, and oracles… you know the list. If he's an erudite, then he's all Shinree rolled into one." Groaning, I crawled up the wall and stood. "And with the Crown of Stones, his only real limit is what he can handle before he passes out. Once he does…"

I swayed. Shadows grew where they didn't belong.

"Whoa," Jarryd said, steadying me.

"I'm okay." I forced Malaq's face into focus. "Certain spells suck more energy from us than others. No matter who this man is, he can only last so long."

"That goes for you, too," Malaq said. His gray eyes tightened. "We need to get you a real healer, Troy. A Shinree healer."

"Later."

Malaq crossed his arms. "Later you could be dead."

"I wish everyone would stop saying that," I snapped.

"Have you looked at yourself? I would say you're pale as death, but you have…" Malaq squinted, "I don't even know what the hell that is all over you. But it is colorful."

"I know," I said. "But first, you need to listen. Draken's magic user is exposed. He has no *nef'taali*," I said, reverting to Shinree. "After opening the door, resurrecting the eldring, controlling them, casting through one, and burning these people—some of these wounds are definitely made by magic. He'll be empty. If we can find him—"

"Gods, man, slow down," Malaq said forcefully. "You're not making sense."

I started over. "In the early days of the Shinree Empire there were entire armies of magic users like me. But casting battle spells, casting anything that relies on negative energy and emotion like what I do—like was done here—takes a higher toll than other types of magic. You cast too many times in a row and you're unconscious. The bigger the spells, the faster you go out. To keep the soldiers safe while they were down, it's said that each one was bound to another man for protection. They were called *nef'taali*."

"Bound how?" Malaq asked.

"Not like you think. Not physically. The soldiers were linked together by magic. It made them closer than brothers, more loyal than liegemen. One would cast and the other would protect him while he was weak. The Shinree who is responsible for this has no one to protect him. He's vulnerable. Now."

Malaq's eyes lit up as he caught on. "You think he's still here."

"I think it's *possible*. Did you see him leave?"

"No. As soon as I could, I came to get you. After I saw Jarryd, and he told me about the eldring, by the time I got back, Draken's forces were gone. I checked the roads all the way to the city, but there was no sign of them."

"If he was smart, he reserved enough strength to make a door out. But if he wore himself down too much, there's a chance he could be close by."

"I'll take it," Malaq said. "How do I find him?"

"I don't have it in me right now to cast anything that would help. You'll have to do it the hard way. Look for Shinree that won't wake up. Look for Langorians trying to blend in. Draken might have left some behind to look after his pet."

"It's a big city, Ian. And with Sarin dead I'll have to go to Guidon. He won't give me men for this."

"Then don't ask. Trust me, *Nef'areen*, they'll follow you. And if you find the man, kill him while he sleeps and bring me the crown."

Malaq gave me a nod. Before he left, he pulled Jarryd aside. While they spoke in muted tones about the best way to prevent my apparent, imminent demise, I walked away. I heard Jarryd's hollered protest, but I kept going, heading to the back half of the cavernous room where rows of massive obsidian pillars outlined a path all the way to Sarin's dais at the end.

123

It was a long, arduous walk. The warm stuffy air and the scent of carnage was not a good combination. It wasn't long before I had to stop and catch my breath.

Propping myself up against one of the tall, round spires, the stone felt good against my skin. It was smooth and cold, polished as perfectly as Malaq's boots. But it didn't help the buzzing in my ears. I closed my eyes and tried to ignore it.

The low whirring continued, building to a steady, deep thrumming.

It thrummed louder. The voices in the room faded into vague murmurs.

Leaning against the column, floating in the droning pulse, I started feeling better. As I did, it occurred to me that the vibrating hum wasn't coming from my aching head. It was stemming from the stone that was supporting me.

Every part of my body that was touching the obsidian was pulsing.

Alarmed, I pushed off the black stone. I turned around, faced it, and there was so much magical energy wafting off the column—off all the columns in the room—that the air shimmered visibly, like heat on a hot summer day. Only, these undulating waves were a lustrous black. *That's different.*

Never before had I seen a stone's aura when I wasn't touching it.

Delirium? I wondered hopefully. *A trick of the light?*

I would have accepted either as an explanation, if the pillars were made of any other substance. But obsidian and I had a history.

It was a principal stone for any magic user. Being known, though, for its dark, violent nature, the soldiers of the old empire relied heavily on obsidian for casting. It was also an integral part of the Crown of Stones. The day I ended the war with Langor, I drew in and utilized so much of the black energy that it bled down from where the artifact had rested on my head. Its aura had leached into my scalp and hair and marked me.

I'd always dismissed the obsidian stains as waste, a leftover of power that had nowhere else to go. Even recently, becoming aware of the shard's connection to the crown, I still didn't understand it. Now, experiencing such an intense, intimate exchange with the same type of stone, I could feel the truth.

The Crown's power had sunk into me that day, and it never left.

The black strands weren't scars. They were open wounds.

And they were bleeding magic.

I looked around at the pillars. It wasn't their energy reaching out to me. It was mine, reaching out to them. *The obsidian's aura is still in me.*

It's been in me all along.

It was a disturbingly seductive notion, that such a tempest could accumulate and exist inside me, and I wouldn't even know. It made me wonder: if I were to touch the dark streaks in my hair, would I feel magic there? Would it be icy-hot and staggering, like touching a vein of raw obsidian? And why would a stone here in Kael, a thing I had passed by countless times before, suddenly awaken it?

Boldly, I reached out. I put my hand on the glossy surface of the pillar, and right away, magic jumped against my skin. This time, I welcomed it. I let it in. And as I did, another source emerged. It welled up from a place I couldn't name, somewhere deeper—and suddenly so much obsidian was flowing through me that I could scarcely see.

It was incredible; the strength, the vigor. I felt exuberant, vital, and alive. A shell of quivering black energy overlaid my skin, and I was too intoxicated to care that it might be visible to anyone in the room. I wanted to drain the column dry and move on to the next, drinking in their magic one by one until the blood turned black in my veins.

There's so much, I thought excitedly. *I could lay waste to Langor.*

I could take out the entire realm and obliterate all traces of their civilization.

If Rella were made safe, then maybe I'd finally be free.

"Ian," Jarryd said then. "Come on."

"Leave me be," I told him.

"Are you all right?"

"I *said*, leave me be."

"They're going to move Sarin's body. I thought you might want to see him."

With effort, I pried my hands away from the column. I stepped back, and I immediately felt like shit. My wounds throbbed faster and harder than my speeding pulse. If possible, my limbs were weaker than before I touched the pillar. And I was angry. I was *so* angry; at Jarryd for interrupting; at myself for being careless. I wanted to dive into that rich, untapped well and let it take the pain away. Let it take everything away.

What did I care for the Kaelish and their decadent ways, for Jarryd and his ridiculous, immature notions that I could save everyone? I wasn't Rella's champion. I was her destroyer. *I could be Kael's too...so easily.*

Too easily.

"You need to be in bed," Jarryd said. "You're not well."

I know. Trying like hell to redirect my rage, I closed my hands into fists. My right didn't want to cooperate, but I forced it, and a twinge of pain shot through my injured arm. It wasn't enough.

I squeezed tighter. The pain intensified.

Tighter, and my knees buckled.

I felt nauseous. But I certainly wasn't thinking about magic anymore.

Jarryd caught me as I was about to hit the floor. He tried to rest me against one of the columns, and I tore out of his grip. "No!" I yelled, stumbling away.

Glancing around, he rubbed an impatient hand over his face. "I have to get you out of here." Jarryd reached for me again. I dodged his hand, and he started cursing. He cursed louder as I walked away.

I went over to the dais. Between the legs of the King's remaining council members, I got a quick glimpse of Sarin. Face distorted in pain and terror, his once strong, solid form was slumped over; eviscerated, bloodless, and limp. Then the crowd shifted, and my view of him was gone.

"Well look who's here," a man drawled from behind me. "It's about time you showed up."

Damn it, I thought, recognizing the voice. Having no choice but to acknowledge Sarin's son, I turned toward Guidon—and swallowed the first words that came to mind, thinking they might get me hung. I swallowed the second ones, too. Accusing the Prince of hiding under a bed during the attack wouldn't go over well. Yet, from his appearance, that was exactly where he'd been.

Lacking so much as a smudge on his soft rectangular face, a wrinkle on his silk clothes, a blonde curl out of position, or a drop of blood on the long-knife hanging from the sash at his waist; Guidon certainly hadn't been in the hall defending his father.

I offered him a polite, but icy, "Prince."

Guidon didn't give me that much. "How is it that Draken has come into my home, slaughtered my people, *my King*, and all you've done is bleed on my floor? Champion of Rella, my ass. If you can't put your magic to good use, then perhaps, Troy, you should be put on a shorter leash. In fact," a slow, sly smile strolled across his lips, "I have one bolted to my chamber wall that's about your size."

"I bet you do. Now, if you don't mind, I'd like to pay my respects."

Guidon put himself in front of me. "You haven't earned the right to see my father. You weren't even here when he was dying."

I raked my eyes up and down the front of him. "Neither were you."

"Filthy, witch," he hissed. "It's appalling how much faith my father put in your hands."

"He might have put some in yours once in a while…if they were more capable."

His nostrils flared. "You go no farther."

"You think you can stop me with words?"

Guidon's hand caressed the hilt of his knife. "The point of my blade was what I really had in mind. But from the looks of you, a nice easy shove might do it." He put out a hand, and I stepped into it. The pressure on my ribs hurt like hell. But the strongest muscle in Guidon's body was his tongue, and even injured, I had no trouble pushing him back a step.

"You might want to try the knife," I suggested.

"Be gone from my hall, Shinree," he fumed. "You are not among friends here."

"I never am."

With a rough jerk, Jarryd pulled me aside. "He's baiting you. Just let it go."

"That fool has no idea what I could do to him," I said in a cruel, breathless whisper. "Before he could even open his mouth to scream, I could suck out his worthless soul and send it into oblivion."

"I'm sure you could," Jarryd said uneasily. "But maybe that's not a good idea?"

"Damn it, Jarryd, he should be the one lying dead on the floor. Not Sarin."

"And you'll be lying on the rack if you don't stop. Guidon is about to be King."

As if on cue, the Prince called out with a flourish, "My loyal subjects!" Backing into the center of the room, he hopped up onto one of the only tables still standing. "In the morning," he said, loud and thoughtlessly cheerful, "General Aldous will lead a force of men into Rella. He will join the newly crowned, Queen Neela Arcana, in her fight against the foul Langorian invasion, and will aid her in dispatching the enemy quickly and mercilessly. Aldous will offer Kael's assistance to rebuild all that was lost, and to help ensure such a heinous tragedy never again happens on Rellan or Kaelish soil!"

When the cheers died down, I spoke up. "General Aldous is an instructor. He has no battle experience."

"That is true," Guidon replied. "But the General will have a contingent of trained soldiers and capable advisors at his side. He will make do."

Jarryd stepped forward. "My Lord Prince, with all due respect...King Sarin pledged three contingents to Kabri, not one."

"Did he?" Guidon's mouth stretched in a taught smile. "What a shame he isn't alive to confirm that."

"Your father granted us aid, not scraps," Jarryd said, struggling to keep an even tone. "We need men, weapons. Supplies. We have a treaty."

"Now that you mention it—Messenger," Guidon said sharply. "It isn't my name on the treaty with Rella. And I am, essentially, King now."

Jarryd's jaw set hard. "Is this an official withdrawal of support? Or do the Kaelish honor all their agreements with duplicity and double-talk?"

"Don't get testy," Guidon warned, jumping down from his perch. "Aldous will fight for Kabri as promised."

"With one contingent?" Jarryd pushed. "That won't be enough."

"Fine," Guidon sighed. "You can have two. But your little Princess might not be in this muddle if she'd spent more time in council and less time in your bed."

"You son of a bitch." Jarryd's voice trembled. "Kael will rot under your rule."

Guidon's hand shot out and wrapped around Jarryd's arm. "Your devotion to Neela, while pitiful, is absolute. So as badly as I'd like to skin you where you stand, Kane, I believe a much more satisfying torment is awaiting you in Kabri." He lowered his voice and said with mock distress, "I fear you may never recover from the loss."

Jarryd jerked out of his hold. "What are you talking about? What loss?"

"You don't know?" Guidon searched through the rage and the passion in Jarryd's eyes, looking for something. When he didn't find it, he let out a muted guileful laugh. "I can't believe she didn't tell you. Draken has extended an offer of marriage."

"Marriage?" Bewilderment dimmed Jarryd's rage. "To Neela?"

"Of course to Neela, you fucking simpleton. Unless your washed-up, half-dead Shinree over there can pull off a miracle, Draken will assume the title of High King. He will unite the Restless Lands under one rule and claim Neela as his Queen. She will be his wife. His lover. The mother of his children. While you, Kane, will be just another filthy peasant conscripted into his army." Guidon leaned in. "Did you know a Langorian soldier's rank is branded into the side of his face?" Wincing, he forced a quiet shudder. "Gruesome, isn't it?"

I moved up next to Jarryd. "Don't let him bait you. *Remember?*"

He didn't even look at me. "No," Jarryd said dully. "I don't believe you."

"Don't then," Guidon shrugged. "But think on this, errand-boy. If Neela let a scrawny, castle servant like you have a taste, imagine what wonders the little bitch would do for a King?"

Jarryd lunged for him.

"Okay," I said, forcing Jarryd back. "That's enough."

"Let me go!" Resisting, Jarryd made my attempt to prod him to the exit, hard and painful. "I'm not through here," he growled.

"Maybe you're not," I winced, slumping against the wall. Fresh circles of red were dripping out of the bandages on my arm. "But I am."

"Better listen to the witch," Guidon clucked at Jarryd. He waved a bored hand then in my direction. "Hear me now, Troy. In honor of my father's good memory, I will endure your continued brief presence in my home. But once you quit my realm, if you dare return under my reign, you will be arrested and chained to my wall for the rest of your life." Guidon was still going on as we left the hall. "And *what* did I say about bleeding on my floor?" he shouted. "Disgusting witch-blood…who knows what it's infected with? Someone get over there and clean that mess up before it stains!"

SIXTEEN

"You did what?"

Wincing at my tone, Malaq strolled farther into the room. Crisp and polished in steel gray and black, his long casual strides brought him quickly to the foot of my bed. He gestured at the mass of bandages on my upper body. "You're still breathing, aren't you?"

I struggled to sit up. "I told you how I feel about King's Healers."

"You did. But I decided you might feel more strongly about staying alive."

That I couldn't argue. "Where did you get him? Sarin didn't keep Shinree healers in the castle."

"Jillyan brought one with her from Langor. And no one was harmed," Malaq said, addressing my concerned expression. "Unfortunately, the man's title does seem to be a bit of a stretch. Draken bestowed him on Jillyan as a parting gift and, if his skill at healing is a direct reflection of brotherly love, Draken doesn't think much of our sister. Anyway, the major damage was repaired before the man passed out. But as you can no doubt feel, the rest was up to that pleasant old Kaelish fellow I saw running from your room a while ago. So don't expect the stitching to be pretty."

"I don't remember any of that," I said, trying. "It's all fuzzy after that drink Liel gave me." I looked at Jarryd, still in the doorway. "When was that?"

"Four days ago," he replied, moving in.

"Shit." I ran a hand through my hair. "I can't afford to lose that many days."

"We can't afford to lose you," Jarryd said simply. "Malaq found no trace of Draken's Shinree in the city, so that means he's still out here. He's still a threat. And you're Rella's only chance against him."

His earnestness made me cringe. "I'm not the one with the Crown of Stones."

"Then we take it," Jarryd replied, as if it were an easy thing to do. "We kill Draken and retrieve the crown from his Shinree. Then you can use it against him. That is the plan, right?" When I didn't answer, he eyed me funny. "You do have a plan?"

"Don't take it personal, Kane," Malaq butted in. He swaggered over to the window and hitched himself up on the sill. "Men like Troy don't work off plans. It's part of his roguish charm. Besides," he yawned. "It's a long way to Rella. He'll think of something."

I shook my head at Malaq. "I still can't believe you bartered with that woman."

"Bartered," Jarryd laughed. "You have no idea."

Malaq threw him a frown. "Do you even know what the word subtle means?"

Jarryd crossed his arms. "I know what dodging looks like."

"Would you prefer," Malaq said stiffly, "that I left Ian in the care of that Kaelish physician with his implements of torture? That saw of his wasn't even sharp!"

"Stop," I told them. I looked at Malaq. "What did you give Jillyan?"

"*He* didn't give her anything," Jarryd said.

"Kane, I swear…" Malaq muttered. "Payment was made. No need to bore the injured man with the details."

"Come on," Jarryd said hotly. "Ian knows anything borrowed from the former Queen of Langor comes with a steep price."

"Steep how?" I asked, and they both looked at me.

A faint grimace pulled at Malaq's mouth as he searched for the right words. Jarryd wasn't so picky. "She asked to bathe you."

"She what?" I barked. "Well that's not going to happen."

"Already did," Jarryd said, giving me his crooked grin. "It's really too bad you can't tell us what happened. It's rumored Jillyan has quite an appetite for Shinree men."

I shivered in disgust. "Vile woman."

"I'm sure," Jarryd said, still grinning. "But if you let her do more than wash you next time, maybe she'll convince Draken to give up."

"Don't be a child, Kane," Malaq scolded. "It was a simple business transaction. Without the loan of Jillyan's Shinree, Ian would be dead." He turned to me. "You'd lost too much blood. The physician wanted to cut off your arm, and you probably still wouldn't have survived the night. And it's not like she harmed you." A slight smile forming, Malaq tried to smother his amusement. "Most likely it was just the opposite."

"Gods," I groaned. "Couldn't you have just offered her money?"

"Jillyan doesn't need money," Malaq assured me. "However, she did ask one more thing. She wants to see you before you leave Kael."

"I think she's seen enough of me already."

As Jarryd laughed heartily at my expense, I leaned back against the headboard and closed my eyes. Despite being in and out of sleep for days, I was tired. Tired of hurting every time I breathed, tired of owing my life to people I didn't know.

"I don't like it," I said. "Why would Jillyan of Langor do anything for me?"

"Why don't you ask her?" Malaq suggested.

I opened my eyes and aimed them straight at him. "I don't want to ask her, Malaq. The way I see it, your sister—"

"Half-sister," he interrupted.

"Fine. Your *half-sister*," I said, letting him have the distinction, "is as much a conqueror as Draken. She's just going about taking Kael a different way."

Malaq shook his head. "I disagree. Jillyan is smart. Even-tempered. Tough. Most importantly, she doesn't approve of Draken's tactics."

"She told you they aren't aligned?"

"Not exactly. Her conversations tend to be a little enigmatic."

"Must run in the blood," Jarryd murmured.

It was my turn to laugh, but the pain in my ribs cut it short.

Holding my aching chest, I went for the large blue bottle on the table beside the bed. Inside was relief, according to the Kaelish physician. If it worked half as well as the brew he'd given me in the hall downstairs, it might alter my opinion of the man.

Leaning sideways, grinding my teeth and trying to pretend my ribs didn't feel like they were snapping out of my chest, I closed my fingers around the bottle's neck and tugged it closer. Popping the top, I tipped the bottle, and poured a steady stream into my mouth.

"Foul is it?" Malaq's aristocratic nose crinkled as he watched me. "Most anything a Kaelish healer prescribes isn't fit for my prize winning sow."

Swallowing, I smiled to myself, knowing there was no way Malaq Roarke kept pigs. "It's *coura*," I said, wiping a shaky hand across my mouth. "Although I'm sure a few herbs are mixed in somewhere."

"*Coura?*" Surprise softened Malaq's jaw. "I would have thought Ian Troy would have ground the herbs in his teeth before taking in a drop of Langorian liquor."

"I would," Jarryd said. "*Coura* tastes like horse dung."

I grinned. "You get used to it."

"So." Malaq shifted the discussion. "When do we leave for Rella?"

"We?" Settling back on the bed, I looked at him. "This isn't exactly a jaunt in the country, Malaq."

"I've ridden on a road a time or two before, my friend," he assured me.

"We aren't taking the road. Going through the mountains is more direct."

"More dangerous as well. Those trails wash out at a moments' notice."

"But if the weather holds, they'll shorten our trip by a week or more."

Malaq shrugged. "The trails it is then."

"I'm not stopping every ten minutes for you to clean off your boots," I warned.

"I'm a Prince, Troy," Malaq said crisply. "Not an old woman."

"Glad to hear it. Now, do you mind telling me why you're going? Royal blood or not, if the Arcana's wanted you, they would have sent for you a long time ago."

"Nicely put. But this has nothing to do with my mother's family. Once we cross into Rella, I'll be leaving you and heading northwest into Langor."

In mid-swallow, I almost choked. "I thought that Peace Envoy crap was a joke."

"Not at all. Sarin knew my parentage and upbringing would gain me an audience with the right people. And from there…let's just say it won't take much to stir up a little trouble." Malaq leaned in. "Not everyone was happy when Draken confiscated Jillyan's throne. From what I'm told, Langor is ripe for a little insurrection."

"Hold on." I couldn't believe what I was hearing. "You're going to Langor to incite civil war? In hopes of what...stretching Langor's resources, provoking a rebellion? Why? So some other, power-hungry tyrant can take the throne?" My pulse pounded at his arrogance. "Draken will kill you on sight."

"Draken will find a use for me. I'll make sure of it. And it's high time I cleaned up my family's mess."

"You seriously can't think you're responsible for any of this."

"You do. You said as much that night at the Dirty Owl...or whatever it's called."

"Wounded Owl. And that's not what I said at all."

Emotion leaked into Malaq's voice. "I need to do this, Troy. I need to see my past, make peace with it if I can. Destroy it if I have to. I thought of anyone, you might understand that."

I sighed and rubbed the weariness from my face. "Who knows of this?"

"Now that Sarin is gone? You." He glanced at Jarryd. "Him."

"No," I shook my head. "It's too dangerous."

"I don't believe that's your call."

Silent throughout our exchange, Jarryd piped up. "I already told you, Malaq, trying to convince those butchers to lay down arms is a waste of breath."

"Perhaps." Malaq stretched out lazily on the sill and crossed his booted feet. "But it is my breath to waste."

"And your life," Jarryd responded boldly. "Walking into a nest of vipers armed only with your tongue. Fool," he spat.

"Actually, Messenger," Malaq smirked, "I'm quite skilled with my tongue. Just ask the maid."

"Gods!" Jarryd threw his hands up. "Do you take nothing serious?"

Malaq's grin widened. "Are you always so quick to quarrel?"

Loud enough to shut them both up, I said, "Jarryd." I raised the only arm that would move and pointed at the hearth. He followed my terse direction with an aggravated scowl, but it vanished at the sight of his father's sunstone clasp sitting on the mantle.

"Damn," Jarryd breathed in shocked relief. He picked up the clasp. "I didn't think I'd ever see this again."

"I wasn't going to let that happen." Wincing, I scooted down into the pillows. "I saw the look on your face when I asked for it. I knew it was important to you."

"So much was lost in the looting. This is all I have left of him." Holding it reverently in his hands, Jarryd looked up from the stone. "Thank you."

I nodded. "Now get of here—both of you. And close the damn door." I pulled the covers up and shut my eyes. When I opened them again, Jarryd and Malaq were gone, but the door was still open.

Cursing them profoundly, I rolled off the bed. Moving hurt less than expected, thanks to the healer's herbs, so I went to the window first. I didn't mean to linger. I planned to close the drapes, then the door, and go back to bed. But there were tinges of red on the horizon. Dawn was reaching up toward the sky, dotting light and shadow across the green of the Kaelish mountain range, and the longer I stared, the more the view became similar to the rocky peaks that skirted the disputed land dividing Langor and Rella—the same unsteady ground where Draken and Aylagar had warred and where my people's empire once stood.

And I began to see different mountains on a different morning.

The shadows became Draken's prowling army. A gleam of light in the valley became the glint off a sea of colliding blades. I gripped the sill and the soft supple strands of ivy clinging to the stones outside felt like skin before my magic touched it. The wind- tossed, fall-colored leaves were grains of the red sand desert; swirling across the wasteland that I created with the Crown of Stones.

It was nothing more than exhaustion coupled with imagination. I knew that. But I was suddenly there, on the battlefield, carrying the suffocating weight of desperation on my chest, enduring the familiar hunger that came with feeding on little more than blind rage and hatred for days on end. Fatigue pulled at my arms and legs. Wrath and resentment spurred me on. The guilt burning in my eyes was self-inflicted, inspired by the shame of casting strength on men that had long since lost the will to fight.

But I kept them going. I had to, to save Rella. I had to wait for the fleeting moments when I could sneak away and cast in secret. It was the only way to stay free, to stay by her side. Aylagar made it clear from the beginning that if I didn't abide by her orders, I would end up with *Kayn'l* in my food and a chain around my neck.

Yet, while my heart beat for the woman, my blood raged for every man that died when my spells could have made a difference. It was that constant internal struggle that made loathe what I'd become. What we'd all become, *even her.*

All I'd wanted was for it to be over.

Gods, I thought in panic. *Is that what happened?*

Had I wanted it to end that badly?

Had I really been filled with that much hate?

Taren was right. I held back for so long. No wonder I killed them all.

I dug my fingers into the stone sill and tried to silence my mind. I didn't want to think. Not about the war. Not about Aylagar. It was strange, how eager I was to push the memories away, when a short time ago I would have embraced them. For years, I'd clung to every guilt-born, wine-induced recollection like a lifeline. Using them to curb my appetite for magic, letting them trample me into submission.

Not anymore. I was too much of a fraud. A hypocrite. I swore on Aylagar's dead body that I was through, that I wouldn't let magic own me again. Now tremors were racing up my arms and down my legs, and my hand was wrapped around the obsidian shard, ready to relieve them. *One spell,* I thought.

Just one to clear my head. One spell and I can think straight.

Accessing the obsidian the crown had left inside me, I instinctively thought: *calm.* And a breath later, my anxieties receded. My mind felt lighter. The tension in me dissolved like cobwebs in a pounding rain, and my muscles began to loosen.

Just a little more…

I barely heard the sound behind me.

I didn't feel the hand on my shoulder until Malaq spun me around. I opened my mouth then, to curse him—I was a hairsbreadth away from a moment of much-needed relief. But shock stayed my words.

Malaq, the man who let nothing show unless he wanted to, was looking at me with outright bewilderment, disappointment, and concern. He was granting me a rare, open, honest display of emotion. And I'd done absolutely nothing to earn it. "This isn't fair." I said, my voice shaking. "You don't know me."

Malaq dropped his hand from my arm. "I know you're better than this."

"I'm not."

"Jarryd thinks you are. He's counting on you to save his home. A lot of people are counting on you. People who will die if you get caught casting in here. Because, mark my words, Guidon will take great pleasure in punishing you."

"I know that."

"But you don't care." Upset with me, Malaq shook his head. "Is the pull really that great? Is it so compelling that you would risk everything?"

I swallowed. "It never stops."

"But you stopped. For ten years you shut it out."

"*I'm trying*, Malaq. But I can't. Not anymore. It's different now."

"Different how?"

"I..." *It's in me*, I thought, but I couldn't bring myself to say it.

"You might believe that magic means more to you than anything or anyone. That you have no other reason to fight but that Rella commands it. But I know better. I know what you could have done the day you channeled the crown. How much farther you could have gone. You could have ruled the world, Ian. Obliterated it. Instead, you removed yourself from it. You walked away. For us—for all of us. Call it guilt if you want. Call it penance. But shutting down a part of who you are for the safety of others...that sounds pretty damn courageous and self-sacrificing to me." Turning to leave, he paused. "I came back to tell you. Guidon agreed to send an extra contingent to Rella. It's a small victory, but I thought you'd want to know."

"It isn't a victory, Malaq. If more men go to fight, more men will die."

"That's really how you see it?"

"As long as Draken's magic user has the crown, yes. If I don't get it back, Neela Arcana could have ten contingents and still lose her throne."

He stared at me a moment. "What do you know about her?"

"Neela? Not much. We met once," I said, recalling the rainy afternoon of Aylagar's funeral. Shy and still very much a child, Neela had been devastated by her mother's death. Yet she'd held it in far better than me. "She was young. Eleven. Twelve, maybe. Why?"

"I wouldn't count her out just yet." Malaq backed away. "When do we leave?"

"Dawn."

As I closed the drapes, I heard Malaq's footsteps retreating. When they'd faded completely, I crossed the room to close the door he'd left open—again.

Half-way shut, I pushed it the rest of the way, and met resistance from the other side. "For the gods' sake, Malaq," I groaned, "go away." Yanking the door open wide, I found Prince Guidon Roarke and a dozen Kaelish soldiers filling the corridor outside my room.

I groaned louder.

"Troy," the Prince said stiffly. "I'm glad to see you on your feet."

"Are you?"

"Of course. If you'd expired in here, the entire room would have stunk of dead Shinree for months."

I grinned a little. "Now it just smells like your wife."

Guidon's face drew tight enough to shatter. "If you were mine, Troy, I would bleed you every day. However..." he paused, straightening his golden, brocade coat. "There are those that see value in letting you live, so I will stay my urges. For now."

"Don't hurt yourself on my account, Prince."

"King, actually. I was crowned yesterday."

"My condolences to your people." I put a hand on the doorknob. "I appreciate you coming to visit, but if there's nothing else...?"

"Actually, there is." Guidon stepped back. "I believe I have something of yours. Or at least, so the little trollop claims." Reaching into the huddle of soldiers, Guidon pulled a woman out of their midst. I had a second to register her identity as the winegirl from The Wounded Owl, before Guidon gave her a hard shove in my direction.

Catching Imma as she stumbled in to me, I turned on Guidon. "If you've harmed her, these men won't be near enough to protect you."

"Settle down, Troy. The girls from her part of the city are a bit too mouthy for my taste."

Guidon strolled away. His guards followed, and I gave my attention to the woman in my arms. I tried to look at her face. I remembered it being beautiful. But I couldn't get beyond the fact that her dress was two sizes too small for her curves. Or that the tan fabric fell perfectly over her hips and hugged her upper body, tight enough to force a good measure of plump pale breasts to erupt up over the top of her tightly cinched bodice. It was a nice look. I just wasn't sure how she could breathe.

"Did they hurt you?" I asked her.

"They didn't dare," she replied. "Not once they found out I was here for you."

"I don't understand."

Imma twisted a strand of long rusty hair leisurely around one finger. "That fine friend of yours came to see me today. Tall. Dark hair. Fancy clothes."

"Malaq?"

"That's him." I could hear the approval in her voice. "He thought I could help with your recovery." Gently, she traced the layer of bandages on my chest. "I'm all yours till morning, Shinree. And I've been paid enough to buy anything you want."

My mind started working. "Anything?"

"Use me as you wish. That is…if you're up for it." Imma pressed her body closer. Feeling me harden against her, she lifted her lively blue eyes. "And you most definitely are." She played at kissing me a moment; drifting her mouth over mine. Then, giggling, Imma wriggled out of my grip and twirled away toward the bed.

"Things got pretty messy the other night," I said, going after her.

"So I heard." Absently, she played with the laces on the front of her dress.

"I'm glad you got out."

"Uh-huh." Imma pulled at the bow. The loops slid apart. The bodice gaped. "You can keep talking, if you like." Leisurely, she reached down and grabbed the hem of her skirt. Bunching up the fabric between her legs, she lifted it to her thighs. "I can start without you." Imma spread her legs wider.

Her fingers disappeared beneath the skirt.

She threw her head back and let out a low, aching moan.

I put both my hands up to stop her. "Wait." Going to the door, I kicked it shut and locked it. By the time I'd double-checked the lock and turned back around, Imma's dress was on the floor.

SEVENTEEN

Running the brush across Kya's flank, I stopped to stare at the leather wristlet tied around the outside of the brace on my right arm.

Diamond. Emerald. Garnet. Kyanite. Citrine. Fire agate. Hematite.

Good choices, all of them, I thought, fingering the row of gemstones pressed into the braided leather. It had been three days since we left the city. Three days since I woke from my night with Imma to find her gone, my wounds healed, and the trinket of stones on her empty pillow. Since then, I hadn't been able to stop toying with it, or trying to figure out what it meant.

Evidently, the shapely Kaelish winegirl I'd spent half a day and a night with, wasn't a winegirl at all, or even Kaelish. Because while I'd slept beside her, she'd been awake, erasing all remaining physical traces of my scuffle with the eldring.

My best guess? Imma and the Shinree woman who attacked the Wounded Owl were one and the same. She'd used a glamour spell to disguise herself as the winegirl and infiltrate the castle. Then, after healing me, she'd left the gift of stones like a calling card, and vanished.

It was a bit of a kick in the teeth, but not entirely unexpected. The attraction I'd felt toward Imma at the tavern hadn't been normal. Yet, my suspicion of her unnatural allure had inexplicably disappeared with her. And I hadn't remembered it at all when she was taking her clothes off in my room. Still, if Imma were working with Danyon and Lareth as part of the ambush, then her earnest attempt to get me out of the tavern didn't fit. Neither did her covert mission to the castle to heal me.

What I really didn't like was her insinuation of a connection to Malaq. Was that done only to gain my trust? Or was there more to it?

Who is she?

Deep in thought, as Malaq slammed his spyglass shut, I looked up. "Anything?"

Standing high atop a boulder perched at the threshold of a steep cliff, he shook his head. "Nothing."

"Damn it." I threw down the brush and stood. "It's getting dark. He should be back by now."

"Relax, Ian. Give the kid some rope."

"Jarryd doesn't know these mountains, Malaq." I looked at the empty trail. "I should have gone with him."

Malaq jumped down and came away from the edge of the bluff. Standing over me, he picked a burr from Kya's mane and tossed it. "You do realize that Jarryd survived Draken's raid on Kabri? That he fled Rella with Langorians on his trail for days and still made it out alive? All of which tells me he can manage to skewer a rabbit or two for dinner without perishing. And even if those furry bastards band together to mount a resistance, I believe he is more than capable of deflecting their wrath. Without you."

"Fuck off, Malaq. He's Rellan. That makes him my responsibility."

"I see. So this guard-dog role you appear to have taken on is only a result of your forced service to Rella? It has nothing to do with you actually being fond of Jarryd? Because the gods know there's nothing likeable about the kid. He's lazy, doesn't pull his weight, always yammering on about something. And his jokes are terrible."

"Are we talking about Jarryd…or you?"

He grinned. "Face it, Ian, Jarryd Kane isn't like us. His blood isn't a stigma. He's never been ostracized. Made to feel ill at ease in his own skin. To doubt his place. He doesn't know what it's like to have this kernel of discontent always in the back of his mind, telling him that with all the tribulation surrounding his existence that it has to mean something. That he was born for a reason. And finding that reason…that's what keeps us going. Not him though," he shrugged. "That boy felt his reason from day one."

Malaq's lecture was long-winded, but dead on. "Rella," I said.

"He loves that land. He carries it with him. Her people. Her Queen. What do you think gets him up before dawn every damn morning? Not that I mind having breakfast ready when I wake, but it would be nice if I didn't have to eat it with him hovering over me, harping about how it's time to get on the road."

I snatched up the brush and put it away. Sliding a hand down Kya's front left leg, I lifted it and checked the grooves of her hoof for debris. "I'll be honest, Malaq." I put her leg down and glanced at him before I picked up another. "It's hard for me to accept you as feeling out of place or ill at ease with anything."

"Have you ever had half a barrel of fish stuffed down your trousers?"

I blurted a laugh. "Can't say that I have."

"I was a half-Langorian boy growing up in a Kaelish fishing village, Ian. I wasn't exactly well received." Malaq wandered away. He went over to our small fire and sat down. I finished Kya's last two hooves, gave her one of the carrots Liel snuck out of the kitchen for me before we left the castle, and then joined him.

"Pig slop," I said, throwing myself down.

"What?"

"I had a bucket of it dumped over my head once. I was living in this little Rellan farm town on the mainland. It's called Ula?" He shook his head like he hadn't heard of it. "The locals didn't like me talking to their girls. There was this one…" I smiled. "Anyway, it's not fish, but I still chased the little bastards down and made them eat it."

"How old were you?" he chuckled.

"Thirteen, I think."

"So you were always this charming?" Still chuckling, Malaq shook his head. "What about the girl?"

"Katrine? We got pretty close. As far as I know she's still there." I pictured her the day I left for war; curly red hair spread out in the hay; brown eyes going closed as I slid my hand under her dress. "I haven't been back in a while."

"From that expression on your face it seems she might be worth a visit."

My smile grew faint. "I tried, after the war and the crown but…I was in a bad way. I was dangerous. I *am* dangerous," I said plainly. I gave him a sober look and said what I'd been thinking for days. "Malaq, if I was made to cast right now, sitting here with you…"

"You'd have time to put distance between us."

"We don't know that. Not for sure."

"It's a risk," he conceded. "But so is that soup our absent friend keeps making for dinner. The way I see it, his bad cooking will do me in before one of your spells."

Malaq held his flask out. I took it without hesitation. After a long drink of the sweet warm wine, I looked at him. His features were relaxed. His posture was loose. It was clear: Malaq didn't see me for what I was. He was too busy thinking he'd found some kind of kindred spirit. But he was wrong. I hadn't spent my life searching for the reason I existed. I'd been trying to run away from it…and failing miserably.

He doesn't get it. How easy it would be for me to slip up. How much it takes for me to sit here with these stones on my wrist, with the shard touching my skin.

To not think about how it would feel to let it sink in.

I took another drink to quell my thoughts. "You should pack up and head home."

"Home?" There was a touch of surprise in his voice. "Where exactly is that?"

"You know what I mean. Go back to your stepfather. To the life you made with him. This isn't for you."

"What isn't? Curling up on the cold ground, careening through forests, climbing mountains for hours on end—by myself, since Kane's always riding ahead fretting over the distance and you're always a mile back, sleeping off your last spell in the saddle. I couldn't imagine a better time. Besides." He leaned back and stretched his long legs out across the ground. "If I wasn't here, you'd miss me."

I tipped the flask at him. "We don't have enough wine for me to admit that." I took another mouthful and passed it back. "That night at the Owl, what were you really doing there? It's not exactly a place for royalty."

"Didn't we cover this? I was looking for you."

"And you found me how?"

"A Shinree riding through the city streets like he's on fire…it wasn't that hard."

"What about Imma?"

"Imma?" Malaq tilted his head, thinking, and I recalled the morning we left Kael. At seeing my lack of bandages and watching me take to the saddle without issue, Jarryd had given me a point-blank, what-the-hell stare for at least a minute. On the other hand, Malaq had shown no shock, concern, or even a smidge of curiosity. Not that I could condemn him for that. Malaq was naturally nonchalant. And if he had truly paid for Imma's services, I would have heard about the depth of his generosity ten times by now.

Since I hadn't, I wanted to believe that meant he was innocent. That he had nothing to do with the Shinree woman who'd played me. But I'd been forced to make assumptions about Malaq's character from the beginning, taking him as he presented himself, honest and reliable. I'd accepted him at face value because I'd been drawn in, swayed by whatever indefinable element Malaq Roarke possessed that earned him devotion so easily. I'd let my guard down.

I couldn't remember when that had ever served me well.

"Did you send her?" I asked abruptly.

A dent formed in his brow. "Send whom where?"

"The Kaelish girl that isn't Kaelish. Did you send her to me?"

The dent deepened. He looked at me over the rim of his flask. As he tipped it, I searched for trickery or deceit in his eyes, but as usual, they were veiled and discreet, and incredibly controlled. "No…?" he said at last.

"You didn't pay her? She said you sought her out and paid her."

"Did I?"

"You tell me."

"You do realize I have no idea what you're talking about."

"Forget it."

Malaq closed the flask and tucked it in his pocket. "How about a couple of questions for you, my friend? Questions that actually make sense."

A noise disrupted the quiet of the forest. It repeated, and I shot to my feet.

Gripping my sword, I moved to investigate, but Malaq intercepted. Putting himself in the way, he said deliberately, "Why is it that one day you can barely move, and the next you're fit to ride in the saddle longer than we are? Or maybe I just imagined you being turned on a spit of eldring claws?"

The sound continued; faint pops and cracks of twigs underfoot.

I glanced in the direction of it. "You're seriously doing this now?"

"At first, I thought you'd paid Jillyan for another session with her healer. But I know how you feel about Langorian women."

The footfall grew louder. I pulled out of his hold and stepped toward the sound.

"I'd love to hear where that pretty new bracelet of yours came from, too," he said, and I stopped.

Looking down at the wristlet, running a finger over the stones, I wondered if Malaq was asking (days later) because he realized I suspected him. Or was it simply that he did everything in his own time?

"So it's silence, then?" he said. "That's what I get? Why am I not surprised?"

Jarryd broke through the trees. Bow in one hand, a rabbit and two squirrels in the other, he walked between us, oblivious to the friction. He glanced up. "Hungry?"

Malaq looked at me with genuine irritation. "Don't touch that pot, Kane. It's Troy's turn to cook."

Stumbling on the uneven ground, Kya bumped into me from behind. She nudged my back with her nose, and I picked up the pace, pulling her faster down the hill.

I was doing my best to focus on the terrain, to keep Malaq and Jarryd in my sights and not fall behind. But my mind kept drifting, spinning with a myriad of concerns that had grown to preoccupy me, day and night, since leaving Kael. I couldn't sleep with the thought of Draken's army inflicting suffering while I was too far away to stop it. His alliance with my Shinree enemy confounded me. As did Imma and her motives, and Guidon's desire to get into bed with the Langorians (literally). His bride's uncharacteristic generosity to someone she had every reason to hate was just as baffling.

The moment when I was being cast on through the eldring ate at me as well. It was a gap I couldn't fill, no matter how I tried. Pain had made the whole thing a blur, and it was maddening. I couldn't recall the words of the spell. I had no idea if I'd killed the eldring before it was completed, or if my enemy had finished his conjuring. If he had, then something was coming. And when it hit, I was going to get blindsided hard.

It was also weighing on me how swiftly my appetite for magic was increasing. When we'd first left the city, I'd been able to tolerate the symptoms for a while. Now, going long stretches without casting shredded my nerves down to nothing. The harsh fact that replenishing them put my companions in jeopardy wasn't helping.

I did try to be cautious. When I cast, I used Imma's gift instead of the shard, so I didn't risk waking the crown. I channeled only what was necessary to refocus me, and only when I couldn't stand the feel of myself—which was pretty much all the time.

They aren't safe with me, I thought. *I should leave. Veer off the trail and go.*

I don't need them. They're a distraction, a hindrance. It's better if I sever our connection now, before they become too reliant on me.

Before I have to watch them die.

Malaq slowed his pace. Atop his mount, he halted and waited for me. When I caught up, he started moving again, keeping time with me as I walked Kya beside him on the trail.

Sensing a question on his lips, I asked, "What is it?"

"Something's been bothering me," he confessed. "I can't figure why a Shinree would support Draken at all, let alone help make him High King."

"Yeah, I've been going over that one myself."

"Langorians care nothing for the slave laws. They raise your people like cattle. Work them to death in the mines. Atrocities rarely breed allies, Ian, and even if they did, with a magic user this powerful, what could Draken, or any Langorian, offer the man that he couldn't just take for himself?"

Ahead of us, Jarryd turned in his saddle. "What about protection?" Seeing our blank-faced reactions, he brought his horse around and came back toward us up the hill. "The day Kael was attacked, Ian—" he gestured at me, "said something about the ancient Shinree, about how they bound themselves together. Maybe that's what our magic user did. He agreed to help Draken in exchange for protection. He could do a lot worse than having a Langorian as a permanent guard."

"None of my kind would ever bind with a Langorian like that," I said, shooting him down. "The process is too complex, too sacred."

"It could explain the man's relationship with Langor," Jarryd offered.

"No, you don't understand," I told him. "You aren't talking about a partnership or a treaty. Or even the blood oath you took to serve your King."

"Then what am I talking about?" Jarryd's blue eyes were crisp and challenging. "You said it yourself. Channeling the crown makes him vulnerable. So vulnerable, that Malaq had a good chance of finding the man in Kael. But he didn't. Maybe, that's because someone had a deeply personal interest in getting Draken's magic user to safety. A selfish interest. Like being magically bound together." Jarryd shrugged a shoulder. "I don't know about you, but selfish sounds like a Langorian to me."

"It does," I conceded. "But this kind of magic, taking on another self… it's no light matter. Memories, abilities, feelings; a part of each person goes into the other. And it's for life. Once the link is established, it's permanent. The two parties will communicate sensations. Share their memories. Feel each other's emotions and pain."

Jarryd balked at my explanation. "Why would anyone want that?"

"Look past the obvious," I scolded, and he frowned. "You take away the need for words between two men in battle, give them access to each other's skills and experiences, and they move as one. Eventually, over time, everything—every move, every sword strike, every need—becomes something far beyond instinct."

"And the Shinree had an entire army like that?" Malaq whistled, imagining the possibilities. "What of you, Troy? You carry a soldier's blood. Did you ever have a…what did you call it?"

"*Nef'taali*," I said. "It means my other, or other half, other soul. There is no direct translation. And no, I told you. It isn't done anymore." I gave Kya's reins a tug and started down the hill. "There's a stream not far ahead. We can stop and refill."

I had no doubt they'd both taken offense to my gruff tone, but after a moment I heard Malaq prod his mount forward. "Anyone up for fish?" he asked, coming up behind me. "You did mention a stream."

Taking up the rear, Jarryd grunted. "Prince Malaq Roarke catching fish from a stream? This I have to see."

"I'll have you know, Kane, that I am an excellent fisherman," Malaq replied. "One of the advantages of being banished to a tiny village on Kael's southern shore is that there's little to do but fish. And there are no finer waters."

"If you believe that," Jarryd countered, "then you've never been to Kabri."

"My naïve, young messenger," Malaq laughed. "The bay in Raymorre is a blue you could never imagine. The sand is silk. The fish practically jump onto the shore to be eaten. In no way could Kabri's drab rocky slopes compare."

I kept walking. I listened now and then, to ensure their debate didn't come to blows. Malaq enjoyed riling Jarryd simply because it was an easy thing to do. I suspected it would eventually earn him a punch in the nose. Today though, their conversation remained lighthearted. Jarryd relented to a chuckle. Malaq threw his head back in genuine laughter. It was a much-needed relief of tension. I might have even joined them in it. But as I glanced back, the late afternoon sun glinted off the edges of the serpent clasp at Malaq's throat, and I started thinking about what Draken would do when he saw it. When Langor's egocentric King realized Malaq had something that belonged to him, death was a good possibility. Slow torture was more likely.

If, by some miracle, Malaq actually managed to talk his way into Draken's good graces, I couldn't imagine he would last long masquerading as a son of Langor. Pretending to be one of them, living inside the walls that echoed his mother's screams. It would break him, perhaps even before Draken did.

Stopping once more, I looked up at Malaq. "Draken's keep. Do you know why it bears the name Darkhorne?" I could see by his face that he didn't. "The castle was constructed over seven hundred years ago on a summit halfway up one of the tallest mountains on the western shore. It was commissioned by one of the members of the Ruling House of the Shinree Empire. It was to be a palace. But no Shinree ever lived there."

"They didn't build it either," Malaq said as he and Jarryd came to a standstill. "Darkhorne was constructed entirely by Langorian slaves and Shinree whips."

I nodded. "What else do you know?"

"It's difficult to get in uninvited."

"The whole area is difficult," I corrected him. 'The ground is unstable. The mountains are stripped bare and full of abandoned mines. There are no trees, no cover. It's desolate and dreary no matter the season. The keep itself is well fortified. It's built on great deposits of hornblende. One of the dark stones."

"So that's where the name came from," Jarryd cut in. "What does it do?"

"On its own? Nothing. But when a Shinree channels with hornblende nearby, it takes over. It sickens good intentions. Twists even the most carefully crafted spells. Hornblende was a favorite tool for assassins and traitors, especially during the last years of the Empire, when the ruling houses were fighting like spoiled children. It was easy work, tricking a man to kill someone he thought to heal. All they had to do was plant a sliver of hornblende near their mark and the deed was done."

"Seems effective," Malaq agreed.

"But before then," I said, "before it was known what hornblende would do, countless died from spells gone wrong, Langorians and Shinree. They died in the mines, in the slave camps—on the steps of the very keep they sought to build. Ultimately, Darkhorne was abandoned. It stayed that way a long time. Until your forebears, Malaq, broke free and founded their own realm. When the first King of Langor was crowned, he claimed the keep as his own. He had it completed and ordered the mine underneath be worked by the condemned, turning it into the most feared prison in all of Langor."

"I'm not Shinree," Malaq said. "The hornblende won't affect me."

"It's a dark place, Malaq."

"It's a place made of rock, like any other."

"Goddamn it." I shook my head wearily. "Why does every conversation we have end with me wanting to wrap my hands around your throat?"

In no mood to hear his response, I turned around and resumed my trek down the steep stony path. I pulled Kya as quickly as the terrain would allow, and gradually the ground flattened. The trail widened. Rock gave way to patches of dirt and grass. Trees replaced the barren cliffs we'd been following all day. Saplings at first, and then thicker, more established groves, popped up to line both sides of the path. Not far ahead they would close in tighter. The trail would narrow again. It would dip down and curve into the deep woods, where it would stay for some time. When it came out again, the dirt would change over to sand. The vegetation would thin and Rella would be visible on the horizon. Not long after, Kabri.

Even with the spell pulling me back, I didn't want to go.

Pushing his mount past Malaq, Jarryd came to ride beside me. He leaned down, grinning. "Care to wager how long it'll take our Prince to catch something?"

"The wager won't work if we're both betting against him."

Jarryd's grin widened. "I think I have a biscuit left he can use for bait." Standing in the saddle, he twisted to rummage through his packs. "There it is. One left."

"You sure you want to waste it?"

"Oh, it's not a waste." Closing the flap of the bag behind him, Jarryd chuckled, "Especially if he falls in."

As Jarryd turned back around, I caught the brief flash of something in the air.

Arrow, I thought. But I had no time to voice a warning. Steel split flesh with a spurt of red as the barb tore across the side of Jarryd's face.

EIGHTEEN

The next arrow stuck in his saddle. The third mine. Scores more riddled the ground as I yelled for Malaq to take cover and hauled Jarryd down off his horse.

We headed into the trees, but it was no better there. Langorians soldiers filled the forest. More rode in to block both directions of the trail. Weapons were drawn, orders were shouted, and we were surrounded. The soldiers held position, but they were doing so reluctantly. Every Langorian in sight was salivating with the urge to attack, except one: Malaq Roarke.

Malaq was the only man among us not on edge. Having chosen not to heed my warning, he sat in the saddle, his rowdy mount stomping the ground, while he assessed the situation with a calm, curious eye. In flawless Langorian he demanded to speak to the officer in charge, and I left him to it; turning my attention instead to the blood emptying out of Jarryd's head.

"On the ground." I pushed him down. Jarryd leaned back against a tree, and I squatted beside him to examine the horizontal slice dividing one side of his face. Carving a path just shy of his mouth, all the way across his left cheek, the arrow had cut fairly deep, but clean. Where it exited, through his ear, was another matter. A good measure of flesh had been ripped away. What was left behind was torn and mangled.

I needed water and bandages.

I looked at Kya. She was just out of reach. I knew any move I made for her would be seen as a threat, but asking permission wasn't going to work either. It was a waste of time appealing to our enemy's sense of decency. They didn't have any.

Removing the dagger from my boot, I improvised. "Thought I was going to have to part with some hefty coin to replace that nice tunic you bandaged me up with in Kael. But I'd say this makes us even." Stretching out the bottom of my shirt, I put the blade through the hem and cut it off. Dividing the cloth further, I bunched up one of the pieces and pressed it against his face.

"I can do it myself." Jarryd yanked the cloth out of my hand.

I resisted the urge to yank it back. Drawing a sword, I laid it across his lap and said emphatically, "Last resort only. Got it?"

"This feels pretty last resort already. There's at least—"

"Stop counting. It won't change their numbers." Naturally, I'd already tallied them, and the result wasn't good. More than a dozen mounted troops were scattered across the hill, and at least twice that many were in the woods and on the trail. There was no way I could have missed a force so large. Magic had definitely masked their approach.

One of the mounted soldiers broke off from the rest. He moved off the road and into the canopy of trees. As he headed straight for us, Jarryd's hand tightened on the grip of my sword. He started breathing faster.

"Come on..." he muttered, and I almost took my sword back.

"Stay put." I put a hand on his shoulder as I got up. "And keep your mouth shut."

"To hell with that." Jarryd started to stand, and I shoved him right back down.

Clipped and harsh, I said, "Don't. Do. Anything."

He gestured at his face. "I'm just supposed to take this?"

"For now." He started to object, and I cut him off. "Don't start fights you can't win, *nef'salle*." I thought the Shinree expression of friendship might soften both my words and his reaction. I was wrong. His eyes were charged with so much rage. I could almost see the memories of Kabri's fall shooting through his mind.

"I can't just sit here," he said tightly. "I won't."

"You will. Or I'll knock you out myself."

Upon us now, the Langorian brought his warhorse to a causal stop. I gave Jarryd one last, stern look and then raised my eyes. My intention was to take measure of what I was in for, but my goal fell apart as I got lost in the multitude of scars crisscrossing the man's body. In addition to the recent, circular symbol of rank branded into his cheek, on his face, his neck, and both arms and hands, were ruts and furrows, raised jagged lines, pockmarks, and uneven blotches of burned skin. Nearly every visible piece of him was disfigured, damaged, or marred in some fashion. Even his nose had the look of being broken at least twice. I didn't even want to imagine what the rest of him looked like.

Yet, gruesomeness aside, the man was no tavern rat like Danyon. His head of thick, black hair was combed and contained. Instead of a wild beard like most of his kin, he sported only a small tuft in the middle of his chin. He carried no extra weight, either. Sizeable muscles protruded from his sleeveless leather vest, as if his body had been built by years of hard work.

"Troy," the man said cordially. "Captain Krillos, at your service." Smiling down at me like an old friend, he crossed an arm over his waist and bent in a dramatic bow. As he straightened, and our eyes met, his held no animosity whatsoever. Only a simmering amusement and far more intelligence than most Langorians were blessed with.

"Captain," I nodded. "I didn't think Langor had any high ranking soldiers left from the old days. Or any soldiers for that matter."

"I was out of your line of sight, Shinree. We all were." Grinning openly, he spread his arms in a sweeping gesture at his men. None were quite as distinguishable as Krillos, but they were all rough and nasty looking.

"Where? Prison?" I asked, and the captain's jaw tensed. "Gods," I laughed. "I'm right. You weren't even in the army during the war. You were in a cell."

"Captain Krillos!" Malaq called out. "I believe you would do better dealing with me. I've been dispatched by the realm of Kael to discuss peace with your King."

Krillos slid his eyes to Malaq. "I know who you are."

"Is that a threat?" I cut in.

"Troy," Malaq cautioned. He raised a hand to silence me. I didn't like it, but Malaq seemed to think he could handle the situation. So I backed down, and prepared to watch him waste his refined diplomatic skills on a man whose head should be in a bag on my saddle.

"If you know who I am, Captain," Malaq said, with a frigid smile, "then you are either witless or disloyal. Unless, you have another explanation as to why you have accosted my party and have yet to address me with the honor in which I am due."

Krillos backed his mount out of the trees. He returned to the path and halted in front of Malaq. "My deepest apologies, My Lord Prince," he said; sounding more facetious than sincere. "It was not my intention to offend you."

Carelessly, Malaq drew Natalia and rested her across his lap. "Then, what is your intention, Captain?"

"To bring you home to Langor," Krillos answered.

I jumped in. "As a prisoner?"

Krillos tilted his head at me. "Our task is to bring the Prince safely to Darkhorne." He glanced between us. "Or did you think King Draken unaware?" His grin was wicked, yet lighthearted, as if he found the whole thing entertaining. "He knows you're coming, Prince. He knows you're all coming."

"Then I look forward to a proper welcome," Malaq said evenly. "But, as you can see, Captain, I already have an escort."

"A Kabrinian pup and a used-up witch?" Krillos grunted. "These men aren't fit to escort a Rellan goat herder." He laughed, and a vigorous round of chuckles ran through the troops.

"And what of you, Captain?" Malaq asked. "Are you fit?" His tone was quiet and a little bit frightening. "Would you give your life to protect me? Would you give it now, if I asked?"

Krillos went still as stone. "I'd prefer not. But whatever we were before, we're now avowed soldiers of Langor. We're duty-bound to protect you, Prince. Honored as well, if you have half the character you've shown so far. But you travel with known enemies of the realm. Your brother doesn't approve."

"I owe my brother nothing." Malaq's gray eyes burned. "I owe you even less."

"That you do." Krillos bowed his head. "But even I know these two are questionable company for a Prince of Langor."

"You dare judge me?" Malaq laughed. It was a dark, menacing sound unlike any I'd heard from him before. "I choose my own companions and my own enemies. And I choose carefully. I suggest, Captain," he said, equally sinister, "that you do the same."

Krillos said nothing. He just stared at Malaq, and Malaq stared back, and the silent contest of wills went on long enough to make me sweat.

Wisely, Krillos broke first. "You would know best," he said, with barely masked impudence. "I'll honor your wishes and leave you with your *chosen attendants*. But I'm taking that with me." His dark eyes fell to the shard at my neck.

"Why?" I asked him. "What does Draken want with it?"

"How would I know?" Krillos smirked. "Maybe he wants to give a bauble to his bride on their wedding night…if he finds her soft Rellan flesh pleasing enough."

Jarryd bolted to his feet. "Neela will never marry Draken!" He stepped toward Krillos. I put an arm out to stop him, and he bared his teeth at me.

"Damn it, Jarryd," I snarled back. "Don't make me hurt you."

"That's right, Troy," Krillos snickered, "control your pup. I'd do it myself, but I've filled my quota of Rellan beatings for today." Leaning back in his saddle, he waited for his men's laughter to die down. "So, if you don't mind… the stone?"

"Sure," I said. "I'll give you the same terms I offered the last dead man that asked for it. Take it. If you can."

"Now, that," Krillos said, a twinkle of excitement in his eyes, "is the best offer I've had in a while. But, I'm sorry to say, I don't have time to grind your face in the dirt today. I have another task in the area that needs completing."

I took a guess. "You're going after Kael's troops."

"We are. But rest easy. Draken and Guidon have a temporary accord. Our orders are only to observe the Kaelish and report back their numbers."

"And if they raise arms against you?"

"That would be foolish."

One of his men leaned in. "We were sent for the Prince and the stone, Captain. We can't go back empty handed."

"Actually you can." I pulled my other sword. "If you go back now, Krillos, your hands may be empty, but they'll still be attached."

"Ian," Malaq cautioned. "There are better ways to settle this."

"It is settled," I told him. "Isn't that right, Krillos? You're under orders not to engage us." I gave the Langorian a deliberate smile. "Draken knows it would be a waste of men to try me."

"Cocky bastard," Krillos murmured. He shook his head, laughing to himself. "You surprise me, Shinree. I like that. It's almost a shame you'll be dead soon. And I don't have to do a damn thing to make it happen. Once the Arullans catch up to you for Aylagar's murder, I'll just haggle with them for the stone over your headless corpse."

"Kill them, Ian!" Jarryd bellowed at my side. "Don't let them leave here alive!"

Krillos let out an amused snort. "Did you lose too much blood there, Messenger? Your witch—brave and dashing as he is—can't possibly kill us all."

"Oh, I think I could." I looked down at the stones at my wrist and started spinning them round and around, drawing his attention. "It's just a matter of how."

"That's a bluff," Krillos said brashly. "You don't have the stomach for magic anymore. Haven't cast a spell in years, I'm told."

"You were told wrong." A bit of the mirth faded from his eyes as I laid it out for him. "You were set up, Krillos. Draken doesn't care about you. If I kill you right here and now he'll just pick some other witless fool to run errands for him." I called to the stones. One by one, they began to glow. "Or, you could take him a message. Tell Draken I won't deal with his lackeys. Let him get his own hands dirty for once."

"Meaning?"

"If he wants something he can come ask for it himself."

"You realize," Krillos frowned, "that I might not survive that conversation?"

I shrugged. "I can live with that."

He frowned a moment more. "All right. I'll give Draken your message. And if I'm still alive after, you and I will take this up again. Soon."

"I look forward to it."

Giving Malaq a quick nod, Krillos spun his horse around and took off up the hill. In his wake, the mounted soldiers fell into line and followed. The ones on foot came out of the trees and marched away.

As the dust settled, Malaq turned to me. "I'll make sure they don't double back."

He took off in pursuit. I put my weapon away and looked at Jarryd. One hand gripping my sword, his other gripping the sopping red cloth, the entire side of his face and neck was painted in blood. It dripped down, darkening the white of his shirt and trailing off his arm to speckle the long stalks of grass around his legs.

I walked over and yanked my sword from his grasp. "Give me this."

His voice was rough and disturbing. "Why? Why did you hold me back?"

"Jarryd, if you draw on a Langorian, you better be ready to kill him fast and quick, or you die. You draw on fifty Langorians…you just die."

"Men like Krillos slaughtered my King, Ian. They slaughtered Sarin."

"And they would have ripped you to pieces just as fast."

"If I killed one, it would have been worth it."

"Really?" I got right in his face. "Are you so afraid of Neela marrying Draken that you'd rather die than see it happen?"

His blue eyes tightened. "Fuck you, Ian. Just…fuck you."

Slamming the sword in its sheath, I shoved past him and walked away, struggling not to be tired or frustrated, or any of the things that were making me want to beat the shit out of him until he saw reason.

Not that it would work. I recognized Jarryd's absolutes and reckless passion all too well. I understood his need for justice no matter the cost. I knew what it was like to be ready to go up against the enemy with nothing but anger and vengeance.

I also knew how easily it could get him killed.

I turned back around. "Krillos will bring me Draken. Draken will lead me to his Shinree and the crown, and that's what's important right now. That's my priority."

"Draken is the priority. His army—they need to be stopped. You didn't see what they did in Kabri, what they're doing all across Rella."

"I've *seen*, Jarryd. I know what those fucking animals can do. But what if Malaq can truly destabilize the realm? What if he can start enough of an uprising that Draken will be forced to call his troops home? The occupation would end without any more Rellan or Kaelish soldiers dying. It would just be me and Draken's magic user left to finish this."

"It will never happen that way. A revolt like Malaq's talking about takes time. Time my home doesn't have. And you know as well as I do. If Malaq goes to Langor, chances are he'll be dead inside of a day."

Shoulders slumping some at the thought, I nodded. "I know."

"But you can stop that, Ian. You can save Malaq, Kabri, all of *Mirra'kelan*, if you just kill Draken now. Wish him and all of his kind dead, once and for all. I know you can."

"If I had the crown, yes, I could." Excitement overtook his drawn features, and my expression turned fierce. "Do you have any idea what the cost of something like that is, Jarryd? Do you even care?" I didn't want to know his answer, so I didn't wait for it. "I do. And I'm not paying it again. Besides." Exasperated, I ran my hands back over my dusty hair. "There's more to consider than just Draken."

"What *more*?"

Jarryd stared at me with expectant, curious eyes. As he did, I thought of all the motives and agendas, the implication and rumors, the mysteries and impossibilities that had been bugging me for days. And I laughed. "The fuck if I know. Maybe I'm making connections that aren't there, making myself crazy over nothing. All these fragments, these pieces I have—the crown, Draken, his Shinree, Imma…the shard. Maybe none of them fit together."

Bewilderment shone through the blood on his face. "Pretending I know what you're talking about, have you thought that maybe the only thing these pieces have in common is *you*?"

I wasn't laughing anymore. Jarryd had such a way of seeing to the heart of things that it made his innocent, offhanded statement feel like something else. Something I didn't like.

"Just so we're clear," Jarryd said then. "If you don't kill Draken, I'll find a way to do it myself."

"Go ahead. But you're no good to her dead."

Jarryd flinched like I'd punched him in the stomach.

"I have something for that." I went over to Kya. Unbuckling one of the packs on my saddle, I pulled out the blue bottle the physician had given in Kael. "There's not much left," I said, walking back and shoving the bottle in his hand. "But it's the one thing that old coot did right."

Jarryd uncorked the stopper. Without wavering, he drank.

"You two won't ever work," I said, watching him. "No matter what happens with Draken, Neela won't give up her crown for you. She might smile and pat your head. Bestow favors and gifts to keep you interested. Royal concubines receive many special privileges." His scowl was brutal, but I finished anyway. "If that's enough for you, go ahead. Stand quietly by in the shadows. If it isn't, then turn your back now."

Cautious of his wound, Jarryd wiped the spill from his mouth. "It's not like that. Not anymore. Hell, I'm not sure it ever was."

"Then if the past is where Neela belongs, then do yourself a favor and leave her there. Otherwise, her ghost will follow you to the grave."

"The way Aylagar follows you?" It was a sincere, innocent question. Justified, after the speech I'd just given him. But twice in a matter of minutes Jarryd's candor had flustered me and I stood, gaping at him, until Malaq came back. His mount slid to a dusty stop between us, and Jarryd walked off.

Cloth against his bleeding head, bottle gripped in his teeth, Jarryd climbed awkwardly up into the saddle and started down the trail.

Malaq stared after him. "How is he?"

"Not good," I said. "Where are they headed?"

"Back to that valley. Where the main road curves in close to the mountains."

Picturing the place, I frowned. "Aldous will be days from there yet."

"If Krillos has orders, he'll wait. Which will keep him off our trail for a while. Give us time to get our impetuous, young friend patched up. Maybe get some sleep. Real sleep," he said, with meaning. "I'll even take first watch."

"No. I'll do it."

"And forget to wake me again like last night—and the night before?" He allowed a faint showing of worry into his voice. "Do you think I haven't noticed? You can't keep going on magic alone, Ian. You need sleep."

"What I *need* is to look after Jarryd." I swung up onto Kya's back. "Unless you want to handle the stitches? It's not quite like skinning a fish, but…"

Malaq sighed. "Just don't nursemaid the kid. He wouldn't like that. Besides, the wound isn't fatal. He's not going to die tonight just because you got some shut eye."

"He's not dying at all," I vowed. Tossing him a glare, I kicked Kya into a run.

"It was a joke!" Malaq called after me. "Gods, am I the only one out here with a sense of humor?"

NINETEEN

er dark skin glistened wet in the moonlight. The individual beads of water on her body were so distinct and clear, I knew I was dreaming.

But I didn't care.

How could I? The girl standing before me was wearing nothing but a man's mail shirt. The neckline draped down off her shoulders. The hem barely skimmed her hips. The large woven links revealed glimpses of a small frame molded to perfection.

Yet, it wasn't purely her meager attire that appealed to me. A sense of spirit dominated her face; a flawless, dark brown circle, framed by an unbound mane of black curls that hung down to brush her thighs. There was an abundance of playfulness in her brazen smile and mischief in her wide, round, dusky-colored eyes. They gazed at me, suggestive and confident. And I instantly thought: Aylagar.

I couldn't deny the girl's resemblance. The color of her skin and hair, the slant of her nose and shape of her face were more than a good match for Aylagar. There were nuances though, aspects of the fantasy that my mind had gotten wrong. Foremost, the girl in my dream was only half Arullan. She was young too, with a slender frame, and I never knew Aylagar that way. Having more than a handful of years on me, she had born two children by the time we met, earning her the healthy curves of a woman's body.

Despite that, Rella's Queen had been every bit the warrior; strong, vibrant and determined, calculating and assertive, fierce and passionate. I'd once likened Aylagar to a storm trapped in a bottle. There had been nothing naïve, carefree, or innocent about her.

The beauty moving away from me toward the edge of the pond didn't exactly strike me as innocent. But a sense of freshness, a youthful, untroubled exuberance, showed in her every step.

Pausing to dip her bare toes in the water, she reached a slender arm back in my direction. Her fingers stretched out—and I was suddenly standing beside her; watching her lift her shirt off over her head.

Slowly, it slipped through her fingers.

She let go of the mail. It hit the ground with a clink. I reached for her, and she ran, laughing and diving under the surface of the water.

A moment later, she came back up in the middle of the pond like a rising fountain. Unruly curls kinked about her face and shoulders. Longer strands fanned out behind her. She laid back and small waves bobbed over the curves of her breasts; caressing them.

Undressing quickly, I threw everything I owned in a heap on the muddy bank. I put my swords on top and waded in after her. The water was impossibly warm. I sunk down into the liquid darkness and she drifted into my arms. Her small body fit so seamlessly against mine. I had the distinct and sudden impression that it belonged.

There was a mutual sense of security and trust in our embrace. She felt safest with me above all others, and I was stronger with her. I was comfortable. Relaxed and content in a way I wasn't accustomed to. I was completely at ease with myself. I had no anxieties, doubts, or misgivings. No regrets. It was similar to the bliss that came with channeling magic, but better somehow—if it wasn't make-believe.

I should wake, I thought. Something told me it was wise to flee her presence now. Before the false feelings she aroused in me became too hard to forget.

"I have to go." I started to push her away.

She lifted her head off my shoulder. "Stay." Her eyes pleaded, as dark and wet as the water around us. And as I looked into them, I knew her. I had no idea what the girl was called or where she came from. But I knew our life together. I knew her body and her heart. I knew she was mine.

"You..." I lost the words. "This can't be right. You're a dream."

She laughed. "How sweet."

"No, I..." My thoughts felt strewn about. "This isn't real. I shouldn't be here. I was..." I looked about, "somewhere else."

"Hush." She brushed her fingers over my temple, smoothing out the frown.

"I wasn't here," I insisted. "I don't even know where here is."

"Yes, you do. Here is where I am. There is nowhere else. No one else. There is only me, Ian." Her voice had gone hard. I was disappointed the Arullan accent I'd expected wasn't there. I'd always loved Aylagar's sound. But I lost track of why its absence bothered me as she said, *"You must protect me no matter the cost. No matter what you have to surrender. Nothing and no one else matters. Only me. Do you understand?"*

"Yes, but—"

"Say it."

"I understand."

She kissed me then, a soft, gentle touch of her lips that left me wanting.

"More," I begged.

The Arullan girl wrapped her hand around mine and towed me back through the water. At the bank, she let go. She walked out onto dry land, and the water fell off her like rain.

I came up from behind. She leaned against me. My body responded instantly to the soft, wet warmth of her. But as stiff as she made me, there was an overwhelming, peaceful comfort at being near her.

She felt like home.

Home...?

I frowned at the notion. It was odd, unfamiliar, and as I tried to figure out why, I was filled with a tense restlessness. The emotion was so palpable, she sensed it.

"The unease will fade, Ian. Just focus on me." She turned to face me. Her arms encircled my neck. Her fingers dove into my wet hair. *"Remember what's important."*

"You," I said.

She took my hand. We sat on the wet moss of the bank and she climbed onto my lap. Wrapping her legs around my waist, her mouth collapsed on mine with an aggressive, demanding kiss that was more about laying claim than anything else.

She shoved my back to the ground. Her eyes flickered with a strange, unnatural gleam. I'd seen it somewhere before.

"Intae'a...love...wait." I tried to sit up.

"No." She pushed me back. Sliding her body down the front of mine, her tongue lapped at my chest. Her hands wandered over the muscles of my stomach. *"You go nowhere."* They moved lower. *"Not ever."* Her lips joined them. *"You're mine."* Lifting her head, she stared at me through a tangle of muddy curls and said, *"Forever,"* with such outright passion and need that I came up off the ground, grabbed her arms and rolled her onto her back.

Letting out a low, impatient growl, I lowered my body down on top of hers. Her legs fell open. I slid inside her, and she smiled. Watching me, her fingers sifted through the hair over my eyes. She ruffled the pale strands that hung against the sides of my face.

As she let them fall, it came to me that there should be color there.

"Wait," I said again. "This doesn't feel right."

Grinning, she pushed her hips against mine. "Really?"

"That's not what I mean."

She thrust again, harder. "Is this right?"

"Stop," I scolded her. "There's something—"

She thrust a third time, and I stopped caring. "To hell with it."

I plunged in deep. She laughed again, breathless and manic, as we fell quickly into a seamless rhythm of sliding skin and swelling desire. Seizing each kiss like it might be the last, her entire body consumed me. Mouth, arms, legs; wrapping and kneading, stroking and gripping with a clear sense of dominance.

She wanted to own me. And I let her, because I was no better. I beat against the soft walls inside her. I pushed her strong, dark legs up higher, shoving in harder, as if I had some great yearning to feel the end of her, to have her taste in my mouth, her smell on my skin. I wanted to burn the sensations into me so I wouldn't forget.

So I could keep them with me for when she was gone.

Looking down, I watched her writhe beneath me. I felt the muscles in her thighs tremble. I listened to the sounds of her release and realized how perfect she was.

The Arullan girl was my sanctuary. The moment should have been flawless.

But a word had popped into my mind, and I couldn't shake it. It was playing over and over, above the pounding of blood in my ears, worming its way in, trying to break my concentration: wake.

I didn't know where it came from, or what it meant. Lost in the folds of her, I had trouble caring. The word only became truly important when her body stiffened, and a gasp that was more fear than pleasure escaped her.

Pulling out, I sat back on my heels. I croaked out a wheezing, dry-mouthed, "What?" She didn't answer, and our ragged breathing sounded huge against the silence.

Then her eyes slid past mine. They widened.

She shook her head in fright, and a chill raced up my spine.

The air prickled along my skin.

Ever so slightly, the space around us tightened.

I grabbed the girl's arms and pulled her up. "Run." Gathering her clothes, I glanced at the thin dress and shawl in my hands. They were dry and free of mud, and as I shoved them against her bare chest, I couldn't remember her wearing them.

The inconsistency was disturbing, but I shook it off. "You have to go." I pushed the curls back from her face and kissed her. "I won't let them hurt you. I promise."

Eyes damp with fear, she nodded and backed away. As the waist-high grass swallowed her, I crawled the short distance to the bank where I'd left my cloths, boots, and weapons. Yet when I reached the spot, it was all gone. There was only a pair of worn gray trousers that weren't mine.

Having nothing else, I slithered into them. I checked the bushes, but my belongings weren't there, either. I had a nagging feeling that something was terribly wrong. The girl, the pond, my presence here; it all felt off.

I raised a hand to my throat. It was bare.

"No." I looked at the ground. Panic raced through me. I couldn't remember losing the obsidian, or taking it off. In fact, I couldn't remember anything. Where I'd been, what I'd done before. I was unarmed, in the woods, in the middle of the night, and I had not the slightest inkling why.

I jumped as a voice broke through the dark. "Just how does a man with so much power fall so far?"

Spinning around, I found him standing in the shadows at the water's edge. Dressed in gray and crimson, dark hair bound at the back of his neck, King Draken of Langor stared down his hawk-like nose, eyeing me like a rabbit in a snare.

He tilted his head higher. "So what is it they call the Champion of Rella these days? Slayer of Bandits? Defender of Worthless Peasants and Cheap Whores?" Draken let out an exaggerated sigh. "I admit, Troy, I expected more of you."

Jaw set, I nodded at him. "And I expected you to be babbling incoherently, sitting in a corner and pissing yourself for the rest of your life."

"Then I suppose we are both disappointed."

"The madness I gave you with the Crown of Stones was permanent, Draken. How the hell did you break the spell?"

"Who says it was broken?"

As I pondered that, Draken narrowed his deep-set eyes and gave me a cold, menacing stare. There was a hint of sedate distance to it, making his intimidation seem almost accidental. It was a gift, and I'd forgotten how aggravating it was. How his slightest smiles were strategic and meaningful. How even in battle he could be striking and stoic; nothing out of place; nothing showing he didn't want.

Like Malaq.

I drew a startled breath. Anxiety settled into my stomach like a heavy weight. "This is wrong. This isn't where I was."

"Perhaps not. But it's where I want you." Draken wandered closer. "Now… Where to start?" His black-gloved fingers traced the thin stripe of beard that ran the length of his jaw. "Oh, yes. That nice little bit of dark meat you were enjoying. I don't suppose you'd call her back so we can share?"

I lunged for him, and hands came out of the bushes. Gripping my arms, wrapping around my chest, as they pulled me back, I resisted; shoving an elbow into solid plate mail, a fist into a closed helm. I kept trying, but they were too well protected. I couldn't land a decent hit. My bare feet kept sliding in the mud. I had nothing to deflect their spiked clubs as they swung into me—striking legs, back, and shoulders—driving me closer to the ground.

A solid punch to the jaw whirled me around. Something heavy hammered the back of my head a few times, and I was down. "Chain him," Draken ordered.

Shackles locked about my wrists and ankles. A burly Langorian with metal gloves yanked me to my knees. He grabbed a handful of hair and wrenched my head up higher. "Pay respects to your new King, witch."

I pushed out a heartfelt, "Fuck you," and his fist sunk into my side.

Draken squatted in front of me. "Comfortable?"

Winded, blood spattered off my lips as I breathed, "I'm good."

Draken blinked. He cleaned his face with the back of his gloved hand as he stood. "As you are no doubt aware," he said, still wiping at his chin, "there are many levels of pain. You, Troy, are about to learn them all. Quite intimately, I might add."

"Did I say fuck you, yet? My head's a bit fuzzy."

"Oh, how I would love to kill you," he confessed with an eager, angry laugh. "But, I suppose we must have compromise in a situation like this."

His words were odd. "Whose situation? Mine? Or yours?"

Draken flicked a speck of mud from the cuff of his sleeve and straightened his tunic. "One neither of us would be in if you had simply killed me with the rest of them. But my death wasn't satisfying enough for you, was it, Troy? It was far more pleasurable to twist my mind and destroy my soul." The leather of his gloves creaked as his hands clenched. "You left me aware. Did you know that? I knew what you made me into. What I lost. I couldn't come back from it, of course. I watched the world go by from inside my little prison," he tapped the side of his head. "And every day the madness grew worse."

"You destroyed your own soul, Draken. You made your own prison, with your terrible deeds, your acts of savagery and cruelty. All I did was wish it back on you. I gave you the torment and the agony of your victims...all of them, all at once."

"Yes, and it was quite clever. And effective. I would even go so far as to say," insinuation fell into his voice, "inspiring."

"Glad you enjoyed it." I forced my sore, bloody mouth into a wide grin. "But that was then. Now, I just want your head on a spit."

Draken waved a hand. In response, his men pounded me some more. A knee rammed into my chest. Another sunk in between my legs.

The beating went on, and I lost a moment.

Screams faded in and out like thunder in the distance.

Letting go of the pain, I centered on them.

They became closer. Clearer.

Familiar.

I lifted my head. The tall grass parted. Draken's soldiers stepped out onto the bank dragging my Arullan girl out of the weeds by her hair. "No..." I struggled to get up as they tossed her around between them. One drew her body up next to his.

He pressed a knife against her throat.

The tip of the blade pricked her neck.

"You son of a bitch—let her go!" I pulled at the arms that held me.

"Don't!" she shrieked. "Ian, please. Please don't."

I swallowed. "Intae'a... I can't just let them—"

"You have to," she broke in. "He said...he said..." Sobbing, her voice quivered. "If you fight them, they'll hurt me."

The knifepoint went in a little deeper. The man laughed as she screamed.

"Let her go!" Twisting and jerking, struggling to push the soldiers off, I flung myself onto my back and kicked out with both feet. I hit one man in the groin, another in the stomach. I knocked two more down with a sweep of my legs, evaded the last one, and got up onto my knees.

As I reached my feet, she cried out in a deafening plea, "STOP!"

Pulse hammering, harsh breath ripping through my lungs, I looked at her. I looked right into her panicked, petrified stare, and did as she asked: nothing. I let my captors take hold of me again. I watched hers slide a rough hand over the front of her dress. Pulling the fabric aside, he groped, digging dirty fingers into her breasts. He laughed as she squirmed, while I just stood there. Not looking away. Not helping her.

I couldn't. I was rooted to the ground. I was held in place. Not by the strength of my restraints or the fear of what they might do to her. I was transfixed by her dark eyes, as the terror in them began dissolving into something else.

Then everything dissolved.

There were only her eyes, reflecting back at me memories I didn't live. I saw nights I never spent in her arms. Days with her that never happened. An avalanche of emotions that weren't mine poured over me. They felt so pure, so real.

I wanted them to be mine.

And then they were.

Our life together was perfect and tranquil. My weaknesses, my failings, meant nothing to her. Without question, she loved me.

At least she had. Now that I'd failed her, all that was gone.

"How could you let this happen?" she wept bitterly. "You promised, Ian. You said you'd protect me." Frostiness tainted her voice. Her tear-stained face turned ugly. "They're going to kill me, and it's all your fault."

She was right. But I couldn't bear those being her last words to me, so I turned to Draken, and groveled. "Don't do this. If there is a drop of mercy and goodness anywhere in you, you son of a bitch...please. Draken...I'm begging you. Don't do this."

He smiled. And I knew that I'd lost her.

"NO!" Thrashing again, flailing and fighting, I yanked at the chains. "You want someone to hurt? Go ahead! Hurt me, goddamn you—HURT ME!"

Draken released a slow, gratified sound of contentment. "Oh, but I will hurt you, Troy. I've been waiting so very long to hurt you as you did me...with madness and despair, grief and anguish. By the time I'm finished, you won't remember what it's like to feel anything else." He nodded to his men. Grabbing the chains, three on each limb pinned me down. They held my head still, forcing me to look on as Draken tore open the front of her dress. He pulled a knife from his belt. Excitement gleamed in his eyes. "Ten years." Tenderly, he ran the tip of the etched blade between her breasts. The stones forged into the handle glowed bright against her bare skin. "Tell me, Troy, does this hurt?" Draken jammed the knife into her chest. "What about this?" Swiftly, he yanked it out. Her body convulsed. And like he wanted, I felt it.

I felt each and every stab of the knife as it went deeper and deeper inside her.

Ripping and tearing, oblivious to her strangled cries, Draken gutted my beautiful Arullan girl. He butchered her until blood sprayed like rain on the wind.

When he was done, he tossed her shredded body to the ground and walked away.

Lying beside me in the mud, her distant eyes were wide and full of reproach.

Her dark skin glistened wet in the moonlight.

TWENTY

I sat up, sucking in air and crying out, "Gods—" and stopped. My sudden mobility was startling, my surroundings confusing. It was still dark, but there was a warm fire, no pond, and thank the gods no girl, and no Draken.

No knife. No blood.

I collapsed back on the grass with a shuddering moan. Soaked in a cold sweat, panting through the burning ache in my chest, I tried to calm down. I stared up at the gathering clouds and struggled to think of nothing. But the shifting, bloating shapes above were abnormally dark and ominous. They converged on the full moon, growing and flowing. Eating up the light like puddles of blood spilling over the ground.

"Not real," I muttered. "Not real. Not real."

Not real.

I tightened my fists to stop the trembling running through my arms. They were weak, like the rest of me. My whole body felt used up and sore, as if my encounter with Draken and his troops had actually happened.

Dismissing the ridiculous thought, I ran my hands over my face, gathered my strength and sat up. I blew out a few deep breaths, trying to relax. But I couldn't stop shaking. Foreboding hung over me. I couldn't lose the feeling that enemies were everywhere. Lurking. Watching. I was afraid.

It wasn't a feeling I was used to.

Nightmares, I was well acquainted with. It had been a while, but I'd suffered through my share, usually fashioned from a mix of bad wine and bad memories. Many had featured Draken and Aylagar over the years. But this one was particularly disturbing. And it wasn't Aylagar. I'd dreamt of someone else. Someone I had never seen before. *Someone who didn't even exist. Someone beautiful,* I thought, unable to resist envisioning her face in my mind. It was odd how perfectly I could picture her; naked beneath me on the wet grass, her round eyes full of desire. She was smiling. Her mouth opened in laughter.

Blood dripped off her lips.

Alarmed, I squeezed my eyes shut and pushed the image out. Needing to fix my thoughts more firmly in reality, I looked over at Jarryd. Deep under from the *coura* and herbs, he was fast asleep near the fire. I'd closed his wounds hours ago, and a hefty amount of bandages now covered one side of his head. His skin was pale, but he was breathing normally. If I could keep the infection out, he'd be all right. He was in for some bad scarring, though, and I owned no magic to prevent it. Neither could I do anything to improve the look of his mangled ear. Jarryd needed a skilled Shinree healer, which would be hard to come by in the middle of the mountains.

Not that Rella will be any easier, I thought. The realm was occupied territory, and standard Langorian tactics were to seize all Shinree healers for their own use. If we couldn't find one, Jarryd was going to have to live with what was done to him for a while, and that worried me. He didn't need more fuel for his vengeance against the enemy, or another excuse to risk his neck. The young fool was already locked on that course as it was, and it annoyed the hell out of me; because he had choices. Choices I didn't. *Choices I never had.*

I'd pretended I did, for a while. After the crippling blow I dealt to Langor, I'd convinced myself they were no longer the threat they once were. Rella would have no need to call me back. I wouldn't have to use magic in her name ever again.

The more time passed, the more I believed it was true. *Ten years,* I thought. After seeing Draken in the dream, it felt like yesterday.

I could still hear his voice. *Does this hurt?*

An abrupt snort came from one of the horses, and my heart lurched.

No other sounds followed. I knew it was probably nothing. But our mounts were tied at the edge of the glen, just beyond the reach of the fire. I couldn't see them well from where I was, and the dream had left me jittery and exceptionally paranoid. Too paranoid to sit on my backside and wait for another ambush.

I got up. It was a slower process than usual. I had to stretch out the creaks before I could stand straight. Moving was unpleasant, as well. I felt stiff and bruised all over as I rounded the fire. Having dwindled substantially, the flames provided little light, and in the gloom, I stumbled over something on the ground. It was Malaq's empty blanket.

I glanced around. His things were still under the tree where he'd unpacked. His mount was with the others. But he wasn't in sight. "Malaq?"

Jarryd stirred. The horses swished their tails and eyed me suspiciously.

"Malaq," I said again, louder. "Damn it," I muttered, when he didn't answer. I was as angry at him as I was at myself. I'd let a dream preoccupy me so much that I hadn't even noticed his absence.

I called for him a few more times as I walked the perimeter. I searched for broken leaves, bent limbs, or tracks that didn't belong. I scanned the tree-tops for uninvited visitors and checked the dirt for signs of a struggle. There was no indication of anything out of the ordinary. Only a few imprints of Malaq's long, casual strides leading out of the camp.

Running through the short list of places he could have gone took about two seconds. If he'd ventured into the trees to relieve himself, he'd be back soon. Then I could let into him for abandoning his post after badgering me about keeping watch. Though, with the woods so quiet, he should have been able to hear me calling him.

I stared in the direction of the stream. Malaq had made the trek several times for me since making camp, certainly enough to know his way there and back.

But he wasn't back.

Goddamn it, Malaq.

I looked at Jarryd. The last thing I wanted to do was leave him asleep and defenseless. Yet, if Malaq had gone to the stream in the middle of the night there was no clear reason for it. And from what I knew of Malaq Roarke, the man didn't do much of anything without a reason.

Going back to my own blanket, as I picked it up, I summoned the hematite at my wrist. I drew its energy into me, felt it sink hard and thick in my veins. Imagining the spell's outcome in my mind, I whispered the words and let go. The gray auras flowed out of me, seeping from my veins, my skin, out of my hands, and over the fabric in my grip.

Magic merged with the woven strands. They shimmered. The color dulled.

A little woozy, I walked over to Jarryd. I spread the blanket out on top of him and stepped away. The material shifted slightly. Then it blended with the shadowy ground and took Jarryd with it.

The spell was a cheat. One that had come in handy often during the war, when Aylagar sent me on long scouting missions over the border. It was the only way I ever got any sleep in Langorian territory. Unfortunately, the concealment wouldn't last more than a couple of hours, and if anyone stepped in the space Jarryd occupied, the spell would collapse. But it was better than nothing.

Eying the empty ground in front of me, I knew Jarryd couldn't hear me. I said it anyway. "I'll be back soon." Then I grabbed a sword and headed into the woods.

———

Between the clouds and the overgrowth, little light filtered down onto the narrow path. Branches and thorns grabbed at my clothes. Limbs smacked my face and raked my exposed skin. It had only been a few minutes, yet I was wearing half the forest.

It was my own fault. The route to the stream wasn't a lengthy walk, or a hard one. I knew the way. Yet, I kept losing track of it. My thoughts wandered. I couldn't get my head straight. Still unnerved by the dream, I was flinching at every sound. The shifting silhouette of the trees in the wind resembled hunched figures lying in wait. My legs felt unusually weary. My pulse was racing.

When I found Malaq, I was going to wring his royal neck.

At last nearing the stream, I picked up on a faint, muffled masculine voice. As I drew closer, the voice became more distinct. Closer; and I recognized Malaq's familiar lilt. My nerves as they were, though, I didn't call out right away. Instead, putting my hard earned camouflage to work, I lowered myself down to the forest floor and crept forward.

Edging my way up to the thick layer of tall grass that bordered the water, I stopped just inside the cover of the weeds. I parted them for a peek, and spotted Malaq. Pacing back and forth around the bank, he didn't appear to be in danger. Though, he was uncharacteristically accepting of the mud kicking up on his trousers, and his dialog was unusual. Spewing out harsh, straightforward quips about Langor's unprovoked attack on Kael, Malaq was using the same tone and style of words he'd used with Krillos; abnormally cold and to the point.

Crawling on my belly, I got closer and scanned the area. I was looking for movement that wasn't Malaq. A spot of color or shadow to indicate he had company. But there was no visible evidence that anyone else was nearby.

Then Draken of Langor spoke. "I have listened to your words, brother, as was our agreement. Now, it is my turn," he said with authority, and the King launched into a speech that attempted to justify his run of recent murders.

Yet, there was still only Malaq, standing alone with gray eyes fixed on the surface of the stream. I watched him closely. His rapt attention of the water didn't waver. As Draken kept talking, Malaq kept staring, and I understood what was going on.

Draken's voice had no physical source. Not here anyway. It was coming from, or more accurately, traveling through, a communication font. A spelled source of water, designed to carry voice and image both over large distances (and out through another chosen body of water), the font was a common tool for aristocrats and Kings. Sarin had one sitting in his chamber, though he'd sworn to me he hadn't used it in years. The life energy needed to operate the device wasn't something he could abide.

Draken, however, always true to form, didn't give a damn about the cost. But his use of the font meant he was nowhere near the stream. It meant I couldn't touch him. I couldn't kill him. And the way he was dismissing Sarin's death as the mercy killing of a useless, old man—relegating the slaughter in Kabri to that of a tedious burden; killing Draken of Langor was suddenly all I could think of.

The notion was pervasive. I couldn't understand how staggeringly fast it had taken me over. Draken's cruel, careless words had ignited a fast-burning, dangerous rage inside me. I tried to let it go, to dismiss or even dim the thought. But it was unshakable.

Breathing hard, my muscles twitched with the need to act. Sweat beaded on my skin despite the cool night air. The impulse to come out of hiding, to storm down to the stream and ram a sword straight through his smug intangible face was so great. I could barely keep it together. Only one thing kept me prone in the mud: my abrupt, violent urge for retribution didn't feel right.

I didn't feel right.

Almost overnight, my desire for justice and revenge against Draken had magnified. My itch to hurt him, to make him suffer, had soared to the height of a full-blown compulsion. I was actually shaking with the need to see him dead. Only, the fury that was driving me had absolutely nothing to do with our past or the current situation in Rella. It came from the smell of the grass and the sight of the rippling water. It was born of Draken's voice coming out of the dark and the mud clinging to my skin.

The entire scene was my nightmare come to life.

All that was missing was the Arullan girl and the knife.

Breathless, my heart pounding like a thousand hooves against the ground, I tried to stop listening for Langorian soldiers skulking in the grass. I tried to stop staring at the stream in hope that she was there, waiting for me.

But the wind in the trees was her distant scream. The fine mist as it started falling was the splatter of blood. The grass tangled around my boots: chain.

Draken yelled, startling me, and the fantasy disappeared like it never was.

"Can you not see that Troy seeks to destroy me?" he bellowed, and the grass around the stream rustled as frightened creatures scampered through the weeds.

"You threaten what he is bound to protect," Malaq said briskly. "Troy has no alternative but to interfere."

"You take his side?" Draken raged. "Against your own kind? Against me?"

"Your men attacked us," Malaq countered.

"You travel with my enemy!"

"I suppose," Malaq said, backing down some, "that I have come to consider your enemy, my friend. I realize that discomfits you, but…you and I are blood, Draken. I haven't forgotten that."

"Then prove it. Prove your allegiance and kill the witch while he sleeps."

I rested a hand on my sword. Malaq seemed to take forever to answer.

"No," he said ardently. "No murder, Draken, not for you, not for anyone."

"Oh, my dear, brother," Draken chuckled. "Are those your mother's delicate Rellan values you inherited? Or perhaps your stepfather's Kaelish foolishness you borrowed?"

"I am made of many things, *brother*," Malaq responded.

"We shall see exactly what you are made of soon enough," Draken said with promise. "In the meantime, I suggest you lose your fanciful notions on the journey, or you will find Langor a difficult place indeed." The water churned and gurgled. When it stilled, and the spell came to an end, Malaq's shoulders sagged like the strength had gone out of him. He dropped his head in his hands.

I pushed up from the muddy ground. No longer caring for stealth, I trampled through the stalks of tall grass toward the water's edge, prompting a startled Malaq to pull his blade.

Seeing me, he lowered it. "Ian," he breathed.

"That was an interesting meeting," I said.

His posture stiffened considerably. "What did you hear?"

I stopped beside him. "Enough."

"I didn't call to him. Draken instructed me to come here. His voice came through the damn water in my flask." He shook his head. "It was unnerving as hell."

"He's pushing you, Malaq. Killing me is a test."

"I know."

"He'll ask again."

"Then I'll tell him no, again. No matter how things go I won't come against you."

"Don't make vows you can't keep."

"Damn you, Ian." Malaq slammed his sword away. "Have I done anything that would make you question my word?"

"You haven't seen the level of manipulation Draken's magic user is capable of. I have. He can make you do things you never intended."

"Then protect me from him. Protect me from Draken. From all of it. Or can't you defend as well as destroy?"

I struggled to cage my temper. "I won't be there to protect you, Malaq. You're walking right into Draken's hands. The odds of you surviving are incredibly slim."

"Even them," he challenged me.

"How about I just kill Draken instead?"

"That won't solve anything."

"It'll solve one thing."

"Yes, he'll be dead. But you'll only be temporarily ending the conflict. Whereas, I can stop this war and prevent any more from coming after. I can save Langor. Save Rella from a future riddled with the constant threat of attack."

"That's optimistic. And arrogant."

"Is it?" Malaq stepped closer. "A true and lasting peace between all the realms...can you imagine it? I know you want to. I know that, despite the Arcana's claim on you, and your tough talk about how much you hate it...you hate the thought of war even more. But you, and Jarryd, you're right about one thing. Going to Langor is dangerous. So I need something from you, Ian. I need a way to protect myself."

"There's nothing I can do, Malaq."

"Right," he nodded. "I suppose this is the part where you tell me I'm as good as dead? Or that my faith in you is sorely misplaced?"

My jaw clenched. He was right on both counts. "If I help you, and you die there..."

"It won't be your fault." Earnest persuasion shone in his eyes. "I know what I'm getting into. All I'm asking for is a bit of an edge."

"What you'll need is eyes in the back of your head."

"Can you do that?" A spirited grin broke through his grim stare. "Seriously, that would really help. It would look a bit odd though."

"Gods," I grumbled. "Why the hell does Jarryd bother arguing with you?"

Malaq's grin became an outright smile. "Then you'll do it?"

I ran a hand over my face, thinking. "I can write a shield spell. Wrap it around something you own, something you carry with you. Except, if you're in the keep, surrounded by hornblende..." I trailed off, going over outcomes and options. "I can't plan for every contingency, Malaq. No matter what, you'll still be in danger."

"Just do your best."

"My best won't be good enough. It won't be even close." I started for the trail, needing to leave before temper pushed me to say more.

"Only one man will die at Darkhorne, Ian, and it won't be me."

I stopped and turned around. "So you're an assassin now, are you?"

"I'm whatever I need to be to get the job done."

"Well, if you do—get the job done. If you kill Draken, you damn well better have a plan to get out. Because his men will track you down. And when they're done cutting you into tiny pieces, they'll go into Rella and into Kael and exact revenge for your actions." I gave him a hard look. "Did you learn nothing from what your mother did to Taiven?"

Dropping his gaze, Malaq ran both hands back over his hair. It wasn't his usual careful checking to be sure nothing was out of place. It was an anxious, helpless gesture that I was surprised to see him admit to. "Before I kill my brother, I'm going to convince him to name me his heir."

I was back standing in front of him in two strides. "Heir to the throne of Langor? Gods, Malaq, do you even want that?"

"I'm a prince, Ian. Of course I want to be King."

I wasn't sure I believe him. "And what happens when you give up your life to sit on that throne and Langor doesn't change?"

"It will change. The mishandling of the realm goes back long before Draken and his father. When Jillyan became Queen all she could do was hold the pieces together. But I'm not like them. I can make a difference."

"You don't belong there."

"Then where do I belong? Not in Rella. Certainly, not in Kael." His gray eyes tightened. "Maybe Langor is where I should have been all along."

"Don't do this, Malaq. You aren't one of them."

He looked at me a moment then pushed past me for the trail. "I am now."

TWENTY ONE

*S*he stood in the open doorway, staring out at the rain. "Walk with me?"

"Maybe later." Pulling her back against me, I slid my hands down over her hips and kissed the side of her neck. "I have a better idea."

"Maybe later," she giggled. Wriggling out of my grip, she ran down the porch and out onto the wet grass. Spinning in circles in the rain, damp spots spread across the front of her dress and turned the pale green dark. "What's the matter, love?" she laughed. "Doesn't the big hero like to get wet?"

I grinned, but the expression wavered. I had an odd, nagging feeling that I'd forgotten something important, that something was out of place.

I couldn't imagine what. I had everything.

Snow covered mountains rose high in the distance. A forest of tall, thick pines ringed the valley. Our house was secluded. It was small but sturdy. Smoke rose from the chimney, and I could smell dinner on the fire.

It was perfect. The girl was perfect, like a dream.

She walked farther away. The rain fell harder. Mud flew off her bare feet. The hem of her dress was soaked and dirty.

Slipping on my boots, I grabbed a cloak off the wall. By the time it took me to duck into the house and come back out, my beautiful Arullan girl was no longer alone.

Whimpering softly, blood oozing from a cut lip, she was encircled by more than a dozen heavily armed Langorian soldiers.

Dropping the cloak, I ran down off the porch and into the yard. I went for a weapon, but there was no sword at my hip. I glanced at my empty wrist, thinking something should be strapped there to help me defeat them.

Thunder rumbled across the valley. Lightning ignited the gray-green sky, and Draken was suddenly standing beside me. "Feeling puzzled, Shinree?" he asked. "Helpless, perhaps?"

I wiped the rain from my eyes and looked at him. "Where did you come from?"

"Gods, but you've grown weak." He threw a gloved hand across my face. "Soft and pitiful too," he said, watching me stumble in the thickening mud.

Finding purchase, I came up swinging. My fist connected hard with Draken's jaw, snapping his head to the side. I drew back to strike him again, and he'd somehow moved out of range. There were only his soldiers now, piling on top of me, knocking me to the ground. Six sword points pressed against my throat.

She spoke then, a soft tremble of my name. "Ian..."

I shook the curtain of soggy hair from my eyes. My Arullan girl was kneeling beside me. There was so much blood. I couldn't find her face. Then rain rinsed the blood away, and I stopped breathing.

From forehead to chin, her face was in ribbons.

Draken grabbed a fistful of her long hair and wrenched her away. As he dragged her toward the house, he shouted at his men, "Bring him!" Sparing a glance over his shoulder, Draken flashed me an ominous smile. "It isn't time to wake up yet."

TWENTY TWO

Cupping my hands under the surface of the water, I drew them up and splashed my face. Icy cold, the shock was bracing, but I wanted the tiny brook to be wider. I wanted it deeper. I wanted to sink down and let the water close over my head for a few, still moments of calm. I longed to feel nothing for a while, to be clean. It seemed like it had been so long since I'd felt clean; longer still since I'd slept without dreaming.

It scared me how much I'd gotten used to that. How quickly I'd accepted the fact that every time I closed my eyes, Draken and his men would be there. *She* would be there. The Langorians would beat and torture me. I would watch the Arullan girl suffer and die. I would wake sweat-covered, dry-mouthed, and shaking, as I had for almost a week.

That was my life now.

The pattern had played out only twice before I realized I was stricken with a dream-weave; a type of healing spell typically used to repair a person's mind after trauma. It wasn't meant to be violent. It wasn't normally sophisticated or involved. The dreams didn't usually occur in rapid, unrelenting succession. One or two were all that were required to fix a patient's mind. My mind, however, was being steadily destroyed.

It was twisted, but clever. My Shinree enemy knew I didn't have the kind of magic to counteract such a spell. He also knew I had no access to anyone that could.

I had to endure it, which was getting harder with every passing moment.

Day or night now, as soon as I drifted off, the dream kicked in. Every sound, every touch, I experienced in that world (both pleasure and pain) was exaggerated and acute. Many of them lingered, like phantom sensations. So that, even hours after waking, I could still feel the heat of her body pressed up against mine.

Flinging the water off my hands, I stood. The sun was high. We should have been off hours ago. But riding hard and wet for days, pushing the horses on washed out trails, cramming ourselves into what leaky cover we could find when it got too dark to see. We were all sorely in need of a little sunshine and solid ground.

Except, as we slept in and dried out, the people of Rella were dying.

Scrambling up the steep bank, I reached the top where our horses were tied, lazily eating their fill for the first time in days. Still, it wouldn't take long to get them going. They were used to the routine, as was Jarryd. Up since dawn, he'd cooked breakfast, broken down the camp, and packed.

Malaq didn't share Jarryd's urgency. Perched on a fallen tree with bare feet and a bare chest, he was scraping several days' growth off his face while attempting to carve out a goatee. Apparently, the way he was gripping a much too small mirror between his teeth and a much too large knife in his hand, shaving wasn't one of Malaq's many skills.

"Since you're about to cut your damn throat," I said lightly, "I'm going to take a wild guess and say someone did this for you back home."

Malaq lifted the blade from his skin. He removed the mirror from his mouth and sighed wistfully, "Myra. She ran a bath for me every day at noon. I've never seen a girl look so fantastic in bubbles. She had hair down to her ankles," Malaq said proudly, as if he'd grown the strands himself.

"Her ankles?" Jarryd chuckled in disbelief.

"Don't be jealous, Kane…even if it does put that tired brown mane of yours to shame." Malaq paused, waiting for Jarryd's irritated squint to know he'd irked him. Receiving it, he went on, "There was barely room for me with her ginger curls in the tub. They would kink around her curves and her…" leaving off, Malaq sighed again. "I wonder if Myra would consider moving to Langor?"

Walking between us, Jarryd threw in a curt, "Not if she's sane," and kept going. Reaching his horse, he picked up his saddle and settled it on the animal's back. "We're up pretty high. I'm going to see if I can catch sight of Kael's troops."

"You'll need a spyglass," I told him.

Mischief glinting in his eyes, he glanced at me. "I borrowed Malaq's."

"Help yourself," Malaq replied dryly. Suspending his work, he looked at me sideways. "Come to think of it, I haven't seen you regale us with your shaving prowess since we left Kael, Troy. Don't tell me you have a spell for grooming."

"No," I grinned. "No spell, *Nef'areen*. Shinree just don't sprout beards as quickly as the rest of you."

"Lucky bastard. We Langorians are a decidedly hairy lot. I suppose though," Malaq said with regret, "I'll have to let it grow once I reach Langor."

"Might help you blend in," I said.

"Blend in?" he scoffed. "It'll keep my face from freezing off. Do you know how bitterly cold those mountains can be?"

"You need to eat more," Jarryd offered.

Malaq blinked at him. "Excuse me?"

"Add a few dozen rolls to your gut, you'll blend *and* you won't feel the cold."

"I won't see my feet either," Malaq argued. "And what's the point of custom made boots if I can't see them?"

"You got me there." Peering over the back of his horse at Malaq, Jarryd ran a finger along his own stubbly chin. "Missed a spot."

Frowning, Malaq inspected his face in the glass. Jarryd went back to readying his horse, and his light expression gave way to a familiar look of intensity. The way he moved, with purpose and focus holding his face tight and making the red puckered skin of his scar stand out, told me his mind was already there. It was at the cliff's edge, staring down over a sprawl of Kaelish colors, trying to calculate how long before they reached Rella's shores.

I wasn't sure if it was Neela Arcana, a sense of duty, or simply that he'd lived in one place all his life, but every delay ate at him. For Jarryd, being away from home was like having a piece missing from him. Kabri wasn't like that for me. No place was, and I envied him.

"Go then," I told him.

"Really?" he said, overtly skeptical. "That's it? No dire warnings? No lectures? No armed escort?" Jarryd swung up into the saddle. "No list of reasons why I shouldn't ride off alone?"

"Told you not to nursemaid him," Malaq muttered under his breath.

I flung him a glare that went entirely unnoticed. Tempering it, I turned back to Jarryd. "Don't be long. We'll be leaving soon."

He gestured at Malaq. "You better tell him that." Urging his mount up the slight incline to the trail, Jarryd rode off. As he disappeared from view, I squashed the impulse to grab Kya and join follow him.

Behind me, Malaq offered his opinion. "Restless, isn't he?"

"Finish up," I told him. "We need to get going."

"It's a shame. What he's setting himself up for. But I guess it's to be expected. Jarryd is Kabrinian, after all. They've lived on hope so long it's in their veins."

I didn't reply. I wasn't interested in listening to Malaq talk around a subject. Walking past him, I went over to Kya, shook out her blanket, and draped it over her back.

"If Kane finds Kael's troops dead," Malaq went on, "or in the hands of our friend Krillos, he isn't going to let a thing like that go." Tugging a cloth out of his pack, he wiped his blade and mirror clean. "He isn't going to listen to reason either." Putting everything away, Malaq looked at me. "So what are you going to do?"

"I don't know." I picked up my saddle and hoisted it up onto Kya's back. "Knock Jarryd senseless and drag him to Kabri?"

Malaq hesitated. "Effective, but…not the answer I expected."

"You want me to go after Krillos? Sorry, Malaq. I'm not backtracking days out of our way to protect some old Kaelish general who wandered too far from home."

"Fair enough. How about then, just for argument's sake, Krillos keeps his word, and Kael's soldiers actually reach Rella alive. What happens then?" Tugging a dark green tunic from his pack, Malaq smoothed out the wrinkles and pulled it on over his head. "Even if something remains of Neela's army, they'll be outnumbered and overwhelmed. Considering Draken has a Shinree and…well," he paused to flatten down his hair, "the Kaelish aren't exactly known for their bravery in battle. But if you joined the fight and help them…"

"Magic has no place in war."

"That sounds like Aylagar talking."

"Maybe. But I'm not fighting in anyone's army. Not again. I don't want to be made out to be a champion, or a hero. I couldn't live up to those names last time, and I certainly can't now. But if I take back the crown, and remove that power from Draken's reach, it might be enough to cause him to retreat. If not, then at least the battlefield will be level."

"So then what, the two sides can go about killing each other like old times? While you bow out and run off to play mercenary again?"

"I didn't say that."

"You just said you weren't joining the army."

"I don't need to wear a uniform to defend Rella."

"No, you need a reason." His stare had weight to it. "When we met, I wasn't sure you had one. But you do now. In fact, I'm starting to think you've had one all along."

"I'm too tired for games, Malaq. But if you're looking for my source of inspiration…there's only one."

"The spell. Right. Sorry," he sighed. "I don't believe you."

I eyed him as I tightened the girth. "You don't believe me?"

"Oh, I'm not saying that whatever spell was put on you to fight for the Arcanas didn't serve as proper motivation. Or that King Raynan didn't set out wanting you to be some rabid, mindless cur he could sick on his enemies. But we both know you're not that. You care about what happens to people, Ian. You put yourself on the line for the Rellans ten years ago, and you're doing it now. I've seen the way you are with Jarryd. I watched you take a beating in Kael when you could have cast to save yourself long before that. Defending a place, preserving a belief or a way of life—maybe you are compelled to do those things. But fighting *for* it…that's something altogether different, my friend."

Malaq fell quiet. I didn't like his uninvited appraisal of my life. But I was still trying to decide if he was right when he threw something else at me.

"What happened to that set of swords you used to carry?"

"I've had lots of swords."

189

"They were spelled, I believe."

Tying a bag onto my saddle, I paused to look up. "You weren't in exile all these years, were you, Malaq? You know too much to have spent your life trawling for fish."

"Of course I was in exile. Officially though, I was only exiled from Kael's city."

"Ever been to Langor?" I said, going back to tying.

"Not yet. I hear it's quite cold."

"What about Kabri?"

"Once or twice. They weren't exactly official visits though."

I nodded. "I see riding next to Jarryd has taught you to loosen your lips."

"And I see you tried to change the subject."

"Actually," I finished my last knot and looked up, "I ended it."

"Damn you, Troy, I know Raynan Arcana formally presented you with a collection of Shinree weapons the morning you left to join Aylagar's forces."

"He did. It was quite a ceremony, actually. The way he talked me up, praising the results of my training, I thought myself invincible. I was sure I'd be back inside of a year with Langor's signed surrender in my hand." Memory darkened my tone. "But that was a private ceremony, Malaq. My tutors, his councilors, a few visiting lords. Can't imagine how you could have learned of it." I gave him a hard stare. "Just how many times did you go to Kabri?"

"Never mind that," he brushed me off. "If you have special swords to protect you, why aren't you carrying them?"

"Because they aren't special. I could press stones into the handle of any weapon and it would work just as well. Besides," I thought back to the day I sat my swords down in favor of the Crown of Stones. "Those blades have seen enough blood already."

"Understood," he conceded. "But we're nearly halfway to Rella, and you haven't uttered a word about how you plan on getting your hands on the crown."

"I thought you said men like me don't work off plans?"

"I *may* have overstated that a bit."

I threw him a brief grin. "I need to make Draken's magic user vulnerable. Give him a target. Something to attack until his magic runs out. When he's defenseless, I can kill him."

"What's the target?"

"Me."

"Great. Now how about a plan that doesn't involve you dying?" I said nothing and he moved closer. "Ian, you took out two armies with the Crown of Stones. How are you going to withstand that kind of power if he turns it on you? For that matter, what's preventing him from unleashing it on you right now?"

"Nothing."

"So then nothing is preventing him from crushing Kael's troops, either. I mean, why wait until they start advancing on Kabri's city wall? Why not wipe them out before they even reach Rella's border?"

"Because two Kaelish contingents, a handful of injured Rellan soldiers and a few farmers armed with shovels, is a waste of the crown's power. All the man has to do is magically enhance Langor's weapons and shielding, increase their soldier's strength and aim, and then let sheer numbers do the rest."

"And you're sure of this because…?"

"Because it's what I would do."

Nodding thoughtfully, Malaq rubbed his newly carved goatee like it itched. "Even so, there's no way Draken is going to let you reach Kabri alive."

"Draken won't kill me. Not yet."

Malaq gave me a look. "You can't be serious."

"I know it sounds crazy."

"Crazy? Not all. Considering, a few nights ago my brother asked me to—what was it he said? Kill the witch in his sleep?"

"Don't ask me to explain."

"Sorry, my friend. But I'm asking."

"I can't," I said. Because no matter how hard it was getting to hide the effects of the dreams, telling him meant admitting that I was losing control. It meant confessing that I was relying on words from a nightmare. That reality and fantasy were blending so much that when Draken insisted over and over in my sleep that he had taken a vow not to kill me, I believed him.

And I could barely stand the way Malaq was looking at me now.

"I need you to trust me on this," I said.

"Trust you?" He smiled slightly. "All right. We all have secrets. But if I let this go, I need the same trust from you in return. I need you to leave Draken to me."

Avoiding his stare, I reached for Kya's bridle. I pulled it over her head, stalling, searching for a level head, a morsel of restraint; a way to give him what he wanted. It wasn't so long ago that I'd argued with Jarryd in favor of Malaq's plan. But since then, the dreams had altered my viewpoint. So drastically, I couldn't imagine giving up the chance to kill the murderous bastard with my bare hands.

"No, I want Draken dead," I said. "Not in two months, or six, or a year. I want him dead now, Malaq. Dead in a way you can't possibly understand. The things he's done…the things I've watched him do." My teeth clenched as I recalled the methodical way Draken cut the dress from her body. The slow, meticulous way he carved her skin. "You wouldn't ask me this if you knew—"

The light shifted. Shadows fell.

She crawled toward me on the ground, hand outstretched, tears streaming through the cuts on her face.

I reached for her.

Shackles locked about my wrists.

A whip sliced through the skin on my back.

I stumbled into Kya. My throat was parched from days without water. I could feel the blood soaking through my shirt, the wrenching pain in my arms from being left to hang for hours on end.

Closing my eyes, channeling the rage into my fists, I willed the illusion away.

When I opened my eyes again, Malaq was standing on the other side of Kya, gaping at me. I didn't know what to say. I scrambled for an excuse.

Then I realized he wasn't looking at me.

Head tilted back, Malaq was staring with a furrowed brow at the thick covering of foliage above my head. "Malaq," I said warily, "what are you looking at?"

"I don't want to alarm you, but…" his focus tightened. He drew his sword.

Giving Kya a slap on the rump, as she moved clear, I pulled my weapons and turned. I was prepared to swing, but there was nothing to swing at.

"Malaq," I said again, angry this time.

"Higher." He put his blade under one of mine and aimed it upward at a cluster of dark billowing clouds. "Before you say anything, just watch."

For a full minute, nothing happened. Then, impossibly fast, the clouds dropped until they were touching the treetops. They lifted, dropped, and lifted again.

The third time, they settled and started expanding.

Swelling and puffing, like smoke bullied by an angry wind, the dense, dark vapor stretched—as if it were being pulled. Fanning out, increasing in size and density, the odd indistinct material was spreading rapidly across the web of branches overhead of our position. Obscuring the vegetation as it traveled, shrouding the canopies and mushrooming out over empty air, it dipped swiftly, diving like a swarm of insects to blot out the lower limbs and obscure the underbrush.

Gliding farther downward, then out across the ground, the cloud-like darkness flowed smoothly over the grass, rolling like a flood of black water.

Abruptly, the flood rushed in from all sides.

In a heartbeat the hill behind us was lost in shadow. The trailhead disappeared a moment later, then the bank leading down to the brook, then the horses. In seconds, all that remained of the glen was a swiftly diminishing circle of grass and light, with us in the middle.

TWENTY THREE

Dust stirred as Malaq pivoted around. "Do something," he said. "It's trying to hem us in."

"It already has. And I can't cast with you here, Malaq. You know that."

"Where the hell would you like me to go? Through that?" He pointed at the dark fog pouring over his bags on the ground. "Not fucking likely."

As it pushed closer, I growled at him. "You're running out of time."

"I'm not leaving you here. If I go, you go."

"Damn it, Malaq, I need you practical right now, not noble."

"I'm afraid you're not getting either." He gestured again at the cloud bearing down on us. Faster and faster, it began pulling itself together and apart, bunching like dough in a baker's hands. "Whatever is happening…it's happening now."

As the mist continued squeezing and expanding, pieces tore away. They drifted over the ground, misshapen and vague. Dividing further, twisting and lengthening, compressing and forming, the batches of gloom molded together. Suddenly, we were surrounded by several groups of tall, featureless man-like figures.

Lacking a scrap of detail or clothing of any kind, the beings lacked faces as well. They had no skin or hair, or any discernible texture. Their bodies were solid darkness, indistinct, willowy, and ghost-like.

I watched them close in. Eight. Twelve. Sixteen. Twenty.

"I know what this is," I said, losing track. Their numbers were growing too fast to count. "They're shadows."

"Shadows of what?"

"Us."

"Sorry, Troy, but last time I checked, I only had one shadow."

"At any given moment, yes. But how many do you think you make in a day?"

I felt Malaq's glance. "So they're all coming? Every shadow I've ever made is coming to kill me?"

"Not all of them. It depends on how long Draken's magic user has been gathering them up. If he's tracked us since we left Kael then…" I slid him a look.

"Gods, but I hate magic." Malaq drew himself up. "What are you going to do?"

"I don't know. I read about this spell once, but it's old. Really old."

"I'm guessing old means bad. Can we kill them?"

"Let's find out." I rushed forward. Cutting through the center of the two nearest black silhouettes, my blades went in easily. Extracting the weapons left gaping holes. Splashes of red misty tendrils spurted into the air.

"Blood," Malaq said happily.

The sprays of red faded to black, and the holes closed.

He groaned. "Now what?"

I raised my swords to try again—and took a startled step back. The blood decorating on the ends of my blades was moving. Darkening and swirling, the stains wrapped around, joined together, and slithered up the length of steel. "What the hell?"

I shook both weapons. The black threads fell off one sword, but clung to the other. Swiftly dancing up and over the hilt, mist the color of night swept cold across my hand. As it crept onto my fingers, they began to tingle and ache. My skin, where it made contact with the sword, burned.

I tried again to jiggle the tendrils loose, but a heavy, lifeless sensation had settled into my hand. It deepened. Going suddenly numb from the tips of my fingers to my wrist, the sword slipped from my grasp. The darkness sloughed off me then. Clinging to the weapon as it fell to the ground, it curled away from the cold steel like a wisp of smoke and drifted off; leaving me to stare down in horror at my frozen black skin.

I felt no pain. I couldn't feel anything. It was like my hand wasn't even there.

Behind me, Malaq let out a triumphant roar. I turned just as Natalia separated a willowy head from its body. The figure became two pieces. The pieces broke apart into flimsy wisps and disintegrated.

He decapitated two more. They disappeared and didn't reform.

Malaq had found their weak spot.

I raised my remaining sword. With so many targets, and Malaq's strategy, I felled six in rapid succession. Our opponents were slow and weaponless. All I had to do was slice off their heads quick enough to keep the blood from sticking to my sword.

There was a catch, of course. No matter how quickly we worked, they kept coming. The shadows were multiplying faster than we could kill them. Some crept between us. Others pressed in, tightening their circle. The rest blended together, uniting into a large, shapeless mass that was surging toward us like the great swell of an ocean.

The waves flowed closer. My moves turned careless.

I had no room to maneuver, no time to aim.

Malaq let out a yell as the undulating black enveloped his boots. Tendrils crawled up his chest, wrapping around his arms. They spider-webbed across his body; pulling him to his knees; freezing his skin and turning it black.

I called out to him as I cut into the swell. I swung madly to reach him. But more and more strands of misty dark blood were spilling up my sword. And the puddle of blackness was creeping rapidly up Malaq's neck.

Slinking across his face, the shadow inched higher. It closed over the top of Malaq's head, and he was gone. Only one hand remained visible. Rigid and black, incapable of movement, it stuck straight out, like he was reaching for me.

I dropped my sword. Calling to the stones at my wrist, I summoned the obsidian and lunged into the blackness. My fingers closed over his. As the icy strands began to flow over me, the remaining shadows moved in quickly. Rolling in from all sides, more dripped down from above to join the mass, and I started casting.

With no thought but to save Malaq, I used the diamond on my wrist to momentarily link his essence to mine. The hematite became a shield to protect him from being drained by the spell (an utterly desperate move that had no valid reason to work), the citrine to stop our hearts, and the garnet to infuse us with a big jolt of stamina to start them again. I had no plan for the obsidian. I simply felt more confident with its energy pulsing through me, so I channeled it, too. Considering I was about to ask magic to bring us as close to death as we could go, I needed the boost.

I threw the magic out. There was no enjoyment in it. Not as I was, on my knees, bitter cold, with blackness thick as tar climbing up my legs. My hand, clasped with Malaq's, was frozen and stiff. My bones ached with the piercing cold. I could feel my heart slowing, the beats spacing farther and farther apart.

My gut said that if the shadows believed we were already dead they would stop trying to make us that way. And it looked like I was right. As Malaq and I grew lifeless and unimportant, the bulging, shadowy mound reacted. It poured down off our bodies like a black tide in motion, sweeping up its errant pieces as it flowed away. When it had them all, the spell divided again, into four thick, bloated man-like shapes that rolled and tumbled from the glen.

With their retreat, light returned to the clearing. It didn't help much, though. I was getting what I wished for at the brook: the cold to close over me, the nothingness.

Light was pointless now that I was dying.

Except—

There was the blurred form of a horse and rider on approach. As it grew near, I tried to focus on it, but in the forefront were the four remaining shadow-men. They were headed back toward the forest, dissolving, and I was afraid to let them go. I kept thinking: *if they escape with the life they stole, would we ever get it back?*

Jarryd slid off his horse and ran toward us.

My voice trembled as I forced out a word, "Head."

I wasn't sure I'd spoken loud enough for him to hear me, but Jarryd didn't miss a step. He threw down his bow, took up Malaq's abandoned sword, and started swinging.

TWENTY FOUR

"Here." Jarryd pushed a cup of something warm in my hand. The steam rose up, found its way to my nose, and the smell made my mouth water.

"Thanks," I said. "Looks great."

Sitting on the ground across from me, blowing the heat off his meal, Jarryd looked over the rim of his cup and inclined his head in the direction of the man stretched out on the ground between us. "Any change?"

I looked at Malaq's sickly pale skin. I watched his chest move under the blanket in little shallow breaths, and I knew he was alive. But he hadn't moved. Since I woke up two days ago, crawled over and sat down beside him, neither had I.

"No," I said. "He's still the same."

"I skinned an extra rabbit. Found a couple of eggs, a patch of strawberries. He'll need to get his strength back when he comes to."

"Good idea," I said. But I needed to say more. Jarryd had taken out the last of the shadows. He'd hauled Malaq and I up across our horses and found a place to make camp. He'd kept us warm, fed, and safe for days, while I'd sat on my ass in a fog of guilt, praying for Malaq to regain consciousness. I'd left everything to Jarryd. And it had taken a toll. Visible dark circles ringed his blue eyes. His braid was half undone and pieces were sticking out all over. Dirt darkened his hands and streaked his torn tunic, as well as the crumpled skin of his swollen, scarred face. "You look like hell," I added.

"Me?" He flashed his usual, uneven grin. "Seriously, Ian," he said, the expression fading. "Get some sleep. I got this."

"I can't." I knew too well what sleep would bring. "It's my fault he's like this."

"The fuck if it is. You're the reason he's alive."

"What I did, Jarryd, casting against the shadows with Malaq so close... it was irresponsible. Dangerous." I wrapped my hands as tight as I could around the mug, soaking up the warmth. "What if he never wakes up? What if something went wrong? I had no idea what I was doing, trying to protect him from being drained by a spell. Gods, what was I thinking? My magic kills people, it doesn't save them."

Jarryd didn't reply to that. "What about you? Are you feeling any better?"

"Some," I said, sparing him the truth. He didn't need to know that, as life came back to everything the shadows touched, it hurt like hell. My muscles and joints throbbed. My insides were trembling from a cold I couldn't shake. I was so far beyond tired, I wasn't sure there was a word for it.

"Can I ask you something?" Jarryd said. "Before I left, Neela told me about that." He gestured at the black shard around my neck. "After what happened with the war and Aylagar, why do you think King Raynan gave you a piece of the Crown of Stones?"

"Honestly? I have no idea. I was a mess that day. I was angry. Not thinking clearly. He handed it to me, and I took it."

"They say you asked to be locked up."

"I did. I begged for *Kayn'l.*"

"And?"

"The King refused. He didn't want his personal weapon tainted by drugs. He said that if I wanted to stop using magic, I had to find a way that wouldn't interfere with my duty to protect Rella. He suggested I try a tincture of amethyst shavings."

"What the hell is that?" Jarryd grinned.

"This man, one of the tutors King Raynan hired for me as a child, he told me about a time when Rellans thought they could glean a bit of magic for themselves. They ground up stones and used the powder to made potions, salves, even teas. They believed their concoctions had medicinal properties."

"Did they?"

I shrugged. "My mother used to say that belief could make anything so."

"Why amethyst? What did it do?"

"It was said to curb addiction. Wives would put it in their husband's food, hoping to calm their drinking or gambling. Don't know how they didn't taste it. It's a nasty mix."

"Wait…" Jarryd looked disgusted, and a little excited. "You actually tried it?"

"I was desperate. I would have tried anything."

"So it didn't work?"

"Oh, it worked. I didn't drink or gamble once the entire week. I was too fucking sick. I couldn't even get out of bed."

Jarryd laughed. "Sorry. I suppose it wasn't funny."

"No," I chuckled. "It wasn't." My thoughts turned back to the crown. "It was an innocent gesture, King Raynan breaking off the shard. Symbolic, I guess. He had no idea how strong the crown was. He certainly didn't know the piece would stay linked."

"I'm not so sure about that. The King had a Shinree oracle at the castle."

"Most kings have oracles. Half of them double as concubines."

"I don't think that was the case. I heard she was a child. Very gifted for her age. King Raynan kept her hidden away somewhere in the castle. He would disappear for hours visiting her. He never spoke of the visions she gave him. But one night, when Neela was young, he confessed he'd never had any true affection for Aylagar. That he already loved one dead woman, why waste time with another destined for the same fate."

"What are you saying? That he knew Aylagar would die?"

Jarryd leaned closer. "The castle guards have been on constant high alert for the last three years. Patrols go out twice a day looking for signs of an invasion. Last winter, new guard posts were established at the border with Langor. Right after that he ordered the castle to be searched. King Raynan was looking for where you hid the Crown of Stones."

"I never told him it was in the castle."

"Exactly. We all thought he was going mad. But I think he saw this coming. Draken. The crown. All of it."

"Even if he did, oracle magic can't be trusted that implicitly. The choices we make every day alter the future."

"Maybe that's what King Raynan was trying to do. He was trying to alter the future *away* from what he saw by breaking the crown."

"It's not broken," I said, "it's…" Jarryd's words prompting a sudden change of perspective, I thought back to the swamp. Taren said the circle was seamless and whole…until I found it. "That's it." I looked at Jarryd in shock. "Missing a piece must cause some sort of disruption in the crown's power. Some decrease in strength."

"Then I was right. King Raynan did know. He saw a vision of the crown falling into enemy hands. He knew that breaking it would diminish its magic, so he gave you the shard to try and thwart Draken's plans."

"It does seem that way."

"But if that's true, then putting the shard and the crown back together…"

"Restores it to full power."

Jarryd looked queasy. "Son of a bitch, Ian. You can't let that happen. You can't let Draken make the crown even more powerful. There has to be a way to destroy it, to break the connection. Isn't there a text that can tell you how it works? An old book or a scroll?"

"Not that I've seen. I've heard songs and stories, but they're mostly about the crown's creator, Tam Reth."

"Reth…wasn't he the last Shinree emperor?"

"The only one. Before him my ancestors were governed by a Ruling House, a council of nine members. Reth was among them, but he wasn't like them. He wanted to cross the waters and find new worlds to conquer. The rest of the House disagreed and dismissed him from the council. That's when he created the Crown of Stones and the formula for *Kayn'l*, wiped out his rivals, and named himself Emperor. He reigned only a year before the quake, but it was a bloody one."

His face grim, Jarryd got up and went to the fire. Suspended above the flames was a crude spit of damp wood and a small cooking pot. After smelling the contents of the pot, he stirred it a few times and added more twigs to the fire. "None of this would be happening if you'd been there." He poked at the fire. "The King should have never turned you out."

"You're right. He should have hung me."

Stirring one last time, Jarryd put the spoon down and looked at me. "The war was draining everything good out of Rella. Maybe you didn't see it. Most of the soldiers didn't. They were too focused on the battle in front of them. But I saw it. The other children saw it too, the women left at home…we all knew. It wasn't just people and crops we were losing. Our way of life was crumbling and disappearing. There was so little left by the time you found the crown. No matter how you did it, no matter the consequences…the war had to end." He stared into the pot. "Rella was bleeding, Ian. You stopped it. And for that, we turned you out. It wasn't right."

Jarryd went back to tending his stew. He said nothing else on the matter, and I was glad, because I had no idea how to respond. The absence of resentment in his expression, the lack of blame he placed on my shoulders; even after all the time we'd spent together I still didn't understand it. Jarryd hadn't revealed so much as a hint of deep-seated loathing or resentment. He hadn't once admonished me, even in jest. He truly accepted what I'd done to his people.

How? I thought. *The Rellans lost near an entire generation of men because of me. How does anyone stomach that?*

Jarryd's view had to be unique. Others couldn't possibly share in his perspective.

But what if they did?

What if I wasn't reviled and feared in Kabri as I always believed?

Is it possible? I wanted to know. I was equally afraid to ask.

Mercifully, the dilemma was taken from me when Malaq began to stir.

With an embellished groan, he stretched like he'd just awoken from a nice afternoon nap. Bewildered and groggy, eyes half closed, Malaq rose up onto his elbows. He wrinkled his nose in disgust. "*What* is that smell?"

"Stew," Jarryd replied. He cocked an eyebrow. "I suppose you can do better?"

Malaq looked weak, almost frail. His skin was ashen. But his mouth worked fine. "Without question I can do better. I'm not ashamed to say I've spent a good deal of time in the kitchens. And my stepfather does employ the best cook in all of Raymorre."

"Of course he does," Jarryd frowned. "What's her name?"

"Narice," Malaq said fondly, which inspired Jarryd to roll his eyes. "She's just a petite, little thing. But I'm telling you, Kane, you put some spice in that girl's hands, the way she rubs it on..." he offered a low, hoarse whistle. "You wouldn't believe what that girl can do to a slab of meat."

"So tell me." Jarryd was struggling hard not to laugh. "What does Narice wear when she's in the kitchen rubbing your meat?"

Malaq grinned. "I'll give you one guess."

TWENTY FIVE

I could still see the hammer smashing into my fingers. I could hear the solid snap of bones breaking. Fragments were ripping up through my skin, and I wanted to knead at the pain. I wanted to tug at the chains; they'd been digging into my neck all day.

They weren't, of course. But my mind said otherwise. My dream world was leaking into my waking one so drastically now. I could scarcely tell the difference.

Last night, when the Arullan girl was beneath me on the soft grass, it was hard to accept that she hadn't been there at all. Not when I could feel her on my skin. Smell her on my clothes. Hear her scream.

The loss of her always felt moments old. It burrowed in repeatedly, tightening my chest, sinking into my gut, forcing me to constantly remind myself that she wasn't real.

None of it is. Why can't I remember that?

My throat constricting with false grief, I was suddenly too wrecked to even hold the reins. I pulled Kya to a fast stop and nearly fell off the saddle. My struggle to stay on didn't go unnoticed, either. Malaq looked back and neither distance nor the waning afternoon light did anything to soften his frown. It was deep and pondering, yet at the same time: emotionless. The expression bore an eerie resemblance to Draken, and I was glad when Malaq turned around and rode on.

He and Jarryd grew smaller. Their details washed out. The two men became dark silhouettes against the forest and the ground between us grayed out.

My eyes grew heavy. The gray turned white.

Cold, I wrapped my arms around myself, but it did no good.

Snow had stolen my warmth. It burned in my open wounds.

I was shivering uncontrollably, though not as hard as my body wanted. The shackles were too restrictive. I could barely lift my head. All I could do was watch.

She cried, and Draken beat her until the sound died in her throat.

Blood spilled from the corner of her slack mouth. It seeped across the ground, and the snow turned red.

I shook awake with a start. Gasping and shivering like it was mid-winter, I clung to Kya's back, wanting to flay Draken alive more than I wanted to breathe. Bloodlust and eagerness constricted my muscles. Black irrational thoughts took my mind to violent places. A vicious wave of brutality broke over me. Anger turned to rage. Rage became hysteria. What little reason I had left fell to pieces, and I suddenly, desperately, needed someone to bleed besides her. *Any Langorian in sight will do,* I thought hungrily, eyeing the one riding ahead of me on the trail.

I shifted a hand to my sword. Without a sound, I slid the blade free of its sheath. I kept the weapon low and out of sight as I eased my horse forward. Picking a spot in the middle of the man's broad back, I pictured my steel sinking down inside, and my throat dried in anticipation.

Giving the mare more speed, I persuaded her to the edge of the trail. I lined her up until I had the best angle for a quick, clean kill.

I raised my sword to strike.

"You're taking me too literal," the Langorian said then, brusquely. "When I say I hate magic, it doesn't mean I *really* hate it. I just hate it being used on me."

His companion answered, but I was deaf to his reply. I was too taken aback by the anomalies in my target's accent. The rhythm was too slow, the inflection too smooth.

Slowing my approach, I listened to him again. I studied his frame more carefully and realized it was wrong. The cut and style of his clothes were amiss. His voice, his coloring, even his perfectly groomed hair were all off the mark.

The man wasn't at all what I needed him to be.

Grinding my teeth on the disappointment, I started weighing the killing of an undeserving stranger against my desire for revenge. Every Langorian deserved to die for something, and if it would bring me a measure of peace, then it was his turn.

Yet, taking his life would change nothing. Killing him wouldn't save her. It wouldn't make her go away. *She can't go away. She exists in me.*

With that sobering thought, my blind fury began to dwindle. As it did, wrath and tension dissolved. My impulse for violence shrunk, and reality shifted back into focus. I couldn't remember where I was or what I was doing. Kya was beneath me, moving over the wooded trail at a moderate pace. A sword was in my right hand that I had no recollection of drawing. My fingers were wrapped around the hilt. My entire hand was white and throbbing with the strain.

I glanced up. Malaq's mount was just ahead of mine. Jarryd's was a pace in front. As they chatted, my eyes were drawn to Malaq's back. A strange eagerness filled me, and I saw my sword plunging in.

Uttering a loud panicked gasp of comprehension, I yanked Kya to a clumsy halt—and Malaq picked that exact moment to look over his shoulder. His blank gaze moved from the shock on my face to the blade in my hand. He watched the weapon shake in my grasp. He stared at the shame in my eyes. But he didn't ask why it was there. After a brief, tense hesitation, he turned back around; oblivious to the bile rising in my throat or how badly I was trembling. He didn't notice that I needed both hands to steady my sword enough to put it away.

I felt dirty. Deceitful. Dangerous. I wanted to run.

But what kind of man left his companions in the wild, with Langorians and eldring and magic everywhere? *Not a sane one,* I thought. *A rational man would stay and defend them. A decent man would keep his misery hidden and his lunacy under control. He would find a way to protect the people that depended on him.*

Distraught, I pushed the hair out of my face and got Kya moving. I caught up to them as Malaq was making an offhand comment about the lack of decent inns in the Kaelish backcountry. He paused to glance at me. "You're strangely quiet today, Troy."

"You talk enough for both of us," I replied gruffly.

"So you are mad," he nodded. "You know, you shouldn't misjudge my complaints for ungratefulness."

"And you shouldn't arrogantly put yourself at the root of all my moods."

Malaq's jaw worked a bit. "I appreciate what you did with the shadows. All I'm asking is that the next time you save my life, you make it hurt a bit less."

"How about I conjure you a nice comfy bed to recuperate in, too? Maybe someone pretty to roll you over once in a while and clean your royal backside?" The venom in my voice had been unmistakable. *Sleep*, I thought, my hands tightening on the reins. *I just need sleep.* "Sorry," I muttered.

"Don't be. Give her yellow hair and we're even." Malaq kicked the roan's sides. "My horse needs a run."

As Malaq's mount sprinted up the trail, Jarryd looked over at me. "Something you want to talk about?"

"I wouldn't know where to start."

"We've got plenty of time," he said, and I was tempted. The weight of the dream was heavy on my chest. Perhaps if I told someone, maybe I could breathe again.

"Troy!" Malaq's voice rang out from up ahead. "You sure there's a house here?"

"Try slowing down!" I hollered back. "Trail's on your left! There's an old oak with a huge knot in the trunk—about the size of your head!"

"Nice," Jarryd chuckled. "You've used this place before?"

"Many times. It's been abandoned for years. Half the roof leaks. There's holes in the floor where the forest has grown in. But the structure is mostly sound and the brush is good cover. Decent shelter might also make our Prince happy for a few hours."

"Throw in some bubbles and a Kaelish girl and you might be right."

Stopping, I angled Kya to face the barely visible, narrow grassy lane shooting off from the main trail. An overgrowth of wild flowers and thorn bushes spilled out into the passage. "Looks like he found it," I said, pointing out the fresh hoof prints and splashes of squashed pink berries decorating the ground. "The path twists a bit, but the cabin isn't far. We'll be there before Malaq has a chance to get his feet up."

Jarryd gave me a look. "I wouldn't count on it."

———

The clearing was large and circular. In its center, fenced in on three sides, was a one-story cabin in perfect condition. Stacks of neatly chopped wood butted up against the house. Row of trees bearing pale yellow blossoms ran the length of the fence. Steam escaped from the open top of a small bath-house on the right. In the front, a sturdy lean-to, overflowing with hay, gave shelter to a sleepy gray gelding and a white cat so plump I had my doubts it could walk.

"Your abandoned house isn't abandoned anymore," Jarryd said, guiding his mount around a group of flustered chickens. "Someone lives here."

"No one lives here," I argued. But that was hard to maintain with plumes of smoke rising from the stone chimney, giving off the scent of fresh baked bread. Carefully tended sprigs of lavender outlined the front porch, and a cozy orange glow was bursting out the front window, promising comfort and warmth.

It was relaxing and inviting. Everything a weary traveler could want.

And it immediately put me on edge.

"Ian." Jarryd tossed his head, directing me to where Malaq's horse was drifting out from behind the lean-to. Saddle empty, reins dragging, sniffing the ground as he wandered, the beast was abnormally quiet and content.

"Stay here." I threw a leg over the saddle and slid down. My boots trampled a flourishing vegetable garden, but I didn't care. The tender leaves weren't real. None of it was. A few weeks ago, when I'd come through on my way into Kael, the cabin was exactly as I'd described it to Jarryd; run down, vacant, and overgrown.

Drawing the sword off my back, I started toward the porch, and Malaq opened the front door. A mug in his hand, he paused in the threshold and leaned carelessly against the frame. He tipped his drink at me. "What took you so long?"

"Get your horse," I told him. "We're leaving."

"Why?" He seemed uncaring of my urgency. "Staying here was your idea."

"Not *this* here, Malaq. *This* here doesn't exist."

"I don't know what you're babbling about, but we aren't disappointing our hostess. Not after she so graciously opened up her home." Stepping aside from the doorway, Malaq bowed. "May I introduce, the enchanting lady Imma?"

She walked out onto the porch. All bouncy and suggestive, with one side of her skirt hitched up to her thigh, large auburn curls caressing her face, breasts jutting, and a brazen, sensuous smile—Imma was provocative to the bone. But she was no lady.

I looked back at Malaq. "Have you lost your mind?"

"Not lost," Imma spoke up. "Misplaced."

"Damn it." I raised my sword. "What have you done to him?"

"Troy," Malaq sighed. He stepped gallantly in front of her. "Put that away."

"She isn't what you think," I warned.

Jarryd came up beside me. "Malaq's right, Ian." He put a hand on my sword, wanting me to lower it. "You'll scare her."

I gave him stern eyes. "That's the point," I said, and he let go.

Imma sashayed out from behind Malaq. "It's so nice to have visitors. And such handsome ones at that." Smiling with the perfect mix of lustful curiosity and shy innocence, she gestured at the cabin. "Come in, please. The fire is warm. The table is full of food and drink. You all look so weary. A nice rest would do you good."

Mindlessly, Jarryd moved toward the porch.

I put my arm out to stop him. "I don't think so."

"You think too much," Imma said sweetly. "Why don't you let your body decide what it needs? Take off your boots. Sit by the fire. Indulge in a hot bath and a good night's rest. Surely you've earned a little respite." Slowly, she dragged her fingers across the neckline of her inadequate bodice. "A little pleasure?" She tugged at the bow holding it together and the air grew tense. Suddenly, I remembered the smell of her hair and the feel of her skin with impossible clarity.

Whatever spell she was using to make her more captivating (and us more compliant), it was working. Only, I'd seen the show before. I was very aware that the skin I remembered touching didn't belong to the woman wearing it.

"We aren't staying," I said, loud and emphatic.

"Of course we're staying," Malaq replied. He hitched himself up on the porch rail. "Look at this place. Look at *her*. Why would we want to go anywhere else?"

"We could use a few days' rest," Jarryd said then, casually, as if Kabri was no longer a thought in his head. "Unless we're imposing?" He smiled at Imma.

"Oh, not at all." Her eyes shifted from his to mine. She wet her lips. "I've been waiting for you."

TWENTY SIX

If I still had any dreams of my own, I would think I was having one now. The food, the furnishings, even the girl was flawless and perfect, tasty enough to grace a King's hall. Unfortunately, we weren't in a King's hall. We were in an abandoned, ramshackle cabin in the middle of nowhere. Everything we were seeing, tasting, smelling, and touching had been created by an incredible amount of stone magic. Half of it was probably illusion.

The absurdity of it all was one reason I'd spent the evening helping myself to a seemingly never-ending bottle of wine. Another was being forced to listen to Malaq regale us with tales of his youth while Imma hung on his every word—and his body.

Mostly, she'd left Jarryd alone. I'd staked my claim pretty quick, sitting him beside me, interfering with every conversation she tried to start with him. I'd made my intention to protect Jarryd clear, but Imma only needed one of them bent to her will to get me to stay. And she definitely wanted me to stay. Each time our eyes met, she gave me a look that reminded me what I was missing.

Not that I needed it. A good mix of desire and resentment had been running through me before I'd even entered the house. Now, after hours of Malaq's wandering hands and Imma's lingering stares, only two things were keeping me from throttling them both: the disturbing realization that I had less of a claim to the fake Kaelish girl across from me than I did the fake

213

Arullan girl in my dreams, and the absence of pleasure in Imma's eyes when Malaq touched her. She didn't enjoy his attentions. She was faking it.

For me.

Imma was looking for a trigger, a way to spark something; anger, lust, unease. It didn't matter as long as I gave her something to use. So I swallowed the jealousy with my wine and gave her nothing.

"I didn't realize Malaq was so charming," Jarryd said with a yawn.

I tapped my mug against the bottle on the table. "A little more of this, and I'll be making eyes at him too." Jarryd laughed long and hard at that. The sound was a welcome one, and I nodded at his cup. "More?"

"No. I'm done." He pushed his plate away and stood, prompting Imma to shoot to her feet.

"I'll make you a place by the fire," she said kindly. "And a warm cup of tea."

Jarryd hovered at the table. "It's your call, Ian. If you want to go, we go."

I looked up at the tired in his eyes. I looked over at the pleading in hers. Malaq's were half closed as he leaned back in his chair, with his feet on the table and a bunch of grapes in his hand. He popped them into his mouth one by one and sighed contentedly.

It *was* late. All three of us were tired, and I was drunk. Yet I was wary to be under the same roof with Imma. There were too many things I didn't know about the woman. And that was exactly why I had to stay. "No sense sleeping on the ground," I told him. "We'll head out at first light."

Jarryd stepped away. "I'll get the horses settled."

"Why don't you let Imma take a look at that wound on your face? Maybe she has something for it."

Jarryd hesitated. "I don't know…"

"Someone else can handle the horses tonight." I centered persuasive eyes on Malaq, but he'd moved on from grapes to a crunchy red apple, and he didn't seem to notice I existed. "A little help?" I said to Imma.

She bent down in front of Malaq and placed her palm against his chest. "The horses need tending, My Lord. After, it will be my pleasure to see to your sore muscles."

Straightaway, Malaq set his half-eaten apple down on the table. He swallowed the last of his wine and stood. "Anything for you, lady."

"At least let me help," Jarryd offered. "With four of them it'll take you all night."

"No need, Messenger." Gracefully, Malaq swung his cloak about his shoulders. "It just so happens that I am an excellent groomsman." He snatched a lantern off the wall and bowed to Imma as he went out the door.

Gods, but she has him, I thought, guilt swaying me back to believing no good could come from staying. But as Imma gave Jarryd a cup of something warm, I tried to overcome my doubts.

"Drink this," she said to him. "Settle by the fire and wait for me there."

Jarryd sniffed at the mug. Sipping gingerly, he wandered over to the hearth and sat down.

Imma glanced at me as she collected the plates. "You're worried."

"Shouldn't I be? You're toying with them."

"If you were more obliging I wouldn't have to."

"If you were less shady I might be more interested in obliging."

"Will the truth make you more willing to listen?"

"Probably not, but it might make me a little less pissed off."

With a huff, Imma stormed off into the kitchen, leaving me to wonder, as I had all night, where she was getting the food for her spells. Malaq and Jarryd hadn't been affected and Imma didn't appear to have lost a lick of energy.

She came back for the cups. I let her have mine, but I put a hand on the bottle and looked at her. "How much have you cast on me?"

"Why? Must there be a sinister reason to explain why you're drawn to me?"

"I'm drawn to you because you're dressed in the skin of an attractive woman."

"Or." She leaned down. Her skirt brushed my leg, and I came close to grabbing it. "Perhaps you sense what lies beneath my masquerade?"

Settling the wine on my chest and my feet on the chair across from me, I looked her over, trying to envision Imma as a Shinree. I couldn't. Her glamour was that complete. "Nope," I shrugged. "But thanks for this, by the way." I lifted my wrist with the stones wrapped around it. "I know that night we had in Kael was fun, but you didn't have to get me a present."

She frowned. "We need to talk."

215

"Then talk."

"Not here. Outside."

"What about Jarryd? Can you help him?"

"I can speed the natural healing process. Anything more would make him suspicious. And it's best if my identity remains unknown."

"What did you put in his tea?"

"I didn't poison him, if that's what you think. And there isn't anything in the wine either." She scowled at the bottle in my grip. "If there was you would have been dead hours ago."

Imma went to the door and walked out. Hauling myself up, I brought the bottle with me and followed her onto the porch. Waiting for me on the bottom step, rubbing her arms to ward off the evening chill, the last slender rays of sun streamed across Imma's shoulders. The golden yellow set the red in her hair on fire, and I was tempted to sink my hands down into the flames. As a substitute, I took a drink.

"I could have killed Jarryd Kane a long time ago," she said, her thoughtful gaze on the trees. "But I have no designs to harm him or Malaq."

"No designs? What the hell does that mean?"

"It means they are unimportant." She crossed the yard and apprehension crept a little deeper into my gut.

We made our way to the bathhouse. Imma opened the door. We went inside and it was clear right away: the high-walled, wooden structure was as detailed an illusion as everything else she had created.

Stone benches lined the interior walls. Rows of candles graced the corner shelves. A large, round, metal cask sat in the center of the room. The rim was low and even with the floor, as if the ground beneath it had been dug out and the tub dropped into the hole. No visible heat source warmed the water, but it was unmistakably hot. Beads of moisture dripped down the walls. Continuous curls of steam rose up from the surface of the tub to escape through a circular opening in the domed ceiling.

Even with the outlet, the air inside the bathhouse was oppressive. It dampened my hair and stuck my shirt fast to my skin.

Peeling the moist fabric away from my chest, I moved farther in. I watched Imma carefully as she put her back to me and reached for the door latch. I wasn't exactly comfortable being locked in with her.

The bolt fell into place. She paused with her hand on the lock, and her body began to shimmer. It blurred. The space around her clouded and shifted, and for a moment, as the glamour spell fell away, I couldn't see her at all.

Then the air cleared. The light returned to normal.

Imma turned around, displaying her true form to me for the first time. "Do you prefer the barmaid?" she asked, and I knew at once that I didn't.

TWENTY SEVEN

The winegirl had been nothing but sex and curves. The woman standing in front of me now was tall, slender, and draped in a modest gown the color of dry autumn leaves. She was lithe and graceful, with skin that reminded me of honey. And watching her move toward me was like watching water flow.

"You haven't answered my question," she said, in that same breathy voice that was in my head at the Wounded Owl. Her pale brows arched. "Or maybe you have."

I couldn't deny her insinuation. Saying I preferred Imma would be a boldfaced lie—if I could speak. Which was questionable, seeing how I was awestruck by the look of her, and by how totally ignorant I was as to what pure Shinree blood coursing through a woman's veins actually looked like. As a child I couldn't appreciate the rarity of my mother's appearance, visually or symbolically. Seeing it now though, as a grown man, I was fully aware that I was staring at the past. I was looking at the power and the splendor our people once had. It was stunning.

She was stunning.

Her hair, in particular, enthralled me. It wasn't white so much as it was colorless, to the point of being practically transparent, even crystalline, in appearance. Fine and silky straight, the strands were cut at jagged angles to lay perfectly over her smooth brow and high prominent cheekbones. The tapered ends brushed the base of her neck and curved in at the line of her jaw, framing a heart shaped face that had an interesting, ethereal quality about it; delicate yet impossibly strong at the same time.

Her whole body was like that, fragile yet firm. Even her hair looked almost breakable, yet with the countless tiny stones woven into the strands: imposing.

Pressed into leather thongs and entwined within the multiple small braids hanging down both sides of her head, a good number of the stones were glowing. Their light created a pulsing, iridescent halo that was breathtaking.

Donning a slow, languid smile at my reaction, Imma came forward until we were nearly touching. We were close in height. I could see every detail, and she let me. Saying nothing, not moving, she allowed me to study her. And as I did, it came to me that she wasn't beautiful in the way that Aylagar had been: exotic, confident and aggressive. Neither did she stir in me anything of contentment or blind obsession, as did the Arullan fantasy girl of my dreams. I didn't feel overpowered by lust as I had with the Kaelish winegirl.

In fact, the Shinree woman was affecting me in a far different way than any woman had before. I was mute. Mesmerized. I had the urge to put my hands against her small breasts, simply to feel her chest rise and fall. I was preoccupied with how her skin glowed wet from the heat of the bathhouse. How her hair picked up the colors of the stones and shimmered with light. She met my eyes, and the striking rainbow of magic reflected in hers was quite possibly the most beautiful thing I had ever seen. It pulled me in and held me captive. So much, that with the soft upturn of her thin, pink lips and the touch of her hand as it brushed my face, I found that all that I was going to say—all that I had planned to accuse her of—was gone.

I cleared my throat. Remembering the bottle in my hand, I took a drink. After another, I found my voice. "I've never seen anyone like you."

"Pity," she said.

"That spell you cast in the tavern…?"

"You're welcome."

My interest shrank some at her blithe tone. "A lot of people died that night."

Eyeing me, she pulled the wine out of my hand, wrapped her lips around the rim and tipped the bottle high. I watched the muscles of her neck move as she swallowed, and the room suddenly went from hot to unbearable.

Licking the spill from her mouth, she pressed the bottle back in my hand. Her fingers lingered on mine. "I simply did what you would not."

"Which was? Cast among innocent people? Use their lives to feed your spells?"

"Innocent?" Frustration clouded the magic in her eyes. She shook her head, making the braids bounce and the myriad of stones clack together. "How can you care so much about what happens to the other races, yet do nothing to save your own?"

"You make it sound like I'm happy our people are enslaved."

"No, you're apathetic. You see us as deserving of what Fate has decreed."

"We earned what Fate decreed. Our ancestors enslaved the Langorians. They terrorized everyone else. They weren't good people."

"Haven't we suffered enough for their deeds? Isn't it time for us to be free?"

"That's a nice sentiment. But the same problem still stands. Our people need to be controlled. Without *Kayn'l*, their urges would return. They would crave magic again."

"As they should. It is a natural thing."

"Natural and deadly. They would use it as they please."

"They would learn restraint."

"Just like that?"

"You did."

"Do you think it was easy for me? It took being responsible for the deaths of thousands to give me a reason to hold back. All they'll have is revenge. Like you."

"It's not revenge I seek, Ian. It's liberation. Something you could have given us a long time ago with the Crown of Stones."

My burgeoning anger turned to suspicion. "And how would I have done that exactly? By challenging five hundred years of law single-handed? Or by wiping out everyone that isn't Shinree?" I stared at her a moment, and it became clear. "That's what you would have done, isn't it?"

"I would have done what was necessary. I don't fear what lies inside me."

"Maybe you should."

With a hiss of aggravation, she brushed past me. I half expected Imma's scent of lavender to follow in her wake, but that was gone. Everything of

Imma was gone. The woman who was sitting down and pulling off her boots was nothing like the spirited girl who'd caught my eye in the tavern. That girl didn't exist, not anymore at least.

"Your name isn't Imma," I said, staring at the smooth arch of her foot, the graceful bend of her ankle. "Is she dead? The girl whose essence you stole?"

Ignoring me, the Shinree woman stood and unhooked the chain girdle from her slim waist. It hit the floor with a clank, and the gown billowed out away from her body. "My name is Sienn Nam'arelle," she said proudly. "I am of the Erudite."

"Nam'arelle?" I didn't bother masking my skepticism. The name she claimed was one of the oldest in Shinree history. A family of miners, it was said they were the first to discover our people's innate talent for stone magic. They wrote the first spells, started the first schools. They created the Ruling House and were one of the most preeminent families in the history of the empire. For any erudite to have survived its violent fall was hard to imagine. For one of the original and most powerful of our kind to have been allowed to procreate and produce descendants, for centuries after, seemed impossible. "There hasn't been a teacher born in hundreds of years.

"I am born," she said, as if those three words were the answer to everything.

"Are you the only one?"

"Are you? Is Ian Troy the only Shinree to have the craft of war?"

"There are other soldiers among the slaves. But they aren't like me. They weren't made from pure Shinree blood on both sides."

"You are right in that," she said, undoing the leather tie on one shoulder of her dress. As the first knot came undone, it became clear that the ties weren't decorative. They were holding the garment together. And she was actually going to take a bath in the bathhouse.

Sienn went for the other shoulder. "Regardless of what you've been told, Ian, no lines have died. They have simply been suppressed. I am proof of that." The tie came loose. As the dress began to fall, it unsettled me. I wasn't sure why. As Imma, when she'd wasted no time disrobing in front of me, I took full advantage of her boldness. Yet, as the cloth fell over Sienn's body to puddle about her bare feet, her oddly-timed, complete lack of modesty had me backing away.

"You don't seem very suppressed," I told her.

"I was liberated almost two years ago. I've had time to adjust."

"Two years?" That surprised me. "Who freed you?"

"I believe you call them rebels. They're labeled as weak and ineffective by the other races. Discarded like trash." Sienn stepped over the rim of the tub. Water rose up around her slender backside as she sunk down inside the cask. "In truth, they are simply people as any other." Her body disappeared beneath the surface. The tips of her hair floated around her face, darkening. "They are free people," she added.

"Why did they release you? Did they know what you are?"

"They were raiding camps all over Rella, looking to grow their numbers. Their leader came into possession of a record book from the slave camp where I was born. He discovered a mistake in the log where the name of my line had been misspelled for generations. The imbeciles had no idea what they had."

"I'm sure your new friends are taking good care of you."

"They are," she said, missing my sarcasm. "They've given me tomes and scrolls full of spells, information on my ancestors. With their help I have become what I should have been all along. And with the knowledge I gain, I repay them."

I squinted at her. "Repay how?"

"Imparting my wisdom, enlightening their minds…as any teacher would do for those anxious to be taught."

"You're training a band of thieving dissidents how to enhance their magic? How to tap into other lines? You can't be serious."

"They're slow learners. My ways are difficult for them. Being Shinree is difficult. They've been ignorant of what it means their entire lives. As was I."

"These precious pupils of yours have been harassing Rella's cities and villages for years. And now you're making them stronger? Instructing them how to do real harm? Don't you see how quickly this could get out of hand?"

Apparently she didn't. Unaffected by the shock and concern in my voice, Sienn offered a nonchalant shrug and leaned gracefully back in the water.

Floating serenely on the surface, her hair fanned out behind her. Water lapped against the sides of her breasts and the curves of her thighs.

The moment was remarkably similar to my first encounter with the Arullan girl. Nevertheless, I was very aware that Sienn wasn't a dream. She was here in front of me, accessible and, evidently, uninhibited. I was fairly certain she was mine for the taking—if I could get past her lies and her not-so-subtle evasions.

"What do you want?" I asked her.

"You."

Her response was as irritating as it was arousing. "Anything else?"

Sitting up, Sienn tilted her head to the side. Water trickled down out of her hairline and over the planes of her face as she held the pose, considering her words or (more likely) debating how truthful she should be. "Magic is so much more than attack or defense," she said at last, which was not an answer at all. "I can help you move beyond that. I can teach you to cross the boundaries that blood has drawn, to retain your strength when casting, and avoid an unwanted magic-price. Ian," she said my name with what sounded like sincerity. "You don't have to be at the mercy of your cravings. I can train you to control your need for magic, or at the very least, how to live with it."

"Thanks, but I'm living with it right now." I took a long, slow swig of the wine.

"Perhaps I can show you a more constructive way?"

"Such as?"

"Learning to let go of what drives you to cast. And what limits you."

"I'm a soldier, Sienn. You can't change that."

"Owning a particular blood is not the issue. Guilt, empathy, anger, pain—love. Emotion blocks your abilities. It clouds your judgment. Weakens your will."

"Then if I want to cast like you, I have to feel nothing?"

Sienn smiled like I was a dense. "I feel. Emotion merely does not shackle me. I can separate myself from it whenever I need to."

"You say that like it's a good thing."

"Ten years ago when you wielded the Crown of Stones against Langor, emotion drove your casting. Things happened you did not intend. Now, you live in fear of it happening again. And that fear chokes your abilities. It suppresses them. You don't need chains or *Kayn'l* to make you a slave, Ian. You do it to yourself every day."

My jaw tensed at the eerie familiarity of her words. They reminded me of the ones that came out of Taren Roe's mouth in the swamps. "What's the cost for this help you're offering, Sienn? I had to sell myself to get you to save Malaq's life back in Kael. Is that why you're here, to collect on my debt?"

"Not at all. I ask only that you meet someone. His name is Jem. He leads us toward a new future. He believes that with your help we can—"

I cut her off with a wave of the bottle and a rude bout of laughter. "That's what all this is about? Your spell at The Owl, breaking into the castle, seducing me, this elaborate ruse... You're trying to recruit me?"

"We could do great things together."

Looking at the wisps of hair curling about her face, at the water breaking over her taut pink nipples; I was pretty sure I wasn't thinking of the same great things she was.

"How did you find me in Kael?" I asked. "Were you tracking me?"

"I was in the city when that foul Langorian arrived."

"Danyon," I nodded.

"He wasn't very discreet, asking questions, threatening the merchants. He hired some locals as spies, so I tracked them. I assumed one would eventually spot you."

I stepped up to the tub, squatted down and felt the water with my hand. "You tried to get me out of the tavern before the ambush."

"I tried to keep you out of the city entirely. My boundary spell alerted me when you were close. That's when I cast on that the page—the jittery young one with all the hair?"

"Liel," I said, smirking at her description. "Why him?"

"He had an honest face, and I knew you wouldn't question his ties to the castle. It was painfully easy to make him believe it was his duty to bring you to King Sarin."

"You do realize these are people you're casting on? They aren't here for your amusement." Flinging the water off my hands, I stood. "Are you behind all this? Stealing the Crown of Stones, stealing my magic, bolstering Draken's conquests? Are you allied with Langor?"

"If I had the Crown of Stones, Draken would be dead and enslaving a Shinree would be punishable by death."

"Your rebel friends were in Kabri when it fell. They did nothing to help while the Rellans were being slaughtered. Which makes your claim of no alliance sound like complete bullshit."

"The Rellans are not our problem, or our enemy. Draken's attack simply gave us an opportunity to rescue many of our kind. We have no alliance with anyone."

"How do you know? Maybe you're esteemed leader is keeping you in the dark."

"He would never."

"Then you're just choosing to look the other way."

"I have no idea what you mean."

"A Shinree who is adept at crossing bloodlines is working with Draken of Langor. He resurrected the eldring, stole the Crown of Stones, and murdered both Rella and Kael's Kings. And he just sent a nasty spell my way. So right now," exasperation lent an edge to my voice, "I need you to wake the fuck up to what's really going on and give me the name of anyone you trained that might even be close to capable of wielding that kind of power."

Her lips pursed. "It isn't one of us."

"What about this man, Jem. How well do you know him?"

"Jem is my savior."

"Really?" That was the second time I'd heard that term recently. "Is that your assessment of him, or more of a self-appointed title?"

"It's what he is. Jem pulled me out of slavery. Fed me. Clothed me. When the *Kayn'l* wore off, and I was lost, he was there. As I am now for him. To my dying breath I will aid Jem in ending the Law of Suppression and bringing freedom to the Shinree."

"That's quite a goal. And quite a vow," I added, finding the level of passion in her voice worrisome. "You think he can do all that?"

"I do. Jem is a persistent man. A driven man."

"Is he a man who would use the Crown of Stones to make Draken High King?"

"A Shinree would never support a Langorian."

"Yeah, well there's been a lot of *never* happening lately." I flopped down hard on the bench behind me. "I'm starting to think the word doesn't mean what it used to."

Sienn watched me a moment. "You really are troubled by all this. Perhaps, if you unwind the answers will come? I can help with that." Lowering her lids, she gave me a persuasive smile. "If you so desire."

What I desired was to lick the streams of water off her body, but I could barely keep up with how fast she was switching tactics. From one minute to the next Sienn was bold, demeaning, aloof, seductive, and a little bit too desperate.

Gliding toward me, the water broke around her body. It fell away as she stood and stepped out of the tub. Droplets fled the ends of her hair and ran swiftly down over the pale skin of her breasts. The wet soaked into my breeches as she knelt down in front of me and placed her hands on my knees.

I took a shaky breath. "This isn't a good idea."

"Shhh." Her hands slid; up my legs, my stomach, my chest, my shoulders.

"Sienn, don't." But it was a weak protest. I wanted her hands on me. I wanted mine on her. To find out if she responded like Imma, if she felt the same, tasted the same.

Her fingers wandered over my face. I grabbed them. Water trickled off her skin onto my wrist, and it was still hot. If it were real it would have cooled by now.

I jerked away and stood. "Is this a spell? Did you cast this on me?"

"Your lust?" On her knees, she looked up at me and laughed. "No, Ian. Fate pulls us together."

"Fate doesn't like me."

"Perhaps he likes me." Multi-hued eyes on mine, Sienn began crawling, catlike, up the front of me. "You like me, don't you?" Slowly, she rubbed her wet, naked body over my swollen groin, wound her arms around my neck and into my hair, and said, "You like me a lot."

Held hostage by her eyes, my mouth moved reflexively toward hers. "More likely it's magic. Another way for Draken to distract me from the Crown of Stones."

"Such a wary man," she teased. "Do you always look for something to mistrust?"

227

Putting a hand on her moist, bare hip, I pulled her in tighter. "I usually don't have to look very far."

Sienn opened her mouth to reply and I pushed my tongue inside. Her responding kiss was slow and sensual. Her hands roamed with a measured, easy pace, as if she was in no hurry to discover me. *Not like Imma. Not at all,* I thought, pleased. I liked the idea of leisurely exploring every inch of her.

Yet, tension had my entire body strung so tight it ached. And the more Sienn's tongue stroked mine, the deeper her fingers kneaded my arms and back, the more I wanted to push her down on the bench, the floor—up against the wall. Where didn't matter; only the outcome. I was desperately in need of the one thing I was never allowed in the dreams: release.

I dropped the bottle. My hands on her ass, I steered Sienn toward the wall and a blur of light flashed across my eyes.

Transitory, gone by the time we made contact, I dismissed the odd light in favor of Sienn's mouth. It was incredibly supple, her tongue agile and demanding.

The flash repeated. It lingered briefly, granting me a moment of form and color that were alarmingly familiar. *No,* I thought. *Not here. Not now.*

It came again, a burst of vibrancy. It blinked in and out until Sienn vanished altogether and suddenly—

It was dark skin I was touching. A young, round face I was kissing. The damp body against me was small and strong.

Long curls of black hair fell wet over my arms.

Full breasts pressed against me.

Trying to banish the apparition, I yanked Sienn closer. I kissed her harder. The mouth beneath mine responded, but there was blood on the air. It was on her skin, her lips. I tasted it on her tongue.

Pulling away in disgust, I looked into a set of wide Arullan eyes.

A bruised mouth said, "Save me."

I cried out—a wordless scream of rage—and the illusion shattered. The girl was gone. Sienn stood naked in front of me with a disturbing mix of humiliation and fearful dismay in her eyes, and I knew I should say something. I just didn't have the strength.

Despondent and breathless, I turned away. Sienn pulled me back. Her smile compassionate, she silently and gently smoothed the hair from my face.

There was genuine kindness in the gesture, and I hadn't expected that.

"I'm sorry," I said. I folded her into my chest. I wrapped my arms around the small of her back and pulled her close. It wasn't an advance. There was nothing sexual in the embrace. I just held her, drinking in the quiet, breathing in the steam.

Gradually, like she knew I needed it, Sienn put her arms around me. I couldn't deny it felt nice. Her embrace was warm and accepting. It made me yearn to slow down and relax, to stop fighting against the dream and against myself. It tried to convince me to let go of the indignity and the pretense, and admit that I wasn't okay. That I was barely holding on and I needed help. I just wasn't sure I needed it from her.

With difficulty, I broke away and stepped back.

"You're going," she said; with more anger than surprise.

"It's for the best."

"Why? Because I'm not Imma? I'm not some barmaid you can lead around like a puppet? Some whore you can pay and walk away from? Is that what you want from me? Is that all you want for yourself?"

I looked straight into her eyes. "No. It's not."

"Then listen to me, Ian. Fate wants us together. I know you can feel it. Open yourself up. We are the same." Sienn took my hand and placed it over her heart. It was beating strong and fast. I felt the pounding echo up my arm. My pulse stepped up to match hers and they formed a perfect, synchronous rhythm that seemed to resonate through us both. "It's wondrous, isn't it?" she said, watching amazement creep into my eyes. "I can show you how it's done. I can show you so many things. With my instruction, your magic will rise to heights you can't possibly imagine."

I hid my disappointment in a dark, angry laugh. "Damn, you're good," I said, moving her aside. "But you're wasting your time." I went to the door and drew the bolt back. "No matter how many tricks you play or how many times you take your clothes off, I'm not joining your damn cause." I gave Sienn one last, regretful look, and left her.

TWENTY EIGHT

The guise of Imma gawked at me from the kitchen. Underneath it, Sienn emoted nothing with her borrowed Kaelish face. She simply stared, waiting for me to pull myself together and come clean. She was entitled to it, having just bore witness to my violent waking. Watching my mind shifting back into reality, hearing me choke back a startled cry as recognition of my surroundings settled in.

I'd be a fool to try and convince her nothing was wrong.

I just didn't have the nerve to tell her that while the rest of the house slept soundly, roused by the gentle pre-morning light streaming through the windows, I'd been in a dark cave, hanging by my wrists over a pit of fire, awakened by my own screams.

I could still feel the hot smoke in my lungs.

Needing water, I reached into one of the bags piled beside me on the floor, and knocked into something. As it tipped, rolled, and smashed into the stone edging of the fireplace, I realized it was the bottle I'd left in the bath-house. Even after dropping it, and now banging it into the hearth, it was still intact, and as full as it was at dinner.

Bottomless and unbreakable, I thought gratefully.

Snatching it up, I found the courage and looked at her. Still, I said nothing, and neither did she. The alarm in Imma's eyes made clear Sienn's wish to know what was wrong. The longing in mine said I wanted to tell her. Yet she didn't ask, and I didn't offer. Neither of us was willing to speak first, and the moment stretched so long it could have easily turned awkward. Instead, it became something else, something intimate and vulnerable. It became the bathhouse all over again, with that same sense of crushing desire rising in me and the same, inexplicable attraction building between us.

It grew rapidly, making the impulse to go to her, to confess the dreams and beg her to make them stop—to strip off her dress and take her right there in the kitchen—so powerful, I could scarcely sit still.

"Sienn…" I said.

Jarryd ploughed through the front door. His abrupt presence startling us both, as Sienn jumped, I stood. Something hit the floor in the kitchen. The bottle fell from my hand, bounced, and didn't break. There was a table and six chairs between us, but we both looked guilty as hell.

If it were Malaq, he would have noticed the tension in the room right away and offered some witty comment that I wouldn't have found funny. Jarryd, however, shut the door, placed his bow on the table, and didn't react at all. Preoccupation glazed his stare.

"Everything all right?" I asked him.

"I guess," he replied. "Something had Malaq's horse going for a while."

"See anything?"

Shaking his head, Jarryd slid the quiver off one shoulder and shrugged with the other. "You know that damn beast of his is quicker to rile than I am."

I managed a smile. "We should get going. Where's Malaq?"

Sienn pointed to the floor-to-ceiling curtain dividing the back section of the house. "It was late when he finished with the horses. I let him have my bed."

I didn't ask what else she let him have. "Wake him."

"I'll do it," Jarryd said.

As Jarryd moved off, I grabbed my sword belt. I was strapping it around my waist when Sienn came over. She tried to catch my eyes, but I wouldn't let her. "I'm going on ahead to the trail," I said, pulling on my coat. Slipping on my other sword, I ran a shaky hand through my hair. "I need to cast."

"It's more than that," she said. "You look terrible." Sienn reached as if to touch me, but I bent down to pick up the rest of my things and she lowered her hand. "I wish you wouldn't leave. If you stay we can talk this out."

I settled the bags on my shoulders. Looking at her, I struggled for words, but I couldn't think of any that would get us past where we left it last night.

Then voices filtered out from behind the curtain and I stopped trying.

"Stall them," I told her. "I don't want them getting caught in my spell."

Moving around her, I went out the front door and down the steps. Jarryd had the horses ready so I threw my packs on Kya's back and tied them on. I could hear Sienn's boots treading softly on the dew-wet grass as she followed me out.

"I thought you might want this," she said.

I glanced back at the wine bottle in her hand. "Thanks." Taking it, I stuffed it in one of my bags. When I turned again, I found myself resenting the fact that it was Imma I was seeing and not Sienn. "Can you break a dream-weave?" I asked abruptly.

The question didn't seem to make sense to her at first. Then it did. "On you?" I nodded, and she frowned in response. "I assume it wasn't traditionally done?" I nodded again, and her expression deepened. "I've never worked with one."

"Oh." Her tone lacked the confidence I needed. "Never mind."

"Wait. How many dreams have you had?"

"I don't know. A lot."

"Then it's likely too late to reverse the damage."

"What damage?"

"It depends on the caster's intensions. If the goal of the dream-weave was to make you deathly afraid of spiders, then I can cast a spell that will keep spiders out of your dreams from now on. But the dreams you've already had, the experiences and sensations they triggered, are imprinted on your mind. They're woven into who you are." Distress softened Imma's eyes. "I'm sorry, Ian. But they're true memories now."

"No," I shook my head. "You have to take them out. There has to be a way."

"That's the deadly side of a dream-weave. If it isn't properly managed, or if it goes on too long, it wraps around your mind. It merges with your other memories, making it impossible to remove the false ones without drastically altering who you are."

"I'm already altered." Anguish lowered my voice. "I *see* things."

"Is that what happened last night in the bathhouse?" I said nothing, and she came closer. "With focus and concentration you can train yourself not to run when a spider drops from the ceiling. You can learn to live with it."

"Spiders," I laughed. "If only it were that simple."

"Come back inside, Ian. Let me try to end the spell. You clearly need sleep."

"No. We've been here too long already."

"Give me an hour. If can banish the dream, you'll never have to see it again."

Her words sounded so final. "Never?"

"Is that not what you want, to be rid of what comes to you when you sleep?"

"It is. But…"

Never? An irrational panic tightened my chest, and I suddenly realized how precious it all was. How precious the Arullan girl was to me. She was a figment, a ghost. A piece of bait that Draken and his witch threw out for me to catch. But the hook was in me so deep now. The torture, the pain of watching her die, was nothing.

It was the thought of losing her, of never being home again, that terrified me.

I grabbed hold of Kya's reins. "I have to go."

"You're in no shape to ride. Let me stop this."

"And then what?" I shouted, making her flinch and back away. "If I stop dreaming, what am I left with? Memories? Obsession? A craving that can never be satisfied? How am I supposed to live like that? How am I supposed to live without…" *her,* I thought. I put my boot in the stirrup and took to the saddle. "Ask him, Sienn," I said, turning Kya around. "Ask your friend, Jem, about Draken and the crown. And if you don't like his answer, then get as far away as you can. Because I'm coming for him." I gave the mare a kick." And you damn sure don't want to be there when I do."

TWENTY NINE

*M*y ears split with her cries. My wrists burned as I pulled against the chains, trying to move that last, final space that would let me touch her before she died.

"It doesn't have to be like this." Draken stepped over her body like a puddle of mud in the street. "No more pain. No more of this." He nudged her leg with his boot. "You are in control, Troy. More in control than you realize, of many things."

Leaning back against the wall behind me, I held up my shackled hands. "If I had any say in my life, do you think it would have come to this?"

"Actually I do. Life. Death. Fate. They are yours to command and mishandle. Not your gods. You Shinree put far too much faith in them."

"It's funny how everyone that speaks of faith and trust seem to have nothing but betrayal on their minds."

"You should take my advice, Troy."

"Fuck your advice."

Draken made a low, angry sound. "Then rot."

THIRTY

I wasn't sure how long I'd been lying on my back in the rain, or when the rain even started. It was nothing but a fine mist now, but my hair and clothes were soaked. The fire was out. It was almost dawn. There was just enough light to see the covering of branches we'd lashed together and wedged into an overhang of rock to serve as shelter for the night. The sun didn't quite reach inside beneath the bows, where Malaq and Jarryd were sleeping. They hadn't stirred yet, but they would soon. Then we'd get back on the road, where I'd spend my day pretending I wasn't looking for *her* in every shadow.

It was all I did now. Bide my time until she came to me again.

My mind was deteriorating so fast. I was afraid that when we finally reached Kabri, I wouldn't give a damn about it anymore. I was afraid I wouldn't even be me.

A faint shuffling disturbed my thoughts. On instinct, I reached for my sword and found an unfamiliar heavy, black boot standing on the sheath.

Another delusion, I thought. But I changed my mind as I looked up past the man's boots and under the edge of his cloak, where stone-laden swords hung off his hips. Rows of smaller gemstones studded his leather gloves. A plain, bronze mask hid his face from view. Escaping from one edge of the mask was a single shock of colorless hair.

I rolled the other way and stood up. "I was wondering when you'd show."

His deep voice filtered out from behind the mask. "I thought we should talk."

Of a similar height, I looked him in the eyes. All I could see was magic. "I'm surprised you came in person."

"I considered inhabiting one of your companions as I did Roe. But that might have gotten us off to a bad start." At my glare he gestured at the shelter. "They are unharmed."

"That's good of you." I bent over and grabbed Sienn's bottle from my pack.

"Not that I understand why you care. You can't believe they would have the same concern for you, a Shinree? You're nothing to them. Especially to the Rellan. You're a weapon, a tool for regaining his kingdom. A thing to be used and thrown away." The man shook his head. Another piece of white hair came loose from the mask. "It doesn't matter," he said. "The Rellans, the Kaelish, even the Langorians, are the past. *We* are the future. We will shape the world. Dominate it. Advance it in ways the lesser races couldn't possibly conceive of."

I nodded like I was picturing his description. What I was really doing was wondering how his big head fit in the mask. "Mind if I ask who rules in this imaginary future of yours? Because if it's a power-hungry Shinree, and an insane Langorian tyrant, you better take me out now. I'd rather not live to see it."

An emotion I couldn't place moved him forward. "I will not have you dead."

"I know of only one reason to conjure shadows."

"Those were merely to get your attention, to convince you to see things my way."

"How long were you planning on convincing me? Until I stopped breathing?"

"If necessary. But perhaps when I returned the air to your lungs, you would have been a bit less petulant."

"Don't count on it." Pulling the stopper out of the bottle, I sat down on a small grouping of rocks. "What of Malaq? Would you have saved him from the shadows?"

"Taiven's bastard? That half-breed means nothing to me."

"That half-breed is Draken's brother. Or aren't you two cozy anymore?"

"Draken has no patience for fools. Malaq Roarke elected the dangerous path with you over safe passage with Captain Krillos. There is nothing more to be said."

"So I stay alive because I'm Shinree. But everyone else is fair game?"

"You leave me little choice."

"As you leave me."

His magic-filled eyes tightened. "Would I come here if I were that easy to kill?"

"Yeah, I think you would. I think you assume that I share your misguided sense of brotherhood. And you want something. So let's get it over with." I took a drink and pushed to my feet. Reaching into my shirt for the cord, I pulled the obsidian out so it was visible. "Come on. I'll even let you have the first move."

His breath came hard and fast as he stared at the shard. He stood a while, mentally drooling over it. But that's all he did.

"I don't get it," I said. "I keep making that offer, yet no one takes me up on it. Why is that?"

With what seemed like great effort, he lifted his eyes. "The obsidian's aura has merged with yours. It clings to you on a level you aren't ready to recognize."

"Meaning?"

"You must remove it voluntarily. Another can do so only after you are dead. And I won't give that order. Your potential for greatness is far too promising to waste."

"Thanks. But you're really not my type." His responding growl of irritation made me grin. "Since you mentioned it though, does this potential of mine have anything to do with what you just said…about the stone's aura merging with me? How is that even possible after I've cast it out?" I pointed the bottle at him. "You can throw 'why' in there too, if you like."

"I'd rather not. What I can tell you is that the obsidian identifies you as a potential path toward re-unification with the crown. It wants to be whole again."

"It's a rock. It doesn't want anything."

He laughed at my ignorance. "You have so much to learn."

Grinding my teeth on his gall, I said, "Okay then, *wise-one*. How did you get to be so damn well-informed? I've never heard of any writings that speak of the Crown of Stones in such detail."

"Of course not. Your knowledge of our history is limited, as with most slaves."

"I'm not a slave."

"It would be easier if you were. Then you might have learned at least some semblance of obedience. For, if you don't start cooperating soon, life will become quite unpleasant."

"From where I'm sitting, it's been unpleasant for a while now."

"It could be worse. Don't you understand that? I'm holding Draken back for you. If I can't make you yield, he will kill you—as slowly and painfully as possible."

"That's what the dream-weave is for? I'm no good to you dead, but if I'm crazy I'll hand over the shard and follow you right off the fucking deep end."

"I couldn't have you continuing to oppose me. I had to do something."

"To convince me?" I corked the bottle and dropped it. Leaning forward, elbows on my knees, arms crossed, I thought about the knives in my braces and wondered: *can he cast faster than I can throw*. And: *if he's dead, will the dreams stop?*

"The dreams will worsen," he said, as if divining my thoughts. "Your fixation on her will grow beyond tolerance. You'll see her when she isn't there. Hear her voice when others speak. Perhaps, you already do."

"She isn't real."

I heard him sneer. "If you surrender, I will stop the spell. You have my word."

"I'd rather have your head."

"Gods," he snarled, "how can you be so cavalier? Inside of two, maybe three months, you'll be crawling on the ground begging for mercy. And if you think to break my dream spell, that won't be easily done. There is too much intent behind it."

"Your intent or Draken's? Or are they one in the same?"

He didn't expect that. Recoiling, the man dropped his gaze. "You wouldn't understand." He turned away. As I stared at him, watching the rain pick up, my choice of words and his lack of a ready answer, brought to mind what Jarryd said back in Kael.

His idea, about a Shinree sharing souls with a Langorian, had seemed preposterous then. It didn't seem anything near that now.

"You're tied to him, aren't you?" I asked. "That's how Draken's madness was tempered. You joined souls." He didn't answer, and I pressed him. "You gave Draken of Langor a part of your sanity, your personality, and it tipped the scales. It gave him back what I took from him ten years ago with the Crown of Stones."

"It was the only way."

"Son of a bitch." I hadn't wanted to be right. "How much of Draken's madness is in you?"

"Enough to make him fit to rule."

"Draken was *never* fit to rule."

"Do you forget that with our bond I have his memories?"

"That must be fun."

"Draken was always a spoiled, malicious sort. A callous, violent bully, if you will. But you, Troy…you're the one that ruined him."

"Are you fucking serious? You're blaming me for what he's done?"

"Draken was not always as he is now. He was shaped…by his father, by kingship, by war…by you. Your spell changed him. It's changed us both."

"No—that was *your* doing. You made his madness your own. Not me."

"You shouldn't take offense. I'm actually quite fascinated by the impact one little working can have on so many lives. What Draken garnered from me in our exchange, his intimate knowledge of our people…I irrevocably changed his perceptions of us. Then I put him on his throne. The King of Langor is indebted to a Shinree." He laughed to himself in cold, dry amusement. "The power our kind hold is far greater than what can be contained in a stone. You'll see," he said with promise.

"I hope so. Because I certainly don't now. I don't have a fucking clue how you could do it. How you could resurrect one of our people's most sacred traditions for that merciless bastard. After all the suffering he's brought to this world?" I walked over, gripped the man's shoulder, and spun him around. "Tell me you were forced into this somehow, coerced, tortured, anything. You couldn't have done this freely."

"I did this for the Shinree!"

I looked at him, baffled. "What are you hiding? Take off the mask."

"No." He yanked loose. "Not yet."

"Take it off. I want to see the face of the man reckless enough to risk his soul for...?" I stopped. "What exactly are you getting out of this?"

"When Draken is named High King he will revoke the slave laws. There will be no more breeding. No more *Kayn'l* to make us impotent and weak. The Shinree will have their own place in the world, their own land. We will have a new empire."

"With you as our ruler? Is that what Draken promised you?"

"We will regain our place. And no one shall take it from us again."

"Damn. And I thought I was losing touch with reality." Laughing, I backed away. "You know, I'm not blind. Or indifferent," I added, thinking of Sienn. "But what you're doing...Draken's soul has twisted whatever good intentions you once had."

"You think me a monster."

"Yes, I do...Jem." Beneath the cloak his body stiffened. "Yeah, I know who you are. But what I don't get is how you go from leading a group of thieving dissidents to thinking you can rule an entire race." Walking back to my blanket, I picked up my sword belt and put it on. Jem didn't try to stop me. We both knew I wasn't going to draw on him. With the magic he was channeling a blade would be useless. I just felt better wearing it. "Where did you come from? You couldn't have been free all this time or you would have been stirring up trouble long before now."

"I was as all the others, a slave without a name. I was nothing." He stared a long moment at the ground between his boots. Head bent slightly forward, rain gathered and ran like tears down the sides of his mask. "It's ironic, really. She was simply trying to bring her brother back. She had no idea what freeing me of the *Kayn'l* would lead to. No vision, no notion what Draken and I could accomplish together. And no spine to see it done. He should have killed the useless bitch instead of marrying her to the Kaelish."

"Wait. Are you talking about Queen Jillyan, Draken's sister? She freed you?"

Jem shirked my question. "Think about it. A land united by one king and allied with the Shinree people. No threat would be worthy of our time."

"It's certainly ambitious. But you can't believe Draken will let you live to see it."

Jem whirled around to look at me full-on and more hair tumbled free of the mask. The short strands draping across the bronze plate were dark before the rain hit them.

Magic-scars, I thought, *from the crown.*

Like mine.

"Draken is *Nef'taali*," Jem said then, matter-of-fact. "He would never harm me."

"Even carrying half his soul, you can't see how black it is?"

Jem repeated himself. "He would never harm me." But there was a strange, sad helplessness in his voice. I couldn't tell if the man was naïve, confused, or just plain delusional. Regardless, he was dangerous. I couldn't risk a confrontation with Jarryd and Malaq so close. I had to put him off.

"So," I said, "you're here to offer me a job? I've never built an empire before. What's the pay? Hope it's better than what you gave Taren Roe."

"I don't appreciate being ridiculed."

"Then stop talking in riddles. Tell me what you want. I'll consider your offer."

"You aren't ready to consider anything. You're still clinging to your first instinct to kill me. You would have tried by now, except you're afraid to cast with your companions here. Even to stop a monster such as me."

"Unlike you, Jem, I don't take casualties lightly."

"You talk of the dead like they're all my doing, like you have no hand in this."

"I didn't raid Kabri. I didn't kill Raynan Arcana. Or Sarin."

"No, you boast and threaten, waste my time with insults and bravado— because war is nowhere in sight. It's a memory. A notion. But I promise you, Troy, Rella *burns*. It *bleeds* while you stand here judging and defying me." Crossing the camp in long angry strides, Jem stood before me. His breath raged wild through the mask. "Would you like to see? To know what your stubbornness has wrought?" Raising an arm to the side, he opened his gloved hand. His eyes on me began to glimmer and shine. "Would you like to witness their suffering? Count how many die while you hold onto that little trinket around your neck out of spite?"

Whispers left his lips, and my muscles stiffened. "What are you doing?"

Paying no heed to my question, Jem traced a shape in the air with his finger, once, twice, three times. On the fourth time around, an outline formed in the dark. It was faint at first, but after another pass, four connected lines of dim white light came into being.

The lines pulsed. The lights brightened. The shape they made grew taller. It changed and stretched until the banded strands of energy ran fast and hot and colorful, all along the edges of a distinct door-like pattern. Outside the door was night. Inside, was undulating darkness punctuated by tiny random sparks of magic. They popped in and out of existence faster than I could focus.

Holding my breath, I reached out. As if reacting to my approach, the sparks jumped. Warmth radiated from the center and gathered in front of my outstretched hand. It was incredible. "Did Sienn teach you this?"

"Sienn is a woman of many talents."

I edged up to the threshold. "Where does it go?"

"Step through and find out."

"No." I glanced at him. But the door tugged my eyes back. "I don't think so."

Jem moved up behind me. He leaned in, whispering, "It wasn't a request," and pushed me.

THIRTY ONE

I hit the dirt face first. Picking my head up, my first breath was smoke. Dust came next, rising thick from the road as Langorian warhorses thundered past. People rushed by me on all sides, bumping, jostling. Screaming. Fire raged into the night sky, consuming walls and rooftops, so close I could taste the heat and feel it on my skin.

Gathering myself up, I tried to get my bearings, but I had no idea where I was. I grabbed the arm of a stout Rellan woman carrying a small bundle against her chest. I pulled her aside. "What's happening? What village is this?"

The woman gave me a strange, vacant look. Tear trails stained her dirty cheeks. Ash darkened her skin and clothes. She said one word, "Draken," and the bundle in her arms started crying. Tiny hands struggled to break free of the wrappings.

I let her go and drew my sword.

"That won't do any good," she wailed. "Fight, run…it makes no difference. We will all die." Sobbing, she staggered away, and the current of the panicked crowd carried her down the road. She blended with the sea of terrified faces fleeing certain death, and the years began to melt away.

I remembered other villages, other women fighting to carry their babes to safety.

I remembered most of them didn't make it.

A sharp elbow to the gut snapped my mind back to the present. It wasn't intentional. The crowd was simply growing in speed and number, and I was in the way.

Making myself more so, I pushed back into the heart of the throng. I returned to the exact spot where I'd appeared a moment ago. But there was no sign of the door. The spell was over. Wherever Jem had sent me, I had no apparent way back.

Only, he hadn't dumped me in some random Rellan village being raided by Langorian troops. From what I knew of door-makers, they couldn't open one unless they, or the person they were casting for, had a strong connection to someone on the other side. Since Jem didn't give a damn about Rellans, his anchor wasn't a villager. And if Jillyan discovered him in the mines, he probably didn't hold much love for the average Langorian soldier, either. *A King isn't average*, I thought. And there was no stronger connection between two people than a bond of the soul, like what Jem shared with Draken.

I stared at where the woman and her child had disappeared. She hadn't merely said his name out of fright. *Draken is here.*

With a sudden rumbling crash, the row of buildings behind me collapsed. The night exploded with a blast of light and fire, propelling me forward onto my knees. Towering waves of black smoke and dust rolled over me. A rain of embers and debris pelted my hair and clothes.

Brushing the ash and cinder off as I stood, sprinkled in between the cries of the crowd and the roar of the flames, I caught the brief, faint echo of shouting men and clanging metal. It was coming from behind the stampede of villagers. It was what they were running from.

I pushed free of the horde and veered off the main road. Taking to the alleyways, I weaved in between buildings. Flames shot out the windows as I passed. Billows of dusky smoke challenged my sight, making it hard to dodge the flying glass and splintering wood. I could barely make out the bodies I was tripping over. Still, I took time to check each and every one. They were all dead.

Following the sounds of battle, I made my way through the maze of destruction and came out at the edge of town. Draken was nowhere in sight. But I found what I was looking for. Stretched across the road, fifty or so

Rellan guardsmen in white, blue, and black were struggling to hold the line. Another thirty were fighting on horseback.

The blaze was raging at their backs. They were enveloped in a haze. All choking and fighting blind, it was possible they had no idea that well over two hundred Langorian soldiers were bearing down on them.

Looking to tip the odds, I tightened my grip on my sword and dove into the fray.

And it was like no time had passed. As if only hours ago I'd been fighting under Aylagar's command, in these exact same conditions, possibly in this exact same village.

My instincts felt the familiarity as well, and as I cut through the Langorian force, my swings and evasions were an unconscious reflection of my experience with this particular enemy. I knew their limitations as well as my own. I knew the weak points in their armor and their weapons. I understood the way they fought, fast and hard without a thought to precision or aim. The occasional variations on their attacks didn't throw me. I watched for signs of how their massive bodies moved to tell me which strike was coming next. Mostly, though, Langorian troops went for the kill with every blow. Considering their size it was an effective tactic on helpless or untrained men and women.

I wasn't either of those things. Throwing all they had into every swing left them wide open, and I had no trouble finding my way in.

Swerving from a swift moving axe, I lunged, pivoted, and sunk the length of my blade between the joints of the armor of the man in front of me. I slammed an elbow into the throat of the one at my back, just below the edge of his helmet.

Deflecting blow after blow, I kept them off me. But I was surrounded. I was in the center of it all, where the bulk of the enemy was pushing forward. So far, I'd taken only glancing blows, but that could change in an instant. To stay alive long enough to help the Rellans, I needed more than steel.

Turning to the stones at my wrist and gathering the obsidian inside me, in one breath I wished for strength in my blade, the stamina to wield it, and the speed to avoid my enemy's attacks. In the next, I cast.

Magic flew swiftly out of me. Pleasure swept in just as fast. As men started dying in a wide circle around me, power rippled across the sword in my hand. It sped down through the muscles in my arms and legs, and my sight came back in time to see the soldiers at the outer reach of my spell go down. Mounted, as their life drained away, their massive warhorses succumbed as well. The foam of exhaustion already bubbling from their mouths, the frantic animals let out terrible, desolate wails as their tall, muscular bodies went limp and slammed hard to the ground.

One after the other—five, ten, fifteen of the great beasts fell, trapping the dead and the living beneath them and sending a heavy spray of dust into the already murky air.

It was a dramatic sight that brought an instant hush over the battle. Soldiers on both sides disengaged and turned to stare through the haze at the wide circle of Langorian bodies surrounding me. Silent but for their heavy breaths, what was left of the enemy held position. But they didn't advance. They knew me. They had just witnessed the hunger of my spell drastically reduce their numbers in mere moments. They were afraid what I might do next.

The Rellans knew me too. I watched their faces carefully, waiting for them to cower. And it moved me greatly to see that they were far from afraid. To the contrary, it was clear; in me, they saw a chance for something other than defeat. They saw hope.

A rousing cheer rang through the Rellan ranks. They rushed forward. The Langorians met their charge. The two sides ran straight into each other, and once more, screams and the sounds of metal filled the night. Adding my cries to theirs, I swiped a club from the nearest corpse and joined in.

Leaving the Rellans do their job at the front, I went the other direction to attack the back half of the enemy column. My opponents tried to avoid me, but it wasn't possible. Guided by intuition, driven by resolve, magic fed my blows. With one hit of the metal club in my hand, shields and helms split. My blade slashed through leather and chain, even steel, as easily as the flesh beneath. Swords broke in half. Skulls caved and kneecaps shattered. Never before had I cut through a line as quickly or precisely. Never had a hasty battlefield spell been so powerful or so flawless.

All I'd set out to do was give myself an edge. It was something I'd done hundreds of times under Aylagar's command. Instead, I was slaughtering them.

I wasn't even breaking a sweat.

Running out of challengers, I turned to look for more. The Rellan soldiers were outnumbering their enemy now, but a decent-sized cluster of Langorians were still at the edge of the village. There, soldiers on horseback were tossing torches through windows and onto rooftops, working to bring down the last structures still standing. Those on the ground stood with weapons-ready, as the rising flames forced the villagers outside—like lambs to slaughter.

I dropped the club. Swinging up onto an empty saddle, I kicked the warhorse beneath me into a fast run. Passing a few enemy stragglers on the road, I slashed them open and kicked them to the ground as I raced by. Pushing as close as I dared to the blaze, as I slid to the ground, the nearest building buckled and caved. Dozens of villagers stumbled from the burning doorway. Eyes blinded by smoke, they ran down off the crumbling porch, straight into the arms of the enemy.

Swords flashed. Bodies crumbled. Butchering old women, children, even those already injured, the Langorians showed no mercy.

I started forward to teach them some.

Then a short figure emerging from the flames caught my eye. It zigzagged down the broken steps and out into the street. It broke through the mushroom of black smoke and became recognizable as a young boy. Small, slight, and obscured by the cloud, he'd managed to stray away from the massacre. Unfortunately, he didn't stray far enough before succumbing to a fit of coughing and falling to the ground.

Loudly, the boy wailed over and over for his mother.

I looked over at the Langorians. They had yet to notice him. Neither were any of the villagers reacting to the boy's call. Many were already dead. Others were begging for their lives. Men were being tied and beaten. Women struggled against pawing hands.

There was a chance the boy's mother was among them. But even if she were, and even if I could save her, his crying would draw the enemy before I could get back.

The boy first then.

But there was someone on the hill behind him.

Just beyond the town, about halfway up the grade was the shape of a tall man on horseback. Swathed in black, bathed in light and shadow from the flickering flames, as the man descended the hill, he stared down on the death and devastation like a proud father. His back was straight, his broad shoulders square. He held his head high, as if beholding such vicious deeds brought the man nothing less than sheer satisfaction.

His name rumbled from my mouth, "Draken," and the cries of the villagers and the boy became background. All thoughts of saving them vanished. Anticipation coursed through my veins. Hatred burned in my gut. I was enmeshed in the chaos of my dream-fueled vengeance. Suddenly nothing existed but the man in my sights…and my need to see him dead.

I ran toward Draken. As if sensing me, his head snapped in my direction. Tapping the sides of his mount, he started moving faster, and I hurried to meet him. I was so focused on finally getting my hands on the bastard, that when a piercing wail rang out behind me I didn't even slow down.

It came again. This time, the wealth of terror and desperation in the cry opened a crack in my single-minded objective, and I spun around.

The boy was still in the road. I had run right past him.

On his back, on the ground, he was dwarfed by two hefty Langorian soldiers. Slapping him down as he tried to stand, kicking him as he crawled away, their huge, round bellies shook with laughter at the child's frantic attempts to fend them off.

They drew their weapons, and I ran to intercept.

Coming up behind the men, I raised my sword to swing—and my body suddenly lurched backwards.

Still on my feet, I tried again. I tried to force myself forward. Yet, I couldn't gain any momentum. It was like an arm had wrapped around my waist and it was pulling, dragging me back. But there was nothing there.

Struggling against the invisible force, blinding sparks erupted around me. The air twisted and warped.

An axe swung for the boy's head, and I sunk rapidly backwards into a rush of wind and color. Darkness swept over me then. It cradled me. Then it vanished, and wet grass came at me fast. I landed on my side in the near dark, out of breath, and covered in filth. The mountain air was clear, quiet, and full of rain.

There was no smoke, no flames. The burning village and the boy were gone.

"No!" I cried, scrambling up from the ground. "Send me back! You fucking send me back right now!"

Through the mask, Jem's eyes ran over me. "You have been busy."

I looked at my hands and clothes, at the blood and the soot. I pictured the boy and imagined the axe biting into his neck. "You fucking bastard. I could have helped them. I could have killed Draken!" Blood pumping furiously through my veins, teeth clenched, I rushed up into Jem's face. "Send me back NOW!"

"Such rage," he said with delight, "such pure aggression. This must be what you were like when you channeled the crown. When you stripped the land to desert and painted it with blood. Oh, what a glorious sight you must have been." Jem's eyes gleamed eagerly. "I need you to be that way again."

"I don't give a shit what you need." Feeling my battle spell fade, the crushing fatigue I'd been living with for weeks returned anew. I shoved my blade away. "Go. If you aren't here to kill me, just…fucking go."

I could hear his angry, rasping breath. I expected more ridicule or another round of threats. Instead, Jem let out a roar and moved to strike me. He was a little slow.

Catching his jab with my left hand, I went for his mask with my right. I started to rip it off when he reached up and closed his free hand around my wrist.

"I said not yet." Jem tightened his grip. Steadily increasing the pressure, pain penetrated deep into my arm. Blood stopped flowing to my fingers. I couldn't feel them.

Magic was enhancing his strength.

Having no choice, I let go of the mask. But my submission wasn't enough.

Retaining his crushing hold on my wrist, Jem tightened it. "You will learn obedience," he promised. He squeezed harder. I felt things compressing. Bending. Breaking. "One way or another…you will learn."

Releasing his fist from my left hand, I clipped Jem hard across the jaw. I hit him a second and a third time. I tried to pry his gloved fingers off. In retaliation, he clamped down with a tremendous, crushing force. He delivered one last, brutal squeeze, and the bones in my wrist snapped like kindling.

At the sound, Jem smiled. When I didn't cry out, though, his eyes widened. "To withstand such pain in silence is commendable. Perhaps I misjudged you."

I responded with a gasping laugh. Had I breath to spare, I would have set him straight. Bone had penetrated skin, and I would have been screaming. If not for the Crown of Stones overriding the pain.

Like many things lately, I couldn't explain it. But at the points where our skin made contact, I could feel the power in Jem's veins. I felt the place where he channeled from: a deep well, dark and cavernous. I recognized the auras that filled him as they swirled and pulsed in vibrant color. The heat of his wrath and his intense cold determination; I sensed how it blinded him. And I knew that somewhere inside the man, he was conflicted.

"Leave!" he shouted. But I didn't even know how I got in. Then Jem whispered in Shinree, and everything inside me came to a standstill. My heart constricted. My lungs emptied. Muscles turned flaccid and organs seized. Pain severed our odd link.

It was only Jem's unwavering hold that kept me upright.

Shoving his other hand in my hair, he pushed my head back, wanting my eyes. "I hadn't thought to find you so disagreeable, so…contrary. You're going to force me to break you, aren't you? I really didn't want that." Jem sighed and released me—my broken wrist from his hand, my body from his spell.

I cried out then. Able to feel now what he'd done to my wrist; I'd just traded one agony for another.

Shock took hold fast, and I started shivering. Blood dripped from beneath the brace on my arm. It ran down over my hand faster than the rain could wash it away.

Clinging to my rage, I fought to stay standing. "I won't let you keep the crown."

"You will never get near the Crown of Stones."

"I don't need to get near it," I blustered. "Not anymore."

"You are developing faster than I expected. I admit that. But by the time you realize what's happening, it'll be too late."

Trembling so hard I could barely speak, I stammered out an unimpressive, "G-go f-f-fuck yourself."

"I see my mistake. You've spent the last ten years building up a tolerance to temptation. What I need is a concentrated attack to break through your armor." Jem reached out. He put a finger on my forehead. "Let's see what a couple years' worth of dreams will do to soften your resolve."

"No..." I tried to move, but his slight touch held me in place.

He started whispering again. The forest began to change. The trees blurred.

Ghostly images of armed soldiers flickered in and out of view.

I threw a desperate glance at Jarryd and Malaq sleeping in the shelter, hoping the sight of them would somehow keep me here. But their bodies were already fading.

Air whipped around me bitter and cold. Snow pelted my face.

I shook the fantasy away. "Don't do this."

Jem stopped chanting. He looked at me. "Are you ready to give me the stone? Will you help me create an empire like the world has never seen?"

She stood behind him, at the edge of a frozen pond.

Wearing nothing but a warm, woolen cloak, she beckoned me.

I struggled to focus. "I will never let you have that much power."

Behind the mask, Jem's eyes tightened. "Then I bid you sweet dreams."

THIRTY TWO

Voices pulled at me.

"Ian, wake up."

I wanted to open my eyes. But her body was curling up, pressing against me.

"God damn it, Ian." Nervousness strained Malaq's voice. "I know you can hear me. Wake up!" Anger too. He threw a punch at my face. Distantly, I felt it.

He grabbed me to throw another.

"Malaq, stop," Jarryd intervened. "It's no good. And…he's hurt enough." Jarryd touched my right arm and pain had me nearly coming up off the ground—more than enough to wake me. But it didn't. "What are we going to do?" he asked.

Malaq's reply was simple. "We keep moving."

"He needs a healer," Jarryd argued.

"I know. I'll figure something out."

"We can't travel with him like this."

Malaq was quiet a moment. His boot kicked my leg. "Why the hell won't he wake up?"

I'm trying…

"Where are you going?" Her hand caressed my face. "I'm right here."

Screaming, I tried to throw them off. I tried to tell them to stop, that I could feel everything. But the words wouldn't come. Nothing responded like I wanted, my voice, my body.

All I could see was blackness.

The sun burst out from behind the clouds.

I shaded my eyes from the sudden brightness.

"What's wrong?" Her slender, dark fingers entwined mine. "I thought you wanted to go for a walk."

"I do," I said. "I'm fine."

"This way." She tugged at me. As we strolled, blossoms kicked up from the meadow. They took to the breeze, floating on the air, turning it pink. I waved them away, but she let them fall as they pleased; a burst of color settling on the pleats of her drab, muslin skirt, a subtle trimming clinging to the gently swaying strands of her long black hair.

Glancing at me, she smoothed a curl behind her ear. "Tell me again."

"Again?" Laughing, I shook my head. "No way."

"Come on" she begged, wrapping her arms about my waist. "It's funny."

"It's not funny. It's humiliating."

"Right," she grinned devilishly. "Which makes it funny."

I tensed at a sound. "Did you hear that?"

She squeezed me. "Quit stalling!"

"No, there was an echo, like someone yelling."

"You're going to kill him!" Jarryd shouted.

"I'm not going to kill him," another man replied tartly. "But you need to secure him better. I can't have him thrashing about right now."

His voice…

Langorian, I thought. I struggled harder.

Weight pressed down on me.

Quietly, Jarryd said, "It'll be over soon. Just hang on."

She pulled at my arm. "Please? It's a great story. Just one more time?" Nuzzling against me, she flashed a coy smile and batted her eyes.

"You're shameless, you know that?" She batted more, and I relented with a sigh. "I didn't know he was a woman."

"You really couldn't tell?"

"With the hair on her chin?" I shuddered. "No, I couldn't tell."

"And when her money was gone, and she started betting with pieces of her clothing?"

"Her armor was solid steel."

"So you thought you'd sell it..."

"Dice was never my game, but it was the first time I'd been given leave, and I'd heard some of the troops talking about this seamy little inn near the border. I spent my whole three days in that goddamn filthy place. I'd gone through my coin and then some. The barkeep was eyeing me to pay up. A few of the men were egging me on. Course they'd been there dozens of times. They knew what I was headed for."

"Back off, Rellan," the Langorian barked. "I may not think he's worth the shit stain on my ass, but you brought me here to fix him. So I am."

"If you don't, you're dead." Jarryd warned.

The Langorian grunted. "And when Krillos discovers you stole the only physician in his camp, so are you. Then we'll break your broken witch a little more and lay him at Draken's feet."

"Shut your fucking mouth," Jarryd snarled. Steel sung as it left its sheath.

"Kane," Malaq said sharply. "Put Troy's sword away."

"This is a waste of time, Malaq. He's not going to help us."

"He will," Malaq said. "He has to."

"Why, because Prince Malaq Roarke abducted him out of bed, dragged him through the woods, and commanded him to? He's going to slit Ian's throat the minute you turn your back."

"Then I won't turn my back." Malaq's tone tempered. "Why don't you get started on the litter? I'll stay here and keep an eye on our guest."

Walking again, she dragged me with her. "So when did you figure it out?"

"By the time we'd both lost our shirts I had a pretty good idea those weren't muscles on her chest. Then she started insisting I take her upstairs. Said I could earn my coin back."

"Did you?" she laughed.

I made a face. "She was all over me, chasing me around the room, goods flapping, while the whole damn tavern laughed. I barely made it out alive."

"Stop," she giggled.

"Seriously. I had visions of suffocating under those things for days."

"I'm glad you survived." Her laughter waned. Desire shone in her eyes.

"Me too." Bending, I kissed her. My fingers on her face, I ran them through her curls, over her arms and across her back.

With a gasp, she flinched. Warm wetness spread beneath my hands.

She went limp against me as Draken yanked the blade out of her back.

Behind her, he smiled. "Shall we play?"

———

"Ian…" Jarryd said nervously. "Ian—Stop!"

He tackled me and we grappled for the knife. It skimmed my chest as we rolled.

"Fight harder, Shinree," the Langorian sneered. "Put on a good show and maybe Draken will let her die quickly."

I swung my head into his. He recoiled enough for me to get both hands on his arm. Twisting it, I forced the knife closer to his body. I pushed.

I felt the blade penetrate flesh.

"Son of a bitch!" Jarryd bellowed.

Shoved, I fell. My face hit the ground. Hooves stomped near my head.

They moved away, replaced by boots.

"What happened?" Malaq said.

"Fuck," Jarryd muttered. "He fucking stabbed me."

"What? Where the hell did he get the knife?"

"It was in my belt. I didn't think… Fuck!"

"Let me see it." Malaq whistled. "I guess taking him on your horse wasn't such a good idea. We should have stuck with the litter."

"That last section of trail was too narrow. It wouldn't have fit."

"The blade's in pretty good," Malaq said plainly. "Ready?"

I heard Jarryd take a deep, uneven breath. He let out a clamped-mouth groan as the knife came out. "Goddamn it…" he panted. "What the hell is wrong with him?"

"I don't know," Malaq replied. "When we reach Rella we'll find a healer."

"Where? And what good will it do?" Pain roughened Jarryd's voice. "This isn't simple delirium. It's been too many days. There's no infection. No fever. This has to be a spell. Some kind of attack."

"Draken's magic user," Malaq agreed. "I told Ian he was going to come after him hard. But I didn't expect this."

Weariness thinned Jarryd's plea. "What do we do?"

Break it, I thought. *You have to break the spell.*

I tried to tell him: *Sienn. Find Sienn.* But the words were stuck in my head.

"We go on," Malaq said grimly. "That's all we can do."

Gods, why can't I wake up?

"What are you doing out of bed?" Her bare feet padded across the floor. She came up behind me and snuggled into my back. "It's cold without you."

"I can't sleep."

Reaching up, she kissed me between the shoulder blades. Her warm breath drifted over my bare skin. "I didn't say anything about sleep."

Hands coming around, she grabbed my wrists. Her grip was strangely tight.

"You think this is really necessary?" Jarryd said.

Malaq sounded surprised. "Five minutes ago you were ready to throttle him."

"It's not his fault."

"He stabbed you in the leg, Kane. Next time it might be somewhere a little more vital. I'm tying his hands and that's it."

"Let's go back to bed." Still holding my wrists, she pulled me across the room.

"You don't understand. I need to wake up."

"You are awake, silly."

I looked at her. The morning light hit her face. Her dark skin seemed almost transparent. "No. I'm not."

THIRTY THREE

The world was flying by in shades of brown. Flailing hands grabbed at me as I slid, caught in a hail of stone and dirt, and a tangle of arms and legs that weren't all mine.

I got a brief, inverted glimpse of the vertical drop I was plummeting down, then—*wham*! Something hard and flat stole my breath, and my momentum.

Coughing and groaning, I picked my face up from the dirt. I squinted though the dust, trying to make out who was beside me. "Jarryd?"

"What the hell was that?" His boots kicked pebbles in my face as he hauled himself unsteadily to his feet. "Are you trying to break both our necks?" he shouted, "or just mine? You goddamn, stupid...."

Jarryd went on. I didn't interrupt. I'd fallen halfway down the side of a mountain. I was winded and choking, my throat was dry, my body sore. I hurt too bad to squabble.

Eventually, Jarryd paused in his tirade to wipe a residue of blood and dirt from his lips. "Son of a bitch," he groaned, throwing an irritated glance up at the rise. Our empty horses were at the edge. Alongside them, peering down, was Malaq; no doubt glad to be monitoring our ensuring battle from a safe distance. "At least you're awake," Jarryd said, raking a hand over his tousled braid, ruffling the dust. "Maybe we can actually reach Kabri now...if you don't kill me before we get there."

"Gods, but you've grown surly."

His patience stripped, Jarryd lunged at me. "And just how the fuck else do you expect me to be? With you pale as death and raving like a mad man." Backing off, he looked me over. Something he saw made the tempest in his eyes die down. Distress settled into the dirty lines on his face. "Do you remember anything?"

"Some." I stared at my bound hands. My right wrist bore a splint and bandage that extended near up to my elbow. The stones Sienn gave me were wrapped around it, but my braces with the knives were gone, as well as both my swords. "Malaq was right to tie me," I said then, my eyes moving to the dressing on Jarryd's right leg. Having slipped out of position in our fall, the stitching had come loose from his recent stab wound. Dirt clung to the torn, wet edges. "I didn't know it was you," I said.

"It's fine." Jarryd gave his usual half-shrug. Taking the dagger from his boot, he bent down and cut me free. As soon as the rope snapped my splinted wrist began to ache.

Rubbing it gingerly, I scanned the surrounding area. "How far have we come?" Tilting my head back, I looked at the sky. It was clear and bright, but I remembered rain.

I remembered...

I drew in a sharp breath. Surreal images and sounds assaulted me. Random illusions surfaced, piling in, one on top of the other.

Her cries, the beatings, Draken's proud face; I recalled it all, swiftly and vividly.

How she felt under me, alive and warm—next to me, bloody and screaming.

Frantically, I whispered, "Not real, not real, not real," struggling to convince myself that I hadn't been at the mercy of Draken's men. I hadn't been in the girl's arms.

Dreams. They're just dreams.

But the conjured nightmares only pushed deeper, blending and overlapping. Repeating. Penetrating. Until pain and nausea doubled me over and whatever was in my stomach, came violently up and out onto the ground. Thankfully, it wasn't much.

Breathless, shivering despite the warm sun, I wiped my mouth on my sleeve. I looked down at my trembling hands and expected them to be red with blood. They were brown with dirt. *Idiot,* I scolded myself. *It's a spell. It's not real.*

She doesn't love me.

Because I let her die. I always let her die.

"Ian!" Jarryd called. "Are you hearing me?"

Confused, I looked at him through a curtain of sweat and dust-coated hair. He looked back, just as puzzled, and we watched each other like that for a moment, with me shaking, and him shaking his head like he had no idea what to do with me.

Malaq interrupted. "Are you two going to stay down there all day?" he shouted.

"A rope might speed things along," Jarryd yelled back. He sat down next to me. "You've been unconscious for twelve days."

"Twelve?" I swallowed. It felt far longer. "There was a Langorian. A physician?"

Jarryd nodded. "We watched him the whole time. I think he did all he could." Jarryd slid his knife away. He reached down and pulled me up. "Malaq was going to let him go, but the bastard came at me."

As Jarryd turned away to survey the ridge above us, I ventured across the oblong rocky shelf that broke our fall. Looking over the side, I gasped, "Shit." It was an alarmingly long way down. Inching back, I glanced up. Then back down. I studied the path of our descent. And it was clear: we should have been dead.

Somehow, miraculously, we'd landed in the one and only place on the entire mountainside that would stop our fall. If we'd gone over the cliff at a different angle or a few steps further along the trail, we would have missed the shelf entirely and kept going all the way to the rocky ravine at the bottom.

I turned around. I felt a deep need to apologize. I'd nearly killed us. But Jarryd wasn't on the slab anymore. He was on the slope, attempting to climb back up with his bare hands. "You sure that's a good idea?" I asked him.

"I swallowed half the mountain, Ian. I need a drink, and I'm not waiting for Malaq to braid a new rope…or whatever the hell it is he's doing up there." Catching hold of a gnarled root sticking out of the slanted ground, Jarryd gave it a yank to make sure it was secure. Sinking the toe of his boot into the dirt, he used the root to pull himself up.

It was a taxing but efficient climb, as Jarryd moved seamlessly from one root or vine to the next. I didn't like it, but he was making good progress.

When he was well over halfway to the top, he called down to me. "You aren't going to tell me what happened, are you? Malaq said you wouldn't. He also said it shouldn't bother me if you didn't." Jarryd looked back at me over his shoulder. "It bothers me," he said, and the vine in his grip snapped in half. He teetered backwards. Boots sliding on the loose pebbles, Jarryd threw himself forward and hugged the cliff face. "It's okay." He blew out a relieved breath. "I got it."

"You should come down. Wait for the rope. It doesn't look stable."

"No, I can do this. There isn't a cliff in Kabri I haven't climbed at least once." Jarryd shifted position. He reached for another vine. As soon as he touched it, the ground beneath him gave way. He struggled to regain his footing, to clutch onto something like before, but there was suddenly no traction. The roots and vines kept breaking. The terrain kept disintegrating at his touch. Everything Jarryd had used for leverage on the way up was refusing to bear his weight on the way down.

"Hold on!" Rushing forward, I scampered up the slope. Just as fast, the loose soil carried me back down. I tried again, but it was useless. The entire side of the rise was crumbling—and taking Jarryd with it.

He slid faster, grabbing in vain at the hill. Nearer, and I realized he wasn't even in line with the slab anymore. If I didn't stop him, the ravine would.

Jarryd tumbled closer.

He sped past me. And I jumped.

THIRTY FOUR

Throwing myself across the slab, landing hard enough to hear it crack, I caught the cuff of his sleeve in my right hand. My grip was sure. I had him. But the mountain was coming down on top of me, pelting my legs and back. I was sprawled out on the rim of the narrow jutting rock, and Jarryd's body was dangling over empty air, dragging me slowly and steadily across the sandy surface. I needed something to offset the draw of his weight. Or we were both going over.

Eyeing the approaching edge, I extended myself back across the shelf, groping for a niche or a ridge. But I had nothing to grab onto except the other side of the shelf beneath me, and nothing to grab it with but my broken arm.

I stretched. The splint restricted me.

Straining harder, clenching my teeth on the pain, I managed to reach my target. I wrapped my fingers around the edge. I gripped as hard as I could, and we stopped—with an abrupt jolt that sent agony reverberating from my fingertips to my collarbone.

Waves rolled up and down my injured arm, and into my hand.

And my grip on the ledge began to slacken.

"No... Damn it. Jarryd!" I cried, trying to make him stir. But he hung silently in my grasp while the spasms worsened.

My nerves were jumping and seizing. I couldn't stop my fingers from opening.

I let go, and we started sliding.

Grinding my jaw down to nothing, forcing my throbbing hand to bend and grab on, I dug into the rock. Fire consumed my entire arm as I clutched the side of the ledge with everything I had. It still wasn't enough. My hand was torn. I couldn't get any more out of my damaged wrist, and I didn't have it in me to pull Jarryd up one handed.

I was done.

"Malaq!" I shouted. There was no response. "Goddamn it!"

Straining, I pulled at Jarryd again and the heavy cloth of his tunic began to rip. I heaved harder. The rip widened. My grip weakened.

There was a way. One conscious roll of the dice I didn't want to make. *It'll work. It has to.*

The skin on my palm shredded further. Jarryd's lifeless body pulled on me.

I did it before, I thought. *And Malaq lived.*

I stared down at Jarryd. "So will you." Determined, I took in the aura of the citrine and wished for a boost of strength. With the same intensity, I clung to the obsidian inside me and commanded it to protect Jarryd. I ordered the spell to leave him alone, to gather what it needed from the trees, the animals in the brush or the birds in the sky. I prayed for it to feed on anything but his life.

A burst of pleasure, then a shot of energy, coursed through me. Strength bled down through my wounded arm into my fingers. All at once my grip held, and we came to another jerking halt that hurt like hell.

Bearing down, able to clutch the side of the overhang with purpose now, I started hauling myself back from the edge as I pulled Jarryd up. Stupidly, I hadn't thought to dull the pain. By the time I got half of him on the shelf with me, my shoulders and back muscles were raging. My left arm felt like it was being pulled off. My right was completely wrecked. At some point, the splint had snapped and red was spreading out across the bandage.

Ignoring it, I burrowed my fingers into him. "Jarryd," I begged through clenched teeth, "swing your other arm up." Getting no reply, I got angry. "Jarryd, you son of a bitch, you're not dead. You're not fucking dead, do you hear me?" I yanked harder. "If you don't wake up, I swear by the gods, I'm going to throw you down in that fucking ravine and tell Neela you ran off with some fat Kaelish dung hauler's one-legged daughter!"

After a moment of silence, he moaned. Tilting his head back, Jarryd struggled to open his heavy lids. "Dung hauler?" He mustered a faint, breathless chuckle. "That's the best you can do?"

"Fool," I grunted. "Thinking you can climb the side of a mountain like a goat."

Wetting his dusty lips, he threw his other arm up, grabbed on and started crawling over me. He reached the slab and flopped down on his back with a breathless, "Thanks."

I peeled my hand off the shelf and rolled over. "Don't mention it."

A pile of rope hit the ledge between us. "Sorry for the delay," Malaq hollered. "I had to lash all three of ours together for it to reach!"

"Will it hold?" I shouted back.

"Of course it'll hold," he answered crisply. "I tied them, didn't I?"

Jarryd grunted. "Smug bastard."

I took hold of the rope and yanked. "It's good. You first."

Moving like a man three times his age, Jarryd got up. He tied the end around his waist, braced his legs against the slope, and letting Malaq's horse do most of the work, walked his way back up to the top.

When the rope landed next to me a second time, I stared at it. I couldn't climb. I was shaking too badly from a debilitating assortment of relief, fatigue, pain, and a deep persistent panic. I was grateful Jarryd was alive. But the fact that he was, that my spell hadn't drained him, was another example of how strange and unpredictable my magic had become.

Jem said I wouldn't know what was happening until it was too late. He said the shard's aura had merged with me. *Would taking it off break our connection? Would it stop whatever was happening to my magic?*

Only, taking it off was exactly what Jem wanted me to do.

Disheartened, I leaned back against the slope. I stared across the expanse at the heavily forested mountains on the other side and tried to quell my uneasy mind. Blazing afternoon sun beat down on the adjacent green summit. The treetops were bathed in a layer of shimmering light. I took a slow, deep breath and watched a flock of birds circle the peak, dancing in the wind.

It was a stunning view, but for the large section of trees that had gone black.

No clouds were in the sky to make shadows. No noticeable rocky out-croppings or caves were visible. There was just a wide swath of dark trees directly across from my position. *Dark or dead*, I wondered.

I sat up. I couldn't see well enough to be sure.

I thought back, trying to remember my intentions when I cast.

I wished Jarryd safe from the spell. I wished the trees to die…and they did.

It sounded ridiculous. Diverting the magic-price to some place miles away, selecting what a spell drains; those things weren't possible for a Shinree soldier. Not without a tremendous amount of training. Yet, I'd done it. There was no other explanation.

I'd done the impossible.

The proof was on the other side of the ravine, and it scared the hell out of me.

THIRTY FIVE

The sixth cup of the night hit my lips and Malaq gave me judgmental raised brows across the table. "You keep that up," he said, "and tomorrow I'll be tying you to the saddle. Again."

Swallowing, I offered a vague grunt. Nevertheless, he was right. I hadn't eaten, and I was already drawing the stares of every pair of eyes in the inn—not that there were many. While the Faernore was the one stopping place on the entire pass that would put a roof over your head, rumors of war had spread quickly, and the place was near deserted.

"I'm not sure if you're aware," Malaq said, trying a more diplomatic voice. "But you're starting to resemble a man whose been dragged by his horse. You might want to do something about that."

"I just had a bath. Though, mine was a bit less crowded than yours." Recalling the unmistakable sounds of pleasure coming from Malaq's side of the curtain, I frowned. "And less enjoyable."

"Most definitely," Malaq grinned. "But that's your problem, Troy. You're always trying to do everything on your own."

Next to me, Jarryd laughed as he raised a hand to the barkeep. "Another!"

"Well, then," Malaq grumbled. "I guess I'll be lashing you both to the saddle come morning."

"Can't." Jarryd stretched in his seat. He let out a lengthy yawn. "You'd have to untie all that rope first. Shouldn't take too long, though. Not for an expert knot-maker like yourself."

Malaq eyed him. "Jealous?"

"Absolutely," Jarryd teased. "A man of your talents is wasted as a Peace Envoy. Or even a Prince. With your wide range of expertise you should be King. Kick Draken right off that throne in Darkhorne and take his place. We wouldn't have to worry about war then. Malaq Roarke could single-handedly turn the whole damn realm of Langor into lady-killers and fishermen. Well-dressed ones at that."

"King?" Malaq eyed me with a level stare.

I replied with a slight shake of my head, indicating I'd said nothing to Jarryd about Malaq's true reason for going to Langor. I didn't agree with his plan, but it wasn't my secret to spill.

"And here I thought you weren't capable of funny, Kane," Malaq said, attempting to downplay Jarryd's insightful jest. "All it took to let your sense of humor loose was a little flat tasteless ale…and a good amount of my coin." He brushed in disgust at the sleeve of his shirt. "I hope the innkeeper puts my money to good use. Like hiring someone to blow the dust off the tables once a year," he muttered, making Jarryd choke on his drink. "Easy there, kid," Malaq grinned. "Maybe you should call it a night."

Laughing, Jarryd wiped a hand across his mouth. "It's not the drink. It's being here, under a roof, sitting in actual chairs, at a real a table in a place that serves," he glanced in his cup, "something close to Rellan ale. I haven't felt this normal in a while."

"Don't get used to it," I told him, which prompted both of Malaq's brows to rise.

Leaning back in his seat, with contemplative, gray eyes on me, Malaq played with the coin in his hand, tossing it into the air and catching it.

On his fifth time through, I reached out and grabbed the coin. "Whatever you're thinking," I said, "stop. I'm fine." I handed him the coin.

He started tossing and catching again. "It's not your reflexes that concern me."

"Then what?" I sneered. "You want me to feel normal too?"

Malaq slammed down his coin. "How about you just go back to being delirious? That's certainly preferable to this god awful mood you've been in for the last three days."

"Three days ago I almost threw Jarryd off a cliff. I think that entitles me to—"

"Feel sorry for yourself? Get over it, Troy. I've wanted to throw Jarryd off a cliff a time or two myself." Malaq paused to shrug at Jarryd's questioning glance. "But I didn't. And neither did you—at least, not intentionally." Flinging himself back in his seat, Malaq picked up his coin. He tapped the edge a few times on the tabletop and moved on. "I had a chat with the barkeep. The bridge to Rella is a two day ride from here. I'm thinking we can do it in one."

"One's good," Jarryd said.

"I knew you'd say that," Malaq smiled. "I'll be leaving you after we cross. If retrieving the crown doesn't go as planned, once I'm settled in Langor, I'll get you whatever information I can."

"Sounds risky," Jarryd said. "They'll be watching you."

"I'll manage," Malaq replied.

"Not if you're dead," Jarryd snapped back.

"I have no intention of being dead."

"If Draken catches you betraying him, that's exactly what you'll be."

"He won't catch me," Malaq assured him.

"I've heard," Jarryd said in earnest, "that Langorians take traitors out into the mountains, break their arms and legs, and leave them for the skin bears." He nudged me with his elbow. "What do you think they'll do with our Prince here when the bears are done? Ship his bloodless remains back to Kael? Or leave him to rot?"

"I take it back," Malaq frowned at Jarryd. "You're not funny."

As usual, Jarryd popped off a comeback, but having learned weeks ago that enduring their banter was an ineffective use of my time, I found a better one; in the form of a shapely woman at the front counter. Dressed in typical barmaid fashion, with plenty of exposed skin and flowing hair, her features were mostly in shadow. I couldn't tell if she was pretty or plain, and I wasn't sure it mattered. She wasn't dark enough to be Arullan. She wasn't make-believe. Moreover, the idea of a few hours of warm, tangible flesh in my hands was extremely appealing.

Something real, I thought. *Something solid. Just for a little while.*

Taking up a tray from the bar, the girl made her rounds to the other patrons. As she came our way, I didn't even look at her. I waited until she sat the mugs down. Then I grabbed her wrist and pulled her onto my lap.

I regretted it the instant I saw her face.

Coiling an arm around my neck, Imma planted a vigorous kiss on my lips. "This is extra, Shinree. And you haven't even paid for the wine."

"You haven't brought us our food yet either," Malaq jumped in. He gave up the coin he'd been playing with and put it on the table. Studying Imma appreciatively, but without a lick of recognition, he added four more to the pile. "Off you go," he waved at her.

Imma didn't budge. "This one," she messed up my hair, "doesn't want food."

"This one can wait," Malaq retorted, bringing a chuckle out of Jarryd; who also appeared oblivious of having met Imma before.

Already, Sienn had cast on them both.

"Perhaps it isn't food you crave, My Lord," she goaded Malaq," but a distraction. Our oracle is exceptionally talented."

"Is she?" Wariness lent an edge to Malaq's smooth tongue. "Does this oracle tell you which of us will more easily part with our coin?"

"Oh, I'm not that foolish, My Lord," Imma replied with a languid smile. "Oracles are for amusement only. The future is far too fluid to live by. The visions you receive too unpredictable. Each breath could bring you closer to what you saw. Or push you farther away."

"Nice speech." Malaq stroked the tuft of hair on his chin. "Tell me, pretty girl. Is there a reduced fee for the two of you...and a hot meal?"

Jarryd snickered into his cup. "Careful, Malaq, your manners are slipping."

"That's what happens when I go too long without proper nourishment."

"There are other ways to feel sated, My Lord." Inclining her body in Malaq's direction, Imma leaned across the table. She ran a hand up his arm. "It's not commonly known, but an oracle can offer more than a forward glimpse. For an additional fee, you can view the past through the body of one whose blood you share. Such as a father or," pausing, she said compellingly, "a mother."

Morbid curiosity sprang to life in Malaq's eyes.

"Don't," I said, trying to squash it.

"Take the journey, My Lord," Imma prodded.

"Back off," I told her. "He's not interested."

"Oh, I think he is." With one finger, she caressed Malaq's hand. "I can show you the answers to all your questions. I can give you the raw naked truth."

Indecision settled on Malaq's face. It wasn't a look I wasn't used to.

And it really pissed me off.

Grabbing Imma's hand, I yanked her away from him. "I said… Back. Off."

Sienn glared at me in angry silence through Imma's blue eyes.

I glared back just as fiercely. "You really don't want to try me right now."

Malaq reached for his drink. As he took an abnormally long draw from his mug, Imma's lips formed a grin that made the room grow hot.

"And what of you, Shinree?" she asked. "Do you desire entertainment? Would you like to…come with me?" she purred, and a chill ran over my skin. What the sound of her did to me was so unfair. Her touch was more so, because as Imma's fingers brushed my face, I felt Sienn beneath. She was warm and full of magic, and as she once more whispered, "Come," the world shifted.

The dank, smoky room around me melted rapidly away.

I was suddenly elsewhere.

THIRTY SIX

Fine wood furnishings and intricate tapestries of Rellan design decorated the shadowy room. The fire in the hearth was out, making the air cold and the light dim. A few candles were lit. Their flames danced wildly over the gray stone walls, fighting to stay alive against the fierce wind whipping through a broken window on the far side of a large canopied bed.

The place was familiar. I'd been here, but I couldn't grasp when or why. I could feel the answer in my head, but I couldn't pull it out. I had vague impressions with no details, notions instead of actual recollections. It was frustrating as hell. But it was no dream. I hadn't gone through one of Jem's magical doors, either. I was here, in this place, in my own body. Yet even that was off.

I was anxious and out of breath, like I'd been running. The splint was gone from my wrist. Exhaustion and the various aches I'd felt for weeks were absent. I wasn't feeling the ale or the slightest craving for magic, and my clothes were different, right down to my boots. The shard was missing from my neck (which was disturbing), but I still had the wristlet. However, the leather cord that held the stones together was worn and frayed by age.

The same culprit had brought unfamiliar lines to the backs of my hands. Some were naturally made. Others were magic-scars; dark, coiling streaks that extended up under the cuffs of my shirt and, presumably, kept going.

I was in the future. I was in my future.

Sienn is the oracle.

"Son of a bitch."

I cursed her a few more times as I glanced around. I found a way out, a single door. I hesitated taking it, though. Future-me must have run in here for a reason. Yet, leaving might lead to a clue as to where and when I was.

I stepped in the direction of the door, and a burst of pain shot through my left hand. Wincing, thinking an injury, I turned it over and found more scars. Unlike the others, these weren't made by magic or time. The shapes decorating my entire left palm had been deliberately carved with a blade.

They were very old and very distinctive Shinree symbols and runes. But I knew the characters. I'd seen them positioned this way before, arranged to represent a particular kind of spell that had one specific purpose.

No...

I couldn't have.

I traced the raised white lines with my finger. I went around the circle and over the individual symbols scratched in the center. I followed the entire design, trying to accept that it was real. That it was on my skin—that I'd done it to myself.

At some point in my life, at a point before the time I was seeing now, I would do as Jem had done with Draken. I would employ the ancient Shinree ritual to bind my soul to another. I would take on another person's memory and aspects of their personality, and change us both forever. *Why?*

I clenched my scarred hand shut, trying to understand. What could drive me to do such a thing, to alter my life so drastically and permanently?

It wasn't for certain. The future I was in might never come to pass. But it felt true enough at the moment, especially with the ache coming through the scar.

From what I knew of a soul-bond, the discomfort wasn't being caused by the wound itself. It was an alarm, a warning sign. It was a distress signal to alert me that my 'other' was hurt. It was an excruciating, dizzying distress signal that had the room spiraling so violently, I had to catch hold of one of the bedposts to keep from falling.

I clung tighter, gasping, watching the room blur as I willed the pain away.

Maybe it worked. As after a few minutes, both the pain and the vertigo eased.

Gingerly, I lifted my head and gazed over at the door. I wasn't so keen on leaving anymore. The door was the exit, but it wasn't the way out. Enduring the vision until the gods were through fucking with me—that was the way out.

Pushing off the post, I turned toward the bed, and jumped back a step; startled by the sight of a woman's body lying atop the disheveled silken covers. With the faint light, I hadn't noticed her until I was up close. Now, I couldn't imagine how I'd missed her.

Stretched out on her side, a mass of long, curling, black hair covered her face. Her elegant dress, miles of golden delicate fabric, was crumpled and torn. The rips revealed glimpses of a small frame and a good measure of dark leg.

My eyes followed the curves of her body. They were achingly familiar.

They should be, I thought; I saw them every time I closed my eyes.

Staring harder, I shook my head. I glanced about the room. "No, this isn't…"

I looked back at her. It didn't make any sense.

"You can't be here. You…" I sunk my hands in my hair and staggered away. "No. No fucking way. You can't be here. You *can't*."

I was awake, in the future. I was in my future and the Arullan girl was here. *That could only mean…*

Heart in my throat, I dropped my hands. *Gods, help me. She's real.*

But it was more than that. I was here with her, and the shard was gone. *Did I do it? Did I give Jem what he wanted in exchange for her?*

I jumped again as she let out a low moan. Stirring slightly, she rolled onto her back. Her hair slid with the movement, exposing first a single soft shoulder and a slender neck. Then a soft, round face, full lips, long, thick lashes, and a delicate brow.

The sight of her was like a current carrying me downriver.

Helpless to withstand the pull, I knelt beside the bed. With equal amounts of dread and longing, I pushed a stray ringlet back from her closed eyes.

She didn't react, and I got bolder.

I slid a finger across her cheek, over her lips, and down her chin. I caressed her throat. The modest collar of her gown was lined with white velvet. I traced it from shoulder to shoulder, brushing lightly over her soft skin.

My throat dry, I tried to stop there. I really did. But desire had replaced the blood in my veins, and before I knew it, I was leaning down and touching my lips to hers.

I edged closer. My knee hit something on the floor. A silver goblet, it spun away from the bed, striking the leg of a nearby table and bouncing back noisily over the stones. As the goblet reversed and rolled my way, I held my breath. I watched her, waiting.

She didn't even twitch. She remained still and quiet. Vulnerable. Unaware. *Defenseless.*

What am I doing?

Backing away, clenching my hands to keep from touching her, shame hit me like a fist in the face. Disgust drowned my need in one fell swoop. Suddenly able to see past the fever on me, it was clear that her features were slack. Her limbs hung limply. Her lips were pale. The movements of her chest were abnormally slight. As if each breath was considerably less than the last.

I moved closer. I looked harder. I put my ear to her chest and was appalled at how slow her heart was beating. Her skin was cool. Her body bore no wounds. There was no outward evidence of anything wrong. There had to be though.

She was dying.

Strength deserted me, and I sat down hard on the floor. I leaned back against the bed, head buried in my hands, trying to come to grips with finding her and losing her in the same moment. The hurt was too much.

Only it wasn't simply grief I was feeling. There was a conflict in me that was utterly foreign where the Arullan girl was concerned. All I'd ever wanted in the dreams was to save her. Yet, here in the reality of my own future, I found myself considering what it would serve to let her die.

Will it change anything? Can I forget her if she's gone?

Dead has to be easier. There'd be no hope that way.

The thoughts running through my mind were repulsive. I was horrified, panic-stricken by ideas and perceptions that hadn't formed yet. Inclinations I might never have.

Running a shaky hand over my face, I took a deep breath. I took a few more, trying to focus; to remember that I was in the Faernore sitting at a table with Malaq and Jarryd. Nothing I was seeing was actually happening. Odds were it never would.

But it could. It could all happen.

Because she's real.

She's out there somewhere. She's out there right now, I thought, and comprehending that, admitting that my dream girl was flesh and blood and attainable, the impulse to find her was crushing. It was a sudden, consuming urge, so deeply imbedded within me, that as I looked at the girl sprawled out across the bed, for a brief moment, I didn't see her. I saw the path to my destruction. And I asked myself, *what would I give up to have her?*

The answer was obvious. *Everything.*

"Son of a bitch!" Snatching up the goblet, I spun and threw it across the room. It hit the wall, dropped, and rolled. Silence followed, and in between my angry ragged breaths, there was sound.

It was slight, a faint scrape on the stones.

I got up. I came around the end of the bed, and there was another body. This one was male, unmoving, and slumped face down below the shattered casement. Broken glass littered his clothes. Rain darkened his brown hair. Blood spread out in a wide pool around his upper body. It ran in channels across the grooves of the floor. My eyes were drawn to the thickening red streams. Watching them, I felt odd, weak.

Another twinge ran through the scars on my palm.

Shaking it out, I went over and squatted down beside the injured man. I couldn't see his face, but I didn't need to. I knew him. We were connected on a level that went beyond memory or friendship. We were bound for life. Only for him, that life was nearly at an end.

Carefully, I rolled him over. "*Nef'taali?*" I expected the ancient word to feel odd on my lips, but it was strangely comforting. I said it again, urgently. "*Nef'taali?*"

His blue eyes opened. Choking on the swell of blood in his mouth, he coughed out my name, "Ian. I knew you'd come."

Sitting down, I lifted him gently. I tried to pull him onto my lap without hurting him, but it wasn't possible. The gash across his stomach had nearly split him in two.

"Gods...Jarryd." My eyes roamed over the wound. "I'm sorry."

"Not your fault. You told me to stay away." He tried to smile. "I didn't listen."

"You never do." I shook my head. Seeing him like this was hard, but the pain it brought my future self was devastating. I could barely separate from it to speak. "How? How did this happen?" I asked, but I wasn't referring to his injury. My ancestors had performed the ritual binding as a means of protection. Why then would I have used it to tie myself to a young, impetuous fool like Jarryd Kane?

What could he ever protect me from?

"I think it was poison," he said faintly. "You have to help her."

"You first."

"Not this time, *Nef'taali*. There's nothing left of me to heal."

"That's not true. Just lie still."

Jarryd gripped my shirt with a bloody hand and pulled me closer. "I couldn't stop it. I couldn't save her. But you can." His hand fell away. He shuddered against me. "Help her, Ian, please. Save Neela."

I thought I misheard him. "What?"

"Forgive her. What she did was wrong. So many things went wrong. But if you let her die..." his head rolled to the side.

"Let who die? Jarryd?" I shook him awake. "Jarryd!"

"Promise me...you'll never forgive yourself if you let Neela die."

My blood turned to ice. My head snapped around to the bed. All that was visible was her arm and a few strands of hair, and I nearly stood, nearly dropped Jarryd in the ocean of blood covering the floor, just so I could see her face again and be sure.

"That's..." I licked dry lips and tried again. "That's Neela Arcana on the bed? She's... No," I snarled, "you're wrong. It can't be her. That isn't Aylagar's daughter. I wouldn't...I couldn't possibly—" my voice seized. The resemblance I'd noticed the first time I dreamt of her suddenly made such perfect sense.

I could almost hear Jem's trap swinging shut in my head.

Why didn't I see it before now? Why didn't I recognize her?

He didn't want me to. Not until it was too late.

It was despicable, what he'd had done to me, but it was cunning. By fixating me on an actual woman, forcing me to repeatedly watch Draken rape, torture, and murder her, Jem had turned Rella's new Queen into a very real, very unobtainable obsession.

An obsession, I thought soberly, *that Draken intends to take for his wife.*

A wet gasp left Jarryd's body. He stiffened and squeezed my arm. "If you can't find your own cause to save Neela, then do it for me. Do me this one last favor."

My throat ached. I pulled him closer. "She never loved you."

"I know." He gave me an unsteady, crooked grin. "Nor you."

Jarryd's eyes fell closed. I felt the strength draining out of him like it was mine. I no longer cared about Neela. I couldn't bear the hole his absence would make in my life, in my very soul. The idea was too painful to live with.

"*Nef'taali*, wait" I said, and then it was gone. All of it; his life, the room, the bodies, the blood; all my unlived memories slid out of view. Future happenings scattered.

In less than the blink of an eye, all that remained of my vision were moving walls, and a bending, undulating floor, as everything shifted out of focus.

When it shifted back, I was in the present. Sienn was still perched on my lap in Imma's form. Malaq was across from me enjoying his drink. Jarryd was beside me, alive.

Mere moments had passed. Nothing had changed for them.

Everything had changed for me.

THIRTY SEVEN

With a yank, I pulled Imma off the table and dragged her to the darkened stairwell at the back of the room. I pushed her up the stairs in front of me. "I don't like being ambushed."

Her worried blue eyes glanced back. "Where did you go? What did you see?"

I pushed her faster. "Stop playing me, Sienn. I know oracles go along for the ride."

"I couldn't. Not wearing this form."

We reached the shadowy light of the upstairs hall, and the masquerade of the winegirl dropped away. Bruises darkened the outline of Sienn's jaw. Finger marks discolored her forearms. Looking at her, my anger subsided. "Are you all right?"

"Are you?" She lifted my right arm, inspecting the splint on my wrist and the heavy bandage wrapped around my hand.

I pulled away. "I asked first."

"I fell," she replied briskly.

"So did I."

Sienn uttered an irritated sound. Pulling a key out from inside her cloak, she unlocked a door at the end of the hall. Sienn went inside the small room. I waited until she'd lit the lanterns and the fire, and then followed her in. I took in the low lumpy bed, the dusty old trunk, and the small stand with a cracked basin and a pitcher of water.

Confident we were alone; I closed the door and confronted her. "What are you doing here?"

"I spoke to Jem." Sienn pulled the tattered, threadbare curtains over the window. "He denied your accusations. He was angry. Defensive. Cruel." She turned to me. Her eyes, clean of magic, reminded me of shiny pearls. "He questioned my loyalty, my faith. He said I failed him, that I didn't try hard enough to win you to our cause. I tried to explain your views, to make him see reason."

"Reason has little to do with the choices your friend is making right now." I hesitated, but there was no good time for what I had to say. "Jem shared souls with Draken of Langor. They're bound together, as *nef'taali*. It's how Draken shed the madness, how he regained what I took from him with the Crown of Stones."

Shock sent a hand to her mouth. "I knew he'd changed. We all saw it, but…" Strained and defiant, she argued, "No. He wouldn't. He'd never join with Draken."

"Whatever Jem gave up in the exchange, it balanced out Draken's insanity. And the pieces of Draken that Jem got in return…there's madness in him, Sienn. I've seen it."

Her stare wandered. "He started wearing these gloves and I thought…I just thought…" A kind of resigned sorrow contorted her features, and Sienn fell back against the wall. "The gloves were to hide the runes on his hand, weren't they?"

"That would be my guess."

Abruptly, Sienn crossed the room. Removing her cloak, she dropped it on the trunk and bent down beside the bed. Reaching into a muddy traveling bag on the floor, she pulled out a large book and held it against her chest. Thick and old, the tome was bound in a wide strip of cracked leather that looked as if it might crumble to dust if she squeezed any harder. "I stole this from him."

"What is it?"

Sienn took a timid step. "There's something I didn't tell you."

"I'm guessing there's lots of somethings you didn't tell me."

She bit her lip. Anxiety was wafting off her. "Jem was born of a soldier line, but I've trained him to be much more. And now, linked to Draken, and with the crown, he…" she took a breath. "Ian, Jem is a Reth."

My brows shot up. My voice followed. "A Reth?"

"Not just any Reth. He's a direct descendant of Emperor Tam Reth. If he were Rellan or Langorian, if he were born of any other race but ours, Jem would be our legitimate ruler. He would bear the title of King of the Shinree."

"King." The word sunk like rocks in my stomach. "And now he has a crown."

"No matter how you feel about him, Jem Reth has the birthright to establish and govern a new nation for the Shinree."

Along with the power, I thought angrily. "God damn it, Sienn. That night in the bathhouse, when I asked you about Jem, don't you think that his blood ties to the creator of the Crown of Stones should have been the first thing out of your mouth instead of your tongue?"

"I didn't believe you. And I don't condemn people for their heritage."

"No, you teach them." Swiftly, I closed the distance between us. "You taught a man with the most powerful warrior line in Shinree history, how to better wield the most powerful weapon in Shinree history, so he can wipe out anyone that stands in his way."

"I didn't know—"

"You showed him how to access other lines, how to cast without losing strength."

"Yes, but—"

"He won't pass out after he casts. He'll have access to spells I don't. How the fuck am I supposed to fight him? I ran a hand back over my hair; unable to believe how fast the situation had gone from bleak to hopeless. "Why didn't you tell me?"

"He asked me not to."

That would have put me over the edge, if not for the complete absence of deceit on her, and my first-hand knowledge of Jem Reth's fondness for manipulation. With his clear lack of scruples, it was only natural he would spell his own people to keep them in line. *He didn't free them. He just gave them a new master.*

"He trained you," I said with disgust. "He trained all of you. You follow him around, do his bidding. Like dogs."

Emotion flushed her face. Short, rapid breaths of anger made her small chest heave and her nostrils flare. Sienn's icy stare put me in mind of a fierce winter storm, and as she found her voice and seethed out a breathless, "I am no one's dog," I couldn't decide if the urge building in me was to hit her, or kiss her. "If you knew him you would understand. All Jem wants is a place for our people."

"No, he wants an empire, Sienn, an empire that he's building with blood. And he's making no apologies for it."

"Jem doesn't second guess. He doesn't regret. That's who he is."

"Yeah, I got that. He takes no responsibility for the lives he's taken."

"You mean he doesn't drown himself in guilt? Jem is stronger than that." She eyed me critically. "Stronger than you, perhaps."

"I got that too. Now, you brought that book to me for a reason. So let's hear it."

Sienn sat down hard on the bed. "Jem came to us a little over two years ago."

"He's been free that long?"

"A few months before me," she nodded. "Apparently, he was quiet about where he'd come from. He just showed up in camp one day with these grand plans. He was committed, knowledgeable. No one remembers how he came to be in charge, he just did. When Jem discovered the mistake with my name, he came personally to rescue me. There was an excitement, an eagerness about him. Jem had secrets, but his decisiveness, his passion for our cause, for life..." A smile wanted to come, but she forced it away. "Then, he disappeared. He came back a week later, and he was different. He was distant and demanding. Impatient. Harsh. I thought it was the weight of responsibility." Sadness shrunk her voice. "It all makes sense now. That week he was gone, Jem must have been in Langor, being bound to Draken."

"That would explain the changes."

"But the purpose of the ritual is to make two souls better, not worse."

"The spell shares and distributes what it believes each needs from each other. It probably saw Draken's madness as one hell of a need and didn't know what else to do but try and distribute it between them. It might still be doing it, altering their minds in some futile attempt to eradicate it from them both."

A little pale, Sienn lowered the book onto her lap. Runes were carved on the front, but her arms were blocking them. "This never leaves his side. I had to wait until he fell asleep to take it." She patted the cover. "According to the title, this is the journal of Emperor Tam Reth. But the pages are blank. I know it's spelled. I've tried everything."

"Then try everything again. If Tam wrote about the Crown of Stones, what's in there could help me gain an advantage." I stepped closer. "I want you with me on this, Sienn. But before we go any further, I need to know. Do you condone what Jem Reth has done? The lives he's taken? Do you believe what he's doing with Draken is right?"

Sienn set the book beside her on the bed. "The Shinree deserve to be free, Ian. The Crown of Stones can give us that. *Jem* can give us that. He could be a great leader."

Not surprised, I nodded. "If that's how you feel..."

"It is. But Jem has gone too far. The Langorians are butchers. I can't accept a future with Draken as our ally. I won't." A tear slid down her cheek. Sienn swiped at it furiously. Another fell. Her shoulders began to tremble, slightly at first, and then harder. "Damn you, Jem," she wept, "how could you?"

I crossed to the bed and crouched in front of her. "I'm sorry, Sienn. Jem Reth isn't the man you knew. Not anymore."

Nodding, Sienn leaned forward. She rested her head on my shoulder. My hands settled on her knees, hers rested on my arms, and we sat like for a while as she cried.

After a time, her breathing slowed. It fell in step with mine, and I felt the anxiety go out of her. A measure of apprehension left me as well, and it struck me that I was more than a little content in our half-embrace. I enjoyed the smell of pine on her clothes, the scent of soap in her hair. I was aware of the places where our bodies touched. Not lustfully. That was there, but below the surface. This was a comfortable moment. A shared easiness that told me I could hold this woman for hours and it would be satisfying and tantalizing in a way I wasn't accustomed to. *Is she right? Is it because we're the same, both of us with pure Shinree blood? Or was it simply the fact that Sienn was real?*

That she wasn't imagination like the Arullan girl.

She has a name now, I thought, and I suddenly felt sick all over.

"Sienn," I said. "I need your help."

She sat up. "The dream spell? Jem cast it on you, didn't he?"

"He claims he doesn't want me dead, but I feel half there already."

"I'll do everything I can."

"Then do it quick, before I change my mind."

Her head tilted. "Why would you do that?"

"Because he's got me, Sienn. He's fucking got me." I pulled away and stood. "What I see when I dream is something I should never want to see again. But there's this part, these moments that are so beautiful, that when I'm not dreaming, I want to be. I crave it. I *need* it," I said, my jaw grinding. "I suffer through all the bad just to have that that one, small morsel of good." I turned from the look in her eyes. "I know how it sounds."

"It sounds like magic. Come here." I sat down beside her. Gently, Sienn guided me to lie back. "You need to dream for me one last time, Ian. But I swear, after that, it'll be over. Whatever demons plague your sleep, you will never see them again."

Sienn was wrong. What plagued my sleep was waiting for me in Kabri. But I closed my eyes and wished that it wasn't.

———

Bit by bit, my Arullan girl's body was coming apart, separating like smoke caught in a strong wind. The pieces were pale, ghost-like. They tore off, shredded and blew away.

The whole world was shredding. But I cared only for her. I felt her leaving, deep in my chest. And I had no idea how I was supposed to breathe when she was gone.

"Wait..." I tried to catch her. She was like sand in my grip. "Don't go. Don't leave!"

The last of her drifted out of sight, and I was alone.

It was dark, barren. Panic and darkness swallowed me.

"NO!"

There was no light without her. "Come back!"

The scream still in my throat, I threw open my eyes.

In the room with me, Sienn spun around, startled. "It's okay," she soothed.

Running both hands through my sweat-drenched hair, I rose up onto my elbows and panted at her. "Is...is it done?"

She nodded. Her smile was tentative, almost placating; a look she no doubt reserved for the sick and unstable. "The nightmare will never come to you again."

I felt a twinge of alarm and locked it away. "Thank you."

"How do you feel?"

"Tired."

She gave me that smile again. "That's to be expected. You should feel better in a few days. You can remove your bandages," she added kindly. "I sealed the cuts on your hand and corrected someone's disgraceful attempt to mend your wrist. I also arranged for private accommodations for your messenger, so I could look at that hole in his leg without drawing attention. I checked on the wound to his face as well. Though, fixing you and your friend is becoming quite a habit."

"Thanks," I said again.

"There's an extra bed for you in Prince Malaq's room. Or, you can stay here." For Sienn, it was a subtle proposition. "I want you to stay here."

So much for subtle.

"I can change back into Imma," she offered, "if you prefer."

"Is that what you think?" Shaking my head, I slid off the end of the bed.

"I don't understand, then. Why don't want me?"

Her voice held such an odd mix of passion, neediness, and shame that the words were out before I could stop them. "What happened to make you like this?"

Sienn's face turned as white as her hair.

"Never mind," I said. "You don't have to answer."

"If it matters to you."

"It doesn't."

"It might."

"No, Sienn, really. I shouldn't have asked."

She took a resolved breath. "It's all right. It may help you understand."

Sienn stood. Hugging her arms to her chest, she moved about the small room, back and forth, passing the fire, walking in and out of its glow. It was distracting. One second the light breached the fabric of her dress. The next it didn't.

I just wanted her to stand still.

"You, Ian," she said at last, still pacing, "perceive *Kayn'l* as a means to curb the danger we pose to the world. And you are correct. But coming off it, being aware of what you did and what you were deprived of… You can't imagine the confusion and the anger, the fear. The shame."

"It must have been a lot to take in at once."

"It doesn't happen like that. For short term use or light doses, perhaps, but for a slave who's made to ingest *Kayn'l* for years, it's a much different process. My senses didn't work right for many days. My mind returned in pieces, in these vivid, frustrating, random flashes. It took months for the details to fill in. Eventually, I remembered." She hugged herself harder. "I remembered men. Lots of men."

She was right. I couldn't imagine. But the look in her eyes got me damn close.

The ache inside Sienn, the animosity toward those that owned her and used her; I could see how it fanned out to encompass pretty much everyone, including herself. It made me think, *this is Jem Reth's doing*. He may have rescued Sienn, but he'd done nothing to help her recover. If anything, his manipulations had broken her even more.

"You're safe now," I told her. "That part of your life, what you did, it's over."

"For me, yes, but so many others are being abused and neglected, Ian, and I want to help them. I want to show them what it means to live, to be free to choose." She gave me a quick smile. "To find someone."

I tried not to flinch. "I hate what happened to you. But we aren't together, Sienn. We can't be. Not now."

"Why, so you can concentrate on recovering the Crown of Stones? I think Jem's spell had you more out of focus than anything I could do in one night."

"I'm not so sure about that." Sienn lowered her eyes, bit her lip, and the gesture went right through me. "I should go." I forced myself to move toward the door. "We'll look at the book in the morning. Maybe between the two of us we can figure out the enchantment. I want to break it before we reach Kabri."

My hand was on the latch when Sienn came up behind me. She pressed her long, lean body against my back. Her arms wound around my chest. I could feel her warm breath through my shirt.

For a moment, I entertained the thought of pushing her away.

Then her hands slid down my stomach.

They moved lower, and I sucked in a breath.

Lower still, and I did nothing to stop them. I couldn't—Sienn's hands held me. They hardened me. Her rhythmic caresses were skillful and intuitive. Her vigorous strokes raised a heat that made the leather between her skin and mine melt away.

Her stroke quickened. Blood thundered through my veins. Tension had my body pulled so tight; easily, she could bring me with just her grip.

If it were Imma, I could live with that. But it was Sienn. Whatever it was between us, it made me want far more than just her hand.

With a growl I seized her wrists and pulled Sienn around in front of me. Lips parted, breath coming quick, desire had her white eyes sparkling like icicles in the sun.

It was too much.

Overcome, I gripped her face. I pushed my fingers into the delicate bones of her cheeks and pulled her mouth to mine. As my tongue pushed in, Sienn fumbled with the sword harness on my back. Sliding the straps down my arms, as they fell away, she unbuckled the belt from my waist, and both my weapons hit the floor. She stripped off my braces and my shirt. As her deft fingers went to work on the laces of my breeches, we stumbled toward the bed. All I had to do was lie down; from sleeping with Imma, I knew Sienn was well versed in pleasuring a man.

Now, I knew why. And it gave me pause.

I couldn't erase what she'd been through. But I could make her forget for a while.

Capturing Sienn's head in my hands, I held her eyes. "Sit down." I placed her on the edge of the bed and knelt in front of her. Her frost-colored hair clung to the sweat on her face. The neck of her dress was off-kilter. I made it more so. Tugging it down off one shoulder, I pulled her exposed breast into my mouth.

Moaning, Sienn arched her back, forcing the smooth mound in deeper.

I lifted her skirt. I ran my hands over her thighs, then my tongue. I was spreading her knees apart when something moved in the corner.

Moved wasn't exactly the right word, though. Nothing was there to be moving. No form. No light. No breeze; the window was closed. There wasn't even a shadow.

I stopped to stare. Sienn pawed at me, trying to win back my attention. But as I focused, I could make out two darker forms hovering inside the larger one. Small and slightly oval in shape, they were aimed right at me. They looked like—

Eyes?

He's watching us.

"Son of a…" I pushed myself back away from her and stood up.

Breathless and confused, Sienn said, "Ian?"

"What's the matter?" I shouted at the corner. "Threats and torture aren't enough, you sick fuck? You had to send your whore to win me over?"

Craning her neck, Sienn followed my gaze. Her expression was wild as she looked back at me, but she didn't even try to come up with a lie. She just sat there.

Furiously, I fastened my breeches. "How could you let him use you like this? Or was that story you told me just a tale to play at my sympathies?"

"What I said was true, Ian. All of it was true. Please," she begged. "Stay with me. We belong together. Fate—"

"Don't!" I reached down and snatched up my gear in one swift lunge. "Don't say it. Don't fucking say it." I threw the door open so hard it slammed back into the wall and bounced off. Catching it as I stormed out, I threw a violent glance at the corner. "She's all yours."

THIRTY EIGHT

Rolling over, my heavy eyes landed on the bed next to mine. Vision bleary, mind groggy, it took me a minute to realize his covers were thrown back and his mattress was empty. "Malaq…" I groaned.

I wanted to roll back over and ignore it. Sleep pulled at me like hands in the dark. My blankets were warm. The bed was a welcome change from the ground. I'd dreamt of nothing for the first time in as long as I could remember, and it felt good. But I'd played this game with Malaq once already, and it hadn't ended well. So I threw my legs over the side of the bed, armed myself, and went in search of him.

The upstairs hall was quiet. The majority of the Faernore's rooms were vacant. The rest were locked, with sleep sounds emanating from the other side. Jarryd was behind one of the doors. I thought about trying to find his room, but between the drink and Sienn's magic, he'd be out cold till morning.

Muffled voices filtered up from downstairs. Heading toward them, I continued down the hall. Flames from the hearth painted hulking shadows on the wall of the stairwell as I descended into the main room. The shadows took form and became the stocky bodies of six Langorian soldiers. Marking their positions, I walked out onto the floor.

One man directed me with a hostile glance and an impatient jerk of his head to a grouping of three tall-backed chairs near the fire. Two were occupied. Having a good idea by whom, I kept a hand on my sword and made my way over.

Malaq, in the middle chair, was hunched down in his seat. Eyes aimed securely downward, legs outstretched, ankles crossed, with a mug of something sitting on his chest, he didn't acknowledge me in the least. Sitting to his left, his brother's hawk-like gaze was on me in an instant.

Adorned in enough black to be night itself, King Draken of Langor took a sip of his drink and smiled. "Troy," he said, revoltingly pleasant, "how good it is to see you. I trust you slept well?"

"Bastard." I threw myself down in the empty chair to Malaq's right. Gesturing at the cloak on his shoulders and the bag on the floor, I said to him, "Going somewhere?"

Maintaining a silent stony vigil of his boots, Malaq replied, "Darkhorne."

Draken laughed; a low, amused sound that instantly stabbed holes in my patience.

I glared at him. "How's my spell treating you, Your Grace? You still *look* crazy."

"Then I am in like company, am I not?" His laughter dying, Draken tilted his head, examining me. "No," he said with disappointment, "I'm not. You're not quite there yet, are you? How unfortunate. I thought the dreams would have crippled you by now." He sniffed. "It would have been nice to have you grovel at my feet tonight."

"I was just thinking the same thing."

He flashed me a tense smile. "Speaking of crippled…how does it feel, Troy, to be using magic again?"

"You tell me. You must have a good idea what it's like for a Shinree to channel magic…since you own half of Jem Reth's soul."

"Ah. I told Reth you were smarter than you looked."

"Smart enough to get his dream-weave broken."

Worry lines contorted Draken's highborn features. "No matter," he said, shrugging them off. "The damage is irreversible."

"I'll find a way. Maybe in that old book Reth kept under his pillow?"

The lines came back. He rubbed at them. "I don't know why I agreed to his damn dream spell. Having you drawn and quartered would have been much simpler."

"Hold on," Malaq barked. Curiosity had finally eaten through his steady demeanor. "What dream spell? What damage? And who the hell is Reth?"

"Reth is a dead man," I said plainly.

Draken spared me a frown. He transferred it to Malaq. "The spell, my dear brother, was to keep your friend busy and out of the way. Break him, if I was lucky. Apparently, I wasn't."

Malaq chewed on his lip. His eyes darted between us like he had a head full of questions and accusations. But Malaq was in a dangerous position. He couldn't afford to show me too much sympathy or appear too eager to cow to his brother. So he lowered his head and drank.

"The book," I said to Draken. "Where did Reth get it?"

"Let's see," he sighed, "where would one find an ancient Shinree artifact?"

My lips curled at his sarcasm. "You dug up the ruins of the old empire."

"Not personally. That was Jillyan's project."

"What was she looking for?"

"Something to tell her how to make me sane. You know, that poor girl was never meant to be Queen. She was such a timid little thing when she was young. Our father never appreciated her...sensitive side," Draken said delicately. "Eventually, he beat it out of her, and Jillyan took to ruling quite well when it was forced upon her. But she never stopped looking for a way to save me. As a result, with all that research, she's developed quite an extensive knowledge of the Shinree. Not to mention a peculiar fascination." He winked at me. "Jillyan does like her pets."

Thinking of what my healing cost in Kael, I said dryly, "So I've heard. How did she learn about the journal?"

"She didn't. Jillyan had no idea it existed until she found it. All she knew was that the answer to breaking your spell must lie within the Crown of Stones. So she went to the one place that might have information on how it worked. It took years—tunneling at night, working in secret to keep the Rellans from discovering. But, eventually, she unearthed miles of structures buried beneath the ground."

"Where does Reth fit in?"

"He was assigned to the digging crew. When he arrived he had no record. There were no papers of sale, no documents of breeding. He didn't exist."

"That had to be a mistake. An oversight," I said, thinking of Sienn and the mislabeling of her name.

"I assure you, Reth's enslavement was no oversight. Under the same impression, though, my sister, ever the curious one, had him weaned of *Kayn'l* for questioning. Imagine her surprise when he turned out to be useful."

"He might have been more useful if you hadn't joined souls and turned him mad."

"Jem understood the dangers of our bond. He is a motivated man who will do anything to free the Shinree. Whereas you, Troy, are content to be Rella's lapdog."

I grunted at him. "Did you come all this way just to flatter me?"

"I came, as you requested: to barter for that little piece around your neck."

"I don't think I said anything about bartering."

"Come now. There must be something you want. Money? Land? A title, perhaps?" Sly and persuasive, he whispered, "Neela Arcana?" and every muscle in my body constricted. "So," Draken grinned eagerly. "You've discovered it's her. What an unpleasant moment that must have been."

I forced my voice steady. "She's not yours to offer."

"How chivalrous," he teased. "She's not yours either. But she can be."

"What about your wedding?"

"I can be persuaded against it. Besides, who am I to stand in the way of a man's dream coming true?" I said nothing and he leaned toward me. "Seriously, Troy, have you thought about what that means? All those nights you started out in her arms, happy and in love. And then woke up alone… with your cock aching. You could feel her on you. Taste her. But you couldn't touch her. Couldn't fuck her. Until now." Watching me, he wet his lips. "Would you like that? Would you like to feel what it's really like inside there? Because I'm betting it's warm, wet, and hungry."

My heart was pounding so hard it hurt. I had to clench my teeth and grip the arms of my chair just to stop a 'yes' from bursting out of me. But I did.

A few hours ago I wouldn't have. Draken's lewd proposal would have sparked a delusion or a phantom touch. Either would have undone me. Now, with the spell broken, Neela was just a painful memory. A deep-rooted temptation I couldn't quench. And that was something I'd dealt with my entire my life.

"No," I said.

Shock dampened the enjoyment in Draken's eyes. "Did you not hear me?"

"I heard you. The answer is no."

Slowly, his dismay slid away. It became a gradual smile, deep and full of meaning. As if he had something else in reserve. "Then perhaps, you would prefer another of Aylagar's brood?"

"Another?" I narrowed my eyes at him. "What are you playing at?"

"Neela is not the only princess in the castle."

"Aylagar bore only two daughters, Draken. One you sent to plague my dreams. The other has been dead a long time."

"Elayna is a few years older than Neela. And a bit used," Draken grimaced. "But she is certainly not dead. I just saw her this morning."

"I don't believe you."

"That's a shame." Draken pretended to inspect his sleeve, brushing at a speck of dust; drawing things out. "Because, trust me, Troy, if you secured her release, Elayna would no doubt show you gratitude in ways you would find most pleasing."

"You're lying."

"I most definitely am not. That woman knows her place is on her knees, and to tell you the truth, I think she likes it." He moved on to shine a dingy spot on the cuff of his left boot. "And rest assured there's enough family resemblance to satisfy your lustful craving for Arcana women." Suspending his grooming, Draken flashed me a wicked grin. "Mother, daughter, sister… really Troy, someone should give you a medal."

My eyes on him were fierce. "I was there when Aylagar got the news of Elayna's death. I saw the message."

"Well, that explains it," he said, feigning exasperation. "Rellan messengers can be so unreliable."

"They found her body in the mountains, Draken. Along with the men you sent to kidnap her. None of them survived."

"If I recall, the poor frozen little thing didn't have much of a face left."

"No, she didn't. The wolves saw to that."

"Well, they certainly ate someone."

"Enough!" I snapped. "Elayna Arcana is dead."

"Elayna Arcana is in a cell underneath Darkhorne lying in her own filth."

Draken and I scowled at each other. Malaq continued (as he had been) scowling into his drink. No one said anything for a long time, and the room seemed to grow smaller, the flicker of flames in the hearth louder.

It was Malaq who spoke first. "My Lord, please tell me this is a ruse."

"Sorry, little brother." Draken gave him a sad face. "I didn't intend to reveal your cousin's captivity like this, but your witch does bring out the worst in me."

Malaq looked numb. "You've really held the true heir to the Rellan throne in Darkhorne for the last ten years?"

"More like almost twelve," Draken corrected him.

"Why?" Malaq said, working hard to hide his revulsion. "You could have ransomed her at any time, used her for leverage. Let her go," he suggested forcefully.

"To be honest," Draken said, "she was forgotten."

"You son of a bitch," I growled.

Draken's brows came together. "I don't think I like your tone."

"Why the charade?" Malaq asked him. "Why make it out like she was dead?"

"Don't be so naïve, little brother," Draken scorned. "The ransom for a child is considerably higher after the mother has been allowed to drown in grief for a while."

"Goddamn Langorian swine," I muttered.

"Don't blame this on me, Troy," Draken countered. "Elayna was overlooked because of the chaos that ensued after the war—chaos you created with the Crown of Stones. All these years you've been tearing yourself up over Aylagar's death, but it was her daughter you should have been grieving for. She became an animal in a cage because of you."

The image unnerved me. Probably though, he was lying. *But if he isn't...*

"So is that a yes or a no?" Draken made a show of trying to read my expression. "It's a fair trade. And if you keep the lights low, she truly does resemble Neela. At least from behind."

"Gods!" I shot up out of my chair. "Do you think I would use Aylagar's daughter that way? No matter what Reth's spell has done to me I would never—"

"Oh, yes you would," he broke in, his voice dripping with pleasure. "All those dreams, all that dark, beautiful flesh. You used every piece of Neela. Many times. But," he said firmly. "If you're truly done with her, and if you don't want Elayna, I'll take them both. There's nothing in Langorian law against having two wives."

Rage burned in my stomach. "Elayna is dead. And the dreams are over. You can't use them against me. None of it was real."

"It was real enough at the time. So real, that when you lay eyes on your little, Arullan beauty for the first time..." Draken left off in a husky laugh. "The spell may be broken, Troy, but can you honestly tell me that you wouldn't give up your own life to have five minutes beneath Neela's skirt?"

Malaq stood abruptly. He emptied his cup in one long furious gulp, went to the bar, and slammed it down with such force that Draken's guards pulled their weapons.

"What's wrong, brother?" Draken called after him. "You don't approve?"

"No," Malaq replied, loud and curt. "I don't."

"It was a harmless spell," Draken reasoned. "Or would you rather I take your friend's heart out of his chest?"

Malaq's glare was frightening. "It sounds like you already have."

Draken trained a quiet, feral look on his brother. It put me in mind of a wolf ready to pounce.

"Draken," I said sharply. "I have a counter offer. Elayna's life for yours."

His dark stare shifted off Malaq and focused on me, just like I'd wanted. "Sorry, witch," Draken said. "It's Elayna for the stone."

"No. It's, you give me Elayna, or I kill you. Now. Tonight."

Draken grunted. "Reth would never allow that."

Turning away, I crossed the room. Langorian soldiers slid out of the shadows. They crept closer as I moved to stand next to Malaq. I reached over the bar. Fishing around behind the counter, I said, "Reth isn't here." Finding a good-sized bottle, I pulled it out and tried to make sense of the poorly scrawled words on the label. "Which means," I glanced at Draken, "that protecting you isn't high on his list."

"If there is danger, he will respond," Draken assured me. "At its simplest form, being *nef'taali* comes down to preservation and instinct. If I die, Reth suffers too."

"There's a bit of good news." Popping the stopper out, I recoiled at the smell and took a sip. "I swear," I said, my face contorting at the taste, "the damn Kaelish will drink just about anything."

"I wouldn't come here without protection, Troy," Draken said tiredly.

Tilting the bottle at his men, I laughed. "These guys?"

Draken hissed. His patience was frayed. Mine had been in pieces before I even headed down the stairs. There was only one place this was going.

I looked at Malaq. Then I looked at his chair. He said nothing, but I knew he understood me. I also knew by the subtle twitch of his jaw, that he was pissed as hell.

I left the bottle on the bar and moved into the center of the room. "I want Elayna released, Draken. And I'm not giving you the stone."

"Well." He motioned to his men. "It seems we are at an impasse."

I gripped both swords and stripped them bare. "No. We're not."

THIRTY NINE

Steel ruffled my hair. The edge of a blade rode along my left arm, splitting the sleeve clean up to my shoulder. Another sliced through the front of my shirt.

Draken's men had good aim and a hard swing. They were noticeably determined to see me dead. Nevertheless, having already dispatched five of them, it was clear they were too slow to get the job done.

My last challenger spared a glance at his dead comrades on the floor. Fear tightened his gaze as he wiped the sweat away and re-settled his grip on his sword. Still, being Langorian, he flashed his best spiteful, contemptuous smirk, let out an abrupt battle cry, and ran at me.

Launching himself forward, as the man drew back to swing, his boot slipped in a wide streak of gore on the floor. Over extended, balance gone, his feet went out from under him. He landed hard on his back, about ten feet away, with a loud, "oomph."

"That was quite a move," I praised, laughing. "I'd clap, but," approaching, I brandished both swords, "my hands are full."

With a wince, he sat up. Sweeping a mass of matted, dark hair out of his face, the man glared at my weapons. His gaze swung to the space between us, measuring it, trying to decide if he could get up before I killed him.

"The answer is no," I said. "But you're welcome to try."

He thought about it. Then, in an abrupt, surprising move, he dropped his sword. Lowering his head, he raised both hands in a gesture of surrender.

It took me about two breaths to decide what I thought of it. "Tell me, soldier. If I was there and you were here…what would you do?"

His head lifted. We locked eyes. His mouth jerked with an ugly, thick-lipped grin. "I would spill your stinking Shinree insides all over the floor."

"That's what I thought." I kicked him in the jaw. He fell backwards, and I shoved both blades in his chest.

Yanking them out, I lobbed a satisfied grin at Draken. Sitting sideways in his chair to observe the fight, he gave me a scowl and turned back around. Malaq stood beside the hearth. He'd been watching, too, but he wore no expression whatsoever.

I put my swords away and joined them. Passing Draken, I ripped the drink out of his hand and drained it. As I was feeling particularly tetchy, I threw the mug into the fire and put myself directly in front of him. "Guess that just leaves you…Your Grace."

He gave me a patient smile. "I didn't come here to fight you, Troy."

I put my hands on the arms of his chair and leaned in. "Then you won't stop me from taking the head off your shoulders?"

Firmly, Malaq said, "I will."

I sighed. "This isn't about you, Malaq. Walk away."

"I'm sorry, Ian," he said. "But I can't do that."

Pushing myself off Draken's chair, I faced him. "Don't make it come to this."

"My Lord," he said to Draken, "with your permission?" Malaq waited for Draken to nod before clamping his hand on my arm. I didn't shove him off. With all we'd been through together, the man had earned a measure of lee-way, so I let him steer me to the base of the stairs at the far end of the room.

There, out of Draken's hearing, my charity ended. "Watch yourself, Nef'areen," I warned, shaking out of Malaq's hold. "You're about to draw lines between us that won't be easily erased."

"And you're letting rage make you reckless. You've shown Draken you aren't as weak as he thought. Now, it's time to back off. You've made your point."

"I'm pretty sure my point won't be made until it's sticking out the other side of your brother."

Malaq pinched the spot between his eyes like it ached. "Ian…"

"Draken needs to die."

"Not today," he whispered.

"And why the fuck not? He's right here, right in front of me." I shook my head. "No. I'm not doing it. I'm not letting that man walk out of here alive."

"You have to. There is too much at risk."

"You don't understand." Memories of Neela lent a shaky, strangled sound to my voice. "You don't know what those dreams have done to me."

"You're right. I don't. I don't know because you didn't tell me. But your inability to put faith in anyone, including yourself, isn't the issue right now." Malaq's voice lowered even further. "If you leave Langor without a King, it will fall under military rule before I can even get there. Without a real, legitimate change in leadership, and a new direction, my people won't stop. They won't let go. They'll rise again in another ten, twenty, or thirty years, and they will keep rising until they're shown another way. Unless, of course, you're willing to do worse than before and wipe out every man, woman, and child of Langor; wipe them all out, so there's no chance of war ever happening again?"

It wasn't a dare. It was quite the opposite, actually. It was the most preposterous scenario Malaq could imagine. He truly believed I could never commit such an atrocity as to destroy the entire Langorian race. He believe it so strongly, I didn't have the heart to tell him he was wrong. I was more than capable. "You expect too much of me," I said.

"I expect friendship."

With an angry grunt I broke away from his harsh stare. Putting my back against the side of the bar, I looked up at the darkened stairwell and wished I'd never gotten out of bed. The sentiment worsened as Malaq pursued me.

"Look, Ian," he said. "We both want the same thing. But killing Draken prematurely will make my push for peace that much harder. And we may never get Elayna Arcana out of Darkhorne alive. You can't tell me that isn't important to you."

"Of course it is. But even if Draken does have Elayna, he won't let her go."

"I will. When I'm King I will free Elayna and any other Rellans my brother has locked away. I will put right all the wrongs my family has brought to this world. You have my word." There was an abundance of strength and purpose in Malaq's voice. And I wanted to believe him. I wanted to put my faith in the man more than I had any other in a long time. He had a way of inspiring hope and fostering devotion that was his own special kind of magic.

But how long would his conviction and charisma last in a place like Langor?

"Malaq," I said, putting a hand on his shoulder. "You are the son of a Langorian King and a Kabrinian Princess, raised by a Kaelish Prince. You are the perfect balance of war and peace, of soldier and diplomat. If anyone can accomplish such a feat as to change nature's course and turn Langor around, it is you. But if Draken lets you live to sit on the throne at Darkhorne, it will swallow you. And when it spits you out, little will be left of the man you are now."

"Brother!" Draken bellowed from across the room. "We need to be going."

My grip on Malaq tightened. "Tell him no. Let me kill him. And I will get you on that throne."

Malaq gave me a long, hard completely unreadable stare. He was about to answer when Draken shouted again. "You might like to know, Troy, that I have a man upstairs with a blade to your young messenger's throat." Draken paused to let the picture form. "If you want him to continue breathing, I suggest you back down."

With a snarl, I started toward Draken.

Malaq grabbed me. "Stop. Think about what you're doing."

I tried to throw him off. "I'm fucking killing him is what I'm doing!"

"Let him go, Ian." Malaq struggled to hold me back. "Let us both go. Do you really want to risk Jarryd's life for this? Ian!" he said again, forcefully, because I wasn't listening. I wasn't even looking at him. I had too much fury and turmoil running through me to focus on anything except whether or not I could live with either choice.

Letting Draken walk out of the Faernore alive, it felt so damn much like giving up—on Neela, on my own need for vengeance. Yet if I let Jarryd die, I was turning my back on someone who would never turn his back on me. I would be forsaking the bond we might make before it even happened. And that was like giving up too.

"Son of a bitch." Grinding the anger down between my teeth, I waved a brisk hand toward the door. "Get him out of here. Before I change my mind."

Malaq gave Draken a crisp nod and released me. "You made the right call."

"Did I?" Watching Draken make his way over with a triumphant smile, I scowled at Malaq. "This is the last goddamn time I stay my hand for you, Prince. Are we clear?"

If Malaq had a reply, he kept it to himself. With me on one side of him and Draken coming to stand on the other, he looked a little stunned. Being stuck in between us wasn't a concept anymore. It was a cold, hard fact.

Looking exceptionally satisfied, Draken let loose a gruff, Langorian command in the direction of the stairwell. A moment later, heavy footfall struck the boards on the floor above. Another moment passed, and the sound hit the top of the stairs. As Draken's guard descended, I measured him to be much the same as the rest of his ilk: big and meaty with enough dark hair and ugliness that the details weren't important. His stare, fixed on me. It was brimming with a mischievous, almost perverse sense of gratification.

The man came closer. As he lifted the dagger in his hand, his expression turned outright malicious. He held the weapon up, in front of his face, and my attention was immediately drawn to the distinctive Shinree runes etched along the glistening-wet blade. A set of brightly colored stones adorned the hilt. The stones were of a particular combination, inlaid for one purpose only: the ritual binding of souls.

I started to form an accusation. But all I could think of was, *how?* How was it that a *Nor-Taali* blade, an ancient Shinree ceremonial weapon, one never meant to see combat, had made its way to a rundown tavern on the edge of Kael? More confounding was how this specific blade was here—because it was mine.

When I left for war, I'd left the dagger (and a handful of other belongings) in a Rellan village, in the care of a friend. I'd never bothered claiming it after, and I certainly hadn't meant for Katrine to guard it with her life. But knowing full well the feisty girl would rather die than deal with a Langorian, I knew exactly what the bastard had done to get it from her.

I just needed to hear him say it.

The soldier reached the last step. I pushed off the wall and blocked him. "How did you get that?"

He lowered the dagger from his pockmarked face and grinned. "It was a gift."

"Katrine wouldn't give shit to a pig like you. What did you do to her?"

"Nothing the bitch didn't enjoy."

"That bitch is my friend."

"Your *friend* was a dirty tavern tramp that begged for more."

Knuckles clenched, I raised my arm to hit him, and a drop of red slid off the tip of the dagger. Time seemed to slow as it dripped to the floor.

It sped up again as I looked back to the blade, and the implication sank in.

The soldier sneered at the comprehension on my face. "Your other friend, upstairs, he didn't beg for more…but I gave it to him anyway."

I punched him. Not once, or twice. I drove my fists into his unsightly face until it looked like a bowl of meat and his legs buckled. Whimpering, begging for me to stop, I grabbed the bastard's head and brought my knee up into his throat to make him shut up. Then I hauled him to his feet and hit him some more.

"Troy did as you asked," Malaq said; his distraught voice in the background. "You said Kane would not be harmed."

"How nice to have earned your trust so quickly, brother," Draken chuckled.

Shoving my opponent away, I started up the stairs. I made it up two before pain struck my leg and I went down.

"Ian!" Malaq called out.

But it was Draken's voice that shook the walls. "FOOL!" he roared. Rushing up to the battered soldier, Draken seized him by the throat and lifted him off the floor. "You were charged with delivering Troy's property to Reth, not pilfering it! Do you have any idea what you've done?"

His sputtered, raspy reply was unintelligible. But his answer, like the question, had no purpose. It wouldn't reverse the fact that the man had buried the *Nor-Taali* dagger deep in my right thigh. That blood was pouring out around the edges of the blade, soaking my breeches and streaming down my leg.

Stealing myself, I wrapped a hand around the grip of the weapon. I needed to get it out, but I hadn't counted on the aura of the stones reacting so promptly to my touch. The second my skin made contact, a rapid surge of magic spread out from the stones beneath my fingers. It progressed down the blade. It ran hot into the wound.

Magic hit my open vein and the lights in the tavern grew brighter, the air heavier.

Jolts of pain attacked my chest. The room grew fuzzy and cold.

I yanked the weapon from my leg, but the harm was done. Jarryd's blood on the blade had mingled with mine. The process to bind our souls was already beginning.

Dazed, I sat where I fell. I looked at Malaq at the bottom of the stairs, gripping the bannister furiously. He wanted to come to my aid, but he knew it would cost him.

I took the choice away and warned him back with a shake of my head.

Draken finished choking his soldier to death and dropped him. As he turned to me, for just a flash, something was on the face of the King of Langor that I'd never expected to see: fear. Then the expression shifted. It became more predictably shrewd and pompous, which made sense.

The first to experience the magic of the *Nor-Taali* in hundreds of years, Draken alone knew exactly what was happening. And he liked it. He liked knowing more than I did. "Do you feel it?" he said to me then, sly and suggestive. "The pain? The disorientation? The messenger's injuries are becoming your own. He's dying, Troy, and you're going to feel every excruciating second of it."

"How?" I winced. "How do I stop it?"

"Complete the ritual. Rewrite your entire life. And his. Or not," Draken shrugged. "The decision is yours. But be quick about it. From the way you're looking, I'd say your Rellan friend is running out of time." He gave Malaq a meaningful, cautionary look. "Don't be long, brother."

As I watched Draken leave the inn, I recalled the vision Sienn gave me.

Fate is giving me a choice. Let Jarryd die now, or later.

Neither worked for me.

Leaning heavily on the banister, I crawled up the stairs. I reached the second floor, stood awkwardly, and glanced down at Malaq. His face was ripe with indecision.

"Go," I told him.

Swallowing, he nodded. "Jarryd?"

"I'll take care of it." Digging into the front pocket of my breeches, I pulled out his black pearl ring and tossed it to him.

Malaq looked at it, then at his empty finger. "When did you…?"

"You sleep like the dead, Prince. Maybe this will keep you from ending up dead while you sleep."

Closing his hand over the spelled ring, Malaq stared up at me. "You're a good man, Ian. For an outcast," he grinned. The expression wavered. Sadness crept into it as he backed up. "I know you don't believe in luck, but I wish it on you all the same."

I forced a shaky smile. "Goodbye, *Nef'areen*." Turning, I limped away down the hall, following the trail of Jarryd's blood on the floor.

FORTY

My right hand shook as I carved the last of the markings on my left, telling myself for the fifth time that I had to keep going. Jarryd was spilling blood from more wounds than I cared to count. Sienn was nowhere to be found, and I was no healer. All I could do was go on. Finishing the ritual was the only way to keep him alive.

It wasn't as selfless as it sounded, though. With each scrape of the knife, I found myself becoming not only accepting, but anxious for what Fate had dropped in my lap. I kept recalling that last, brief instant of my vision. That flicker of a moment as I'd watched Jarryd's life drain away. I remembered feeling like a part of me was dying too.

The gods knew I didn't want Jarryd to die at all. Though for my future self to suffer a sense of loss so profound and debilitating, it had to be over something worth losing, something that surpassed the boundaries of normal friendship. And if tying myself to a Royal Kabrinian Messenger could truly give me that, if I could have something in my life positive enough that merely the idea of not having it was unbearable—contentment, stability, maybe even peace—I wanted a chance at it. I wanted something good that filled the holes longer than magic, or a bottle, or a woman. Until the possibility was in front of me, I hadn't recognized how much.

"So the task is yours, my friend. I only hope you want it."

Completing the final rune on Jarryd's right hand, our connection deepened. A host of sensations flowed in, yet nothing I could explain or pinpoint.

No clear emotions of his that I could sense. No trace of intention or attitude. Those things would come later when the link between us was truly forged. My body would be ready then, to recognize and process them. What I felt now was simply a presence. An awareness of him that went beyond what my eyes could see or my ears could hear.

It was weak and diminishing quickly, but the spell wouldn't take long. Now that blood was shared and the runes carved, all that remained was to call the first four of the seven stones in the correct order. It sounded straightforward. Yet there were few Shinree alive who could do it. I was one of them, but only because of my mother. Being both nostalgic and a taskmaster, V'loria Troy had required me to memorize the most minor details of anything she deemed important. The dagger, a memento passed down through her family line, had been one of those things.

Sapphire first, I thought, as I drew it in. Meant to calm the mind and ready it for the intrusion that was to come, the blue stone created a higher level of awareness. A place where the initial transference would occur, and where later, the regular more routine, exchanges would flow between us. Next was opal. Amplifying our traits and skills, the stone would enhance our memories and experiences, and sharpen everything that was to be shared. Then, diamond to intensify and stabilize the link. Lastly, I drew in the hiddenite to make everything permanent.

Holding their magic in me, I trapped the hilt of the dagger between our bleeding palms and absorbed the remaining three minor stones. I couldn't remember their roles, but as their auras blended flawlessly with the other four, they created a perfect harmony of power inside me.

Vibrating and crackling, it traveled to where our hands met. It swarmed over our fingers. Swirling. Encircling. Tightening. In seconds, we were swathed up to our elbows, held fast by a single, unbreakable force.

Abruptly, a portion split off. It merged again with what enveloped us. Sweeping up my arm to my chest, it plunged into me (into both of us), tore out and split again.

Repeatedly, the glowing, pulsing, white energy infiltrated our bodies, divided, re-joined, and then infiltrated again.

I screamed every time.

Unconscious, Jarryd didn't react at all. But I could feel the force burrowing though me. Collecting bits and pieces, plucking them out and replacing them with something foreign, it was tearing me apart and rebuilding me from the inside out.

In less than a breath I'd lost the ability to grasp my own existence. Three more; and I couldn't find a single notion of individuality. Not even a memory of it.

The spell pulled, shredded, emptied and filled me, over and over, faster and faster, until it was done. Then it tore out of me with half my soul in tow.

———

The cracked boards of the ceiling above me faded in and out. I watched them, but I had no clue why they were blurry. I couldn't remember why I was lying on the floor beside the bed instead of on it. Or why my head felt like a vice was clamped to the outside. I put a hand up to make sure one wasn't attached to my skull, but finding none didn't make the pain any better. It didn't make me care if the indistinct light in the room meant the sun was rising or setting. All I wanted, as I focused on the tangle of gray covers hanging off the edge of the bed, was to pull them down over my head and go back to sleep.

If only the blankets weren't coated in blood.

Tentatively, I reached up. My intention was to examine the stains, but there was a strange scar on my left hand. I wasn't sure how the lines got there, but they were deep and fresh, and in no way random or accidental. The skin of my palm had been carved into a well-defined pattern of complex Shinree runes.

I read one aloud. *"Nef'taali."* And with a force that would have knocked me to the floor if I weren't there already, I knew why the lines were on my hand and whose blood was on the bed. I knew what I'd done. I also knew that I wasn't alone.

I lifted my head off the floor and saw him, in the gloom, sitting in a chair near the window. Brown hair unbound and expression intense, Jarryd was quiet and still. He wasn't looking at me. His fierce blue eyes were fixed on the ceremonial blade gripped in his scarred hand. A crazy amount of blood darkened his flesh and streaked his breeches. Multiple, overlapping, vertical white seams divided his bare chest and stomach.

I gazed at the scars in shock. Hours before, they'd been gaping wounds. Now, they looked months, perhaps even years, old.

Sitting up, I tried to think. Vaguely, I recalled pushing my strength into him. I remembered praying I could give Jarryd enough to keep his body working until I could get him to a healer. Somehow though, between the spell and my commitment to repair him, I must have transferred over a substantial amount of my own energy. So much, that I'd mended Jarryd's fatal wounds completely and weakened myself beyond good sense.

It was a sound theory, given how lousy I felt. But it was worth it. Saving Jarryd had been a much-needed victory. I just wasn't sure he felt the same way. His posture rigid, his face pale and pinched with unease, he hadn't even reacted to the fact that I was awake. *I should say something*, I thought. Yet I didn't know how to justify stealing pieces of a man's soul without asking. *He has to understand I had no choice. I couldn't sit back and let him die. The gods worked too hard to put us together.*

There is reason in this. There has to be.

But the longer he sat, saying nothing, the more uncertainty wormed its way into my mind. Apprehension tightened my chest, and I was suddenly skeptical of the choice I'd made. A choice I had no right to make for him.

Gripping the blankets for leverage, I heaved myself up to sit on the edge of the bed. Elbows on knees, I leaned forward and dug the heels of my hands into my aching forehead and thought, *what have I done?*

Quietly, Jarryd said, "The time for doubt is past, don't you think?"

"I'm sorry," was all I could come up with.

"Save it. The Langorian left you few options."

I stared; wishing he would look at me. "Are you saying you're okay with this?"

"I'm saying it's done."

"So you're just going to accept it, without argument or comment?"

"What do you want me to do? Shout? Scream? Slam your head into the wall?

"If that's what you want."

"Will it change anything?"

"No."

"Then what good is it?"

I had no answer for that. I was too startled by the cold simmering anger that had replaced Jarryd's usual impassioned outburst. *Already he's different.* "How do you feel?"

"You don't know? You can't sense me? I thought that was the point."

"All I can sense is my head." I shook it, and got a surge of pain in return. Groaning, I flopped back on the bed. I closed my eyes and groaned some more.

Footsteps moved across the floor. A small weight hit the bed.

"Here," he said. "I figured you'd want this back."

I opened my eyes. The dagger was beside to me. I had absolutely no desire to touch it.

Gingerly, I sat back up. "Do you understand what I've done?"

Jarryd took a long, slow breath. He went back to the window. His eyes burned through the drawn moth-eaten curtains for a long time. He gazed like he could see something of interest through the holes. He couldn't, of course. Until we reached the border with Rella, for miles in all directions there was only forest.

Still, he went on staring. And the anxious feeling inside of me grew worse.

"I didn't at first," he said, finally. "I should have been dead. I was confused, weak. Then…" absently touching the scars on his chest, he swallowed. "There was this presence. Like something had climbed inside me." Dropping his hand, Jarryd drew a shaky breath. "These things," he pivoted around, "these parts of you…are they in me for good? Can I ever go back to who I was?"

"Everything that makes you who you are is still there. But who I am is in you too, permanently. Experiences, skills, memories, behavior, personality traits, likes and dislikes—the spell copied those things from me and gave them to you."

"All of them?"

"Probably not. It was up to Fate to decide what each of us needed from the other. We may not know the full extent of what he gave us for a long time. It could take days, weeks, maybe even months, for all aspects of the spell to manifest."

"You mean *change us?*"

"Yes, but that doesn't mean it will be drastic."

"How could it not be? How could taking in parts of your life not affect mine?"

"It will. But with time and practice, you can sort through my memories and experiences like pages in a book, absorbing what you want, scanning and storing the rest." Anxiety was getting the best of me. I cut my explanation short. "Jarryd, I knew the consequences. You didn't. And for that I am truly sorry."

He turned away again. I would have felt better knowing what he was thinking. But Jarryd was seeing life through my eyes. He was sharing in the horrors of my past and the mess I'd made of the present, so I had a good idea. Myself, I was more than a little self-conscious. Granting Jarryd access to everything I kept hidden hadn't been a concern when I was saving his life. Now, it was painfully embarrassing. All my private, intimate moments weren't intimate anymore. He would know my childhood fears and blunders. He would grasp the extent of my love for Aylagar. How I'd fallen for a woman I'd known full well had only two uses for me: war and sex. He would understand how close her death had come to ruining me. How defective I was, how brutal I could be, and how deep my lust for magic really was.

Nevertheless, it was the exposure of recent events I was dreading the most. The secrets I'd made of Reth and Sienn wouldn't sit well with him. Neither would the dream-weave and the degree of damage it had inflicted. The rage, the helplessness, the pain and the need the spell had created in me; Jarryd would endure it all through my memories. He would re-live my obsession for Neela and know her as I did. He would feel her. Want her. *Share in her,* I thought, feeling an irrational wave of resentment speed through me. It was followed by desire, jealousy, and other unbecoming things that I frantically tried to force away.

As Jarryd's body stiffened, I knew I hadn't been quick enough.

"Emotional and physical sensations," I said apologetically, "strong reactions and changes in moods. They all travel instantly across the tether that runs between us."

"That's why my head is starting to hurt. I feel what you feel." He sighed and faced me. "How is that a good thing?"

"You can learn to ignore it, to push away what you don't want. We both can."

"You said this wasn't done anymore."

"There hasn't been a pairing of Shinree soldiers in over five hundred years."

"I'm not a soldier. I'm not even Shinree."

"And I don't know how that will affect things."

Jarryd rubbed at the symbols on his palm. "They look so harmless. But I don't even want to go home now. The thought of Kabri makes me feel trapped, bitter."

"That's my fault. Once you can distinguish what's me, you can block out—"

"Neela?" he said sharply. "Can I block out your thoughts of her? Your dreams?"

"I swear, Jarryd, I didn't know it was her. I just found out myself."

His hands twitched like they were aching to wrap around my throat. "Why didn't you tell me about Jem Reth, about his spell? The images I got from your mind… How do you live with this stuff in your head? How are you not angry all the time? Just knowing what they did to you makes me want to rip Draken's fucking head off and shove it down Reth's throat."

"That pretty much sums up it up."

"Gods." He ran both hands through his hair. "Sick, fucking bastards."

"Sick or not, Reth knew what he was doing. He created a lure as any good hunter would. Giving me something I wanted and then snatching it away."

"Something you wanted? You don't even know Neela."

"What he gave me was the kind of life I never thought I'd have. Draken only put Neela's likeness in my dreams so he could use the threat of their marriage against me."

"That Shinree woman, Sienn, she stopped the spell. So the dreams are done?"

"They are. But the way I recall them isn't normal. They're too vivid, too real. It's like I'm there. Like they aren't memories, but—"

Her hands ran over me, broken and bloody. Her lips touched mine.

"They come over me sometimes," I said, a little shaky.

Splatters of warm blood hit my face. Ropes cut into my skin.

Clenching my fists, I pushed the images away.

Her burned arms reached out. "*Save me,*" *she pleaded.*

I slammed my hand against the post of the bed. "Fucking leave me alone!"

Jarryd took an anxious step. "What is it? What do you see? Is it Neela?"

I nodded. "I hoped it was over. That with the dreams gone I wouldn't see her like this anymore. God damn it!" I hit the bed again. "We'll be in Kabri in a matter of days. How am I going to face her? I can feel Neela in my hands, Jarryd. I can *feel* her and she doesn't even know me."

"I know her. I have loved Neela Arcana as long as I can remember. I would give my life for hers, well beyond the oath I took to serve Rella."

"Great," I sighed. "Let's just fight over her now and get it over with."

"Let me finish," he said harshly. "Neela and I were childhood friends. For a while we were close. Then this sharp, shrewd, restrained Princess emerged, and the girl I knew died. I had little choice but to bury her."

"Not far enough, I'm thinking. The way you went after Guidon back in Kael."

Jarryd lifted a shoulder in a faint, half shrug; a gesture that was definitely his own. "The past creeps up. But Neela is Rella's Queen. There is no place for me in her life anymore. There never was. And that can only help you."

"Sorry, my friend, but I don't see how your unrequited love will help anything."

"Understanding the reality of who Neela truly is, recognizing the differences between her and the girl in your dreams…that has to do something to override the illusion. At least make it less powerful. Make her less enticing."

"Or, she could become your obsession as well as mine." I shook my throbbing head. "I'm sorry, Jarryd. I should never have brought you into this."

He gave me an impatient glare. "Closer than brothers. That's what you said back in Kael when you were describing this very spell—when you were adamantly telling me that no Shinree would ever take part in such a thing with a Langorian."

"Guess I was wrong."

"But maybe you aren't wrong about this."

"I've done things, Jarryd. I'm not a good person. Shinree are addicts by nature. If you inherited that from me..." I couldn't finish. Overcome with doubt and rage, I raised a fist to strike the post again, and Jarryd stopped me.

Clasping his scarred palm to mine, he pulled me to my feet. "Is it possible that all of this has happened for a reason? That B'naach, the Shinree God of Fate himself placed your dagger in Langorian hands because he knew it would take something this drastic to make you understand that you aren't alone in this fight. Maybe, he knew you would need more than magic to defeat Draken and Reth. Or, maybe," with a jolt, I felt a great surge of strength leap from him into me, "you just need *more*."

Energy sunk in where our hands came together. It raced through me, and the ache in my head began to dim. An instant later, a different sensation swept in. It was strong and startling, but it was neither pain nor pleasure. It was simply a notion, a conspicuous and comfortable presence inside me that I could only define as something other than myself.

FORTY ONE

We pushed out of the brush at the mid-way point of a lengthy strip of white sand beach. Across the water lay our destination: Rella. Up the beach a ways was the slender belt of rocky land that would carry us across. North of this natural bridge was the beginning of The Shallows, a long, low, narrow river that marked the boundary line of Kael's western border. The slender canal ran up the length of Mirra'kelan, extending past the swampy Border Lands to empty out into the violent waters of the Northern Sea.

South of our position, the main road into Kael sprouted off the beach and disappeared into the trees. Snaking up the coast, the road wound around the mountains, through the harbor villages, and eventually headed north into the city.

The inlet, bleeding out into the ocean as it did, was a busy, well-traveled spot. Villagers from both realms trawled the water. Most days, boats were bobbing in the waves from sunup to sundown, while merchants and their families journeyed back and forth across the bridge looking to trade or sell their wares.

Today, no one crossed the bridge or walked the road. There wasn't a single boat, net, or trap in sight. No fisherman, either. Likely, it was the three Arullan warriors, two eldring, and Jem Reth—standing in a line at the edge of the waves—that had scared them all away.

The eldring were on their haunches, heads down to keep the sun out of their eyes. The warriors, two men and one woman, all midnight dark in skin and hair, were focused and well-armed. Watching me, with boots fixed firmly in the sand and cloak flapping in the breeze, Reth peered sedately and silently through the holes in his bronze mask.

Jarryd leaned in. "Any ideas?"

"Reth wants to bargain. He won't attack unless I provoke him."

"And if he provokes you?"

"Hopefully, it won't come to that. I'll show interest in his plan. Get him talking. Maybe I can find out what's in Tam's journal."

Jarryd eyed me doubtfully. "You really think that old book has the answers?"

"Magic wise, I shouldn't be doing the things I'm doing. If the crown is boosting my abilities, maybe it's boosting his too. If I can find out how, maybe I can reverse it, or use it against him."

"That's a lot of 'ifs' and 'maybes', Ian. I don't like it."

"Yeah, well I haven't had an option I did like in a long time."

"There is another way." Jarryd's hand slid to the quiver hanging off his saddle.

"No. It's too dangerous. Reth won't let you draw on him. And neither will I."

"Well, if I can't shoot him…" Jarryd tightened his grip on the reins. "Let's go say hello." Showering me with sand, he kicked his horse into a fast start. His mount shot down the dune with purpose. The eldring responded by dropping to all fours. Without hesitation, they ran straight for Jarryd on an intercept course.

"Son of a bitch." Speeding forward, as Kya crossed between Jarryd and the fast approaching eldring, I slid to the sand, drew swords, and woke the obsidian inside me all at the same time. I willed the stone's strength into my arms. It streamed down into my blades, and I took up position.

The eldring bounded closer. They squatted to push off their hind legs. I spun. They jumped. Accommodating the eldring's height, I came around swinging both swords in a high arc, and cut across their muscular midsections like they were no thicker than a blade of grass. Their pieces hit the ground like boulders. A fall of brown, brittle leaves drifted down on the breeze to cover their remains.

I'd managed to suck the life out of the only tree on the beach.

Pivoting from Reth's angry eyes, I looked at Jarryd. His expression was no better, but it wavered as he jumped down off his saddle and winced at what was a fair amount of gore on my face. Mopping at it, I pointed to the bridge. "You need to go."

Jarryd responded with a terse, "No way. I'm not letting you face Reth alone."

"And I'm not letting him anywhere near you."

"I'm not a fucking child, Ian. I can fight. I *want* to fight." He held up his hands. "I can kill with these now."

With a hiss I pushed them down before Reth noticed the scar. "Having some of my abilities," I said in a low voice, "and knowing what to do with them are two different things. You can't be reckless with this."

"Reckless?" Jarryd shot back. "I'm whatever you made me." His temper flaring, it rolled in like a storm through the link. I tried to absorb it with some semblance of detachment, but it had only been a day and a half, and I hadn't learned how to do that yet.

"This is still new. It will settle. For both of us," I said, fighting to keep his anger from becoming mine. "But right now, I have to go down there and pretend I don't want to slit that bastard's throat. I can't do that with you in my head, Jarryd. I'm sorry."

Undoubtedly, there was an easy way to halt the constant transfer between us, but I hadn't learned that yet, either. All I had was a trick I'd relied on after the war, when I was doing everything I could to stop casting. It involved visualizing a section of wall in my mind and filling it with the faces of my victims. Trapping my addiction on the other side, I used the guilt of my past to divide me from the temptations of my present.

Now, things were less complicated. I wanted isolation. I wanted to be separate and alone. So I closed my eyes. I pictured the surface smooth and utterly blank. I focused on its perfect, seamless emptiness; on its seclusion and clarity.

I kept with those simple thoughts as I built my wall higher.

Fanning it out, I grew the partition broader and stronger. I lengthened it. Both ends met, and as they slammed together, I felt a sudden, definite break in the magical thread that tied my soul to another—and Jarryd's anger was gone.

I couldn't feel a single physical or emotional sensation that belonged to him. I was aware only of my own mind and body. I was normal again.

Except, normal felt completely wrong.

There was an uncomfortable quiet in me, a disturbing sense of desolation.

Being disconnected had opened up a hole. If I didn't fill it soon, it would get deeper. Its jaws would open wider.

If the hole were allowed to become permanent, it would swallow me.

This is what my future self was feeling in the vision.

This is what it will be like when Jarryd dies.

I opened my eyes. The process to block our link had taken no time at all. Yet it was enough for the two Arullans to get Jarryd on his knees and their swords against his throat. The woman wore little to cover her strong body but weapons. Her fellow watchdog was a short, squat man with an even shorter, squatter face. He was ugly for an Arullan. She wasn't. But they both looked mean as hell.

"Sorry," Jarryd said to me.

"Don't be," I told him.

"Must be a spell," he said, still apologizing. "They moved so fast."

The male Arullan gripped Jarryd's braid and forced his head back. "We can still move nice and slow when we want." Running the tip of his blade down the side of Jarryd's neck, he carved a thin gradual line. "See?" He yanked Jarryd closer. "We're going to have so much fun together."

"Leave him alone," I warned.

The Arullan's slit-like eyes shifted to mine. He slammed the pommel of his short sword into Jarryd's head and shrugged. "Oops."

"If he's not alive when this is over," I vowed, "neither are you." I turned to lay eyes on Reth. He was still at the edge of the waves, guarded by the third Arullan.

I slid my blades away and headed down to the water.

Radiating patience he clearly didn't have; the sand hadn't even stopped crunching under my boots before Reth barked at me. "Idiot! You've joined souls with him?" He tossed a hand at Jarryd. "A messenger from Kabri? A *commoner?*"

"Better than that piece of shit Langorian you tied yourself to."

"Draken is a King! Our joining has taught me how to lead our people."

"You're using a mad tyrant as a model for kingship?" Laughing, I glanced at the warrior next to him. Large and bald, the man's dark face was severely sharp, like staring at a rock. "Bodyguards, huh? I must be starting to worry you."

Reth let out a grunt. "I intercepted these three on their way to collect on a hefty reward for your head. Apparently, with the recent fracture of the Arullan government, old grudges have become new."

"And you had nothing to do with that?"

"Their hatred of you? No, you incited that when you killed Aylagar. As far as the split goes, Draken did offer an alliance to Arulla. Those with wisdom have taken it. Those without will suffer for their stupidity."

"Your new watchdogs will suffer a lot more if they don't release my friend."

"I think you have it backwards. Instilled with my gift of speed, you can't possibly cast faster than they can swing." Reth held a hand out to the Arullan beside him. In silence, the man unhooked a metal flask from his belt. "This," Reth said, taking it, "is the key to your friend's continued health." Removing the cork, he held it out. "Drink."

I leaned in and took a sniff. It was pure *Kayn'l*. "I'm not drinking that."

"I came here to talk. But if you prefer to make it difficult..." Reth gave a nod, and the Arullans holding Jarryd shoved him roughly to the ground. He tried to fight back as they kicked him, but his attacker's legs moved in a blur. It took only a moment for him to stop moving.

"ENOUGH!" I shouted. Surprisingly, they left off. I turned to yell at Reth, and his guard's fist struck my face absurdly fast. In a flash, I was on my back with the man on top of me, the flask in my mouth, and a steady stream of bitter, syrupy thickness pouring down my throat. I went to shove him off, but I couldn't lift my arms. My legs wouldn't respond. It was like the sand itself was holding me down.

"Swallow," the Arullan ordered. "Or the pretty Rellan boy starts losing important parts. Either is fine with me." Grinning, he tipped the flask higher. The *Kayn'l* filled my mouth. It overflowed, shooting out around the edges, rushing into my lungs, sputtering out my nose.

Jarryd screamed, and I swallowed as much as I could. The rest, I choked on.

When the flask was empty my captor let me go. "Tasty?" he chuckled. He sunk a fist into my stomach as he got up.

Gasping and gagging, I coughed out a weak, "Fuck off, Arullan."

"Mind your manners, witch. Or I'll give you something else to swallow." Grabbing his cock through his pants, he let out a coarse laugh.

"Silence!" Reth thundered, and the Arullan's body went unnaturally still. At the same time, the sand shifted, and mine became mobile.

Rolling onto my side, I wiped the gluey black liquid off my face. A good deal of it was soaking the front of my clothes, but enough had gotten in me. Already, I could feel a slight numbness spreading through my body.

I snarled at Reth as I pushed to my feet. "What the hell was that for?"

"Your own good," he answered boldly. "Trying to cast against me would not have been wise. So I removed the temptation." Reth beckoned, and the Arullan woman obeyed. Lingering, the man squatted. He put his blade to the back of his Jarryd's neck.

No!" I started toward him, and the sand tightened around my boots. I tried casting, but felt nothing as I reached for the stones. Pleading with Reth would get me nowhere, so I tore down the wall that separated me from Jarryd and conveyed motion and urgency across the link. I flooded our connection with my own desperation and adrenaline, willing Jarryd to hear me. But the *Kayn'l* had reduced him to a fuzzy thought in the back of my mind and I had no idea if my warning was getting through, or if he was even alive—until, he struck.

In one rapid, fluid move, Jarryd twisted away, wrapped his legs around the Arullan's ankles, and yanked his feet out from under him. The second the man hit the ground, Jarryd kicked him in the face, kicked the weapon from his grip, and snatched it up. Brandishing the short sword in his hand like he was born with it, Jarryd hovered over his opponent. A slight crooked grin tugged at one corner of his bruised mouth as he went down on one knee and, without a word or the slightest hesitation, drove the blade clean through the Arullan's neck.

Jarryd got up and walked away from the body. Watching him, I tried to reconcile the personality of the young man I'd met in Kael with the unflinching kill I'd just witnessed.

I couldn't.

Reth's spell dissolved. The sand eased its grip, and I ran up to Jarryd. "That was..."

"You," he said. But it wasn't resentment burning in his eyes. It was excitement. "Did you see that?" he laughed. "What I did?"

Appalled, I shook my head. "I never wanted this for you."

"Well I've got it." Jarryd rubbed at his chest like it hurt. His face probably did as well; it was a mess of cuts and bruises. "It's a good thing, too. Do you have any idea how difficult it is to stay alive at your side?"

I wasn't sure how to answer that. "You can't be here right now, Jarryd. With the *Kayn'l* in me I can't connect to the stones. I can't protect you."

Jarryd glanced at Reth. "I don't trust this."

"Me neither." I gestured at the bridge. "It looks clear, but there could be sentries on the other side, so don't travel the road. Stay in the trees alongside it and take the first fork. The house at the end belongs to an old healer friend of mine. His name's Broc. It's been years, but if you tell him you're with me, he'll hide you. As long as you don't flirt with his daughter," I threw in.

He gave me a half-hearted grin. "If you don't show..."

"I'll show."

There was skepticism in Jarryd's nod, but he winced his way up into the saddle, turned his mount, and rode swiftly up the beach to the bridge. I waited until he'd crossed over into Rella. Then I grabbed Kya's reins and went back to Reth. "So let's have it."

He dismissed his remaining warriors. As they walked off mindlessly toward the road, Reth said, like an invitation, "Neela Arcana?"

My grip tightened on the reins. "Sienn broke your dream spell."

"I'm not surprised. Sienn is a powerful magic user."

"Maybe you should stop hurting her then. Or someday she might hurt you back."

Reth's white eyes tensed. "Sienn won't betray me."

"Sienn's loyalty isn't real. You created it with magic."

"I enhanced it. She wanted someone to save her. All it took was a little push to believe it was me."

"That's quite a skill you have, finding and exploiting the weaknesses of others."

"I prefer to call it motivating." He cocked his head, scrutinizing me. "I see your mental and physical state has improved since the dreams stopped. You do understand that the reprieve is temporary? That when the woman you crave is standing before you in the flesh, your desire will return anew. And if I hurt her," he paused to smile, "you will do anything to make it stop."

"I won't go against Rella. I can't. The spell that binds me to protect the realm is older and stronger than yours. It will always be the dominant force in my life."

"When Draken claims it, Rella will no longer be. Which means your spell to defend her will have no basis to exist." Watching me expectantly, he stepped closer. "Draken will forgo his marriage to Neela. Cast her into exile somewhere remote and private. She will no longer be a Queen. Just the girl you felt at peace with in your dreams. You can go to her. Live the life you played at. Have a child. Several if you like. There will be no more fighting. No more wandering. Just a happy, stable existence growing old with the woman you love. All you have to do is remove the shard."

I turned from him and wandered out into the waves. Staring at the horizon, watching the evening sun turn the water into a bed of diamonds, as my head fought off the fuzziness of the *Kayn'l*, I struggled like hell to ignore the need in my gut. I couldn't believe how strong it was. I hadn't even known I'd wanted the things Reth offered until he showed them to me. Now, I couldn't stop thinking about them. I couldn't stop thinking about her. There was only one thing he did wrong.

"It isn't love," I said, "what I feel for Neela. What you made me feel."

"You're right. Obsession was better for my plans."

"Obsession and I are old friends."

"Then you know how hard it is to shake. How it clings to you. Suffocates you."

"I know how to fight it."

"Do you?" he chuckled, and my confidence wavered.

I have to, I thought. *I have to fight it, to bury her, like Jarryd did. Jarryd...*

Gods, maybe I was wrong. Maybe he can protect me from something.

Reth was still talking, but I shut him out and delved deep inside; to the place that harbored a part of a soul that wasn't mine. I started peeling back the layers like the petals of a flower. Concentrating on Jarryd's memories of Neela, I rummaged swiftly through them. Every strong thought of her, every recollection and emotion, all the things I'd been dodging since we joined, I reviewed. They flashed across my mind in the blink of an eye, and I began to grasp the impact she'd had on his life. I witnessed their early friendship and their budding adolescent flirtation. I saw the physical closeness that almost was and the frustration that grew as their relationship fell apart. I watched them become strangers as Neela's tenderness, warmth, and trust wilted beneath an emerging coldness. I felt Jarryd's pain as he tried to accept their separate paths, how he'd struggled not to hate her and to instead transform his desire and affection into a fierce undying loyalty.

Converting resentment into resolve, Jarryd's disappointment had become conviction. He'd turned heartache into a steadfast devotion, allowing him to continue to faithfully uphold his oath to Rella's crown.

It was an impressive feat. I was proud to let those parts of him become a part of me. And as I did, as I saw Neela through Jarryd's eyes, the woman he knew started to prevail over the illusion in my head. His version came into focus, and the allure of mine, dimmed. My emotions surrounding her evened out. I felt stronger than I had in weeks.

I knew better, though, than to think I was cured. Or that Reth couldn't destabilize my newly found armor with a few choice words. He was damn good at that. He was also damn good at making me want to kill him. Only, this wasn't the time. He didn't have the crown on him, and I couldn't cast. Without access to magic, remaining in Jem Reth's presence wasn't a smart move.

I grabbed Kya's reins and started pulling her down the beach.

"Where are you going?" he demanded. "We aren't finished." Reth got louder as I kept walking. "Don't turn your back on me. Troy! Get back here. Do you hear me? I *said*, Get. Back. Here!" I didn't, and rage shook his voice. "L'TARIAN!"

Kya bumped into me as I stopped short. "What did you call me?"

There was a short hesitation. "L'tarian."

"My mother was the only one to call me by that name. How do you know of it?" When he didn't respond, I drew a breath and faced him. "I asked you a question."

Reth threw the heavy cloak back over his shoulders. He unhooked the clasp and let the dark covering drop to the ground. "L'tarian was your birth name." Reaching both hands behind his head, he undid the buckles on his mask. "It was chosen by the man who gave you life." He pulled the covering away from his face. It made a soft squelch as it hit the sand. "It was chosen by me."

FORTY TWO

Age and slavery had taken little away from Jem Reth. His chin was sharp and defiant. Prominent cheekbones rested high on a strong face. His tall frame, similar to mine, was impressively built. At one time, standing side by side, there would have been no mistake that I was his get. Now, you had to look real close. My parentage wasn't the only thing he'd been hiding behind the mask.

"Your face," I said tensely. "The Crown of Stones did this to you?"

"You just learned your father is alive and that's all you have to say?"

He was right, I suppose. But how could I say anything else? It was as if someone had taken a shade from each of the crown's stones, blended and twisted them together into a dank, ugly color. And then they used that color to patch my father's face together.

Magic scars, infinitely worse than mine, streaked his nearly bald scalp. The few patches of hair he had left were dull, thin strands that were no longer white, but a murky grayish brown. The same muted, mottled color stained his skin. It bled down in wide, jagged seams out of his hairline, across his brow, over the length of his cheeks, to cross his nose and dip down past his jaw and into the collar of his shirt.

It was repulsive. Yet in his ruin, I saw common ground.

Putting a hand in the fringe of hair over my eyes, I pulled it back, showing him the vague, colored imprints on my skin. "They're not like yours, but…"

Reth looked at me with blatant disinterest. "Power comes with a price."

I let the hair flop back down over my forehead. "Perhaps this one is too high?"

"Do you care, L'tarian?" He eyed me inquisitively. "Do you truly care?"

"What you've done to yourself? Did you think I would?"

"What I thought was to see more of me in you." His lips hooked down in a deep frown. "And a bit less of your mother."

"I am nothing like her."

"Nonsense. Her blood has tempered you. It kept you from your full potential."

"And what's that," I laughed, "to become like you?"

His stained jaw tightened. "The origin of your name goes far back in the Reth line. It actually pre-dates the empire. Do you know what it means?" He answered for me. "Dark Lord. V'loria didn't want such a label for you, but my ancestors deserved to be honored, and you deserved a worthy a name. It was my right after all, to name that which I created. And it isn't every day a descendant of our Emperor is born."

"I don't want to hear this."

"It's important that you understand how you began."

"No. It isn't."

"You will listen when your father speaks." He raised a muddy-hued eyebrow for my reaction. I was too sick to give him one, and he went on. "It was a different time then in Kabri, before you were born. The war you knew was just beginning. But the estimate for casualties on the Rellan side was grim. Raynan's father was yet King, and he decided they needed an edge. He chose me to lead his army."

"You were a soldier for Rella, like me?"

"Not quite like you. Having been on *Kayn'l* all my life, my natural inclinations took a while to emerge. I had to be taught how to cast and how to fight. Raynan and I sparred every day. He was quite the swordsman in his youth."

"And my mother?"

"Being King's Healer and mistress to the Prince, V'loria resided at the castle. She tended me those first few weeks off the *Kayn'l.*"

"So you knew them both."

"Knew them? We were inseparable—and young. So young and full of mischief," he said, an unexpected wave of nostalgia softening his voice. "The night we went to see the oracle, it was only for fun. We hit every dice game in every respectable tavern. Then we moved on to the not so respectable ones." He chuckled briefly. "It was the last time the three of us were content together. After that night, it all changed."

He had me hooked. "What happened?"

"It was just a dirty roadhouse on the edge of the city. But that woman, whoever she was, was one hell of a seer. We were all shaken after. None of us spoke of our visions. I have no idea what they might have witnessed. But I saw you."

"How do you mean?"

"It was disorienting. I was new to magic. I had no idea oracles could take you into lives other than your own. I didn't know I was seeing the future through my son, not at first. I—we—were in the middle of a battle. There was a quake. You fell. The ground opened and there it was." He smiled, remembering. "It was beautiful."

"You saw me find the Crown of Stones?"

"I felt the power when you used it. The rage. It was incredible. They were all dying around you and you didn't see it. You didn't even care. And I knew. I recognized you as mine. I saw what you would be capable of. That you could wield the magic needed to rebuild our empire. I just had to wait for you to grow up, to be ready to accept the responsibility and the honor of taking up where Tam Reth left off. To become a son I could be proud of."

My heart was racing. I ran a helpless hand through my hair and staggered back. "You knew what the crown would do…what I would do…and you let me?" I searched his eyes for some morsel of compassion or remorse, but the nothingness I found turned my stomach. "All those people…all those lives. You let me kill them. The Langorians, the Rellans…Aylagar." I let go of Kya's reins and drew the sword off my back. "Do you have any idea what living with that day has done to me?"

"Yes. And it isn't what I'd hoped."

"You could have stopped me. Warned me."

"When I had that vision your mother wasn't even with child yet. And if I'd come to you later, claiming you would one day annihilate thousands, you wouldn't have believed me. You were just a boy, L'tarian."

"Don't call me that," I snarled at him. "That is not my name."

"You are a child from the Reth line. You carry the blood of the strongest Shinree soldiers to ever live. To hear you deny your birthright pains me."

"Not nearly enough."

Reth's eyes narrowed. "V'loria and Raynan had a plan. By compelling you to devote your life to saving others, they hoped to ensure that you would never know the wonders of the darkness flowing in your veins."

"I know darkness well enough."

"But you shrink from it. You don't use it, don't embrace it."

"Most days I'm not that weak."

"I see it now." He nodded solemnly. "I'm already too late. You will never come to me willingly."

"You never wanted me willing. Forcing magic on me...the eldring... the shadows...the dreams—you've tried to break me from the beginning." Recalling all that he had done, my voice came out as a roar. "Who does that to their own fucking child?"

"I was trying to make you obedient. I thought once you knew who I was, once you saw what we could do together, you would understand. But...it was all for nothing. She died for nothing. Nothing," he said again, raising a hand to massage the discolored skin of his brow. He stood that way a moment, wincing and rubbing his forehead like it hurt. Then, abruptly, he rushed up to me. Agitation quickened his words. "You must understand, L'tarian. I wanted you strong. I needed you confident, focused. I thought it was for the best. She would have stood between us. I couldn't let that happen. But...I was too late." Suddenly despondent, his voice fell. "In just those first few years, she destroyed you."

At the start of his outburst, I'd assumed he was talking about Aylagar. But there was shame and honesty in my father's white eyes. There was pain and regret in his words. And it started a chill of foreboding on my skin. "What did you do?"

"I never meant for you to be alone. I went back to get you, but you had already left Kabri. And I had no idea Raynan would know it was me. Or that he would actually be capable of hunting me down. Drugging me, leaving me at the gates of that Langorian slave camp…he knew what they would do to me. How they abused their slaves. I misjudged how much he loved her, and what to lengths he would go to avenge her death."

"No." The blood drained from my face. "You didn't. You couldn't have."

"I wanted to raise you, to make you ready to claim the Crown of Stones and lead our people. It was too important. I couldn't leave you with V'loria. She would have smothered every part of me that was inside of you. Can't you see that?"

My throat was burning. I could hardly get the words out. "It was you? You killed her? You killed my mother?"

"You were my son, too L'tarian. My flesh. I couldn't stand her ruining you."

"All this time, I…I thought…" burying the grief, I clamped my jaw shut until it hurt; I wanted the pain. It was preferable to the flood of loss and confusion I was drowning in, the feeling that I was a child again, standing over my mother's corpse, fists balled with rage, believing that I had to hold it all in, that I didn't deserve to cry.

Because there were times I'd hated her.

There were times I'd wished her dead.

And then she was.

"My spells," I said painfully; thinking back. "They were always erratic. I practiced for hours, but I had trouble controlling them. I thought I did something wrong, let something slip." I shook my head. "I thought it was my fault."

"Really?" He sounded surprised. "I suppose you would have known whether you were in control of your magic or not… if your mother had taught you focus or restraint."

"Maybe she would have—if you hadn't killed her!"

"The choices I made were for the good of us all. One day you will understand."

He reached for me, and I pulled away. I raised my sword between us and looked at him down the length of it, saying nothing, feeling nothing. I was blank inside. He'd stripped me of everything. Dignity. Pride. Family. He'd molded the course of my life, influenced my thoughts and emotions, and I hadn't even known he'd existed.

"I know what you're thinking," he said then. "But your aim is wrong. I'm on your side. After all, I let your other, the messenger, leave unharmed. I could have turned him to dust. Although," he cocked an eyebrow in thought. "Losing him, having his soul ripped from you, could be just what I need to push you in the right direction."

"If you harm him…"

Reth laughed, trivializing my warning as if I were no more than a foolish child.

His child, I reminded myself, and a shiver of revulsion ran through me.

"Rage all you want, son, you can't stop me. I'm faster than you. Better." Magic swirled across my father's eyes. A gloomy blended shade radiated up from his stained skin. It spread right in front of me, a cloudy combination of auras that flowed across his face like a mudslide running downhill. It traveled to engulf his jaw and throat, and in its wake his skin took on a gray, leathery appearance.

Distraught, I lowered my sword. "What's happening to you?"

"What will happen to you…if you let it. What will happen in time to us all."

The demonstration over, the color left his eyes. The stains stopped spreading and wherever the crown was, the power went back inside it. But he was still blotched and ugly. *Scarred*, I thought, *inside and out*.

An involuntary streak of compassion ran through me. "Let me help you. Maybe there's a way to reverse this, to make you normal again."

"Please, L'tarian," he scorned. "Don't try to save me. It demeans us both."

My empathy squashed, bitterness took over. "You really are a fucking prick, you know that?"

"And *you* are a descendant of the Emperor. I want you to act like it."

"You don't get to want anything from me. You're a murderer. A selfish, heartless, cold-blooded…" I cringed as I saw the truth. "Gods, I'm just like you. We're all like you. War or healing, it makes no difference. We're a race of killers."

Reth's muddy features tightened. "I can see you're in shock. You need time to consider what I mean to you. To understand where you truly belong."

I wiped the anguish off my face. "And if I decide where I belong isn't with you?"

"Choosing to come against me would be a fatal mistake, L'tarian. You will never best me with magic."

"Then I'll find another way."

He stared at me, mouth agape in anger and surprise, and I turned away with a tug on Kya's reins. Reth called after me, but I didn't stop. I didn't want to hear anymore. I didn't care if he struck me down while my back was turned. At the moment, dying seemed infinitely easier than living with what I was.

FORTY THREE

I went past the fork in the road and didn't even slow down.

I had an excuse. It was flimsy, and Jarryd would be pissed. But he was the problem. I was in no way ready to admit to myself that Jem Reth was my father. How could I admit it to Jarryd?

Yet, as I rode up to the edge of town, I knew my avoidance wasn't about being ashamed or needing time to think. I just wanted a fight. I wanted a strong enemy presence to take it all out on. At the very least, I was hoping for a patrol to scrap with. Even a single Langorian scout to beat senseless would have made me feel better for a little while.

What I got was utter desolation, dark streets, eerie silence, and burned-out toppled buildings. Ula was deserted. Even the one place I was sure would be open was quiet as a tomb. And Ansel's Place was never quiet.

An inn as lively and rowdy as any other, Ansel's had the best food and girls outside of Kabri. The linens were clean. The water was hot and the ale cold. Most importantly, the first room at the top of the stairs and everything in it was mine.

I hadn't slept there in years. But if you added my time growing up in Ula before the war, to the brief stretch when I lived here after, I'd slept in that room longer than any other in my entire life. I suppose that's why I paid Ansel to keep it for me. The day I left, I gave him coin enough to buy the whole damn building for that one room. I had no real intention of returning. Back then, my lust for magic had been too hard to control, and I'd grown tired of worrying over a town full of lives. But I'd wanted to know the space was there if I needed it, that the pieces of my past had a home even if I didn't.

Now, as I crouched in the adjacent alley, peering across the dark street and wishing for the slightest sign of life, my reasons for leaving suddenly felt so damn selfish. *If I'd been here, I could have protected them.*

I could have protected Katrine.

They can't all be dead. There has to be someone.

I sprinted across to the porch and up the steps to the front door. Finding it locked, I felt my way around the building. The windows on the first floor were boarded shut, as was the back door. No street lamps were lit, and I cursed the lack of light as I stumbled up the rickety steps to the second floor. It wasn't an official entrance, just a small ledge and a casement with a curtain. But the regulars knew it was here. Left perpetually unlocked, the window was known as a handy escape for wayward husbands dodging their angry wives.

As I snuck up the stairs and opened the window, I was glad to see that much hadn't changed. Parting the flimsy curtain, I peered into a hall that was pitch-black and deathly quiet. Easing one leg at a time over the sill, I climbed inside, and with hand on my sword, moved down the hall to my old room.

Putting an ear to the wooden door, I got nothing. My fingers touched the latch. I turned it halfway. Then I thought about how the dagger that bound Jarryd and I together had been on the other side of the door; so had Katrine and the Langorian soldier that killed her. And I suddenly couldn't fathom how walking into a room ransacked and painted with the blood of an old friend would do me any good.

My bout of wistfulness crushed, I released the latch, backed away, and went downstairs.

The bottom floor, although equally silent, was not quite as dark. A handful of smoldering embers burned in the hearth. A single candle sat on the bar, creating a small, pale circle on the wood. The light was barely adequate for making out the features of the man standing behind the counter.

But I didn't need light to recognize Ansel. I'd known him over half my life.

Weathered and gray since the day we met, Ansel was double my age. A long-retired soldier, with the reputation of being hard-nosed, feisty and foul-mouthed, the one thing no one dared call the man was old. I wouldn't have even thought it, until now.

Fetching a bottle and two mugs, as Ansel brought them over, I noticed the stoop in his once strong back. He walked like it hurt. His bony hands shook as he poured.

I kept the sadness off my face, but Ansel's losing battle with age was a slap-in-the-face reminder of just how long I'd been gone.

Ansel slid a mug in front of me. "Been expecting you." His gravelly voice was just like I remembered. "Ever since Draken slithered up out of his hole." Ansel smiled, deepening his wrinkles. "Can't wait to see you shove him back down."

"Me too." I looked around. "Where is everyone?"

"Curfew. If you don't obey, you disappear." Ansel turned his head and spat on the floor. "Bastards."

"That they are." Saluting him, I drained my mug. Ansel watched me, and I could see the questions in his eyes. But he wouldn't ask them. Having tolerated my youthful indiscretions as a boy (as well as some not-so-youthful ones later on) I knew the man was more patient than he looked. He would wait for me to explain my absence. And I did owe him that. At the moment though, all I could say was, "Katrine?"

Grief tightened his mouth into a thin line. "So you heard."

"Not the details."

"She's dead, Troy. Knowing how won't bring her back. Won't bring none of 'em back. Sure as hell won't make you feel any better."

"I'm not expecting it will."

Ansel refilled my mug. "You go to any village and you'll get the same. Langorians raided the town. They butchered whoever fought back. They pilfered the slaves. Burned a few homes." Picking up a rag, Ansel started wiping down the bar in wide furious circles. "They descended upon this place like flies. They liked the food, the girls. Some of them didn't leave for days." He paused to toss back his drink. "About a week ago, a new batch wandered in. Started bragging about Kabri, spinning lies about how they'd caught you and strung you up back in Kael. None of us believed a word of it. And you know Katrine…she didn't believe them a lot louder."

A brief, cheerless grin tugged at my lips. "What happened?"

"There was nothing nobody could do. They took her upstairs and, well... the pigs were knee-deep in drink and the stupid girl couldn't keep her mouth shut. It was as simple as that."

"They still in town?"

"Leave it alone, Troy. There's too damn many of them."

"I didn't ask their numbers."

He sighed. "I can show you the one that killed her. I tried to smash his face in. His captain's too...ugly, scarred bastard."

"Scarred?" My grip tightened on the mug. "Krillos?"

"Yeah, that's him, Captain Krillos."

"Son of a bitch."

"I hate to admit it, but he weren't too happy about what happened to Katrine neither. He beat the one that done it real good. Took him to the square and made a real example out of him. If it helps."

"It doesn't." I slammed a hand down on the bar. "I let them go. I let them go and they come here. They fucking come here."

Ansel was quiet a moment. "She might have died anyway. You don't know."

Grabbing the bottle, I went to the nearest table and sat down. "I don't want to know."

FORTY FOUR

Light shone through the boards on the windows. Squinting through it, I didn't even try to count the embarrassing amount of empty bottles strewn across the table. A few belonged to Ansel, but at some point he'd gotten smart and went to bed. I didn't.

I'd drained a good amount of his stock, and now I was paying for it. My mouth, dry as dirt, tasted like I'd spent the night licking sludge off the bottom of my boots. The waves rolling in my belly were enough to sink a ship, the hammering in my head; enough to build one.

And Katrine's still dead. And I'm still a Reth.

"Shit." Pushing all ten fingers into my throbbing temple I stood up—too fast, and the edges of the room tilted. Stumbling, my coat caught on the back of my chair. It tipped over, hit the floor with a bang, and the sound hit my head like a bucket of rocks.

Gripping the edge of the table, I rode out the echo. As it faded, a moment of clarity hit me. "Jarryd," I groaned. I tried to open the link, to let him know I was okay; no doubt worry had put him on the path of doing something unwise hours ago. But I couldn't find him. Then I remembered: *Kayn'l.* "Damn."

Detaching my hands from the sticky tabletop, I headed for the kitchen to clean myself up. Heat rushed to my face with each step. A familiar internal quaking had my limbs weak. Though the drug was preventing anything magical, I hadn't ingested enough to dull my senses. I could feel both the cravings and the hangover splendidly.

The wrongness of that might have been amusing, if not for one small problem.

Getting past the Langorians in broad daylight without magic was going to earn me the fight I'd been looking for last night. Only now, I didn't want it.

It was reckless of me to come here. Stupid of me to drink.

Pushing open the door to the kitchen, there was no sign of Ansel, or much else. The bare shelves were layered in dust. The hearth was gray and cold. Most of the counters and worktables were overturned, leaving pots, bowls, buckets, sacks, and their contents, littering the floor.

Spotting a ladle among the debris, I brought it with me to a grouping of casks in the corner and started popping off lids. Some were empty. Some held wine; something I definitely didn't want. When I found one with water, I spent the next few minutes drinking away the drought in my throat. It took a few more of dunking my head in the barrel before I felt awake. More before the cobwebs cleared.

Shaking the wet hair from my eyes, I stole a cloth off the table behind me and uncovered a nice-sized loaf of bread underneath. I stared at it as I dried my face, trying to remember when I last ate. I wasn't particularly hungry, but I needed something to sop up the abundance of liquid in my stomach.

I tossed the towel and picked up the bread. It was a little like eating tree bark. All the same, I'd had worse, and it helped calm the waves. "Better," I muttered, leaning back against the table. After gobbling down a few more mouthfuls of bread and a couple more scoops of water, my head stopped pounding.

In the absence of pain, I began picking up on some stray noises outside.

Curious, I moved to the window. What glass showed between the boards was too dirty to see through, but there were definitely people outside.

A lot of people, I thought, straining to listen to the muffled voices.

Conversation turned quickly to shouting. When it turned to screaming, I ran from the kitchen, sprinted through the maze of tables, and threw open the front door. I burst out onto the porch—and found such a complete contrast to the night before, that it brought me to an abrupt, startled halt.

The volume of townspeople filling the streets was staggering. I had no idea so many were still alive. *Barely*, I thought, surveying their thin, bedraggled bodies. Heads and eyes down, most spoke in hushed, frightened tones, cowering like mice as the Langorians herded them back. Only a handful resisted. Throwing insults and cries of encouragement, the small group pushed forward, straining to see past the ring of hulking enemy foot soldiers blocking their view of the road.

Standing on the raised porch, I had a nice, clear shot of what had sparked such a commotion. I just wasn't as excited as they were. While they saw an opportunity for one of their own to draw Langorian blood, watching Ansel cross swords with Captain Krillos sunk a really bad feeling into my gut.

All eyes were on him. I couldn't pull him out unnoticed.

Not that he would go. Ansel was doing rather well against a man that was younger and stronger than he was. At least, it appeared that way.

Ansel's strikes were definitely well placed. However, his Langorian opponent's sloppy parries, last-moment evasions, and weak return thrusts, were in reality: carefully timed ploys. Krillos was toying with the older man, and Ansel knew it. Frustration was all over his aged face. Desperation was making his movements rushed. A building rage showed in every trembling swing. So did exhaustion. With his strength all but gone, Ansel would soon go for the kill, and give Krillos the excuse he was waiting for.

I shouted from the porch, "Krillos, hold!"

The silence was immediate. Heads craned in my direction. Soldiers raised their weapons. Krillos turned slightly. And Ansel took his shot.

I cried out to stop him. A tall, well-muscled Langorian beat me to it. He brought Ansel down with a hard tackle, and the crowd went crazy.

Naturally, the Langorian soldiers spared nothing beating them back.

Krillos, giving the disturbance a brief curious glance, shook his mane of black hair into place. He slid his weapon away—a long graceful piece that was definitely not standard issue or even Langorian made. Neither was the showy etched scabbard at his waist or the new crimson coat he was tugging into position.

"Shinree," he called out warmly. "I see Fate has brought us together again." He smiled on approach. "I should thank him for that."

"I think you're confused, Krillos. Fate is one of my gods. Not yours."

"And look what your devotion has gotten you." Krillos stopped just inside the ring of soldiers. "Don't worry. I won't tell anyone if you spend more time cursing the old bastard than praying to him. I have my doubts he listens either way."

I gestured out at the town. "I see you've moved on from dogging the Kaelish."

"On, yes, but not up. Though, there are worse assignments than holding this wretched village." He shrugged and pointed at me. "And I see you've come to defend Rella's southern cities with a half-eaten loaf of bread."

Biting off the end, I waved the rest at him. "Actually, Captain, I thought I might stuff it down your throat. Choking on a hunk of stale bread isn't the most glamorous of deaths, but…dead is dead."

"You know," Krillos grinned, "I once heard that a man's choice of weapons says a lot about his character. So I'm wondering, Troy, what exactly does brandishing day-old tavern fare say about you?"

"It says I don't like you." I tossed the bread on the porch. "Let Ansel go."

With authority, he said, "Lieutenant Lork," and straightaway the big soldier got up. Wrapping an arm around Ansel's neck, Lork hauled the older man to his feet. He pressed a knife against his bloody wrinkled face.

I glared at Krillos. "I didn't say let him up, I said let him go."

"I can't do that, Troy. He attacked me. He's a prisoner of Langor now."

"He's an old man."

"This *old* man," Krillos said emphatically, "has been stirring up trouble for weeks. He refuses to obey the curfew. He won't pay taxes to his King—"

"His King is dead."

"This is Langorian territory now. We all bow to Draken. Like it or not."

"Draken doesn't deserve to be King any more than I do."

"No argument from me," Krillos chuckled. "But I wasn't exactly in a position to refute his claim to the throne, or his offer. Eighteen hours a day in the mines for the rest of my life, versus a conditional pardon on Draken's leash…it wasn't a hard choice."

"How about I give you another?" I jumped down off the porch. As my boots hit the road I pulled the sword at my back. The sound rang out above the whispers of the crowd, and the soldiers in the front row shifted uncomfortably. "Let Ansel go. Take your unsightly friends and leave…or stay here and die."

"Give me that," Krillos said, indicating the shard, "and you can have the whole fucking town for all I care."

Teeth gnashing, I hesitated. "Back in the mountains you said something about shoving my face in the dirt?"

"I said grind, but…go on."

"Now's your chance."

Unconcealed interest sparkled in his eyes. "I'm not supposed to kill you."

"You won't."

"Is that confidence talking or wine?"

"Little of both. But you strike me as a man who likes games of chance, Captain. A man who isn't afraid to wager my blurry wits against his skill with a blade." My eyes shifted to his weapon. "A stolen blade by the looks of it."

"It'll be your blade I'm stealing next."

"I don't know," I said doubtfully. "All those years starving in prison, your mind wasting away, reflexes going dull…nerves shot from fear and torture. I'm thinking that living in a cold, dark cell didn't exactly keep you sharp." I smiled with mock sympathy. "But I'm sure it's all come back to you by now."

A twitch of irritation made his scars dance. "Draken will kill me for this."

"I told you before. I don't have a problem with that."

Grinning, Krillos grunted. "One weapon each?"

I undid the sword belt at my waist and let it fall. "If I win, Ansel and I walk."

"Agreed." Krillos gave another glance to Lork. The soldier eased his grip on Ansel and pitched him backwards into the crowd. As he fell, another round of protests and curses were shouted. But Ansel lay alone in the dust, bleeding, hurting, and gasping. Not a single villager had the guts to go to him. *Katrine would have gone*, I thought.

That's why she's dead.

She resisted, and she died for it. Like all the women and old men, the mothers and children, the soldiers who were slaughtered for their bravery and conviction. And this wasn't the first time or the second. The dance was decades old. Each time Langor reared their head, Rella pushed them back. One side attacked, the other returned the favor. Time and again the tide was stemmed, but nothing had ever prevented the storm from brewing again. *Nothing made a lasting impact. Not even magic.*

Damn, I thought. *I get it now.*

I hadn't totally disagreed with Malaq's views before, but all of a sudden, I understood exactly what he'd been trying to tell me. Langor needed permanent change on a massive level. It needed a strong, consistent, moral influence, a ruler committed to peace and diplomacy. One who could inspire devotion without fear, draw them away from war, and teach them how to build a society on more than vengeance.

Langor needed Malaq Roarke.

Surviving on the promise of conquest, emulating the desires and ambitions of their kings, his people had been raised to believe only victory would bring happiness. Malaq was raised on different beliefs. He could show them other ways to live, other paths to prosperity. Yet, forcing the transformation on them by way of a coup would make him no better than Draken. Malaq had to ascend the throne legitimately, and I had to let it happen. Or the cycle would continue.

"Troy!" Krillos said sharply, grabbing my attention. "You sure about this? You seem elsewhere. And I hate taking advantage of a man when he's down."

I shook off my ill-timed thoughts. "Isn't that what your people do for fun?"

"And they say we're narrow-minded." Snickering, Krillos stepped further into the ring. "No magic. I want your word on that."

"Why?" I brushed past the foot soldiers and joined him. "You wouldn't believe me if I gave it. We're sworn enemies."

"That we are, Shinree. But when a man sees the face of hell and finds himself reduced to nothing but instinct, he comes to trust it."

His odd, self-effacing statement caught me off guard. "Then you have my word. No magic. And no interference from your men."

Krillos nodded. He pulled a strand of leather from his pocket and tied back his hair. Unhooking the buckles on his coat, he slipped it off and passed the garment to one of his soldiers. As Krillos turned back to me, I took a step, and popped him in the nose.

"That's for Jarryd." I hit him again. Blood sprayed back on my hand. "That's for Ansel." Pulling my sword, I slammed the hilt across his jaw and then drove the pommel into his stomach. "And that's for Katrine."

Krillos let out a winded groan and doubled over. Quickly, he put a hand out to stop the men rushing to his side. Bent over, catching his breath, wiping at the thick strings of blood dangling from his mouth, he lifted his eyes and shouted, "Who the hell is Katrine?"

"You rape and murder a girl and you don't even bother to catch her name?"

His bloody face blank, I tilted my head in the direction of the inn.

"The barmaid?" he scoffed. "The one with the red hair, that wouldn't shut up?" Clipped and succinct, Krillos said. "I didn't kill her. I didn't even touch her."

"Maybe not, but a good captain takes responsibility for the actions of his men."

"Yeah. I suppose a good captain would." Wincing, he straightened. "It hurts to admit this, Shinree, but I think I like you. We decimate your glorious Kabri, kill Rella's King, pillage and plunder its villages, and you're mad over the death of one little loud-mouthed whore. Gods, but I admire a man who knows what's important in the world: wine, women, and a good honest fight." Red flew off his lips as Krillos laughed heartily. "Perhaps, my friend, you would be better off serving Langor."

"Don't call me friend, Krillos. You are far from that."

Drawing his sword, he advanced. "You let the deeds of my countrymen sway you against me." Krillos swiped at me. It was a lazy move I had no trouble avoiding. "When, deep down, you and I are the same."

"I don't terrorize people. I don't persecute them for sport."

"It's called following orders." Krillos aimed a sudden, vigorous thrust for my shoulder and I knocked it away. "It's not my fault I'm on the victorious side."

"This isn't a victory. It's a massacre." I lunged. Krillos sidestepped then came back with a swipe aimed at my head. Ducking it, I rolled past him. "You," I said, coming up, "Draken, Reth…life means nothing to you. You step on it every day. All that matters is your own goals. Your pride. Your desires. You're coldhearted." I rushed him. Our swords slammed together. "Ruthless." He pushed against me, and I pushed back. "Butchers." I threw him off with a grunt.

Stumbling, Krillos fixed his stance. "Ending the war wasn't your goal, Troy, your desire? Pride had nothing to do with it? And let's not forget all those Rellans you killed in the process. I'm sure they didn't feel stepped on in the least." He snorted at his own joke. "How can you say what I do to serve my King is any worse?"

"Because you like it."

"Everyone gains satisfaction from beating an enemy. In fact, after obliterating two armies, I bet you were satisfied real good." Krillos flashed me a quick smile. "Maybe that's why Fate keeps stomping on you, Shinree. You enjoyed your attempt at genocide a little too much."

I swung hard and fast. Krillos blocked me, but I pressed forward with intent. Aiming high right, left, and then low, I kept after him. Changing up my attack, altering fighting styles to keep him guessing, I pushed Krillos back so far his men had to widen the circle around us. But the wily bastard took everything I gave him.

He's good, I thought. *Real good.*

Dropping under my swing, Krillos dived past me. I pivoted around and found him out of range, leaning on his sword with his brows up; waiting for my response to his last question. "You're right," I said, catching my breath. "Ending the war was my goal, my desire."

His gaze was curious. "And...?"

"I was young and proud. Arrogant. I thought I could handle anything. I saw my Rellan commanders as cowards and bigots. They were afraid to acknowledge what I could do. So they kept me in check because it made them feel powerful and useful."

"Interesting," Krillos nodded. "What about now?"

"Now, some days I can't handle anything. But they're still bigots."

"Damn, Troy," he snickered. "I'm impressed. An admission like that in front of this crowd?" Krillos let out a whistle. "I always did wonder what took you so long. When the story of what you'd done made its way through the prison, my first thought was that it was about time. You could have made a substantial dent in Draken's forces whenever you wanted. Yet, for years you swung those damn swords instead of magic. I never understood it."

"I was raised a soldier, Krillos. I was trained to do without question, to ignore my wants for hers...even if hers were wrong."

"As I said...we aren't that different."

I was somewhat taken aback by that, and Krillos laughed at the look on my face.

"So you bottled it all up," he said, bringing the conversation back, "all the bile and the magic. You stuffed it down for years and…boom!" His eyes and arms went wide. "It came bursting out in one giant life-draining explosion." Shaking his head, he grunted. "Damn, that Arullan bitch really fucked you up."

"She didn't—" I stopped myself. Why was I was still defending her? "Aylagar would have lost before admitting that steel wasn't enough. Even that last day, when the directive came from Kabri to surrender, she refused to let me cast."

"Surrender?" Disbelief made more lines on his face. "I didn't know."

"No one did. Aylagar burned the order. But I saw it. She was going to take us down fighting. I would have gone with her, too. But not before I threw everything I had at the enemy. I figured, if it worked, she could execute me for treason after."

"So what, you rebelled and the Rellans got caught in the crossfire?"

"It was all crossfire. The quake hit before I could cast. Then I held the crown in my hands and I lost perspective…control. I lost everything."

Krillos nodded thoughtfully. There was an odd sense of admiration in his eyes. "Seems to me your fellow soldiers were doomed either way. If your spell hadn't taken 'em out, they would have been shipped to a Langorian prison. And trust me, Troy." Dread tightened his voice. "Death is better."

"But that was Fate's choice. I had no right to take it out of his hands."

"Who's to say he didn't approve?"

"Doesn't matter. Whatever my intentions, using the Crown of Stones was a mistake. It was a terrible…" a peculiar sensation overcame me. I tried to dismiss it and finish my thought. "Mistake," I said, but uttering the word only caused the feeling to deepen.

Something was different than it was a moment before.

For once, my explanation didn't sound like a tired excuse or a flimsy defense. It wasn't an apology or a request for forgiveness. It was simply a fact. One that, for the first time in ten years I wholeheartedly believed as true.

It was crazy. Yet, I understood why Malaq's plan made such perfect sense. Why I could suddenly see the worst moments of my life with a neutral clarity that I'd never had before: Jarryd. Our bond was altering me. And at the most inconvenient time possible.

"It was a mistake," I said again, amazed that I could do so without pain. "I'd never touched magic like that. It blinded my aim, my focus. I couldn't see the soldiers, the consequences." I looked at Krillos. "It was a mistake."

"So it would seem," he said, slow and cautious. He was eyeing me like I was mad. "You know, whatever this is—a confession, a moment of revelation…a spiral into insanity," he chuckled uncomfortably, "I really don't want to interrupt. What do you say we scrap the fight and throw back a bottle instead? We can try this again tomorrow."

Quietly, I said, "Have you ever made a mistake, Captain?"

"Such as?"

"Like whatever landed you in prison."

"That was a long time ago."

"How about being cowardly enough to slaughter children because you were too afraid to disobey? Or maybe…." I closed the gap between us. "Coming here today?"

"Ah," he breathed regretfully. "I see you've snapped back to your old self."

"Actually, this is my new self."

Krillos wrinkled his crooked nose. "If you're going for intimidation, Troy, don't bother. I've been threatened by a lot worse than you. Truth be told, I had a jailor once that makes you sound like a squealing little girl." He flashed a devious grin. "How 'bout we see if you fight like one." Abruptly, he swung.

Turning his strike aside, I rammed his chest with my shoulder. As Krillos slid back, the tip of my sword skimmed across his chest.

After taking a moment to laugh at the thin red line seeping through the rent in his shirt, Krillos came at me. Moving faster, with more purpose and dexterity than he'd shown so far, he delivered a flurry of swings and thrusts. His cuts were strong and fluid, his moves unpredictable and artful. My responding blocks were fast and sure. I kept him off me. But the man had a mean crosswise cut that I had to actually work to set aside.

Finally, we locked blades. Steel struck steel, and the brutal impact ran through my hand and straight up my arm. "Yield," I grunted, pushing our swords toward his face.

"Langorians don't yield," he groaned, pushing back.

"Maybe you should start." Sacrificing my leverage, I lifted a leg and the blades slid closer to my face. Cold steel brushed my skin as I rammed my knee into his groin.

Cursing, Krillos broke off and staggered back. Without doubt, he was one of the most competent Langorian swordsmen I'd ever fought. But if prison had robbed the man of anything, it was stamina. It was clear as we engaged again, matching strike for strike; each time our weapons clashed, Krillos took longer to recover for his next swing.

He couldn't outlast me. The obvious inevitability of that was distracting him.

It gave me an opening, and I took it.

Lodging the tip of my blade into the intricate hilt of his, I yanked and ripped the sword clean out of his grip. I followed that with an elbow to his face. Krillos took the punch, sprung back, and jumped me with enough force to knock us both to the ground.

I rose up to a knife in my face. "Thought it was one weapon each?"

Panting heavily, Krillos relieved me of my sword and tossed it aside. He wiped a wrist across his brow, mopping up the sweat. "You're far too much trouble than you're worth, Shinree."

"Good." I rolled hard to the left. Krillos was too spent to react. As his body rolled off mine and slapped the ground, the knife fell from his grip. I threw him off and kicked it away. For good measure, I kicked him too. Then I scrambled up and grabbed my sword.

Krillos crawled to his. As he lifted it, a clap of thunder shook the square. A slow rain began to fall.

"Walk away," I warned him. "You don't have to fight in this war."

"If I don't fight, I'm dead." Dabbing at his split lip, Krillos stood and faced me. "Perhaps Rella was lenient with such things. But in Langor, desertion means death."

"How about insurrection? You seem like the type to enjoy a good mutiny."

For some reason that made him laugh. "Very perceptive, Shinree. But it depends on which side of the mutiny I'm on."

"Langor has grown stale, Krillos. You've known nothing but war for too long. But it doesn't have to be that way. You don't have to follow Draken."

"Is this your plan? Turn us all against him one by one?" Abruptly, he lunged. I knocked the blow aside with a quick parry, and he resumed his loop. "We're only a few generations removed from being your slaves, Troy. Your people were the conquerors then, and they taught us well." Moving behind me, bile darkened his voice. "So forgive me if I don't run home touting peace and revolution. I just got *out* of prison, remember?"

I gripped my sword with both hands. "I won't let you take her kingdom."

"We already have."

I felt the air move as he swung. *High*, I thought and ducked.

I came up with a vicious swipe. My weapon made contact. I felt the cut go clean through. I pivoted to strike again, but as I came back around, Krillos was slumping to his knees in the mud staring in silent horror at his sword. It was lying in the dirt between us, along with his severed hand. All five fingers were still tightly wrapped around the hilt.

For a moment, there was no sound but the rain. No one in the square moved or spoke. We all stared in silence at Krillos, as the blood spouted from his empty wrist.

Scarred face contorted, he raised his head to look at me. Rage and pain had his entire body shaking. "You…you c-c-cut off m-m-my…hand."

"I told you to leave."

"You…cut…off…my…FUCKING HAND!"

"Is that enough? Or, do I need to finish the job?"

Krillos didn't answer. As he forced himself up, the villagers started muttering to each other and slinking away. His soldiers shuffled their feet, exchanging nervous glances. Some backed up. Most were too afraid to do anything. But one brave soul kept his wits enough to come to his Captain's aid. Calling for a horse, the soldier removed his own cloak. After wrapping the cloth around the gushing stump, he took off his belt and tied the leather strap above the wound. Krillos doubled over with a muffled groan as the soldier pulled the belt tight and knotted it.

Dismissing the man gratefully, Krillos walked alone to his waiting mount. Ignoring the stares and whispers, he hauled himself up into the saddle with not a single sound of pain. He was swaying, shivering uncontrollably, and breathing violently by the time he got there, but I was impressed.

"Get a healer," I told him. "Then walk away. You don't need to die for this."

His glazed eyes found mine through the rain. "It's too late for that, Troy. It's too late for all of us." Regret in his voice, Krillos commanded hoarsely, "Let loose the eldring!" and from within the ranks, a flaming arrow shot high into the air.

"Krillos, no!" I ran toward him.

Intervening, Lieutenant Lork aimed his sword at my chest. "You're mine, witch."

"Stand down," Krillos ordered. "Troy and the old man go free. I gave my word."

Lork slammed his weapon away. As he shoved past me with a growl, I looked up at Krillos. "Stop this. The eldring will tear through this town like a plague. Everyone will die."

"Then save them. That's why you're here, isn't it?"

"I can't," I said with gritted teeth. "I have no magic."

"Well, I guess Fate really is stomping on you then, isn't he?" Clutching his bloody arm to his chest, Krillos kicked his mount into a run. He turned down the next street, and the moment he was out of sight, Lork gave a shout.

More arrows flew. They were close. I thought they were for me. When I saw where they were headed, I knew I had no hope of making it. I lunged anyway.

I landed at Ansel's feet just in time to watch four steel barbs sink into his chest.

FORTY FIVE

"He's not meat!" Straddling Ansel's corpse with a sword in each hand, I warned the eldring back. "Leave him. Find your meal elsewhere."

Their reply was as I expected. A nauseating amount of saliva dripped from their gnashing jaws and the pack dropped to all fours. Almost in unison, they spread out in a slinking half-circle. Forming three rows of ten, the creatures crept toward me through the rain; gray, leathery noses twitching, orange-red eyes staring patiently.

The first row took off. I had no choice but to leave Ansel and run.

Sprinting through the mud, I glanced back. Most of them fell on his body. Three broke off and came for me. I could hear them gaining as I darted up the front steps of the inn, ran inside, and slammed the door.

I slid the first steel bolt home. Drawing the remaining two locks into place, I leaned back against the wood and listened to my pursuers' wet, anxious snarls on the other side. Claws clicked back and forth across the porch as they pondered a way in.

The clicking stopped. I could hear their snuffling.

Weight hit the door. The slab jumped. The force shuddered through me.

It jumped again as the eldring once more threw their bodies into the door.

Again, and the wood bowed. Again, and the hinges strained.

I didn't have much time. Neither did anyone else. Outside, beyond the walls of the inn, was a resounding, gut-wrenching blend of human screams and triumphant primal howls. The noise was like salt in an open wound. Because there was nothing I could do.

Without magic, I couldn't help the people in town. I couldn't escape through the horde to warn those living in the outlying areas. I couldn't even warn Jarryd.

But I have to. I didn't bring him home to die.

Paring my thoughts down, centering them on one purpose, I put more effort into it than before and managed to locate a trace of our link. It was barely anything. It was a wisp, a distant, dull imprint on the outskirts of my mind. But I clung to the notion of it.

Refusing to let the *Kayn'l* stand between us, I trudged through the miasma of the drug, struggling to push past its confines. Diving deeper, pushing harder, with a determined burst of focused concentration, I went farther inside myself than ever before. Farther still, and I uncovered an untapped store of strength. A pure, quiet confidence—a belief that said I was capable of so much more.

Embracing the notion, I pressed forward. I broke through the haze that separated us, and all at once Jarryd's presence rushed in. I got a deluge of nervousness, concern, relief, and anger. I didn't have time for any of it.

Bouncing back to him urgent necessity and caution, I gave Jarryd a large, vigorous dose of something I tried to convey as "get the hell out and don't come back."

None of it worked. His resistance hit me like a slap in the face. Confusion, temper, along with a swift jolt of sheer insolence, told me he was doing exactly what I didn't want. He was coming to find me.

Frustrated, I banged my head into the door. As if in answer, the eldring banged back. A crack formed in the center of the door, and I clambered away.

They struck again. The crack splintered. Black clawed fingers reached through the fissure. Grabbing onto the fractured wood, the eldring gave a quick jerk, and a chunk of door went flying out onto the porch. Gnashing blood-wet fangs filled the gap, and I bolted for the stairs.

Taking them two at a time, as I reached the top, I darted down the hall. My goal was the roof by way of the window. But as I parted the curtain and started to climb over the sill, my boot hit glass. The window that had been wide open, just a few hours ago, was shut and locked.

Puzzled, I reached for the lock. My fingers gripped the metal latch. An odd stinging sensation bored in through the middle of my back and out the center of my chest.

I looked down for the source and stared in shock at the thick steel bolt protruding from my shirt. Dark wetness was spreading out across the fabric. Numbness was radiating into my arms and legs.

A second bolt exploded through me, alongside the first. I turned, bringing my sword to bear. A third sunk into my side, and I went down.

A man stood in the shadows. He had a large, wooden crossbow in his hand.

Recognizing him, I gasped, "You...?"

Coming closer, Lieutenant Lork squatted down. He surveyed his handiwork with a leering smile. "When you're dead, I will take that stone from around your neck. Then I will take your head and stick it on the end of a pike. Should make a nice standard, don't you think? One look at your rotting remains will send those sniveling Rellan whelps and their gutless Kaelish allies crawling away on their bellies."

I wanted to curse him. I wanted to curse him and his son, and his son's son, and every Langorian that ever dared to draw breath. Except when I opened my mouth, all that came out was blood and pathetic choking sounds.

"Captain's a smart man," Lork said, nodding to himself. "But he doesn't understand war. And Draken? Thinking he could turn you against Rella— break you like a bull. What he doesn't get, *witch*, is that rabid fucking dogs like you can't be broken. You have to be put down. Crushed. Destroyed." Abruptly, Lork's eyes shifted past me. He frowned at the three eldring sitting on their haunches at the top of the stairs. "Wait your turn," he hissed at them. "You can have him when I'm done."

Their oddly colored eyes shined in the dim light. Their growls were eager.

"You need to die faster." Standing, Lork drew his leg back and kicked me.

This isn't right, I thought, groaning as he struck me again. *This isn't how it was supposed to be.* I had a future waiting for me. One I'd seen in Neela's chamber, as she and Jarryd clung to their last moments of life. Another I'd just come to realize; Malaq bringing peace to the realms. And a more vague hope that I hadn't known existed until right this moment: Sienn.

But the vision had been wrong and my hopes way off the mark. I was leaving. I was taking half of Jarryd's soul with me, and I would never know Sienn. Never touch Neela the way I had in my dreams. Never save her kingdom or see my people free.

Shivering, I choked out a blanket, "I'm sorry," to all of them. Then I closed my eyes and waited for Death.

A typical god, he was taking his sweet-ass time getting here.

FORTY SIX

Being dead was different than I expected. It was dark, but warm. Whatever was beneath my naked body was comfortable and smooth. The air had a surprisingly clean, soap-like smell. Most noticeably (and perhaps the most strange), Death had a pair of the softest, gentlest hands. He could hum too. It was a light, peaceful tune he was singing while he ran a wet cloth over my face.

As he moved on to wash the rest of me, everything started to hurt.

It was a general, tender sort of achiness, like strained muscles and day old bruises. My limbs were heavy and my head was a bit sore. Still, if the discomfort was mine for all eternity, I could learn to ignore it.

I wasn't sure I could do the same for the nagging thought in the back of my mind. The one that said I wasn't complete. That I had two gaping, bloodless hollows right through the center of me, and another through my side, rotting and festering.

Why I should care how I looked in Death's house, I wasn't sure. Yet, the thought of not being whole was disturbing. I lifted a hand to find out if it was true—and Death caught my arm. I opened my mouth to argue. Pressure descended on my lips. It was moist, affectionate, and it struck me that I'd never imagined Death to be a woman. Or that she would greet me with a kiss.

Not just any kiss, I thought as her mouth moved passionately against mine.

Death wasn't being hospitable. She wanted me.

Weirdly aroused, I returned her attentions. I assumed it was a game. That once I joined in she would scorn my impetuousness and that would be that. But I'd been wrong about a lot of things lately. And as her tongue pushed into my mouth and her weight rested on top of me, I decided to stop caring if it made sense that Death was seducing me. She was doing a damn fine job of it.

She felt fine too; as a god should. Her body was long and lean. The bend of her backside fit right in my hands. Her breath, sweet, like wine, rode along my skin. It was tantalizing and warm, like her touch. Each stroke was purposeful and abnormally warm.

At the points of contact, where our flesh met, the heat was intense.

It built to a kind of surging vibration. An energy that was so fierce and tangible, I had the bizarre notion our passion would be visible if I were to only open my eyes and look. *My eyes,* I thought dimly, as we kissed.

Comprehension sped through me. *Gods...I'm not dead.*

I flung open my heavy lids to blinding daylight. Pale hair hung in my face like sheets of icy rain. I put my fingers into it and grabbed on. I felt braids and stones.

Sienn.

I turned my head from her mouth. Breathless, I started to laugh, but my elation was cut short by a sharp twinge in the center of my right palm. The ache was distinctive. I recognized it immediately. But it was on the wrong hand.

Sitting up, I pushed Sienn off me. The shove was hard and abrupt. I hadn't meant to send her reeling off the bed. Yet, looking at the scar she'd given me, she deserved no apology.

A match to the one on my left hand that linked me to Jarryd, the one on my right were fresh. The marks were no more than a few days old. And they linked me to her.

"Why?" I thundered.

Sienn trained her white eyes on me. Her hostility was like a window shattering inside my head.

"Gods, woman," I gasped. Her wrath hit me again. "Stop it!"

Wiping my kiss from her mouth with the back of her hand, Sienn's glare slowly wandered from my eyes. It tempered as it moved downward.

Remembering I wasn't wearing anything, I grabbed the sheet at the end of the bed. "You bound us together," I said, yanking the cover angrily up to my waist. "Did you do this for Reth? Is this some kind of sick way to tie me to him?"

Sienn stood and smoothed out her dress. The fabric was a light, airy shade of blue that, next to her white hair, reminded me of winter. So did her expression. "Jem has nothing to do with this. All I did," she said, concise and snappy, "was save your life. Again." With a drawn-out, frustrated sigh she sat down on the end of the bed. "The marks and the link both will fade. They aren't permanent."

"I don't understand." I glanced around. The room was cozy, but sparse. Outside the lone window, a grove of fruit trees flanked a small barn. "I know this place."

The trees were taller than I remembered. But it had been a while.

Behind Sienn, a cupboard stood against the wall. One of the doors was hanging crooked. *Still?* I thought. I'd only offered to fix it ten times.

"This is Broc's house," I said.

"Yes."

"Is he here?" I sat up a little. "Gods, he must be pissed. I don't visit for years and then I show up like this. Where is he?" I'd barely gotten the question out before memories hit me. I couldn't tell if they were hers or Jarryd's, but I saw the house empty. The furniture in the main room overturned. The walls and floors streaked with gore. I saw my old friend's body lying near the back door, gutted. "He's...dead?" I got another flash; a man, much younger. His leg was hacked off at the knee. An axe was buried in his head. "Gods, his...his son," I said, my voice breaking.

Sienn rested a hand on my leg. "I'm sorry, Ian."

I nodded gratefully. "I'd known him since the war."

"I know."

"Broc had a daughter." I swallowed, recalling a feisty young girl with perpetually tangled hair. "You didn't find her?"

"She was probably detained. Whatever happened here, Langorians aren't in the habit of wasting healers."

It wasn't much, but I took it. Rubbing the worry off my face, I looked at her. "What are you doing in Rella?"

"I've been tracking you since the mountains. When my spell failed I thought..."

"What? That I was dead?"

"It crossed my mind. But apparently there was *Kayn'l* in your blood. It interfered with my spell."

"Then how did you find me?"

"I cast again and tracked your messenger friend here. I was with him when you reached out and warned him to leave town." Faint amusement softened her mouth. "He nearly fell over."

"We have a few things to work out with the link."

"I strongly suggested he heed your advice, but he refused."

"Yeah, he's like that."

"Admirable," she admitted. "Charming even, I suppose. But foolish. Like you."

"You think me a fool?"

"I did say charming as well." Grinning, she bit her lip, and I gave up trying to stay mad. It was difficult enough pretending Sienn didn't affect me when we weren't connected by magic. Now, I could sense how being near me made her pulse race, and I liked it. Feeling the desire spreading through her body, how it swelled and gathered heat like a burning ember, made it hard to even look at her.

I looked down at the wounds on my chest instead, and they sobered me instantly.

Though the holes were indeed sealed, Sienn had yet to repair the scars. They were big and messy. Staring at them made me feel uncomfortably fragile.

"Those will be gone soon as well," she assured me. "I had to focus my energies elsewhere. You were dead after all."

My eyes shot to hers. "Dead?"

"Essentially."

"You brought me back? Like I did with Jarryd."

"The process was similar. But without the power of the *Nor-taali* it took nearly everything I had just to link us together. I've been healing you in stages as my energy returns. As you can see, I'm not quite finished."

"Couldn't Jarryd have loaned me strength?"

"He was in no condition for it. The effects of your injuries were coming strongly through the link. He could barely walk by the time we found you."

"And the Langorian?"

"The man that hurt you? Do you think I would leave the swine anything but dead?" Flashes of Lork bloody and screaming passed between us, and I had my answer.

I squeezed my tender right hand into a fist. "And these will fade?"

"As I said. Although, there are benefits to being coupled as we are. For a time our connection will allow you to cross bloodlines, heal, make the rain. You can limit the consequences of your spells, redirect the cost, kill and defend with far more creativity."

"I can access your erudite abilities?"

She nodded. "It's an opportunity you should treasure while you can."

"And when the bond expires? Will I retain any of it?"

"I'm afraid not. Like the marks, the knowledge will fade. But it doesn't have to. Think of this as a sampling of what I have to offer…if we were to make it permanent. You could breach the innermost parts of me. Feel me in unimaginable ways." Sienn scooted up the bed to sit beside me. "Think about the possibilities, Ian. The things we could do together. To each other," she whispered enticingly. "With our souls mingled," her hand slipped under the blanket, "our consciousness and senses joined," she ran her fingers up my leg, "the experience would be…"

Something beyond ecstasy, I thought hungrily.

But even bonded to Sienn, I still couldn't find a single reason to trust her.

She took her hand away. "You're hesitating."

"And you're pushing. Why?"

Sienn said nothing. She looked at me between pleats of jagged white hair as if my question didn't bother her at all.

The cold wave of emptiness coming out of her said just the opposite.

"You're lonely," I said. "Really lonely," I added, and she blushed. "I'm flattered you think I'm the answer to that, but—"

"Oracles aren't supposed to cast on themselves," she said abruptly. "Those with the gift aren't merely observers. They can go beyond inhabiting the body they visit and can actually influence it. They can change things. In the past it's dangerous and forbidden, but in the future…" she shrugged.

"You gave yourself a vision," I guessed. "And I was there?"

"It was just a glimpse. An instant that may never happen, a possible path we may never take. But…we held the marks of joining. I could *feel* you. It was beautiful and real, and…" Sienn let out an uneasy laugh. Almost, it masked the sob in her throat. "Love is something I've never had. And it was only a moment, but…when I see you now… I want it back." She laughed again. "It sounds stupid, doesn't it?"

I struggled to answer. Our blended emotions were wreaking havoc inside me. My heart was pounding. Catching my breath was near impossible. "No," I said at last. "It's not stupid. It's nice." She smiled a little. "But if we're headed for that, then let it happen. You can't force us together."

"You're right." Sienn got up. She turned away, and I had to quell the urge to go to her. "You've been out a few days," she said. "You're probably hungry."

"I could eat." Getting out of bed, I snagged my breeches off a chair and slipped them on. "How does this work? My magic is back. I can sense you, but not Jarryd. Does one link override the other?"

"I taught him how to block you. But you can be aware of us both at the same time, if you wish."

"I admit I'm surprised to see you here. After what happened at the inn…" I got a quick memory of me walking out on her. I felt her anger and humiliation. How my words hurt. How her feelings for my father complicated everything.

I tried to shove her sentiments surrounding the moment away, but they were strong. They begged for attention. All of Sienn's feelings did. They were raw and acute, and it was clear the restraint she claimed was an exaggeration. Her emotions weren't controlled. They were locked away. In reality, Sienn Nam'arelle was a tangle of longing, desire, hope, anger, anxiety, despair, embarrassment, fear and frustration.

Coming off a lifetime of *Kayn'l* had left her in turmoil.

She had found some comfort, at first, in my father's company. Her resulting gratitude and awe of him was apparent. Her affection and devotion to him was real, at least at the start. It was born of the time they spent together. The hours they trained and planned, talking about freeing our people, talking about me. Reth told Sienn of his wish that I stand with him to build the foundation of our new realm. He told her—

Son of a bitch. I cut short the flow of memories and turned on her. "You knew? From the beginning, you knew that Reth was my father? God damn it, Sienn."

"I've left him," she said. "For good."

"And I'm supposed to believe you?"

She threw me a sad, flat look. "I saw him, Ian, his face…his scars. I told Jem I can't follow him anymore."

"How did he take it?"

"I think he wanted to hurt me."

My temper stalled. "I would have made him regret that."

"No, don't say that. No matter what he's become, I can't discount what he's done for me. I was nothing. I didn't even care that I was nothing. Jem understood that. He helped me through it. He gave me purpose." She wiped her damp eyes. I felt Sienn's heartache like it was mine. "I believed him a kind, decent man."

"Maybe he was." I moved up behind her. "I'd like to think there was something my mother saw in him."

"It's still there, Ian—the good. It has to be." She leaned back against me.

Instinctively, I wrapped my arms around her. "Even if that's true, there's no way to reach it. Not with Draken's soul inside him."

"What about the Crown of Stones? Can you use it to somehow undo their bond?"

"I have no idea. Have you had any luck with Tam's journal?"

"Not yet." Sienn snuggled into my neck. I could sense the contentment settling over her. "Jem is emptying labor camps all over the realms. He's established a temporary Shinree village just across the border in Langor."

"Not the spot I would have chosen."

"I know." Sienn reached a hand up behind my head and sifted her fingers through my hair. "But once we're all free of the *Kayn'l*, a proper settlement will be built. Jem hopes to erect it where the old empire once stood."

"And my father expects Draken to allow that?"

"They have an agreement."

"Gods," I grunted. "Those two are made for each other." I brushed my lips against her neck. A chill came over her and we both shuddered.

"Joining with Draken was wrong," she conceded. "But Jem's goal is admirable."

My hands slid down the front of her dress. As they lingered on her breasts, a jolt of longing swept through her and into me. Enjoying it, I murmured, "And what goal is that? Power?"

"Freedom," she sighed absently.

I laughed. "Freedom he's slaughtering innocent people to get."

"Innocent, *Rellan* people."

Her words were like a bucket of cold water over my head.

I spun Sienn around. I tried to feel if she truly meant it, but too many emotions were in us both right now to tell. "Do you really believe that?"

"Yes. No." She shook her head. "I don't know. Jem's guidance is too important to lose. We need his leadership to make a place in this world."

"This world is being torn apart by a war he started."

"The fighting must end, yes, but Jem doesn't have to die to see it done."

"Will he go back on *Kayn'l*? Submit to imprisonment? Slavery?"

"Of course not."

"Then he dies."

"Ian, Jem is your father. He's your family. That's something few Shinree ever get to claim."

"He killed my mother, Sienn."

"Then he is all you have."

"No. You're wrong." I reached out and took her face in my hands. "I have more right now than I've had in a very long time. Maybe ever," I said. Because in spite of the enormous hurdles between us, as Sienn spoke of family I found myself thinking of her. I thought of Jarryd and Malaq, and the gods help me, in some twisted way I even thought of Neela. Not a one of them were blood or kin. I hadn't known them all that long. But they were a part of my life now, whether I wanted them or not. "Whatever this is, whatever I feel when I'm with you, I don't want to lose it, but... I'm sorry, Sienn." I dropped my hands. "I hunt criminals for a living. I hunt them and kill them, and that's exactly what I'm going to do to Jem Reth."

"I'm sorry, too." Resignation tensed her face, and Sienn slammed the link between us shut so fast I stumbled. "I'm calling due the oath you swore to me in Kael."

"Sienn…"

"*No*, Ian, Malaq Roarke was drawing his last breath on that tavern floor—"

"I know."

"And you swore that if I saved him you would honor your vow." Her tone turned sinister. "Take the crown. Kill Draken. But Jem stays alive."

"Or what? You'll kill me?"

Sienn didn't reply, and the room turned as cold as her eyes.

Turning away, I went to the bed. I started tossing the blankets aside, looking for my shirt. But it wasn't there. Nothing of mine was in the room. Not my boots, my weapons. *Nothing*, I thought, and the knowledge of how true that was brought an abrupt wave of anguish sweeping over me. Whether it was hers or mine; I didn't care. I felt very much like a small animal trapped in an even smaller cage.

All I wanted was to escape.

I threw the blankets down and headed for the way out.

"You're always leaving me," she said then.

The pain in her voice cut deep, but I yanked the door open anyway.

"Do you understand what I intend?" she asked.

"Yeah, I got it Sienn. If I kill Jem, you kill me. Not overly fond of the idea. But with two less Reths around, the world just might be a safer place."

FORTY SEVEN

I was really wishing I had my shirt, or at least my boots. If I had, then I would have kept going, down the hall, through the main room, and out the front door. Instead, I was left standing in what appeared to be the command center of the Rellan army, noticeably underdressed.

Ordinarily, I wouldn't have thought twice. I'd dealt with being conspicuous my whole life. But the last thing I'd expected at this very moment was to see General Aldous, a handful of high-ranking Kaelish soldiers, a dozen Kabrinian Royal Guardsmen, a few Rellan generals, Jarryd Kane, and Queen Neela Arcana—assembled around a kitchen table in my dead friend's house.

Engaged in a lively, somewhat heated debate, not a one of them had noticed me. I was seriously considering making a run for it (bare feet and all), until Jarryd ruined my escape plan.

Spotting me, he excused himself from the group. Freshly washed and shaved, with a new white tunic, blue breeches, and his hair tightly braided, Jarryd's appearance was similar to the morning we first met in Kael. But the resemblance was only on the surface. No matter how he scrubbed himself or what clothes he wore, the green smooth-faced young messenger I knew was gone.

It wasn't merely the assortment of healing contusions left behind by his run-in with the Arullans. Though they made him look older, roughening Jarryd's features and giving him a harder, more intimidating air, the injuries only accentuated the chilly jaded expression that had taken over his eyes.

In what had to be a result of our connection, Jarryd's gaze was now that of a more worldly man. A man that had done things he wasn't proud of. Yet, if it came down to it, he would do far worse in a heartbeat. They were the eyes of a survivor, someone who had learned to endure the unendurable. I imagined they looked a lot like mine.

Jarryd reached me. The unsettling quality dimmed with a flash of his usual, uneven grin. "Thank the gods you're up and about." He threw his arms around me in a hearty embrace. "Sorry," he whispered. "If I'd known you were awake I would have warned you they were here." Pulling back, his stare drifted to the marred flesh on my chest. "A lot's happened while you were out."

"That seems to be the pattern."

Jarryd smiled. Then a swift measure of sympathy and uncertainty came over him. "Reth?" he said. It sounded vague, but it wasn't. When I'd dropped the wall to warn Jarryd of the eldring, I'd also made him aware of everything that had happened to me since we parted ways on the beach. Ansel, Krillos— the disturbing details of my meeting with Reth. Jarryd knew it all. He also knew how it had affected me.

"Yeah," I said. "Thanks." I glanced at the gathering across the room. "Think you can get me out of here? I could really use a spell."

Jarryd started to reply when the front door opened. A lanky boy in a heavy cloak and far too much hair over his eyes entered the house. With a careless shove, he swept the mess of strands back, and I recognized the move instantly.

Startled, I glanced at Jarryd. "It's that page from Kael. What's he doing here?" Watching the boy remove a leather satchel from inside his cloak, I noticed a Kaelish uniform underneath. "Don't tell me he enlisted."

"Afraid so," Jarryd replied somberly. "Liel's been assigned to General Aldous as an aid. He actually seems quite proud of his appointment."

Spotting us, Liel rushed over. He offered me a deep bow that sent his curls flopping over his face. "I'm glad to see you well, My Lord."

I pulled him up. "Didn't I tell you not to call me that?"

"Yes, My Lord," he said, tossing his hair again. "Several times."

Grunting, I looked him over. "You're a long way from home, boy."

"I am," he said with a sheepish grin. "The day I rode out into the forest to find you, was the farthest I'd ever been from the city. I could barely stay on my horse. Now look at me," Liel puffed out his chest. "I'm a soldier."

"Riding into the middle of a war is a lot different than riding in the woods."

"You're right." Liel's eyes twinkled. "It's better."

His eagerness troubled me. "Have you ever held a sword?"

"I'll be fine, My Lord. Besides," Liel said slyly, "if I stay by the General's side, I won't be anywhere near the frontline."

"He's got a point," Jarryd grinned.

A chair scraped loudly across the kitchen floor, as a Kabrinian guardsman stood and beckoned to Liel. "Excuse me," the boy said, with another bow and shove of his hair.

I watched him walk away. "He's going to get himself killed."

"Aren't we all," Jarryd replied. He turned me aside. "Reth is in Kabri. Our scouts spotted him a few hours ago."

"Does Sienn know?"

"Probably. She's been working pretty closely with us."

"Sienn's been helping you?"

"Sienn's been invaluable. Her magic carried word to our allies and gathered our scattered troops. Without her making doors for us—"

I put a brief hand on his arm. "Sienn made doors for the Rellan army?

"If she hadn't, it would have been another month before we could coordinate an attack. And we would never have gotten Neela out of Kabri for this meeting."

"Gods, I don't understand that woman. Fighting against Draken while protecting my father at the same time? Between Reth's plan to free our people and Neela's push to drive the Langorians out, it's like Sienn bounces between these hopeless causes."

"Thanks," he grimaced. I started to apologize, and he cut me off. "I get it. It's like she needs something to believe in, something to fix—which could explain her attraction to you."

"Funny," I frowned at him. "Can you sense any part of her in me?"

"Nothing. But I don't need magic to know that woman is full of twists and turns. Then again" Jarryd shrugged, "what woman isn't?"

I looked at him doubtfully.

"What?" he laughed. "You think me a priest because I don't go on about bubble-girls and naked maids like Malaq?" Jarryd leaned in and lowered his voice. "Guess this means you didn't get *all* my memories."

"Apparently not the good ones." He laughed at that, and the motion emphasized the abrasions on his face. I nodded at them. "Why hasn't Sienn taken care of those?"

"I told her it could wait. Her work with the army and healing you was more important." Edging closer, Jarryd lowered his voice. "So how is it... seeing her?"

He wasn't talking about Sienn anymore. "I don't know yet." With the crowd, I hadn't caught more than a flash of Neela's dark skin and hair, but even that much made me nervous. "I don't know," I said again.

"This might help." Jarryd lowered the barrier. Our connection reestablished, and in the time it took to draw breath, we exchanged memories of the past few days. I didn't have much to offer except for dying and waking up with Sienn on top of me. But Jarryd had been busy. After helping Sienn rescue me, he'd cleaned all traces of death from Broc's house. He'd scavenged for food and supplies, practiced with Sienn on controlling our link, met with the Rellan generals, and helped coordinate the arrival of the troops. He'd gone into town to lend a hand in burying the victims of the eldring attack and in burning the remains of the creatures Sienn had disposed of in her quest to find me.

When Neela arrived, Jarryd was out in the yard. He helped her down from her horse and their hands touched. I was afraid of his response, but Jarryd felt only a deep comfortable affection and a great sense of relief that Neela was safe. He experienced a normal honest appreciation of her beauty—but none of my lust or obsession. Not a drop of it was in him. Being exposed to my memories of the dream-weave hadn't altered Jarryd in the least. "I don't believe it," I muttered in shock. "The dreams still haven't affected you. I thought for sure, by now..."

"Your memories of Reth's spell can't harm me, Ian. I know unequivocally that the woman in your dreams is not the same woman sitting at that table over there. The Neela that Reth gave you was perfection. He imprinted her on your mind, and letting her go won't be easy. But the woman you dreamt of was a fantasy. *That Neela*," he gestured at her, "is as real and flawed as the rest of us."

Neela rose from her chair. She looked in our direction, and I backed up. "No. Uh-uh." I shook my head. "I can't do this. I can't be in the same room with her."

Jarryd grabbed my arm. "Hold onto what I've shown you. You'll be fine."

"I'm breathing the same air as the woman I'm magically compelled to desire. Just how is it that I'm supposed to be fine? How can you trust me not to walk out of here, go to Reth, and beg for her?"

"Because I know you. I know parts I wish I didn't. But being bound together has made me absolutely certain of one thing. You, Ian Troy are no coward. You're not weak or selfish, and you would never turn your back on what's right. Not if it meant people would suffer." Jarryd looked past me. "Not even for her."

Neela moved away from the table. As she drew near I tried to be what Jarryd expected. I tried not to be a weak, selfish coward ready to throw everything away for a woman I didn't even love. I didn't want to be that damaged.

I was pretty sure I was though. As when Neela stopped in front of me, I didn't lower my eyes or bow. I didn't do anything to show respect. I stood and ogled Rella's Queen like I'd never seen a female before, while my mind picked out the discrepancies between her and my dream girl.

Little taller than the recent scars on my chest, the real Neela was as small in stature and frame as her imaginary counterpart. The shape of their faces was identical, as well as skin tone, hair, and eye color. But the curls I remembered running my fingers through were either absent, or contained by the large number of braids hanging down to the small of her back. Bound together at the nape of her neck, the mid-point of her back, and again at the ends, the style was efficient for travel, but too restrictive. I didn't like her gown either. The material was course and drab. The square neckline was modest and the bodice ill fitting. Unadorned sleeves of a plain white under-tunic poked out from the cuffs. She wore no jewelry or trimmings of any kind, only a dull chain girdle slung low around her hips.

The bland, unbecoming attire was undeniably an attempt to conceal Neela's royal status. Yet, with the refined intelligence in her eyes, the majestic quality of her features, and the shrewd awareness on her face, there was no masking what Neela was. Not from anyone who cared to look. And there was no hiding anything from me. I knew exactly what lie beneath her noble exterior and the unattractive dress.

No, I don't, I thought. *I don't know this woman at all.*

That became especially clear as she looked me over, openly and critically, like a slave up for purchase, tilted her head back and her chin up, and said, "Well?"

"Forgive him, my Queen," Jarryd jumped in. "Ian is not yet himself."

Neela lifted her thin brows. "If he can walk, he can bow."

"My apologies," I said, bending low. As I straightened, I found her still staring, but her focus was more reflective. Her lips were pursed. Exasperation and dissatisfaction shone in Neela's eyes, and it was pure Aylagar. It was the look she'd worn at every single troop inspection, whether we were to her liking or not.

That didn't mean I would ever confuse mother and daughter. Neela's body was less powerful. Her hair had a thinner texture and less sheen. With a Rellan father, her skin was lighter than her mother's, her eyes more wide and round, and her nose smaller. But Aylagar was present in the shape of Neela's face and the set of her shoulders. They shared the same full lips, the same rounded jaw, although Neela's was clenched far too tight for someone so young. *It should be softer,* I thought, remembering the feel of her face in my hands—the taste of her lips. The sounds she made beneath me.

I searched her eyes, but I didn't recognize them. There was no attraction. No acknowledgment. There was zero awareness of me and barely a semblance of benevolence in her. The way Neela stared, with unabashed frigid indifference, my insignificance in her world was painfully obvious. It didn't put me off in the least.

To the contrary, her sustained, unbearable nearness made my mouth go dry. It made my focus lock in so completely that the rest of the room became indistinct. I could hear her in my head; laughing, crying, pleading. Her sobs mingled with the soft urgent sounds of passion. Shrieks of terror intertwined with cries of release. Neela's pain and pleasure, overlapping in my mind, meshed into one long gasping ricocheting echo, and I lost my breath. I couldn't draw another.

Without her, there was no air. Only her body could sustain mine.

I reached for her.

An abrupt wave of reason roared across the tether that tied me to Jarryd. His sound mind smacked headlong into my mania with an abrupt jolt of common sense that doused the fire in me.

Cracks formed in the delusion, and I fell quickly back into reality.

"I do not tolerate tardiness," the Queen said then, shrill and sharp. "I expect a full explanation, unless you are mute as well as disrespectful?"

"Your voice," I said, dumbfounded. "It's so…cold."

"Ian," Jarryd warned. "Maybe this isn't a good time."

"No." I pried my eyes from her and looked at him. "I'm alright."

Jarryd stepped back, but he didn't look happy about it.

The Queen looked like she didn't know what happy was. Glaring up at me, her forehead was so tight I thought it might snap in two. Breath came out of her in quick, angry waves. It hit my bare chest, prompting a physical reaction that was far lower.

"Not only did you arrive later than anticipated," she went on berating me, "but your recent street brawl and subsequent injury have caused an unacceptable delay."

"I'm fine," I said. "Thanks for asking."

Somehow, she frowned harder. "I am not ignorant of the rigors of your trip. I am merely attempting to convey the urgency of the situation. In the last few weeks Draken has amassed a great army on Kabri's shores. It is imperative that we strike now while they are all in one place."

"How great?"

"Five thousand."

"Damn. I hadn't expected Draken to have so many men."

"They are not all men."

"Eldring," I nodded. "Resurrecting them was a smart move."

"Agreed. But we cannot allow that to cow us. From all across the realm, the sons and brothers of my soldiers have taken up arms. Doratae has sent aid from across the sea. Aldous has brought the Kaelish. Our Arullan allies have just arrived. And with every brave citizen willing to defend their home, we are a respectable number."

"Your Grace," I said formerly, "I believe the Arullans might be deceiving you. Or they simply have a different understanding of the word ally."

Gliding gracefully past me to an empty chair near the hearth, Neela sat down. "I suppose politics are not a popular topic of discussion in most Kaelish taverns, so I will educate you." Back perfectly straight, she smoothed her skirt and folded her hands primly on her lap. "The Arullan government has fractured. The dissension began shortly after my mother died, but it was unorganized. Since Draken's return, the division has become pronounced and problematic."

"The division seems to be centered on my head."

"It is true, one faction still seeks retribution for the warriors Arulla lost by your hand. Once a year for the last ten they have sent an emissary to demand your execution."

"Maybe the King should have complied and delivered me. That is what he did to my father, isn't it?" I said, testing her. "Raynan dropped him right on the doorstep of the enemy."

Neela bristled, though her face lacked both shock and confusion. She knew exactly who my father was. "I'm curious," she said. "Are you implying Jem Reth's confinement was unjust?"

"I'm saying it was lenient. Your father should have hung mine and been done with it. Now, because of his clemency, the job falls to me."

Turning slightly toward Jarryd, Neela said, "I would like some tea."

Jarryd wavered. He didn't want to leave us alone, but he complied with a courteous, "Yes, my Queen."

When Jarryd was out of ear shot, Neela asked, "You and Reth spoke at length?"

"We did."

"But you didn't kill him."

"I had no magic. It would have been a little hard without it."

"Is that the only reason?"

"I do have questions for him."

"His answers would be untruthful."

"Probably. But I don't exactly have anyone else to ask."

"You could ask me," she offered. "Or do you feel I will be untruthful as well?"

"I'm not sure. I don't know you." It came out more regretful than I intended.

"Well then," she blinked, my tone disarming her. "I will tell you what I can. About your mother, your father, whatever it is that concerns you. *But first*, the threat to Rella must be contained."

"Fair enough. There is one thing…" I waited for her nod of consent. "What you've put together here is impressive. But you're sending a mishmash of soldiers into battle, most of which have never fought together, have dissimilar fighting skills and different tactics, against the whole of Langor and a powerful magic user. If you don't have a solid strategy, it will be a massacre."

"Do you believe me incompetent?"

"Inexperienced."

"Then it's a good thing you're leading them and not me. That is, if you've recovered enough to lift a sword. It is considerably heavier than a mug."

My jaw tensed. "I think I can manage."

"Let us hope that you can. Or I will be forced to exert what little influence I have left to ensure the lives of my people—not as Queen of Rella but as wife to Draken of Langor. If that happens, Rella will disappear forever. Draken will look for other kingdoms to conquer. Many more will die. And you, Shinree, will indeed find your head mounted on a mast bound for Arullan waters. Do I make myself clear?"

"Perfectly. But here's the problem." I crossed my arms and looked the Queen squarely in the eye. "Draken has been waiting for this confrontation. Reth turned his back and let you sneak out of Kabri. They are no doubt aware of the exact number of your troops and who your allies are. And I am damn certain they know that I'm standing right here, right now with you. They want this," I said tightly. "Draken and my father want you to make a desperate play to regain your throne. They want me and you, and your allies—all their little annoyances—in one place so they can slaughter us."

"Then you should be prepared."

"Prepared?" I let out a short, scornful laugh and Jarryd's silent call for caution hit me from the other side of the room. "If you charge across the water and try to take Kabri, one army against the other, you will be calling Draken husband in less than a week. But go ahead," I gestured at her. "Maybe you like wearing Langorian Red."

"That was not a very rousing speech, Shinree. I suggest you make your words more inspiring when you address my army. And," her eyes wandered over me in disgust, "cover yourself the next time you appear before me. I am not some shameless Arullan Warrior anxious to bare herself at the sight of your scars. I am Queen. I hold the key to your freedom. And I am not my mother."

I was close to saying something inappropriate when Jarryd came back with the tea. Two cups in his hand, he offered one to Neela, but she shook her head. "Attend me, Shinree," she commanded, rising from her chair. "We have much to discuss."

"Neela," Jarryd said persuasively. "Give him some time. He nearly died."

"Silence, Messenger," she scolded him. "You no longer have the right to address me informally."

Jarryd's confusion inundated the link. "I don't understand."

Her chin lifted higher. "Your services are no longer required. When this campaign is done you will be relieved of your duty to the realm."

"What?" Jarryd balked. "Have I done something to offend you?"

"There was no offense," she replied. "It is simply a matter of loyalty."

Anger overrode his bewilderment. "You can't be serious. I would give my life for Rella. For you."

"Would you?" Grabbing Jarryd's hand, Neela turned it over, exposing the marks on his palm. "You are not the same man who pledged his life to my kingdom."

"I'm still *me*, Neela." Jarryd yanked free of her. "I would never betray you."

"Then tell me," she demanded, "who comes first? Who would you listen to? Which of us would you save? Me? Or him?"

"Stop it," I butted in. "You can't ask him that."

"How can I not?" she shot back. "Look at what you've already done to him. He is different, Troy, inside and out. In time, you will change him into someone I barely recognize, someone who chooses you over me." Her head shook in an anxious, helpless way. "Don't you see? Jarryd is as much a slave to you now as your people are to mine."

"That is not true," I argued.

"You had no right!" she cried.

I countered, with a loud, "Would you rather I left him to die?" and the room went silent. A handful of Rellan guards drew their swords and rushed to flank me.

"Ian, Neela— please." Jarryd wedged in between us. "Liberating Rella is what's important now. Not this."

Swallowing, Neela looked at him. "You understand my position?"

"I do," he said. "I know it couldn't have been an easy decision to make."

"It wasn't," she admitted. "But of late, there have been no easy decisions."

"Then I won't make this one any harder." Jarryd bowed. "I will abide by your command, Your Grace." He came up and met her gaze. "As I always have."

Visibly stunned, tenderness invaded Neela's round, dark eyes and she more resembled the girl I'd dreamt of. But the semblance was heartbreakingly fleeting.

Tightening her face, her body, even her hands as they clasped securely in front of her, Neela clamped off the emotion like binding a bleeding wound. Then she took her guards and retreated back to the table. Her request for my company was seemingly forgotten.

"She can't do this to you," I said. "It isn't right."

Jarryd gave me one of the cups he was holding. "She's scared."

"Scared of what? Me?"

"Yes, but not in the way you think. No one talks to Neela the way you just did. Only her father. And he's gone now."

"So I remind her of her father?" I grunted. "That's great."

Jarryd's grin was short-lived. "Aylagar was a strong woman. Neela doesn't show it, but she's always been afraid of not measuring up. She's scared of appearing weak, doing the wrong thing, making the wrong choice."

"Like she did just now?"

"She had her reasons."

"Bullshit reasons," I muttered.

Jarryd took a long drink. It definitely wasn't tea in his cup. "I've watched Neela shut people out for years." He gave his half shrug. "It was only a matter of time until it was me." Jarryd tipped his mug again, vigorously drowning the resentment and the disappointment. The longing for something he once had.

Deciding to join him, I threw my tea into the fire and went to find some wine.

FORTY EIGHT

What I was doing was wrong in so many ways. Lurking in the shadows, afraid to move for fear of being discovered; the moment was not at all as I'd imagined. Hours ago, when I'd spied Neela retreating to one of the back bedrooms to rest, I'd envisioned her undressing. I'd pictured her lying in bed, braids undone, and clothes off. I'd seem myself walking in to find her waiting. Her arms would be welcoming. She would pull me down on top of her, and there I would stay until morning.

Now, standing in her room, uninvited and unannounced, deliberately and stupidly invading the Queens' privacy, I realized not only was I despicable (and possibly asking for a death sentence) she wasn't anywhere near naked. She wasn't even on the bed. Fast asleep, sitting on the floor, facing the open window, Neela was leaning against the wooden bed frame. Her head was bowed, her shoulders slumped.

It was an oddly casual position. It made the Queen seem downright approachable. It made the idea of crossing the room, dropping to the floor and pressing my lips against hers, rational. She might even welcome it.

I took a step, then another. I took a few more.

On step number six, the floor creaked. Neela jumped. Her head shot up. She spun around on her knees. Even with nothing more than moonlight, the accusation was plain in her eyes. "What are you doing in here?" she demanded.

"I knocked," I offered. I thought the lie might make me sound less guilty.

It didn't.

Livid, she asked, "How did you get past my men?"

"They might have a bit of headache when they wake, but nothing permanent."

"I'm glad you restrained yourself." She stood, hands clasped. "I will require time to deliberate on a proper punishment for your impertinence. For now, I will simply remind you that I have a title, and I expect you to use it." Neela looked down her small nose at me. "Do not assume that because of who your mother was, or because you slept with mine, that you are above showing respect to your Queen."

Her coarseness quickened my pulse. "You are not my Queen. Shinree have no sovereign rulers, only masters. Would you like me to address you as such?"

"I have trouble believing that you, Troy, would willingly call anyone Master."

"There isn't much a Shinree does willingly, Your Grace. The *Kayn'l* doesn't allow it. Neither do the chains."

"I wasn't aware you had developed rebel tendencies."

"Rebel tendencies?" I laughed. "Because I speak my mind?"

"Because you speak out of turn. My Shinree know their place."

"And where's that? Locked in a cage, or tied to the foot of your bed?"

"Whichever you prefer."

I had another snappy reply ready to go, but I held back. The resentment flowing through me was irrational and unfamiliar. It didn't even feel like mine. *Because it isn't.*

"I'm sorry, Your Grace," I said with sincerity. "This is not me."

Nothing moved but a single brow. "Explain."

"The spell Sienn used to heal my wounds is complicated. It left us…" I searched for the word, "tangled. It should wear off in few days."

"Then I suggest, until it does, you do better to control it." She drew an impatient breath. "Is there some reason you decided against requesting a proper audience?"

"I didn't think you would see me. First impressions aren't one of my strong points."

"Agreed. Then I suppose this is about Jarryd?"

"Jarryd? No."

A touch of disappointment alighted on her face. "He didn't send you?"

Now I was disappointed. "Jarryd's been asleep for hours."

"I see." Her expression was thoughtful. "Do you really think me too hard on him? That I was unfair and quick to judge? You may answer freely."

"Does my opinion matter?"

"I suppose not."

"If I say you were wrong, will you change your mind about dismissing him?"

"The decision is made."

"Then you're just looking for validation. Or a fight."

She sniffed. "I'm sure I have no idea what that means."

"It means, Your Grace, that you spend all day hiding behind your forced apathy and your cold formalities. You use them like a barricade. And when it gets too tight inside to breathe, you look for an argument. You debate with someone, anyone that disagrees with you, just so you can let it out. So you have an excuse to feel."

"Watch your tongue, Shinree."

"It's all right. I don't mind if you use me." I edged closer. "I'll be your excuse. Your release." The curve of her mouth pulled at me. I moved in.

Neela's eyes expanded to the size of dinner plates. "Troy!"

"I'm sorry." I stepped back. "I meant no disrespect. I'm not myself."

"I fail to see how a healing can rob you of common sense and decorum."

"That's not it. There are other things going on with me. Things I've been trying to deal with, to make sense of and control, but...I can't." With that admission, my shoulders suddenly felt heavy, my stomach sick. "I don't know who I am anymore. My whole life feels like a lie. My choices orchestrated. My desires fabricated."

"Is this about Reth?"

It wasn't when I came in, I thought. But it certainly all came back to him; my lineage, my connection to the crown, my attraction to her. "Yes," I said decisively. "Whatever you can tell me about him, I need to know. About how all this started. How I came to be."

"Can this not wait, at least until morning?"

"No. I need something real. Something true," I said tightly. "Now. Tonight."

Hesitating, Neela regarded me a moment. "Perhaps you should not prize the truth so highly. It may not be to your liking."

"I pretty much assumed that already."

"As you wish, then." With a breath to compose her thoughts, Neela jumped right in. "For the last five hundred years, since the fall of your empire, Rella has furthered the Reth bloodline for our own use. Generations of soldiers have been produced, born in captivity, kept in secret with their magic suppressed. Many lived and died without ever having cast a spell. Others were weaned off the *Kayn'l*, put to use, and drugged again."

"You kept us as what…weapons?"

"Essentially. But you are concerned only with one Reth, are you not?" She waited for me to nod. "When my father, King Raynan, was a young Prince, it was questionable whether or not he was meant for kingship. He paid no attention to propriety. He spent considerable time drinking and brawling in unseemly establishments, and generally cared little what anyone thought, most of all his family or the royal court."

"I wouldn't have guessed Raynan Arcana had a wild side."

"Very. His open affair with his father's pretty, young Shinree healer, V'loria, earned him the reputation of a Shinree sympathizer. That label was made worse when Reth was taken off *Kayn'l* and they became unlikely companions. Swordsmanship, horses, gambling, all the follies young men engage in, my father enjoyed and yours had been denied. So they indulged together. After a while, Reth began to resent the inequality of their friendship. He found his free will difficult to accept while surrounded by slaves of his own kind. Living in comfort at the castle caused him great guilt. He petitioned for better conditions and increased rations at the labor camps. He demanded new laws be enacted against the mistreatment of slaves. Your father tried hard to improve the Shinree way of life, to change things—the right way."

Relief was heavy in my throat. "Then he wasn't always like this."

"No. Nevertheless, Jem Reth was in a battle he couldn't win. And as that became apparent, he grew bitter. His public outspokenness put a great strain on his friendship with my father. It fell apart completely when Reth's affair with V'loria came to light."

"My mother said I came from an arranged breeding."

"She lied. Whether she loved either of them, I have no idea. But V'loria Troy possessed an allure that neither of our fathers could resist."

"If Reth was causing so much trouble, why wasn't he put back on the drug?"

"By the time the order was given Reth had fled Kabri. Shortly after, slaves were reported missing. Camps were attacked. Sellers robbed. He eventually freed enough Shinree to have a small following, and for a time Rella had quite an uprising on her hands. It was only after Reth's capture that the resistance fell flat. It was as if they didn't know how to carry on without him."

"He was their inspiration, their hero." Sadly, I shook my head. "Gods, I wish I could have seen him like that, before Draken and the crown. Before—"

"Before he became desperate enough to kill your mother?"

"Yeah." I gave Neela a hostile glare. "Before that."

"Jem Reth betrayed my family," she said, getting her back up. "He initiated an unsanctioned pairing that left the King's personal healer with child. A child so dangerous, my grandfather's advisors recommended the pregnancy be terminated. Ultimately, he decided the benefits outweighed the risks, and V'loria was allowed to keep the child. But for a time, Troy, you were nearly never born."

"Am I supposed to thank you?"

"An indication of gratitude might be appropriate." Eyes narrowing, she resumed her story. "After the debacle with Reth, it was decided a new approach was needed and you would be born free. Without *Kayn'l*, no time would be wasted on recovery, and your youth could be spent in training. All that was needed was a way to keep you loyal."

"The spell," I nodded.

"Its purpose was to compel you to defend the realm when threatened. But other methods were needed to cement your devotion since, as you know, spells can be broken. They can weaken over time. Or, on occasion, fade altogether when the caster dies."

Certainly, I knew that. But for some reason I'd never entertained the idea. I'd never thought *this* spell might have expired. "It's still on me though. Isn't it?"

"Honestly?" Neela studied me like the answer was on my face. "I don't know."

I nodded, realizing I felt strangely consoled by her uncertainty. It was better than a definitive answer. Because hearing that my devotion to Rella was truly no longer induced would mean that I hadn't been forced to come back. That the commitment I felt to the realm was my own to uphold—or to break. And if I knew the spell had worn out years ago, before I went to war, that would mean a whole other level of anguish.

Neela continued. "To safeguard against the possibility of the spell failing, you were immersed in Rellan society. Living among those you were born to defend, growing as one of them, you learned their culture alongside your own. Witnessing your mother's healing helped to teach you the value and frailty of life. Just as schooling you in the dangers of magic kept any ethical issues regarding the status of your race from arising."

"Ethical issues…like sympathy?"

"It was crucial that you accept slavery as a logical, necessary solution to the threat magic poses. Otherwise, you might revolt as your father did. Every activity, every moment, was to foster a strong, natural desire to defend Rella. This includes your visits to the front line, where you were allowed to view the battle, and the slaughter, up close."

"I remember that," I said, her words sparking something I hadn't thought about in years. "The Langorians were like giants. The way they tore those Rellan soldiers apart… I'd never seen people die like that before."

"Exposure to the atrocities of combat at an early age instilled in you a deep, unconscious hatred for our enemy."

"What it did was give me nightmares."

"You were quite small. And new recruits are often unprepared."

"You mean they die faster?" Neela offered no response, and her shortage of emotion was telling. "Those Rellan soldiers were sent in for my benefit, weren't they? Sent to die so I could watch?" Still she said nothing, and I plopped down on the edge of the bed; hands on my knees, eyes on the floor. "You controlled everything. Even my hatred."

"It was imperative that you witness the depth of Langorian butchery."

I threw her a scowl. "Is it any deeper than Rellan cruelty? You conditioned me. You shoved it down my throat that the Rellans were good and the Langorians evil."

"They *are* evil."

"That's not the point. What your family did was wrong. But you know that. You know it, and you aren't disturbed in the least that those soldiers never had a chance. That your family, your father, took a boy and turned him into a killer."

"That tendency was already in you. We simply refined it. Rella made you the man you are now." I gave her a look that said exactly what I thought of that, and Neela's eyes flashed. "You were our last chance to get it right. At the first sign of any undesirable qualities you would have been executed in your sleep."

"Taking your mother's life wasn't undesirable enough?"

"That was my father's call. And he made the right one. So did you." Abruptly, Neela's ire cooled. Her stare calmed. "My mother was wrong, Troy. She should have let you at those Langorian bastards from day one. What happened after was on her."

"What happened," I said, trying not to growl, "was that Rella lost its Queen."

"That is regrettable. But Aylagar was an Arullan. She was a warrior. She was Queen. She knew the risks of war. And your tactic won us years of peace. All that you did wrong was to leave Draken alive."

If it was an act, I couldn't see through it. Neela not only appeared to have accepted my use of the crown as Jarryd did, she supported it. She saw the massacre of thousands of Rellan troops as a strategy. And that implied things about her I wasn't ready to believe were true.

"Why a Reth?" I said; letting my concerns about her lie for now. "If your people wanted a soldier, others survived the quake besides us."

Neela seemed reluctant. "Are you sure you're ready to hear this?"

"No. But I have to."

"Then understand, Troy. This is not something I would normally share. It's of a particularly sensitive nature. And I do believe there are times when too much knowledge can be a hindrance. Our own minds our greatest enemy."

"Yeah," I laughed soberly. "I've tussled with mine a time or two."

"Then I will not treat your service to the throne as my father did. If I am to trust you with my realm, you should not be ignorant of its origins. Nevertheless, what I am about to tell you requires the highest discretion."

"I understand. It stays between us. And Jarryd," I added.

"Naturally," Neela frowned. She sat next to me on the bed. "As you might imagine, the catastrophe that befell your civilization was sudden and fierce. The city was buried. Many of the mines collapsed. The land was turned inside out. The shaking continued for months, making the entire area unstable. Survivors were forced to seek shelter in other realms. They begged for aid, but none would take them in. The Shinree Empire had formed their alliances with fear, and most were glad to see it end."

"Why were they begging at all? My people weren't helpless."

"No. They were sick. At first, they thought it was a plague. But no one could identify the source and nothing would ease their symptoms. They had no idea the illness was due to a rapid and merciless cleansing of magic. At that time, most Shinree were not even aware of the magnitude of their addiction."

"How is that possible? How could they not know?"

"The elite castes never went without anything, including magic. The commoners, the workers, used the stones of their professions daily. Channeling was routine, and done with so few restrictions that it masked the extent of their hunger."

"That's a hell of a lot of spells bouncing around. Where did they get the energy?"

"Many kept farms. The higher castes were erudite-trained. They knew how to minimize the cost of their spells so they drained their livestock slowly, over time."

"Their herds must have been massive."

"You mistake me. It wasn't animals the Shinree were farming."

"What then? Crops?"

"To properly answer you, I need to go farther back. You see, my Rellan forefathers were not originally from *Mirra'kelan*. They came from across the sea and claimed the southern half of this continent as their own. What resistance they met was minimal. The natives were a simple people. Passive. Reclusive."

I thought of Danyon's speech at the Wounded Owl. "The Langorians. They owned the land Rella stands on now. It was their home."

"They called themselves something else at the time, and their settlements actually spread far to the west, all the way into what is now Kael. But they were spaced far apart. They had no military might, no structure for defense, and my ancestors subdued the Langorians quite easily. The Shinree were a different story. We had heard of their ways, their sorcery. We knew better than to attack, so we established trade with the one product we had that was unique to this land."

"Which was?"

"Slaves. We sold them the Langorians. My people introduced the concept of slavery to yours, Ian. But they ran with it. The Shinree utilized the Langorians in ways my ancestors never would have. They weren't given shelter or cared for. They weren't merely used as servants and laborers. The Shinree worked their Langorian slaves mercilessly, often to death, in every capacity; in the mines, as amusement in arenas and houses of pleasure—to nourish their spells. Gender and age were no concern. They simply farmed more."

I swallowed; my throat felt too tight for words. "History says nothing of this."

"It wouldn't. When my people learned of the atrocities being committed by the Shinree, they were horrified. Ashamed. Our part in it was not to be spoken of. Scholars were forbidden to write of it. Only one scribe was allowed to record the true events. To this day, his scrolls are kept locked away by a priest. They are taken out only when a new Rellan leader is crowned so that they may understand what truly drives the Langorians to make war with us." Neela turned slightly toward me. "Obviously, this doesn't excuse what they've done. Or what they became. After the empire fell they could have went back to—"

"Back to what? You took their land. My people took their spirit. The Langorians became what they had to in order to survive."

"That doesn't pardon their butchery."

"Of course not. But there's sure as hell plenty of blame for it to go around."

Neela declined to comment. "When the survivors fled the quake, there was no time to pack. Only a few had the foresight to bring stones with them. The rest were suddenly deprived of something that was as natural to them as breathing. As the truth of the sickness became known, all semblance of society fell apart. Civility was lost. Thefts and murders were rampant. Davyk

Reth, Emperor Tam's only surviving son, established himself as their leader. But by then, the situation was hopeless."

"That's when the other races allied against us and attacked?"

"That is what's written."

"But not what happened," I guessed.

"Davyk begged for an audience with Rella's King. He came under the guise of a treaty. Even his people believed his motives were true. But once he gained entrance to the castle, he used magic to murder the King's infant daughter. He threatened more deaths would follow unless he was given protection for himself, his wife, and any of his future line. The King granted his demands, and in return, Davyk gave Rella a way to contain the Shinree threat forever. He gave us his father's formula for *Kayn'l*."

"My ancestor was responsible for the slavery of our entire race?" Neela nodded and I wasn't sure what was worse: saying it out loud or the complete lack of empathy in her eyes. "I always thought the formula was stolen from us. But he just gave it to them? He condemned us all to save himself."

"Rest assured that Davyk was punished for his betrayal. When Rellan Alchemists learned how to produce the *Kayn'l* themselves, Davyk was the first Shinree to receive the drug. Once they were all subdued, a rash of public executions followed. Many called for the entire race to be wiped out. One of the King's council suggested otherwise. He believed the Shinree's magic could be used to our advantage, specifically the aggression in the Reth blood. That was when the breeding of your kind was first attempted. It took time to develop a way for Shinree to create offspring while under the influence of *Kayn'l*. Even longer to understand what lines would overtake others. But once the process was refined it was found we could produce any type we desired."

"So you started farming us. A little ironic, don't you think?"

"Once the route was ventured down, there was no stopping it. With the risk that Shinree magic poses, as the population grew, their numbers had to be managed and controlled. Now, with camps all over the kingdoms, it's even more important. Not so much as a single birth can be left to chance. Even free oracles and healers are required to gain permission from their King before they are allowed to procreate."

"Then I'm supposed to ask you every time I want to—" her scowl stopped me.

"Do you think under your father's rule it would be any better? Reth knows he can't control so many magic users off *Kayn'l*. He has two choices. Keep them drugged. Or use other measures that are far worse. Either way, your people will trade one form of oppression for another. Is that what you want for them?"

"No."

"Then you agree the Shinree need to remain as they are?"

My answer didn't come as quick as it used to. "I don't know."

"Yes, you do. You have an emperor's blood in your veins, Troy. You know there is no clear and good solution for this. And don't tell me they can stop casting because that didn't work very well for you."

With that, Neela's lecture was done. I offered no response and we sat on the bed together in silence. She pretended to straighten the skirt of her dress and I brooded over her comments. Undeniably, they were dead on. It was her callous delivery I had trouble with.

The way Neela saw my people as little more than domesticated animals made me sick. It made me want to shout, to argue our right to freedom—to vow that I could guide them better than my father. And that worried me. For the simple reason that I couldn't be sure if it was Sienn's soul rioting inside me, or if discovering my true lineage had awoken an instinct I didn't know I had; a natural desire to defend and lead my people.

"Is there a problem?" Neela stared down at the bed between us. The covers were balled tightly in my fists.

"No." I unclenched my hands. "No problem."

"Your father will never be anything more than he is," she said, misinterpreting my distress. "Whatever empathy you have, whatever fanciful thoughts or wishes he triggers in you, must be blocked out. You cannot afford to feel anything for that man."

"I'm sorry, Your Grace, but I'm not like you. I can't shut everything off. I can't pretend I don't care. And I don't want to." Anger seeped into my words. "If I stop feeling for myself then I stop feeling for others. I risk becoming like Draken and my father. Men who shed blood as easily as sweat. Rulers who shut themselves off from the people they have sworn to protect."

"Do you mean me? You assume that I order men to their deaths without trepidation? That I have no grasp of what I ask? No compassion?"

"If you do, I don't see it."

"It's not for you to see. It is a ruler's curse to live while others die. To deny that truth, to coddle those who serve you with undo affection, to weep and mourn like their deaths weren't expected, only cheapens their sacrifice. This, I accepted a long time ago."

"You shouldn't have."

"I do what is required."

"What about what you want?" I turned to look at her full on. Behind her, moonlight streamed in through the window. It got lost in the black of her hair and barely lit her face, but I didn't need it. I had memorized every part of her a long time ago. It was the inside I didn't recognize. "How old were you when you stopped remembering how to live beyond the duties of a Queen?"

"Excuse me?"

"When did etiquette become more important than happiness?"

"I don't know what you mean."

"Obligation has lessened you. It mutes your character."

"You overstep, Shinree."

"And yet...you don't stop me." Cautiously, I lifted a hand. Neela stiffened, but she allowed me to place it on her cheek. The feel of her, solid and real, was like pure vigor in my veins. "How long has it been since you let someone touch you?"

"I..."

"Responsibility has made you forget what it's like to be a woman." My hand slid down her face and Neela's breath came faster. "Or maybe, you were never given the chance to know." My fingers glided over her lips to her chin. I gripped it and pulled her face close to mine. My mouth hovered over hers.

"I saw you once," she said, her voice shaky, "at my mother's funeral."

I winced and let her go. "That was not one of my better days."

"To the contrary. You were striking against the crowd of stoic Rellans and proud Arullans, all pretending it was all right that she was gone, that she died a martyr. But not you....the untamed Shinree, full of rage and love, passion and sorrow."

"Mostly rage. And wine," I laughed, "lots of wine." The memory cast a shadow over my mood. "I'm sorry I took your mother away. I should have told you then."

"You didn't have to. I saw the grief on you, the regret." Timidly, Neela rested a hand on my thigh. "As I see other things on you now."

Of course she could see it; being near her had me rigid as a blade.

But she's Aylagar's daughter, I thought desperately. And taking advantage of Neela's bottled passions and clear inexperience—when she was completely unaware of why I was drawn to her—it was a new low for me. "This isn't right," I said.

"I know," she breathed.

"I should go." But my fingers were on her face again.

"Then go."

"I can't." I leaned in. She didn't recoil this time so I pulled her into my arms. I kissed her, and—*mist rose up off the pond. Frogs croaked low and soft in the tall reeds.*

The girl in my arms stirred. A ray of early morning sun fell on the nest of black curls framing her face. "I've missed you," she said sleepily. "I'm glad you're home."

My hands roamed over her body. "Me too." I stretched out on top of her.

Playfully, she twisted away. "I'm not sure I'm in the mood" she teased.

"Really?" I pulled her arms above her head and pinned her down.

Mischief in her eyes, she whispered, "Tighter." I complied, and she laughed.

Burying the sound with a kiss, I nudged my knee in between hers.

I slid her dress up around her waist.

Her hand struck my face.

"Get off me!" Neela cried. Both hands on my chest, she shoved. I reeled back off the bed, and for a second I had no idea where I was. The forest was gone. Walls were around me. Neela stood and shoved her dress down. She was shaking, breathing hard.

Suddenly understanding what I'd done, I couldn't breathe at all.

"I'm sorry," I said, getting up. "I would have stopped. I swear."

"When?" she whispered harshly. "When your seed was running down my leg?"

My stomach clenched. I started to leave, and Neela grabbed my arm.

She was still visibly rattled. But she took a long, deep breath and attempted to collect herself. "It wasn't entirely your fault. If I must go to Draken—"

"I won't let that happen."

"If it does," she said firmly, "if I marry him and I'm not intact...it wouldn't be wise to risk Draken's displeasure for nothing but a momentary amusement. A curiosity, if you will. Surely, you understand?"

It stung but I didn't let it show. "Of course."

"Before you go..." Neela sat me back down beside her on the bed, though not as close. "As Reth empties the slave camps, he's stealing the record books. Everything a registered slave seller is required to track, all the sales, births, and deaths, are in those books. Soon, your father will have information on the bloodline of every Shinree born since the slave laws were enacted."

"He wants to know what he has. And what they can do."

Loud voices broke out in the house. Neela's eyes shot to the door, and she spoke faster. "Whatever he's after, Reth knows the truth now. Or he soon will."

"The truth about what?"

The door flung opened. Light flooded the room, silhouetting General Aldous and the two Kaelish guardsmen who stood behind him in the hall. Barging in, glaring at me, Aldous gripped the sword at his hip. "Arrest that man!" he barked.

Neela stood. "That is not necessary." Her face blank, she adopted a restrained, quiet authority. "As you can see, I am unharmed."

"What I see," the General said scathingly, "is the Queen alone, in the dark, with an uncivilized witch." Snarling, he drew on me. "I should kill you right now."

"General," Neela said firmly. "Stand down." She turned to me then, cold as a brick wall. "You are dismissed, Troy. Assemble your men at first light."

"Sorry, Your Grace," I said, "but I can't do that. They aren't my men."

Her brow crinkled. "I have said that they are."

"I can't lead them. I won't."

"Shinree follow the orders given them. Even you."

Unclenching my jaw was difficult. "You have my sword and my magic. But you can't have both at the same time."

"I can. And I will." Neela's crisp rebuttal reminded me of Aylagar. Lifting her chin, she added, "I am Queen. The decision is mine."

"If I fight alongside your soldiers and cast among them, they will die."

"This conversation is over. I will not discuss strategy with a servant."

"And I will not blindly follow orders simply because you smile at me. I had enough of playing lapdog with your mother."

The room went silent. Icy resentment darkened Neela's stare. "General," she said, still glaring at me. "Escort this man from my presence."

Grinning, Aldous moved around behind me. "Move, Shinree."

"You better talk some sense into her, General," I said, glancing at him. "Putting me in charge of the troops is the wrong move. I have to take Reth out and reclaim the crown *before* your soldiers attack, or it'll be a bloodbath." I gave him a longer, more significant look over my shoulder. "Battle experience or not…you know I'm right."

Aldous paled. For just a moment, I had him. Then he poked me in the back with his blade. "I said, move."

FORTY NINE

Sitting on Rella's southernmost shore, staring out across the water at the island-city of Kabri where I was born, the battle had yet to start, but a small war was going on inside my head. Wary of going back, I was haunted by old ghosts and anxious of what new ones I might make by simply returning.

If challenging my father caused him to unleash the power of the Crown of Stones on the world, the resulting consequence would be all my doing.

The weight of that was devastating.

Thankfully, I couldn't focus on it for any length of time, seeing as the two extra souls residing in me had their own issues. Sienn and Jarryd were respectively unsympathetic and enraged at the suffering of the Rellan people. Their opposing sentiments left me with a great need to avenge their pain, as well as an appalling sense of satisfaction. I was angry, sad, homesick, triumphant, bitter, all at the same time.

We only agreed on one thing. The Langorians had to go.

To see that done I had to confront my father, regardless of the risk and regardless of what it cost me with Sienn. And it would cost me. Welching on an oath like I made to her was a serious matter. Pissing Neela off was not quite as dire, though I could have handled the situation better. Still, the outcome of our quarrel was promising. My words of warning had definitely rattled General Aldous.

After completing our morning march to rendezvous with the bulk of Neela's forces, the general called an emergency meeting where he convinced several high ranking officers that Neela's plan was flawed. That had set off a whole afternoon of arguing.

Not by accident, I'd missed most of it. After helping set up camp in the meadow beyond the tree line, I'd kept myself as far away as I could from both the politicians and the thousands of men fighting on their behalf. I could still hear the soldiers from time to time though, drinking and joking, sharpening their weapons, preparing their horses, checking their armor—praying. I knew the rush they felt, the eager anxiety. How they hated waiting. They wanted to go, to move, to fight. Facing off with Death himself was better than sitting and thinking about how they might not live to see another day break.

I agreed completely. I might have joined them, too. But I needed to quiet the turbulence in me, not fuel it. That's why I'd been spending my time alone, drawing circles in the sand with a stick, and occupying my mind with trivial things. Such as imagining what the land around me looked like before it was broken.

From the teachings of my tutors, I knew that where the tips of my boots rested in the lapping waves had once been solid ground. The water directly in front of me was then flat, open field. It had jutted out far into the distance, eventually sloping upward into a wide towering unnamed mountain. Landlocked on three sides with open sea on the fourth, the mountain's rocky crags and high tor served as Rella's coastline, until five hundred years ago when the same quake that destroyed the Shinree Empire and splintered the kingdom of Kael off in the east, fractured the southernmost portion of Rella. Cracking in a wide, horizontal line near the base of the mountain, most of the flatlands slid in upon itself. What remained was swallowed, as the ocean flowed in and surrounded the mountain; giving birth to an island and creating a new coastline for the mainland.

Seeing great potential in the island, Rella's ruler at the time, vowed to build a city like none had ever seen. He hired the best builders. The best materials were brought in. The planning alone took years. When construction was finally complete, the city of Kabri stood behind a wall twenty men high. Built into the side of a graduated, rocky slope, stone buildings wound halfway up the mountain to the edge of a thick pine forest. From there, a single road led to the top where an elegant five-story castle coiled around from the north side of the island to the east.

With gleaming spires and towers made of a stone so blue it blended with the sky, many of the castle's windows were made with patterned, colored glass. The battlements and the gates were lined with steel. The front courtyard was small, but an ornate elevated gallery in the back overlooked an impressive arena. A portion of the mountain had been leveled to build the arena and spectators found the views at cliff's edge staggering. Contestants knew them as dangerous, and came from all over *Mirra'kelan* to compete. Others, from far-off lands, arrived by the ship-full simply to marvel at Kabri's wonders.

The city's population had swelled quickly to the point of bursting.

Now, all that glory was gone. Most of the city was leveled. The wall had collapsed. The pine woods were burned. Heavy soot streaked the pale stones of the castle like dark, ugly scars. The fortified main section was still intact, but many of the colorful windows were broken, and the spires were no longer gleaming. One tower was missing an entire side. Another had cracked in half. Its pieces lay scattered like old forgotten bones in the silent, empty courtyard.

Everything was black or ash gray; the structures, the clouds, the forest. The only other noticeable color on the island was red. It was on the mass of tents erected on Kabri's beach. It was on the uniforms of the enemy soldiers milling about. High atop the castle's tallest tip it waved; a large flag whose blood-colored background and golden serpent stood garish and haughty against the ruin.

Another flag was affixed to the city gate. A third smaller standard waved outside the main pavilion, glowing in the light of a ring of torch poles shoved deep in the sand. More torches lined the beach, chasing away the approaching dusk and illuminating the huge enemy encampment far better than I wanted it to.

Draken was claiming the island with gusto. I couldn't wait to show him that he was being presumptuous. And now, I had potent reinforcements to do it with. Possessing the steadfast allegiance of a vengeful Kabrinian citizen, and the skills of a powerful erudite, my outlook and my plan both had changed.

Admittedly, it would have been nice to have more than a day to harness Sienn's abilities. A little instruction from her would have been even better. But since closing our connection at Broc's house, Sienn had shown no interest in reopening it—or looking in my direction. That left me to pick up what I could on my own.

Spending hours reviewing her memories, I'd basically soaked up the gest of Sienn's skills without having to practice a single step. I understood how to combat my father with spells he wouldn't expect me to wield. I grasped how to conserve strength and keep myself conscious longer than ever before. The only thing I wasn't able to absorb was diverting the cost of my spells. The process was more instinctive than learned. How I'd ever done it on my own was a mystery, as it had taken Sienn a considerable amount of training. It took time, patience, and concentration.

Concentration I could access in abundance through Jarryd's keen sense of focus. Patience was something neither of us possessed a great deal of. Sienn had it. But that didn't help me with the third element: time. I had none left. I was banking my entire offense on untested borrowed magic and a temporary bond that could snap at any moment. It was irresponsible at best.

But going in blind, without a trial run, was just plain foolish. *I have to test it*, I thought. And the perfect opportunity was staring me right in the face.

I fixed my sights on the island. Slowing my breathing, I called to the fire agate on my wrist. I opened up, but didn't pull it in. First, I closed my eyes and dove into the space where Sienn Nam'arelle rested inside me. Making use of her essence and her knowledge, I integrated my intent with the channel. I envisioned winding them together, so that as I narrowed one, the other complied. Then I let the agate in.

Choking the path, compressing the aura's entryway to no more than a slender rivulet, I kept the flow of power to a trickle. The act wasn't overly difficult. It was frustrating. Siphoning an infinitesimal stream, when I was used to drowning in it, fell drastically short of the invigorating experience I was familiar with—which was exactly the point. Lessening the physical reaction definitely made casting a lot less appealing. I could hardly feel the magic in me. I wasn't even sure I had enough, but I clamped off the current anyway and moved on to the next step: casting outside my blood-bound abilities.

I had the stones. The spells I could glean from Sienn's memories. The only real hurdle was me.

Coming from a more personal source than most other lines, a soldier's magic was reflexive, instinctive, and emotional. It was wrapped in pretty much every negative or base sentiment and behavior there's a name for. Aggression, defiance, pride, lust, anger, bravado, brutality, vengeance, and more, were all a part of me and my craft. But they had no place in other kinds of magic. If I wanted to move beyond the limitations of my line, I had to expel them. I had to relinquish who I was.

For help, I dug deep into Jarryd's soul. I tapped into the well-honed sense of absorption and rapt focus that dominated his skill with a bow. I employed his strong sense of commitment and devotion, using it to isolate myself from the more selfish aspects of my personality. His ability to see to the heart of things became mine. From Sienn, I acquired her knack for curtailing emotion when she cast and used it to inhibit my own. Then, with the three of us united inside me, I breathed.

Taking in Jarryd's single-mindedness, his diligence and drive to excel with each inhale, as I exhaled I used Sienn's tactic and released everything. Every emotion I draw upon when I pull a sword or cast a battle spell—hostility, rage, passion. I shed it all.

The discharge was unbelievably quick. In seconds I was clean. Blank. Unpolluted. I stared at Kabri's beach with a perception of the world that was drastically heightened. All I had to do was give attention to the torches sticking out of the sand and they became instantly tangible. I was an ocean away, yet the wood against my skin was course. The fibers of the cloth were scratchy. Heat seared my skin. I breathed, and the pitch was pungent.

I condensed my awareness down to a single torch. I wrapped my will around the fire, and it didn't burn me. There was no pain. It was a different kind of discomfort. The flames were spirited and volatile, akin to closing my hand over a swarm of angry bees.

It wasn't something I wanted to hold onto for long.

Visualizing the outcome, I cast. I felt a jolt, a stinging pulse of hot energy that jumped and flitted frantically across my nerves. *Just like bees*, I thought, gasping.

There was an odd sensation. I opened my eyes and the aura was bleeding out of me. I was used to that. But I wasn't used to a portion remaining inside, while the rest stretched and twisted away from me like a translucent length of magical rope.

The aura reached across the water to the beach. Its end made contact with the torch, connecting us like a bridge. Putting my hand out, feeling the flames in my grip, I squeezed. Sparks flew from the top. Burning embers sailed into the darkening sky. Without direction, they fell harmlessly to the wet sand and snuffed out of existence.

It worked. But I wasn't done.

Broadening my focus to include every torch on the beach, the rope sprouted branches and attached me to their flames. I opened and clenched my hand, and as before, sparks leapt. Only this time, I held on. I aimed the fires in my grasp. I bid them to take flight, and they soared with a *whoosh* onto the rooftops of the Langorian tents. Flames consumed the fabric hungrily. Bedlam broke out across the camp, and I smiled.

That's more like it.

Opening my grip, I released the fire and the rest of the agate. There was a slight haze around the edge of my vision, but I wasn't blind. I saw the rope vanish and the dusk blaze orange. I saw the schools of dead fish rise up to float on the water. I endured no loss of strength whatsoever, and the sudden waves of hot vibrations that swept through me were gone by the time they'd even registered as pleasurable.

It was the most physically unsatisfying use of magic I had ever experienced.

Still, I couldn't argue with the results. Channeling as an erudite was far less disruptive. I felt charged, confident. I was ready to try my hand at harder spells. I just needed someone to aim at.

But he isn't someone, I thought tensely. *He's my father.*

Footsteps plodded over the dunes behind me. I gave them my attention, but no sooner had I rested a hand on my sword, did I realize who it was; Jarryd's gait had become as familiar as my own. I couldn't sense him, though. I'd shut him out before entering Neela's room last night and had yet to let him back in. The embarrassing sordid details of my encounter with her aside, I didn't think it wise to keep our connection open. With the coming fight (and our inexperience with the link), if one of us were injured, neither of us could afford the distraction.

Jarryd stopped beside me. He joined me in watching the silhouettes on the far shore scurrying about, trying to douse the flames. "I see you found something to do."

"It's better than listening to a bunch of generals debating strategy."

"It was your strategy they were debating."

"Then maybe I should have been allowed to speak."

"Maybe, you shouldn't have walked out."

"I swear I've never seen a woman argue the same point so many different ways."

"Neela's good for that." Jarryd sat down on the sand.

Glancing at him, I started to ask the results of the meeting. Then I got a look at what he was wearing. Dressed in the formal garb of a Lead Archer in the Rellan Guard, Jarryd was a new man. "I thought she was kicking you out," I said skeptically, "not promoting you."

He spread his arms. "What do you think?"

I didn't answer right away. Outwardly, it was impressive. His deep blue fitted tunic and breeches were made of exceptionally fine leather to allow ease of movement. His boots, soft-soled and lightweight, each displayed a built-in sheath and dagger running up the outside. The front of his tunic boasted an elaborate rendition of the Arcana crest stitched with silver thread on a black background. A smaller version of the design ran down both sleeves. On his back were buckles, empty now, but perfectly position to hold a nice-sized quiver of arrows.

The garments were beautiful and functional. And with a thin, shiny steel brace gracing one arm and a supple, black three-fingered glove covering his opposite hand, Jarryd's transformation was daunting. He was born for the bow. Now, he looked the part. I should have been happy for him. But hearing Jarryd vow to fight for his home, and seeing him ready to die for it, were two different things.

"A little flimsy for battle," I said at last.

Jarryd grunted like he'd expected that. "Liel's back," he said, quickly changing the subject. "He delivered your message."

"And?"

"And I still think you should have let me do it. Reth could have killed him."

"Yeah, well Reth *would* have killed you. Was there a reply?"

"Your father agreed to see you alone, tonight, like you wanted. Details are in here." Jarryd handed me a slip of paper. "Since you've been playing in the sand all afternoon, I assume you didn't hear that Neela went back to Kabri."

Shock raised my voice. "She did what?"

"The Queen wants to be on her throne the moment Langor surrenders."

"Goddamn it," I muttered. "When?"

"A few hours ago. Sienn opened a door for her."

I clenched the paper in my hand. *Of course she did.* "What the hell was Neela thinking? If she's discovered..." I left off. All sorts of images ran through my head at the thought of her and danger. None were helpful. "You couldn't talk her out of it?"

"Neela knows it's risky. She didn't need me to tell her."

"No. She needed you to stop her."

"She took guards," he said angrily, guilt pricking at his temper. "And Neela knows that castle better than any Langorian. She'll hide until our forces arrive. Which," he added meaningfully, "will be *after* the crown is in your possession."

"Good," I nodded. "At least she used her head in something."

"Only when Aldous forced her hand. He threatened to take his men home."

"Looks like the General found a piece of his spine on his trip from Kael."

"Nah." Jarryd threw a handful of sand at the water. "He's just worried about his own skin." He picked up another handful and tossed it. "I saw Sienn just now. I really like how you managed to make both women stop talking to you on the same day."

"One of my many talents."

He grinned a little, but the expression didn't last. "The attack will commence after you open the link and give me the all clear. Sienn will raise a fog as cover and freeze the water's surface so the troops can cross. It's unlikely our advance will go entirely undetected, but with her aid there will be an advantage gained."

"Did you notice?" I nodded at Kabri. "No eldring."

"Our scouts report that none have been seen on the island in days. I want to think that means we caught a break, but," he tossed me a glare, "I've got you in my head saying it sounds too easy."

"Let's hope I'm wrong."

Jarryd strained the sand through his fingers a moment. "We received terms for surrender. I didn't get a look at them, but I heard Neela sent the pages back in pieces."

"Nice touch."

"Yeah. But I know her, Ian. If this goes badly, Neela will sign." Concern tightened the scar on his face. "And the new terms will be far worse."

"If this goes badly none of us will be alive to care."

"I want to go with you," he said then.

"To see my father? No way."

"After you defeat him you'll be in a city full of enemies with no strength to fight. You'll need protection."

Slow, deliberate, and precise, I said, "You aren't coming with me."

"I know where you're going. I read the message. I could follow you."

"We both know you have more sense than that."

Jarryd's teeth clenched. "You can't do this alone."

I'm not alone, I thought. "This is my responsibility. Jem Reth is my father."

"And you're my friend. And Kabri is my home."

"Then take it back. Besides, you're mostly dressed for it. Just don't forget that sword I put on your saddle. Or rather, my saddle. You're taking Kya."

"Ian..."

"I borrowed the sword off an Arullan, but it's got good weight and balance."

"I told you this morning. I don't need a sword. Or your horse."

"I put a mail shirt in your pack. If you can stand plate, that's even better."

Jarryd groaned. "I thought we settled this."

"If you haven't digested my memories of the war yet, do it now. Analyze every battle before you step foot across that water. And keep to the rear as long as you can. I don't care what your orders are."

"That much is clear."

"Damn it, *Nef'taali*, you've never seen anything like this. Neela has near four thousand men. Draken has over five. There will be no time to think or second-guess. React. Breathe. Fight. That's all you can do. Fight and stay alive. You got that?"

"Yeah." Jarryd nodded a moment in thoughtful silence. He stood and brushed the sand off his breeches. Glancing up and down the beach, he fidgeted with the brace on his arm a few times. He turned the archer's ring on his finger, round and round.

"Okay," I said. "Spill it."

"I can't stay here, Ian. When this is over, I have to leave Kabri."

Shame pressed in on me. "I didn't mean for this to happen."

"I know." Jarryd stared down at his palm, tracing the lines with his finger. "I guess I go where you go now. It would feel strange to put distance between us."

"That it would," I nodded. "Any place in particular you'd like to go?"

"We could ride up into Langor and pay Malaq a visit."

"Sounds good. We can help him give Draken a push."

Jarryd's face brightened. "Down the stairs?"

"I was going to say off the throne. But I like your idea better."

"So, Langor then?" he said hopefully.

"Sure."

Jarryd turned to head back up the beach. He paused. "I'll see you in Kabri."

"Be safe, *Nef'taali*. I mean it."

"You too." He seemed a little nervous, but as he moved off Jarryd gave me his typical, crooked grin. I tried like hell to believe that it wasn't for the last time.

FIFTY

I jumped out of the boat and into the water. It was high tide. My splashes sounded like thunder as I sloshed through the waves, dragging the small craft behind me onto the shore. I didn't bother concealing it. My father knew I was coming. His note said this side of the island had been cleared of patrols for the night. He claimed it was to prevent some unwitting soldier on rounds from accosting me. A more simple explanation was that he didn't want the Langorians to know we were meeting.

Bound to Draken or not, Reth had his own agenda.

Nevertheless, it appeared he kept his word. If troops were lurking though, I couldn't see them. In the time it took to row across to the island, storm clouds had moved in to make the darkness absolute. *Langorian dark,* I thought grimly.

It was a foreboding notion. One I tried to shake as I held my lantern up and walked a ways down the beach. The stroll was difficult. All manner of things had washed up, and debris was everywhere. Some of the pieces were charred and weed-choked. Others were battered and sun-bleached. An uncomfortable number were suspiciously body-like in shape, and I avoided them earnestly.

Closer to the harbor, the wind picked up. It tugged at the cloud cover. It freed the moon to light my way, and for a second, I thought I wanted that. I thought I wanted to see what Draken had done with my own eyes. Until the rays shone down onto the ruin and my heart dived straight into my stomach.

It was an irrational reaction. I wasn't ignorant of the destruction. I knew what the Langorians could do. I came with Jarryd's memories of the attack in tow. Even if I hadn't, Reth's message warned me not to put in near the dock because of the damage.

Despite all that, I was shaken. I was infuriated—and not because of Jarryd, or even on his behalf. I felt wronged. Although I never truly fit in, I'd spent the first eight years of my life in Kabri. Now, so little remained, that I could scarcely put the memories of my childhood back together.

Where I used to dart among a crowd so thick I feared being stepped on, were piles of sopping black rubble. Instead of mouthwatering smells, the air reeked of mold and rot. The pier, where I would sit and watch the tall ships unload, had been reduced to a single black post sticking up out of the water. Strapped to its length was one lonely wrecked vessel. It bobbed up and down in the dark waves. Empty and gutted, sails shredded, mast cracked, its ashen hull shimmered like a ghostly carcass in the silver light.

I watched for a while, as the sad half-ship dipped and swayed.

When the clouds came back, I turned away and moved inland over the dunes.

Between the deep sand and the thick patches of waist-high grass, it was slow going. But as the terrain leveled, the weeds thinned. Sand gave way to pebbles and scattered boulders, then rocky outcroppings. At the wall of the mountain, a series of long, flat shelves jutted out across the ground. In one section, they went up as well, far beyond the reach of my lantern. I stretched, holding the flame higher, and was still nowhere close to seeing the end of them, or the peak above.

I put the lantern down and started climbing.

Scaling a mountain in the dark wasn't one of my better ideas, but I couldn't afford to waste a drop of magic. And even without light, I knew the ascent wouldn't prove too difficult—it wasn't my first attempt. Last time, I'd been small. I'd barely made it up two slabs before slipping and breaking my arm. Now, taller, older, and stronger, the rocks were spaced perfectly for my height. I could stand on one, reach the lip of the next, and pull myself up with ease.

Doing just that, in no time at all, I was at a height that was certain death if I fell. The view was nice, though. The elevation lent me a vantage point

I didn't have on the ground, and as the moon made another appearance, I noticed two Langorian warships anchored at a bend in the coast. They appeared empty. Darkness and distance made it hard to be sure, but there were no unusual sounds on the air. Nothing moved on board but the tiny lights of lanterns swinging back and forth on the breeze.

Resuming my climb, a handful of minutes (and a dozen slabs) later, a halo of torchlight engulfed me from above. As I squinted into the glare, a hand reached down. It was splotched and striped with gray. Magic pricked the air around it.

Impatiently, the hand opened and closed. I took it and let my father help me up over the top. I was glad when he let go, though. His skin felt peculiar. The contact left my own tingling. I shook the sensation off my fingers as I crawled to my feet and looked around.

The ledge we were standing on was about fifteen paces across and ten deep. Empty air was on my left. On my right was the mountain wall. It continued up flat and steep, but for a single break in the stone about the width of two men. Beyond the gap was a slim corridor. Near the opening, the walls glistened slightly, reflecting the faint glow of a fire from somewhere deep within. Beyond that was darkness.

I turned to my father. I started to speak, and he walked right by me. Head buried in his cloak, he didn't glance. He offered no smug greeting or poorly timed insult. He just took his torch, headed into the slender mouth of the cave, and left me standing alone in the dark. "Asshole," I muttered.

Following him, I entered the passage. The air was damp and musty. The temperature drop was staggering. I was anxious for the heat of the fire, but paranoia won over comfort and I went slow and cautious. Letting the space between us widen, I eyed the steadily rising ceiling for traps. I ran my hand over the smooth, water-carved walls, thinking they might close in.

My suspicions didn't wane as the corridor opened up and dumped me out into a large chamber. Curving high above like a bowl, most of the roof was lost in gloom. Fissures and cracks fractured the walls and floor. Six were large enough to be tunnels. Two were blocked with debris. The others stood open like black gaping maws, their lengths extending back so far, the small fire in the center of the room couldn't penetrate their darkness. The flames did radiate light enough to see my breath, but they produced no heat. The blaze wasn't real. My father stood in front of it like it was, though, with his back to me and his cloak fanned out behind him.

He didn't move as I approached.

"I came to hear you out," I said. "But first, I need to know what your plan is. How you're going to control our people. There'll be a lot of magic flying around once everyone's off the *Kayn'l*. Do you have a safe way of feeding it?"

Reth hissed. "I don't have time for this. Did you come to give me the obsidian or not?" His tone was almost frantic. "I need it now."

"Why? What makes this piece so damn important?"

"Because without it, I am incomplete."

"You? Don't you mean the crown?" He didn't reply, and a chill went up my spine. I crept closer. "Turn around."

"Give me the stone."

Taking the last few paces between us, I went over and took hold of his arm.

"Wait—" he warned.

I spun him around. Firelight hit my father's face, and I gasped, "Gods," and stumbled back into the cave wall.

Reth pushed the hood off his head. "You should have waited." He unhooked the clasp and shrugged the cloak off his shoulders. Shirtless, as the fabric fell away, he turned in a slow circle, so I could get a good, long look. "I wanted to prepare you," he said, but I didn't believe him. My father wanted me shocked and afraid. He wanted me intimidated. Impressed. He got three of the four.

I was far too sick to be impressed.

The nine auras, the power that brought such internal beauty to the Crown of Stones, had made him outwardly grotesque. His flesh, stained an ugly, muddy chaotic blend of color, had the look of variegated clay. Swirled and kneaded haphazardly together, intertwining bands of celestite, sapphire, and magnetite bled into a reddish-purple bruising of ruby and spinel. Twisted splashes of diamond and amber were mottled with topaz. Meandering veins of obsidian streaked strange patterns atop the scars, which looked to afflict his entire body now. Not just in appearance, but in consistency. Perverted and distorted into something still solid, but filmy, like parchment, or the discarded skin of a snake, my father's flesh was almost transparent. Through it, I could see the mass of multi-colored auras inside him, all slithering, rolling, coiling and squirming, like a nest of newborn serpents.

Frozen against the wall, horrified by the magic swimming in him, I thought, *Gods, does it really look like that? Does it look like that in me?*

I drew a shaky breath and tried not to stutter. "What are you?"

His dappled cheeks rose in an arrogant smile. "I am the future. I am how I must be, to save us."

"That's not true. It can't be." Running a distraught hand back over my hair, I pushed off the wall and moved closer. "If we can destroy the crown—"

"Impossible. The stones are forever held together, linked by the magic and the souls of countless Shinree."

"I don't understand. How could it be linked by souls?"

"The crown isn't what we believed, L'tarian. It's not a weapon. And it's far older than we imagined. Tam Reth wasn't its creator. He was its caretaker. One of many," he added. "Tam was simply the one who got tired of hiding what could make him a god."

"Is that what you think you are? That must be one hell of a book he wrote if it can convince you that this," I threw a disgusted hand at him, "makes you anything but an abomination."

"You honestly didn't read Tam's journal?"

"You know I can't. The pages are spelled."

"They are. But the words are visible to any with Reth blood. Something you might have realized that night at the inn…if you'd bothered to open the book instead of Sienn's legs." He paused to relish in my outrage before he went on. "Tam's writings were helpful, yes. But to gather what I needed, I had to go back myself."

"Go back? You mean, like in an oracle spell? Sienn said that was danger-ous. That you could—" *alter things*, I thought. My heart sped up. "What did you do? What did you change?"

"Relax son, I was careful. Though, it was hard to leave. Being in the empire, in the body of the great Tam Reth," he sighed wistfully, "it was a wondrous time. Truly wondrous. And now I'm one step closer to restoring that glory. To returning what was stripped away and making us as we once were." Passion overcame the nostalgia in his voice. "Resurrecting our past will secure the future. Don't you see?"

I really didn't. And that worried me.

I went over and stood in front of him. Magic clung to his body like a heavy odor. It churned inside him. Watching the auras move beneath his skin made my own feel like it was crawling away. Yet, in spite of that, in spite of everything he had done, I felt sorry for him. I felt sorry for both of us. "You didn't have to kill her," I said, "my mother."

"I told you why."

"I was a boy growing up without a father. If you'd come to me and told me who you were, if you'd asked me to go with you…I think I would have gone."

That seemed to throw him, but he shook his head like it didn't. "That's of no consequence now."

"I heard what you were like back then. How you tried to help the slaves. Things might have been different if we'd been together. You might have been different."

Another head shake; more desperate this time. "It doesn't matter."

"You chose your crusade over your own child. Maybe that doesn't matter to you. But it fucking matters to me."

At the resentment in my voice, a twitch of pain ran across his blemished face. Uncertainty and sorrow glistened in his eyes, making my father look as devastated as I felt. But I had my doubts his sentiment was genuine, and I hated myself for wanting it to be. For thinking he might contest my accusation. That he might apologize with actual sincerity or offer me a single word of peace. I wanted him to make me understand.

But that level of kindness just wasn't in him.

"It won't work," I said. "Draken will never allow so many Shinree to live outside of his control."

"You're wrong. We will be an asset to Draken's new realm."

"What about the ones whose blood is too diluted? The slaves that have been on *Kayn'l* for so many generations they don't know what magic is?"

"All are given a chance to prove themselves."

"Why test them? You already have the records. You know their bloodlines. What are you looking for?"

"The same thing I'm looking for in you, L'tarian....worth."

I glared at him. "And if they don't pass? Are they still assets? Or dead weight?" His response was a dismissive, callous shrug that got me thinking. "Gods, you're not killing them, are you? Please tell me you aren't killing our people."

"Don't be foolish. I'm not killing them. I'm selling them back."

"You're making them slaves again?'

"Some considerations must be made to maintain society."

"You son of a bitch." My voice shook. My chest ached that I had come from such a man. "You freed them and then sent them back. Gave them hope and then took it away." I sympathized completely. "Leaving them ignorant would have been less cruel."

"By putting them back on *Kayn'l*, I spared them the humiliation of knowing how truly useless they are."

"Your compassion is staggering."

"So is your ignorance." His tone turned ugly. "The gods gave you alone a chance to stop our suffering. They put the Crown of Stones in your hands, and all you did was hide it. You turned your head. Did nothing. Became nothing. You condemn me for leaving you fatherless, but you let our entire race rot. You're a coward, L'tarian. A disgrace. An embarrassment to our line. Running around with your fucking tail between your legs, bending over at your master's whim...you, my son, are a castrated dog on the leash of Rella. You're pitiful. Pathetic. And without me, that is all you'll ever be."

Reth turned away. He put his back to me and I stood, staring at it, shaking with how badly I wanted to strike him. He was crazy. Cruel. Despicable. He meant nothing to me. His remarks should mean far less. But they didn't.

My father's brutally honest lashing stung like hell. His words, sharp, merciless, and heavy with disappointment, rang in my ears. His condemnation twisted in my gut. His refusal to look at me made my chest tighten. But what sapped the anger from me, and left me feeling like I'd just been pounded on, was the glaring truth of his allegations.

"I can't deny it," I said thickly. "When I was young, I paid no attention to the slaves. I didn't care what happened to them. I was made not to care. Then, after the war, after the Crown of Stones, after...Aylagar, I thought if all Shinree were as dangerous as me, they deserved enslavement. I certainly did.

I begged King Raynan to take my freedom away. *Begged him.* But he wouldn't. So I convinced myself that it wasn't punishment enough, anyway. That *Kayn'l* was too easy. That living with what I'd done, facing it every day, was more of a sentence than slavery could ever be." Sienn's memories surfaced and my voice fell. "I was wrong. I had no idea what it was truly like. But I do now. And we don't deserve it. No one deserves it."

He was quiet a moment. "Wait here." Retreating into the darkness at the rear of the chamber, my father's footsteps grew soft, then loud again as he came back. He had the Crown of Stones in his hand. "It's yours."

Anxiety pulled my muscles tight. "You're giving me the crown?"

"I don't need it." He tossed the circlet. Catching it, as my skin made contact, I cringed; anticipating an explosion of power that didn't come.

Puzzled, I turned the piece over and examined it. Heavy and not quite perfectly symmetrical, the tops of the individual stones were uneven and riddled with flaws. The sides and bottoms were smooth, magically fused, so that each color flowed seamlessly into the next. Where the stone's edges blended was murky and dingy colored and unpleasant to look at. Just like my father's skin.

I glanced at him. Then back at the crown.

The stones in my hand were dim and cold. The glowing sparks, the auras, I remembered jumping inside of them, were gone. The Crown of Stones was nothing but an empty husk. Its power was in him now.

"You're right, L'tarian," he said boldly, "I did make a choice all those years ago when I killed V'loria. I made the only choice I could. Now, it's your turn. Will you go, take Neela and run? Or stay and be named Prince of the Shinree? Revel in the blood in your veins. Be the champion of your own people."

"Go. Stay." Hopeless anger darkened my laugh. "You make it sound so simple."

"It is simple. You belong with me."

"I'm not going. And I'm not staying. There's a third choice." I stepped back and put a hand on my sword.

"This is why you came here?" he laughed. "To fight me?"

"I came, *goddamn it*, hoping I wouldn't have to. I came hoping there might be something to salvage. That I might see a hint of the man my mother loved. To find out if in some, small way you were capable of caring for your own son. But whatever you were is gone. You're a shell of the man that made me. You're empty. Broken. Just like the Crown of Stones."

Reth stared at me, perfectly still. His eyes were full of ire and a little bit of disillusionment. Like he actually thought I might choose him. "You have no idea what I am, son. But you will." Eerily calm, my father raised his voice and said sharply, "Bring her!"

FIFTY ONE

I couldn't look down. If I looked at the ground in front of me, where Neela Arcana was naked, bound, and bloody, it would undo me. Instead, focusing on something I could handle (the Langorian that put her there), I tightened my grip on the Crown of Stones and belted the grinning bearded bastard across the face with it. Then I threw down the circlet and started beating him.

He struggled, but I was in no mood.

Sidestepping his frantic attempt to block me, I seized one of his beefy arms in mid-swing and snapped it over my knee. The scream he let out as the limb twisted and broke was like oil on a fire. I wanted to hear more.

Driving him back into the cave wall with an eager growl, I gripped his big head in both hands and bounced it off the rock until blood splattered out the back.

"L'tarian," my father said tiredly. "Let him go."

"Why?" I shoved an arm under the folds of the man's neck. "Give me one reason why I shouldn't stand right here," pressing in, I cut off his air, "and watch him die."

"Because he didn't hurt her," Reth replied. "I did."

I dropped my arm. The soldier slid from my grip. He landed in a breathless lump on the cave floor, and I backed away.

"Go," Reth ordered him crossly. "Spread the word to make ready for an attack. The Rellans believe they have an advantage," Reth's smug eyes shifted to me, "now that a proper distraction has arrived." He looked back at the soldier. "Bring the Queen with you and lock her up. Some place dark and dirty, perhaps?"

Features twisted in pain, the Langorian put a hand to the back of his dented head. He couldn't move his other arm. It hung curved at an unnatural angle as he inched unsteadily up the wall to his feet. He took a shaky step toward Neela.

Before he could take another, my blade was out and buried in his gut.

Reth groaned as the body fell. "Oh, son, you really are painfully efficient."

Ignoring him, I booted the Langorian off my sword. I stomped on him a few times just for fun. Then I put my weapon away and turned to face Neela.

I didn't want to—she looked that breakable. Bare shoulders hunched, knees drawn up to her chin, she was sitting with her arms wrapped around her legs and her head dropped forward on her knees. It was unnervingly similar to the position I'd found her sleeping in at Broc's house. Only now, finger-like bruises tarnished the smooth skin of her arms and legs. Rope burns ringed her ankles. The red, wet sores were likely left by the same style of heavy binding that was still tying her wrists together.

I squatted down. She seemed not to notice me. I tried making eye contact, but her braids had come undone and too much tangled hair was in the way.

She wasn't moving, wasn't talking.

I glared up at Reth. I had two words for him. "Did you?"

"A small sampling," he confessed. "I wanted to see what all the fuss was about. And I have to say…it was a bit of a letdown. There is simply no fire in the girl."

Closing my eyes, I breathed. *He wants this. He wants me to lose control.*

And I was going to. There was no way around it. Seeing Neela beaten and used in the dreams was bad enough. Every time I listened to her scream, every time she placed the blame on me, it tore me apart. But I was accustomed to it. I expected it. The real Neela's silent suffering, how she sat, withdrawn, unresponsive, and frighteningly calm, was agonizing in a completely different way.

"Neela?" I said softly. "Neela, can you hear me?" My tender tone getting no response, I got short with her. "Look at me," I said, and her body uncurled.

Head lifting, she peered at me through a fall of knotted dark hair. "Troy?"

"I'm here."

Dazed and shivering, she nodded. Quiet tears fell from her red, swollen eyes. The drops ran over the cuts on her cheeks, across her trembling lips, and down the bruises darkening her jaw. A few slid past the scrapes on her neck and in between the lash marks on her breasts. None made it as far as the burns on her stomach, hips, and thighs.

My father had been thorough. Yet, I'd seen far worse, far too many times. I knew how to disconnect myself from appalling atrocities. I'd been trained to get past the outrage, the sympathy, and the anger, and deal with it when the work was done.

I couldn't get past this. I didn't even waste time trying.

"Hold still." Pulling the dagger from my boot, I sawed at the ropes on her wrists.

"I'm sorry," she whimpered. "I've made things worse."

My grip on the weapon tightened. "This is his fault, Neela. Not yours."

"I tried to run, to fight him, but…"

"It's all right. I won't let him hurt you anymore."

From across the cave Reth let out a grumble of impatience. "The stone, L'tarian. Hand it over or she will endure far worse than my attentions."

Choking back a reply, as I kept at the rope, I wondered if my father had any idea the mistake he'd made. *He* put Neela in my head. *He* made my desire to defend and avenge her exist outside of the dream, in hopes of manipulating and unbalancing me. Well, it worked. I was definitely unbalanced.

Just not in the way he thought.

I wasn't crumbling. I wasn't going to fall at his feet and meet his demands. This wasn't a dream where I was tied and helpless. I was in the room with the cause of her suffering and he was real and mortal, and near enough that I could tear a hole in his throat and smile as the blood drained out of it.

The rope broke. Carefully, I lifted it away from the lesions underneath and tossed it aside. "Stay down," I told her. I slid the dagger away and got up. Putting myself in front of Neela, I looked at Reth. "This changes nothing."

"Are you sure? Between Sienn's teachings and the crown, I can heal her. I can take away the memory of her ordeal…if you give me the obsidian."

"You want the stone? Then you'll have to kill me. You'll have to stare into my eyes as you cast and watch the life you gave me fade away. Can you do that…father?"

"If you insist. But you might ask her first." His gaze swung to Neela. "Ask her if she wants to die like her mother."

"No. If we do this, Neela leaves."

"Neela stays. She moves an inch and I will kill her and every Rellan child under the age of ten. I will boil the blood right in their tiny, little veins."

"You wouldn't."

He gave me an ominous grin. "Go ahead, son, ask her. Unless, you're afraid? Afraid that you'll kill her even if she begs you not to."

"Shut up."

"Do you hate me more than you want her? That's really what it comes down to."

"I said, *shut up*."

"This time would be no accident. It would be outright murder. Because you know you have no real chance against me. You're weak. Your spells are inferior. Neela will die, I will win, and you will be left with nothing—again."

"Stop! Just fucking stop!" Shoving my hands in my hair, I started pacing, trying to come up with a solution that wasn't there. I had no doubt that if I tried to get her out, my father would make good on his murderous threats. The only way to avoid it was to give him what he wanted, to put my desires and her wellbeing above an entire kingdom.

That is what the dream intended for me all along.

Yet, while everything (my own life and the lives of everyone I swore to defend) paled where Neela was concerned, my need to retaliate for her pain didn't.

I knelt back down. Neela had stopped crying. Her stare was composed and resolved. It reflected the answer to the question I wasn't brave enough to ask.

I wasn't brave enough to hear it yet, either. So I kissed her.

She tasted of tears and blood. I almost stopped. I didn't want to hurt her. But Neela's mouth moved on mine as if nothing terrible stood between us. Her hands clutched at me like she needed a moment of pleasure to mask the pain.

Her last moment, I thought, and drew back. "I can't. Not again."

"You have to, Ian. Rella must go on, even if I don't."

"What if he's too strong? If you die for this and I fail…"

"You won't fail." Finding my hands, she squeezed them. "You have abilities Reth only dreams of."

"I don't—"

"You do. There isn't time to explain. Just know that he cannot be allowed to live. There is too much risk. And I am not that important."

I brushed the hair back from her face. "If only that were true."

Neela smiled a little. I kissed her again. I soaked up every second, every sensation. Then I left her. I walked over to where my father was standing near the fire. Churning filaments of magic were worming up out of his body, dancing and hovering over his mottled skin like a dark, vaporous rainbow.

The sight of him was as frightening as it was beautiful. Even his eyes, a swirling, muddy hue, were radiating massive amounts of power. Power he was about to aim at me.

Readying myself, I woke the obsidian. I envisioned it as a thick, black shield, shiny and slick; reflective enough to turn aside any direct magical strike. It would only last a couple of hits. It was better than nothing though, so I sacrificed a portion and made one for Neela.

Next, I roused the stones in the wristlet. Inhibiting the flow to a thin stream, like I'd practiced, I braced for his attack. Yet apart from Reth beaming at me, nothing happened. *He's letting me strike first,* I thought. And I knew why. Meeting my spells head on, taking whatever beating I gave him, would prove my incompetence. It would confirm that he was backed by the might of the crown's power, and I was on my own.

Only, I wasn't. Not today. *Not anymore.*

Splitting the emerald off, I directed it at the cave wall. I nudged it up, inside the layers of rock, all the way to the ceiling, and then over. Invading, infiltrating every split and fissure I could find, I pushed the aura, spreading it like veins through the dense structure.

Drilling in deeper, disturbing the mass, I shifted it—minutely at first. Then I increased and intensified my incursion. I broadened the spell to penetrate the entire area above Reth's position. Then I gave it one final, mind-jarring thrust. I drove it in hard, and a loud splintering *snap* ricocheted through the cavern.

My father looked up for the source. Right as it crashed down on his head.

The fall was long and deafening. Dirt and rock rained nonstop. It rose back up in dark, billowing clouds that bulged and bloated to swallow the firelight and foul the air.

I couldn't see. Dust filled my lungs. It swept into my nose and mouth. The grit was like boulders in my eyes. I couldn't keep it out. Even the shield I'd conjured was useless, as the cave-in wasn't a magical attack. It was a product of my lack of experience with elemental spells, and a pure lack of forethought.

Cursing my own stupidity, I threw myself against the wall and felt my way along it, back to the exit. Blind and choking, stumbling like the town drunk through the corridor, I finally tumbled out onto the slab and collapsed. I was hoping the night air would provide relief, but lost in the thick, grainy cloud that followed me, I was still wheezing. I still couldn't see.

Rain plunked down on the top of my head. Grateful to Fate for his surprise show of pity, I lay back and opened my mouth. It was a light shower, barely a drizzle, but bit-by-bit, the sheath of dirt rinsed off my skin and washed out of my eyes. Gradually, the breeze dispersed the brown fog. The air started to clear. I stopped coughing and hacking, and it was suddenly very quiet. *Too quiet.*

There was no way he was dead.

Hauling myself up with a groan, I went back in. The air in the passage tasted like mud. Reth's conjured fire was glowing again, and I followed the faint traces of light through the remaining stir of dust to a mass of rubble in the center of the cave.

Neela was still where I left her, off to the side, lying on the ground, her naked body covered in sand. She stirred, and I released the breath I didn't even realize I was holding. Miraculously, her eyes opened. For a moment, there was encouragement in her gaze. It faded as her eyes fell closed again.

I took in the sight of her for a breath or two. Then I tucked my guilt away as best I could and refocused my mind (and my gaze) on the pile of debris. It was large, sufficient enough to crush a normal man beyond recognition.

I wasn't kidding myself, though. My father was far from normal.

Throwing a fraction of the agate into the fire, the temperature in the room spiked. Sparks flew and bounced from the core. Pulsing, writhing tongues of orange and gold burst up in a glittering flash. Licking the crumbling ceiling, the flames liquefied what they touched and steaming globules of molten rock dropped in a sizzling ring around the blaze.

Forcing the flames back down, I stripped the heat I'd created. I pushed it underground and held it there. I let the pressure build. I let the temperature swell. When I couldn't hold on anymore, I hurled it out through the ground and released it. My aim was perfect. I could tell from the way my father was screaming, as the cave floor underneath him began to melt.

As his muffled shrieks bled out through the rock, I absorbed the diamond, the garnet, and the kyanite, and struck him again. This time, I went with a different kind of spell. One that in his own, twisted way, my father would have been proud of. I made him face his worst fears. I brought them to life in his mind, and the noise that came out of him was a kind of racking, brutal cry that a man should never be made to produce.

It was unbearable to hear. Never had I thought it possible to be stripped raw by sound alone. But the despair, the absolute terror; it gored straight through me. It echoed like an endless accusation through the dusty cave. And somewhere in the din of my father's anguish, under the weight of his desolate screams, I felt myself losing everything—courage, purpose, my hunger for vengeance in Neela's name, the armor of Jarryd and Sienn's souls. The belief in what I was doing.

My resolve had felt stitched together as it was. Now, it was unraveling.

One thing bolstered me to stand my ground: magic. And I clung to it.

It was always the same, one thing. The painful truth of that wasn't lost on me. I just couldn't think on it now. I was too busy leaching off the energy of the Crown of Stones. Amassing inside Reth, its power was overflowing into the air. I could feel it pulsing. I could taste it, unbridled and deliciously unchecked. It was an ocean up against the little dribble I was wielding, and I was jealous.

Even secondhand the crown's power was amazing.

And wrong, I thought. *Something's wrong.*

He's not screaming anymore.

A flurry of rocks flew off my father's chest. He sat up, and a heavy layer of silt slid away from his burned body. Still smoldering, his head turned in my direction. As he caught sight of me, a low monstrous sound issued from his seared mouth. It was followed by a wide spill of blood. More oozed out of the wet blisters that blighted his head, chest, and arms. It seeped from around the strips of scalded meat hanging off his face; bright, red trails against cooked, black skin.

"You…" he shook a bony finger at me. "You have been keeping secrets from me, L'tarian. I don't like being deceived."

I grunted. "Sucks, doesn't it?"

There was a spike in the crown's power. A breath later, the remaining debris exploded off him in a violent blast of airborne rubble. Dust and pebbles pelted me. I ducked and covered my head as the cloud blew over and past me, into the passageway behind me, and outside.

Warily, I stood. Waving at the thick air, through long painful blinks, I watched my father walk through the haze. His breeches were torn and charred. His multihued gaze shone eerily against peeling crisp flesh. A glimpse of jawbone gleamed in the firelight as he opened his dried lips to speak. "You are impressive, though," he smiled, his pleased voice rough. "It should have taken months of training with an erudite for you to manipulate rock and fire."

I declined to explain my link to Sienn. "Guess I'm a natural."

Reth's smile flattened. "You still have much to learn. Such as this…"

His eyes closed. He shuddered, and a film of magic rose up from his wrecked body. Enveloping him, the auras shifted and coalesced into a solid sheet of rolling energy. As the mass adhered to his body, Reth's spasms worsened. I couldn't tell if it was from pain or pleasure, but while he jerked this way and that, underneath the sleeve of magic, the blood began drying up and flaking away. Blisters healed closed. Dead skin shriveled and shed, fluttering to the ground like last winter's leaves. New, colored flesh formed in its wake.

When my father was restored to the same vile state as before, the wrapping of magic fragmented and broke into tendrils. They looped around his body, flashing and coiling a moment, before sinking back inside.

Reth smiled again. "A soldier capable of healing himself would be a formidable foe. I can show you how it's done." He stepped closer.

Recoiling, I drew the sword off my back. "Stay away."

"I don't want to hurt you, L'tarian."

"Since when?"

"Regrettable things have been said and done. But it's not too late to put them behind us."

"They'll be behind us when you're dead."

Reth's stained face softened. A look of longing gripped his swirling eyes. "I held you once. You were so small. You fit right here." He put his hands out and cupped them. "I had so many plans for you then, for us. I imagined us close. Inseparable. I would teach you, and you would look up to me. Worship me. Need me." He stared at his empty hands. Then he dropped them, as if the emptiness was too much. "I know you yearn for my affection, my guidance. I know you need me."

"Like hell I do."

"What you said before, about me being capable of caring for you... *I am,*" he swore adamantly. "I can be. Just tell me that it isn't too late. That you want to be a family—that you need me. Just say it. SAY IT!" he screamed. The veins on his discolored face bulged in rage, and I smiled inwardly.

I'd found his weakness. It wasn't power, like I'd thought. It was me.

I lowered my sword. I gave my father uncompromising eyes, and said bluntly, "Prove it. Renounce Draken. Use the crown's power to rebuild what you've destroyed. Make restitution for what you have done. Then be rid of it. Walk away from magic. If you do that, if you prove that you mean it…if you chose *me,* then we can leave this land together. We can be a family, like we both want. Like we should have been."

Shock held his mouth slack as Reth stared at me a long moment.

Abruptly, he broke our gaze with a nervous twitch of a smile. "What of the future? What of our people?"

"This isn't the way."

"Then what is?"

"I don't have a solution. But we can try to find one together."

"I can't abandon them. I won't."

"And I don't want you to. But you have to send the power back. Letting it live in you like this, it's affecting your body, your mind. Please. Father," I said, as sincerely as I could, "it's hurting you. Let it go." I searched his eyes, looking for a speck of surrender beneath the magic, a glimmer of sanity—anything. "Do this for me."

"You wouldn't ask if you knew how it felt. But you don't. You can't," he said, with a short, desperate laugh. "You have no idea what I have. What I'd be giving up. You can't imagine how this feels!" he shouted, thumping his chest. "Your concept of satisfaction is far too limited. Too ordinary," he said disdainfully. "The most pleasure you can imagine is a bottle in your mouth and Aylagar's little girl down on her knees."

"You son of a bitch. I'm fucking trying here! But you have to give me something. *Anything.*"

"I am." Reth reached out. He placed a gentle hand on my shoulder. "I'm offering you the safety and security that only a father can give his son. A chance to reclaim what was denied us. To take back the years we lost. I'm offering my love, L'tarian. Isn't that what every child wants? Isn't that what you want?"

He was a coldhearted, crazy bastard, but his words still made my throat constrict. The pain in his stare set mine to aching. The weight of his touch on my arm was a lifeline, inviting me to cling to the notion that everything would fall into place if we were together.

It was a nice thought. If only I couldn't see through his heartfelt plea as easily as his marred skin. "Okay." Nodding, I swallowed. "If you want me to accept you, to understand what you're giving up, then show me. Make me see what I'm missing."

"What are you saying?"

"I need to feel it."

Reth gave me an intrigued, sideways glance. "You've thought about it, haven't you? You've wondered what it's like to host the crown's magic as I do. You want it."

"I don't want it," I said, my protest a little too strong. "I'm...intrigued."

"There's no need to be embarrassed, son. You're a Reth. It's natural for you to covet power." I didn't deny it, and his smile swelled with fatherly pride. "Perhaps just a little? A taste, to satisfy your curiosity?"

Running a hand over my face, I forced a heavy dose of anxiety into my voice. "Yeah, sure." I let some eagerness slip in. "Just a little."

Reth squeezed my shoulder. I felt a surge of energy, and the cloth of my shirt dissolved beneath his hand. "I must warn you, son. After this, restraint might not come so easily." He sneered, challenging me to back down. "Are you sure this is what you want?"

I was pretty sure I'd rather face a pack of eldring with a spoon, but I met his arrogant stare anyway. "Do it."

FIFTY TWO

I was lost, weightless. The cave swam in blinding color. An unending explosion hammered through my veins. It thundered beneath my skin, making my muscles twitch and throb, burning me from the inside out.

Reth's voice as he watched me endure was husky and shameless. "You like it. You like it very much." His fingers pressed harder. Enormous power rode along my nerves.

"Gods…." I clung to him, gasping. I thought my heart would burst from my chest. Then I thought it wouldn't matter if it did; no boundary could contain me. Not even my own body. I had no limits. I was more than I'd ever been—more focused and aware, more alive.

"Now do you understand?" he laughed.

"The crown…it never felt like this before. The vibrations are…" I didn't know how to describe it. "This isn't channeling. It's something else, something deeper."

"Yes," he purred in earnest. "And once the crown is joined with the piece around your neck, the power can be stronger, the pleasure greater. It can be endless."

A shock of fear ran through me at how badly I wanted that.

But Neela's army was positioned across the water. Her people were hiding in their homes, holding out hope that someone would save them. Jarryd was waiting anxiously for my signal. If I didn't give it, his belief in me would be forever shaken. The trust he'd so blindly put in me would be gone. I couldn't squander that.

I placed a hand on top of my father's. Centering on the energy passing through his fingers and down into my shoulder, I tracked the flow backwards out of me and into him. I was searching for a beginning, a source. I couldn't find one. The vibrations weren't issuing from a central location in his body. They were everywhere, pumping through his entire system. Tissue, blood, bone, organs, they were all infused with magic.

A portion of the obsidian may have merged with me, but the wealth of the entire crown was becoming a part of him. It was changing him. Into what, I couldn't imagine. I was afraid I would find out, though, if I indulged too much. Already, with what little was in me, the power was saturating and distorting my senses. It was potent and persuasive, insinuating itself like a disease, contaminating my body's most basic functions.

I lost awareness of my limbs. My heart, that was pounding a moment before, no longer existed. I couldn't feel my lungs working. There was nothing but the magic.

I was a raging sea of pure energy.

I didn't understand how Reth could accomplish anything in such a state. I couldn't for much longer. *I have to make a move, now. Before I can't.*

"That's enough." Reth tried to slip his hand out from under mine. When I held on, he laughed. "Don't be greedy."

"More," I grunted.

Worry touched his voice. "It's time to let go, son."

I latched on tighter. I pulled at the stream. Reth tried to hold back, but the crown knew me. And as I heaved swiftly and ravenously at our shared font of power, massive waves of magic rolled out from his hand, down through my shoulder, and into my body. Rapidly, the auras moved within me, spreading, polluting. They were struggling to take me over. Like an infection.

One I had to purge from us both.

Panic gripped my father's voice. "L'tarian—stop!" He pushed and clawed at me.

I gripped him harder.

Dipping into Sienn's spells, I selected one meant to cleanse the body of contaminants, and aimed it on the magic inside my father. I asked the spell to see the crown's auras as an invader, an illness; a fatal threat to his physical wellbeing. Then, harnessing every smattering of power I had at my disposal, I whittled my focus. I refused to let in a stray thought or a grain of emotion. I had one, single purpose, one goal. To remove the parasite inhabiting my father's body.

I cast.

Hardly a breath went by before he flinched. "What are you doing?"

"Curing you." Slowly at first, then faster, as if siphoning poison from a vein, I drew the swirling, snaking streams of colored energy out through his mottled skin.

Reth's body began to twitch. "L'tarian, no," he begged. "Please. You can't take this from me—you can't." He grabbed at me frantically. Horror thinned his voice. "Stop this. Stop it now!" His multihued eyes grew large and damp. They grew larger as the magic began burrowing out faster. Fleeing from more than just his hand, tiny exit wounds were forming all over his stained body.

The same was happening to me as the auras found refuge. But the pin-pricks of blood seeping out of me didn't matter. Reth's screams didn't matter. Neither did the little jolts of pain, or the knowledge that I had fallen to his level. I was too gorged with magic, too bathed in pleasure.

"You tricked me!" he bellowed. "You had no intention of standing by me!"

"Aren't you proud?" I grinned. "You wanted me like this. Willing to destroy my own flesh and blood, able to do what I must whatever the risk. You wanted me a Reth, cruel and despicable, manipulative, and devious. So here I am, you goddamn, son of a bitch—here I am!" I shouted, shaking him. "Do you like it?"

Shrinking some, he scrambled to appease me. "Maybe there's still time. Maybe Neela's still alive. If you go to her—"

"Turn my back so you can crawl away? I don't think so."

"But she needs you!"

"She's dead!" I hollered back.

"Shouldn't you make sure? In the dreams you swore to protect her. Remember?" he pushed me. "Remember how badly you wanted to save her?"

"What I *remember*, is you making me watch her suffer." I heaved him closer. "But you fucked up, Jem. You took it too far. Somewhere in all the twisted crap you put in my head, avenging her must have become more important than having her, because right now...all I can think of is tearing you apart." With a merciless yank, I grabbed hold of the last of the crown's magic, and I drained him dry. I took everything. Every residual drop that the crown put inside my father, I took for myself; leaving him shuddering and gasping with his white eyes rolling back in his head.

There was no more magic in him. No more fight. He was sobbing, teetering.

Helpless.

It wasn't good enough.

"I've pictured this moment for weeks," I said, glancing down at the weapon still in my hand. "I imagined what I'd say. How it would feel." I looked up at Reth. "I thought it would be harder." Holding his gaze, I raised my sword, and drove the blade through his chest. The shock in his white eyes said it was the last thing in the world he'd expected.

It was for me too. I'd laid bare the man's deepest desire and then crushed it, just like he would have. And I had no remorse, no pain over what I'd done. I had only the sensations pulsing through me, and the knowledge that I was teetering on the edge of being profoundly dangerous. *Of being like him.*

The notion tempered me instantly.

In one long agonizing burst, I sent all the magic back to its various sources, all at once. The void it left behind was devastating.

Weak, worn, and empty, I threw Reth off me. The sword pulled out of him, and I dropped it. The weapon had felt too heavy to hold, my grasp of it too slippery; slickened by the amount of his blood on my hands.

As I wiped it off onto on my breeches, I reconnected with Jarryd. A rapid assortment of things slammed into me from his end of the link. I set it all aside, except for his adrenaline. It blew threw me like a wind, dispelling my exhaustion long enough for me to blast him back with a shot of urgency and satisfaction that he couldn't mistake.

I shut Jarryd out again and looked down at Reth, slumped on the ground at my feet. I couldn't see through his tarnished skin anymore. Without magic, the disjointed blend of colors seemed dull and dreary. His body, no longer swollen with energy, was sagging. Some life was in it yet, but the way his blood was draining out to soak the cave floor, it wouldn't be for much longer.

Eyes heavy, breath raspy and shallow, he reached out a silent hand to me.

I backed away from it and staggered over to Neela.

Stretched out on her side, beneath a thick coating of dust and pebbles, she was still and quiet. No breath was coming out of her. I brushed the debris from her face and her skin was cool to the touch. It wasn't parched and gray as Aylagar's had been. My spur-of-the-moment shield spell must have offered some protection. But a quiet peacefulness hung over Rella's Queen that felt unnervingly familiar.

Not this time, I vowed. *Not again.*

With my link to Sienn, I had access to the temporary binding spell she'd used on me in Ula. I could give my strength to Neela. I could do what I couldn't for her mother. I could save her—if there was anything left of Neela to save, and if I had the strength to give her. Which, I didn't. The only way was to supplement it with magic.

A lot of magic, I thought gravely, as my eyes shifted to the Crown of Stones.

On the ground, in the dirt, near the body of the Langorian soldier, the crown was full again. Its colors glowed and pulsed, calling to me like a beacon in the murky light.

I went over and picked it up. Gripping the circlet, I invited its magic inside me once more. The invasion was a lot less dramatic than when I stole it from my father's body. I tried to infiltrate, to fuse with me like it did him, but its pulse was less tumultuous. More stable. I felt still empowered as before, but not suffocated. Complete without being overwhelmed. The combined auras still aroused a provocative sense of superiority and confidence that was hard to ignore, but I had a better handle on the physical effects of the crown's magic than I had just a few, short minutes ago.

I was pretty sure such a quick progression wasn't a good thing.

Nervous, I glanced over at Reth's ruined skin. I looked at what the crown had done to him, and I told myself this had to be the last time. That it wasn't too late already.

That one more spell wouldn't make me like him.

I completed the symbols on our hands in a daze. I cast the spell and threw myself across our newly forged link. There was little of her to grab onto, but I seized what I could find and held nothing back. I poured my life and my magic into Neela, and prayed that it was enough.

As I collapsed beside her, the crown slid from my grip. Using my last coherent thought, I flung its power out of me and back to whatever hell it came from.

FIFTY THREE

My boots struck the stone floor. Aside from my anxious breathing, it was the only sound. It resonated through the empty corridors of the castle as I walked, searching the upper floors. I opened doors, one by one. The rooms behind them were all empty. The curtains were all drawn. The windows closed. There were no fires in the hearths. No lanterns or candles were lit. The air, trapped, chilly, and tinged with gloom, reeked of death and rot. A combination of burned waste, sour wine, tainted food, overflowing chamber pots, and old blood; the foul odor lingered in the dark. It intensified as I went lower, clinging to me as I passed, making my empty stomach cramp like a cold hand clenching it tight.

The discomfort in my gut worsened with every broken dish, slashed tapestry, splintered door, and overturned furnishing—wreckage that was a poignant, graphic reminder of the Langorian occupation and the recent battle. A battle we must have won, or after passing out in the cave I would have woken up chained in a Langorian dungeon instead of in a room on the fifth floor of Neela's home. *Neela's very deserted home,* I thought uneasily. *The damage was extensive. She must have ordered an evacuation.*

Still, someone brought me here. So where are they?

If Sienn were nearby, I had no idea. Her presence inside me was gone. Our bond had run its course, and I was relieved. While there had been certain obvious perks, the longer it took Sienn to discover my default the better. Once she learned that I'd borrowed her erudite knowledge to kill Reth, blatantly breaking the vow I made to her back in Kael, she would seek restitution. Whatever flirtatious game we'd been playing at would be over then, one way or another.

I couldn't sense Jarryd, either. Our link was jammed, but not on my end; Sienn had taught him well. He must have been with me for a time though, since his cloak had been draped over a chair near the bed I woke up in. His quiver was on the mantle, empty. The bow beside it lay broken in two. A scattering of blood stained the wood.

I tried not to let it worry me. If Jarryd had been severely injured in the fight, he would have been lying in his own bed instead of sitting vigil next to mine.

In contrast, my temporary connection to Neela was working a little too well. I hadn't gained any of her memories, but her emotions were exceptionally strong. Coming on me as I regained consciousness, the flux of past and present sentiments and reactions had been too suffocating to make sense of. Instead, I'd been forced to stockpile the whole thing and shut her out. Now, after having a few minutes to consider the experience with a more level head, the improbability that she was even alive, that *I* brought Neela back from the edge of Death's lands, amazed me. I was a soldier. I broke bodies for a living. I didn't fix them. *But I fixed her. I healed her, gave her life.*

Right after I took my father's.

Squeezing my scored hands into fists, I descended the main staircase faster, all the way to the first floor. I imagined I'd have a better chance of finding someone here. What I found, was outright ruin. And far too much blood.

Streaking and spilling, gathering in dark dried pools on the floor, it speckled the ceiling. It splashed the walls, spelling out foul words and promises of "Death to All Rellans," in thick, dripping strokes. Great sprays darkened the fabric of shredded wall-hangings. Doors, torn from their hinges and gouged down the middle, all bore thick unmistakable splatters.

There were widespread singe marks as well. Ashy remains that I hoped weren't human kicked up around me as I walked. Chunks of shattered statues and pottery crunched under my step. There wasn't a piece of furniture left unbroken or a painting that hadn't been cut. Clothing, baskets, linens, cooking pots, vials, bottles, books, papers, and dozens of other personal belongings were strewn about.

The main entrance was just ahead. Normally, it took two men to lift the great slab of wood that barred it shut from the inside. I was willing to give it a try though. Fresh air was on the other side, and I needed some badly.

I was about to grip the thick, heavy log, when I heard the first hint of sound that wasn't my own.

Postponing my exit, I followed the intermittent, distant noise down a long, dark hallway that ended in a set of closed double doors. Surprisingly intact, of the muffled voices that filtered out from underneath the doors, none belonged to Jarryd. Only one belonged to a woman, and it was definitely Neela. Even with a wall up, I could feel a faint impression of her. I couldn't make out her words, but her tone was severe and harsh, like she was reprimanding someone.

If I barged in, I had no doubt that 'someone' would be me. As badly as I wanted to see her, or anyone, I didn't feel like arguing. It was safer to let her finish.

While I waited, I thought I'd continue looking for Jarryd so I backtracked to the main hall. I wandered down another poorly lit passage, with more smashed furniture, more blood, and more defiled pieces of Rellan life. The stale air was even worse here, and it was really starting to get to me.

Stepping over scattered shards of a broken mirror, I went to the nearest window. I gripped the heavy drapes in both hands, and pain shot across my left shoulder. "Ow."

Recoiling a bit, I finished tugging the curtain aside. Sunshine and warmth streamed in. The blackened remains of Kabri stretched out for miles in front of me.

I didn't give it a glance. My eyes were drawn elsewhere.

Dropping my hand, I leaned into the sun and stretched out the neck of my shirt. Bruises, deep and widespread, covered my entire left side. Some of the contusions were the usual greenish purple that comes with real physical damage. The rest were far from usual.

On my shoulder, in the exact spot where my father had shoved the power of the Crown of Stones down inside me, was a large magic scar. Distinctly hand-shaped, the center of the scar was obsidian colored. The 'fingers' extended out, streaking off both sides of my shoulder in an ombre pattern where black, bleeding to red, dipped down to curl in slender bands around my arm. Bending, I picked up one of the larger pieces of the broken mirror and moved my shirt aside. Black to gray stretched down my back.

None of them were the hideous, garbled splotches my father had. The markings the crown had left imprinted on my skin were sharp and well-defined, almost as if they were designed with skill. They reminded me of Arullan skin art, and I thought I could even pass them off as such. *For now,* I thought. *But is this how it starts?*

Is this how my father's scars looked at first, before he channeled too much? Before the crown started changing him?

If he were alive I could have asked him.

"Fuck!" I threw the glass on the floor and yanked the curtain closed. I had yet to hear Neela come out of her meeting, but I was fine with that. My mood had soured too much for company. I wasn't even up for finding Jarryd anymore. I wanted Kya, a bottle, and a long ride to clear my head. There was just something I had to do first. One place I needed to visit that suddenly seemed long overdue.

The castle hadn't changed much in ten years. Once I found the kitchen, I easily located the cellar, and to the left of that, the discreet door to the servant's corridor. Inside the passage, it was cold and tight. A few lanterns on the wall were lit, and I could see my way fairly well. Navigating through one junction, then another, I came to an old, dilapidated stairwell that headed in one direction: down.

Cramped, dark, and dank, with twists and turns, and no railing, the route wasn't very inviting. A slippery deposit of grit covered the stone steps, which were narrow and broken in spots. There were torches on the walls, but the only one in use was at the bottom of the staircase. Its glow was weak and far away.

I took my time. Descending at a careful pace, I stuck close to the wall. It didn't surprise me as pieces crumbled off beneath my fingers. Portions of the castle had been rebuilt and added onto over the years, but the section I was in now was one of the oldest.

As the layer of sand underfoot grew heavier, the light got brighter. I finally caught up to it at a long, wide landing. There were no more stairs, just a dirt wall reinforced by large wooden planks. On my right was a sizeable tunnel that led out to the beach behind the castle. On the opposite wall was the burning torch I'd been chasing. Beneath it, a shadowy oblong nook cradled the cold, waxy nubs of a dozen candles wasted away to nothing.

They'd been burning the last time I stood here, with King Raynan Arcana. He'd told me how the candles were specially crafted, fashioned by Rellan priests who wove ceremonial prayers into their making. Then he showed me where to push to make the wall move.

Using the shoulder that didn't hurt, I found the spot, leaned against it, and shoved. As stone scraped stone, a few fragments chipped off to settle on my boots. Dust wafted, coating my hair and making me sneeze. But there was no resistance. The door-shaped slab swung open wide with a puff of musty, salty air and a brief tumble of gravel.

While I waited for the shower to stop, I reached back and stole the torch. Holding it out in front of me, flames burned away the darkness to reveal a small cave-like chamber. Far below the sea, the walls were round and wet. The rocky floor was pitted. Straight ahead was a massive wooden door, bolted into the cave wall. On my previous visit the door had been in one piece. Now, it was in three.

Crossing the damp cavern, I jumped over the splintered planks and into the next chamber. I could only see a fraction of it. Housing the generations that were laid to rest here, the Royal Catacombs were quite large. Even setting fire to a few of the torches bracketed to the wall didn't help much. They gave just enough light to make the shadowy stone likenesses of the dead dance and sway eerily about.

I moved farther in. The room was a dark, dusty maze of stone crypts. Brushing at the years of grime in the grooves, I cleaned off a few with faces I didn't recognize. Then I found one that didn't have a face at all. Flat and smooth, there was only a name etched into a metal plate at the foot of the lid. There had been no time or resources for more. No chance to pay tribute to the fallen. Not even King Raynan Arcana.

My eyes slid to the neighboring vault. The day I left Kabri, it too had been blank; without monument or rendering. But the carvers had long since made it otherwise, chiseling out an inscription, a body, and a face.

A face I'd thought never to see again anywhere but in my head.

Proceeding to the nearest empty bracket, I rid myself of the torch. Then I went back and walked the length of Aylagar's crypt. Twice. I traced the outer edge, lingering on the rough spots where crude Langorians tools had chipped away the granite in their hasty search for the Crown of Stones.

I blew the sediment away from the side. Underneath it was a short Rellan poem about duty and sacrifice. Adorning the gray stone lid was the recreation of her body. It was unexpectedly intact. *Intact, but wrong,* I thought, running my fingers over the plain pious gown that covered her from neck to ankle. In place of her usual Arullan battle armor, the gown had been chosen to make Aylagar appear more Rellan. For that same reason, her height had been exaggerated, her muscles down-played, and her frame slimmed. The miles of hair I loved had been shortened as well, shaped in a stern fashion and hidden under a wimple—something Aylagar would have died before ever agreeing to wear.

The injustice didn't stop there. The fire in her eyes had been made vacant. The depth of emotion on her face tamed. Even Aylagar's strong, exotic features had been reduced to a stoic expression of unsmiling indifference.

"They didn't know you." Bending, I placed a gentle kiss on the cold, hard surface of her cheek. I ran my hand over hers. Fingers lingering, I waited for the tightness in my chest, the ache that accompanied every thought of her. I expected to hear the thunderous *slam* of the lid falling into place. The sound had echoed inside me for years.

None of those things happened. I wasn't overcome with grief or remorse, or even love. There was no hitch in my throat or sting in my eyes. Standing over Aylagar's grave was one of the most anticlimactic events of my entire life, and it made no sense. Her memory had driven me to more bottles and ill-tempered moods than I could count.

Killing her had nearly killed me.

Then I understood. Aylagar wasn't the catalyst for my pain anymore. She was no longer the standard that I held all other women to. Thanks to my father, Neela was. She was the center of my nightmares. She haunted me now, and it didn't seem fair. Aylagar had to die to earn that right.

Faint footfall alighted in the passageway. As it drew nearer, my perception of Neela multiplied. A moment later, I heard her climbing over the broken door.

Her dress rustled as she moved up behind me.

"That isn't her," she said. I didn't turn around and Neela came closer. "You can't blame the artist, though. My mother was too fierce and beautiful to be captured in stone."

My pulse racing, I stared down at the vault. "You look like her."

"Not really." She sounded a little sad. "I know how you saved me. Thank you."

"Are you all right?"

"It's strange having parts of another person in my head."

"What's strange is that I'm getting used to it."

My jest put a smile in her voice. "When I woke, I could feel you so much I could barely breathe. Now, it's vivid one moment and faint the next."

"I had to block you out. And our connection is fading."

"Already?"

I was wary of facing her, but I jumped on the disappointment in her voice. "You sound as if you'll miss me."

"Perhaps. You are like a whirlwind."

"I've been called a lot of things," I chuckled. "But never that."

"It's true. You're inspiring, but difficult. Your...nature," she said delicately, "influences my words and decisions. It carries my thoughts in directions I would never go. I have found few traits in you that are fit for a Queen."

"Well, you'd make a lousy bounty hunter, so I guess we're even."

Neela gave into a brief laugh. She came to stand beside me at her mother's tomb, and I could sense her anguish. The mental wall between us wasn't working so well.

"You long for her," I said.

"Yes. Do you?"

"Not anymore."

"Then what do you long for?"

"That's a complicated question."

"Let me rephrase. *Who* do you long for?"

It was like reflex. Without thinking, I turned around with her name on the tip of my tongue—and swallowed it. Neela looked too spectacular for words.

Gone was the drab, unflattering dress she wore in Ula, as well as all traces of her ordeal in the cave. Clean and healed, her smooth, dark skin shimmered in the faint light of the torch. Her hair, shiny and debris-free, flowed unbound over the shoulders of an elegant white beaded gown. Instead of rope burns, strands of pearls surrounded Neela's wrists. More adorned the slender silver band on top of her head. Three encircled her throat. One string hung lower, drawing my eyes to the wide scooped neckline of her cinched bodice and the enticing hollow it made between her breasts.

"I brought us something to drink." Neela pivoted away and went back to the exit. A serving girl stood in the passage. I couldn't see what she was holding, but when Neela returned she was carrying a silver goblet in each hand. "Is something wrong?" she said.

"Nothing." Clearing the wobble from my voice, I took the drink she offered me and tried again. "It's nothing."

Neela nodded, but from her expression, she knew I was lying. Or maybe she'd simply expected me to offer more. An apology, perhaps, for what my father did to her. I could have inquired about Jarryd as well, asked how many men were lost in the battle, or if Draken were gathering forces for another attack.

All of those things would have required far more composure than I had. I barely had enough to stand and drink in the sight of her without losing it.

Then she smiled at me, and I couldn't even do that. It was an open amorous smile, like I was the only man in the world, and it completely disarmed me.

My hold on the barrier between us slipped. The wall broke, and Neela rushed in.

Her barefaced emotions and intent invaded me. They were easy to decipher. Her sentiments had one basic theme: Neela wanted me to touch her.

Before I did, I moved away.

"I'm sorry if I remind you of her," she said.

"That isn't..." I glanced back. I could sense her discomfort as acutely as my own. "This isn't about your mother."

"Good." Quiet for a minute, she said abruptly, "I dreamt of you."

"Oh?" I replied, nearly choking on my wine. Recovering, I tried to feel her out, to see if she knew anything about Reth's spell. "Do you have a lot of my memories?" I asked, keeping it vague. "The exchange is different for everyone."

"No, I don't believe I do. A few hazy moments of your youth, perhaps."

"When did you regain consciousness?"

"Two days ago. It's been nearly four since you cast your spell. The entire time, I've been having, what I believe, are your dreams."

Retreating to the wall, I leaned against it, and downed half the goblet in one gulp.

"Is that even possible?" she asked, strolling over, "to share a dream?"

"I suppose," I said, affecting a nonchalance I definitely didn't feel. "We are connected."

"They were quite vivid. Explicit, even...considering we barely know each other."

The color left my face. "I'm sorry if they disturbed you."

"They didn't." Neela took a small drink. "Some say dreams let our most inner thoughts out to play." She sat her goblet down on one of the tombs and came right up to me. We were nearly touching. "Do you really want to do those things to me?" Her eyes wandered down. I clenched my jaw, trying to fight it, but my interest in her was blatant. "Do you want to do them to me now?"

I had nowhere to go. My back was literally against the wall. I didn't trust myself to touch her, even as long as it would take to move her out of the way. I didn't think looking at her was smart either, so I kept my eyes down. I just didn't keep them down far enough, and before I knew it, I was counting the rows of beads that lined her bodice.

That led to mentally tracing the flower-like pattern; down around the collar, over the curves of her breasts and the flat plane of her stomach. I imagined doing it with my fingers. I saw myself reaching out, gripping the bodice and tearing it straight down the front. I could almost hear the beads bouncing as they hit the stone floor.

"Ian," she said. "Look at me."

I raised my eyes. I watched her lips part. She wet them with a slow caress of her tongue, and things tightened in me that were already about to snap.

"You frighten me," she said.

An awkward laugh slipped out. "I know the feeling."

"You misunderstand. It isn't you that frightens me. It's how *I* am when I'm with you." Doing away with the last little space between us, she nestled in close. "I want to touch you. Here." Neela ran an impatient hand down the front of my breeches. "And here." She started stroking me through the leather. My pulse turned painful.

"Neela," I breathed. "What are you doing?"

"If you have to ask, then I'm not doing it correctly."

I swelled in her grip. "You are. But we shouldn't—we can't. Not here."

"So my mother does stand between us," she said with anger.

"No, but…"

"Then finish it. Finish what you started that night when you came into my room…when you laid me back on the bed…when you pushed up my dress." Her caress turned brisk. Blood throbbed in my veins. I was taught, aching. "You awakened this in me. You put your hands on me. Your mouth."

"And you told me to stop," I reminded her.

"Now, I'm telling you to finish it." Snappish, she said, "I am Queen, Shinree. My will is law, and you will obey."

"Obey?" *What the hell is wrong with her?* "Are you ordering me to bed you?"

"Do I have to?"

"No. I'm not a—"

"Slave? I think we both know that you are." Neela seized my rigid cock tighter. Glancing down at her prize, with low lids and a devious grin, she whispered, "At least part of you recognizes my authority."

Resentment clenched my jaw. *It's the dreams. It has to be. The memories, the lust—they're funneling through the link, affecting her.*

"You said you'd show me how to be a woman." Neela took the cup from my hand and tossed it. She brushed her lips over my face, my mouth. "Do it. Show me."

"You aren't yourself."

"I can't be myself. Not ever. Not with anyone." She drew back and looked into my eyes. "Only with you. Only right now."

I shook my head. "It's the spell I used to heal you. It's influencing you, confusing you. That's all this is."

"I don't care what it is. I don't want to do what's right and proper. Just this once, just for this moment, Ian, I don't want to be Queen. I want to be the woman you dreamt of. I want to feel like you made her feel. Just this once."

Frustration mounting in me, I growled. "You don't understand." Her body was rubbing against mine. Her tongue was on my skin. I was so eager to be inside her—to feel the real *her* wrap around me—I was shaking. "If we do this, Neela, walking away after, having to leave you…it will wreck me."

Her lack of concern was unequivocal. "I know."

FIFTY FOUR

Little bits of stone fell away as I pushed Neela back against the wall. More showered her hair as I leaned in. Crushing my mouth to hers, digging my fingers into her arms in a feverish attempt to make her real, I held her there. I liked the feel of her in my hands, the permanence. I liked how she didn't mind my need to dominate her. It was as uncontrollable and irrational as the clear hunger in her embrace.

Frantic and eager, drawing my lips into her teeth, winding her tongue around mine; a familiar, desperate yearning was in her every kiss, every rake of her nails as she snaked her hands under my shirt. It was obvious. Neela shared in my hysteria.

I gripped the captured fabric in my hands tighter. Yanking, I pulled the sleeves off her shoulders and ripped them down over her arms. The bodice tore, spilling beads down the front of her like tiny icicles. White against the black of her skin, they clattered to the floor, just as I imagined.

As Neela shrugged out of her ruined sleeves, the pieces of cloth fell around her hips. She stood before me, half-naked, with no tension whatsoever on her face or in her body. She was giving herself to the moment—and to me. I think I stopped breathing.

"Are you all right?" she asked.

"No," I said honestly. "Not in the least."

Basking in my loss of composure, an impish grin tugged at Neela's lips. It faded into a more serious expression as her fingers slid between the laces of my breeches. She loosened them, one after the other, with ridiculous, painstaking precision, seeming not to notice that I was dying with every second that ticked by. Just as deft and slow, she removed my shirt. Regarding me first with her eyes, then her hands, Neela traced the contours of muscle on my chest, arms, and stomach. She bent down and did the same with her lips, and a chill ran over me.

I pulled her up. I kissed her, gently this time. I moved my lips over her chin and down her neck. Caressing her shoulders, gliding my hands down to the small of her back, I made my way leisurely around to her stomach and up over the curves of her breasts.

Supple and damp, they were more than I could hold in my hands. Her nipples were dark and erect and I gave them attention, caressing them, rolling them in my fingers. I plucked one into my mouth. Neela moaned, and her pleasure burst over me like a cloud break. Her desire, the sensations I provoked in her, all came hurtling at me through the link. The outpouring was unbelievably strong. The feel of her was extraordinary. I didn't even consider shutting her out. Together, we were a seamless, unending wave of tingling nerves and burning skin, rushing blood and pounding hearts. Every sense, every touch intersected and overlapped; the heat rising between her legs; the crushing, merciless pressure growing in me.

Neela's lust added to mine was a towering wave of desperation and madness.

When it became something beyond measure, I picked her up and threw her down on the first surface I could find.

As I separated the leather of my breeches, she lifted her dress. I gripped her bare thighs, pulled Neela's body toward mine, and her warm, wet flesh swallowed me whole.

She was tight. Sweltering. Soft.

She opened up.

And I fell.

Her body was the door. Her thrusts were the perfect, eager snare. Her walls, like hot silk soaked in honey, were the treacherous boundaries of a bottomless abyss.

They closed in. I fell deeper.

I had no control, no grip. I plunged past reason and conscience, tumbled past tenderness and attraction. The catacombs, our link, restraint—they all became background noise as I plummeted into the one thing left in the dark with me; the waiting arms of the dream.

I felt it happening. There was no fighting it, no breaking free of its embrace. Defiling my sense of pleasure, the spell polluted my desire with an impatient, lust-fueled frustration. It stripped my morality and corrupted my affection. It warped my passion into a kind of voracious, selfish depravity, until I had only one motivation, one concern: my own primal need for release.

In consummating my obsession, its focus had shifted. *She* was unimportant. Her body was paramount. It was a means to an end, a path to satisfaction. And I used it as such. Slamming into it without respite, my thrusts were brutal, long and deep. My touch turned rough, my kisses harsh.

I had a dim sense of fingers clawing at my arms, of breasts jutting and bouncing, and legs wrapping in a frantic attempt to slow me down. Her cries prompted a scattered notion that I might be hurting her, but I didn't stop. Her pleasure, or discomfort, was secondary to how badly I was burning. How hollow and starved I was. All that would fill me was to empty myself in her.

Yet, I couldn't. It was quickly becoming apparent that no matter how fast our bodies hit, or how far I pushed inside, it wasn't hard enough or deep enough to satisfy.

It never will be.

There is no relief to be had in her.

And that was the point. It was the crux of the spell. It was one final jab from my father that the lure he dangled in front of me, the life he offered in exchange for the stone, was unattainable. Even if Neela came to care for me, my desire for her would become tainted by constant frustration. The thing he made me want more than any other—the allusion of utter contentment I felt in the dreams—would be forever out of reach.

Even dead he plots the course of my life.

Panting, I pulled out of her and stepped back. Damp curls clung to her face. Sweat glimmered like dew in the flickering light. Passion glazed her eyes and it was almost enough to make me believe I was wrong.

Then I saw cuts open on her skin. I heard laughter that wasn't there.

I reached out to Jarryd for added strength and got nothing. I gripped Neela's arms, trying to stay in the here and now. But the wet on her skin felt like blood.

With a sound of revulsion, I let her go.

Neela tried to pull me back. "What's wrong?"

I flung her off me. "Everything," I snarled. "You. Us. You don't know how badly I need you to be real. How I need all of this to be real. But it's not. It won't ever be."

Her brow tightened. "Calm down."

The hiss of drawn metal came out of the dark. Past the torchlight and the gloom, something was in the doorway. The shape of a man, it moved slightly.

Watching it, I said, "You turn everything upside down. I can't trust myself with you. I can't trust my own senses. I know we're alone. Only, I swear...*I swear* I can hear him in the room with us."

"I heard it too." I went for a weapon and her hand shot out to stop me. "I heard a servant, Ian," she said, slow and persuasive, "that's all." Holding my gaze, she spoke louder. "Come out of the shadows, boy."

There was a noticeable hesitation. I held my breath through the whole thing.

I let it out when a lanky figure crawled clumsily over the broken door and fell into the chamber. Gripping a torch in one hand, he kept his head lowered and his eyes down as he picked himself up. Clearly, this was the last place he wanted to be. It was also the last place I thought to see him.

"Liel," I sighed. "Gods..." I ran my hands over my face, wiping away the sweat. The panic was harder to shed, but I took a few, relieved gulps of air and recovered enough to pull up my pants.

Liel's recovery was going to take a bit longer. His face held significantly less color than my eyes and he wasn't even coming close to looking in our direction. "Pardon me, Your Grace," he muttered. "It's the Langorian Ambassador. He's returned and is asking for you."

Neela spared him a frown over her bare shoulder. "I'll need some time. See if you can scrounge up something to feed him while he waits."

I looked at her. I was hoping for an explanation. But she just turned away, with her emotions all over the place. There was dread, fading desire, and a lot of humiliation. She was ashamed of her appearance, which was not exactly pristine. Her hair was sticking out all over. A visible sheen of sweat layered her skin. Smudges clung to her once-white gown, which I had completely wrecked. I'd done the same to her usual poise and dignity, and she was having trouble recapturing it.

Mostly though, she was nervous as hell.

"The Ambassador wishes to meet with Troy as well," Liel added.

"Me?" I said in surprise. "What does he want?"

Liel's voice was strained. "I couldn't say, My Lord."

I peered at him through the gloom. "You survived the battle without injury?"

"Yes, My Lord. But many were far less fortunate." Liel raised his eyes. He looked straight at me. "Many that should be here aren't."

"That's enough," Neela broke in. "Troy is aware of the rigors of war."

Liel's gaze plummeted like a stone. "Yes, Your Grace," he said, his normally impeccable posture slumping. His floppy curls seemed to go flat and lifeless, too. As if the weight of worry pressed them down. Even more peculiar, he hadn't bowed once.

I might have chocked it up to simple embarrassment. After all, the boy did just catch me fucking Rella's Queen on the tomb of her ancestor. Except, it wasn't shame he was exhibiting. It wasn't fatigue either, or trauma from witnessing his first battle.

Liel was radiating fear, anxiety, and a good amount of despair.

"That will be all," Neela said to him. "Tell the ambassador I'll join him shortly."

Eyes on his boots, Liel nodded. He fled the chamber like it was on fire.

Neela slid off the top of the crypt. I stepped back, giving her room to pull herself together. I would have helped, but she shimmied into what remained of her sleeves and flattened down her rumpled skirt in silence. She combed a hand through the tangles in her hair, looking anywhere but at me. Running her fingers through the strands, a few got stuck in the pearls on her head but she worked them out on her own. The front of her gown (in two pieces now) gaped stubbornly open, and the longer Neela fumbled with the material, clutching the tattered fabric to her breasts like a shield, the more I was certain she was looking for ways to avoid me.

"The castle is quiet." I snatched up my shirt and slipped it on. "Were there no celebrations?"

451

"Not really." Still holding her dress together, Neela didn't look up. "There is a lot of work to be done."

"Funny," I said, tying the laces on my breeches in quick, angry motions. "I didn't see anyone doing any work."

"Oh?" Her tone was careless, but I felt a ripple of anxiety bounce between us.

"There are things you aren't telling me."

"There are things you aren't privy too."

"If the healing spell had gone differently, I would have been privy to everything. As it is, all I can feel is how much you're lying to me right now." I put up a barrier and choked off our link. Point blank, I said, "You won, Neela. The Langorians are gone. You have your throne back. Yet, you aren't happy. Why?" Her absence of an answer tightened my voice. "Where are all the people, Neela?"

"I don't know what you're talking about."

"My father is dead. Langor is defeated. Yet, that poor boy that was just here looked too afraid to breathe. I want to know why."

Neela stared at me a long moment. Then, so soft I could barely hear her, she said, "We didn't win."

"What?"

"We didn't win."

"I don't understand."

"We lost, Ian. The war is over and we lost."

I tossed my head in defiance. "No. We're here, in Kabri, in the castle. There's no battle outside. No enemies camped on the beach or patrolling the halls." I got louder. "We won, Neela. Your ragtag army defeated Draken's forces or we wouldn't be here."

"Yes. They did. I was told that with Sienn's help we knocked Draken's numbers down to half rather quickly. We took heavy casualties, but the city was ours within the day." She took a halting breath. "The next morning, the warships came."

"I saw a couple ships on the other side of the island. They looked empty."

"They were scouts. The rest came shortly before dawn. Thirty vessels landed under the cover of the morning mist. An alarm was sounded, but the beasts poured out."

"Eldring?"

"They fell on my men, my allies, like a swarm."

I gulped down the sickness in my throat. "What about Sienn? She could have—"

"Sienn was nowhere to be found." Neela took a deep, grief-filled breath. "You were right, Ian. Draken knew I'd put everything I had into this battle. He let me think we had a chance. But we didn't. We never did."

"Then how did you and I get back to the castle?"

"Once the battle with Draken's forces had swung our way and victory was clear, Liel and Jarryd came for you. They had no idea I was even missing. They found us both unconscious and brought us here before the eldring attack."

"If Draken owns Kabri, why am I not in a cell?"

"I've made other arrangements."

"What arrangements?"

"Before we get to that…." Neela's gaze wavered. "Ian," she said, timidly, as if fearing my reaction, "your father's body wasn't in the cave."

"What?" Devastated, I stared at her. "Are you sure?"

"I had all the tunnels searched."

I said it like a curse. "Sienn."

"That was my thought as well. Is it possible she took him for burial?"

"Sienn is blind where Jem Reth is concerned. If she has him, he's not dead."

"That is unfortunate."

Rage melted my shock and distress and I roared at her. "Goddamn it! I should have seen this coming. I should have known she wouldn't just sit back and let me kill him. Damn it!" I spun around and struck the wall behind me. Stone crumbled, but not enough, so I hit it again. "That fucking bitch—she healed him. She fucking healed him!" An uneasy thought came over me and my voice dropped dramatically. "The crown?"

"Gone as well."

Briefly, I closed my eyes. "Why the hell did you keep this from me?"

"I've accepted terms. I knew you would try to intervene."

"Damn right, I'll intervene."

"You can't, Ian. It's done."

"It's not even close to done. I still have magic."

"And Draken has my sister."

I lost some of my zeal. "We have no proof. He could be bluffing."

"I can't risk it. If I marry Draken, he will let her go. He'll pull his men out of the villages. There will be no more killing, no more executions. Kabri will be rebuilt. You will be spared."

"I never asked you for that. And I don't give a damn about the city!"

Neela's voice went up to match mine. "I do!" It went back down. "I won't be powerless as his Queen. I will be in charge of rebuilding the realm. And Draken allowed me to pick a Regent to look after Rella's lands. Someone I can work with to ensure my people are taken care of. Marriage is the only way to guarantee that some trace of Rella survives, Ian. It's the best possible solution for everyone involved."

"Except you."

She paled a bit. "This is my fate."

"It doesn't have to be. If Elayna is at Darkhorne, then I'll get her out. I promise. Just, don't do this. Don't marry him. Give me some time. I'll find your sister."

"I have no time to give. I leave for Langor in the morning."

I knew the look on her face. Her mind was made. "So, if I hadn't questioned you just now, your plan was to deceive me, sleep with me, and then what...? Creep off and leave me here in ignorance until I stumbled onto the truth?"

"Yes."

"Well that's a shitty plan."

"I was trying to protect you."

My glare was cruel. "Bullshit."

"You're like no man I've ever met. You rouse things in me I didn't know existed and..." her confidence wavered, "I wanted this one time, this one moment." Blinking, on the verge of tears, Neela shook her head. "I thought if I could keep you out of it, if could keep you alive, that maybe someday we could..." she left off with an awkward smile. "It's a fool's wish, I know. I'm sorry. I shouldn't have lied to you. Forgive me?"

It was straight up, unabashed feminine wiles at work. The way Neela's sad round eyes pleaded with me to trust her, to forgive her and not be angry.

She deceived me, tricked me. She was still doing it. But despite that, and even knowing she was under the influence of the dream weave—knowing she didn't really want me, I had the impulse to grab her and run. To take her away from Draken and my father and anyone who would ever think to hurt her.

But staring at Neela felt like things tearing apart inside me. And with her scent on my skin and the taste of her still in my mouth, I couldn't think.

I needed distance, space. I started from the room. "I'm going after my father."

"You don't even know where he is."

"I'll find him. And Draken."

"Let it go, Ian. Rella is gone. There is no one left for you to save, nothing left for you to do."

Her words brought me to a halt. "You told me that before," I said, recalling the first night I dreamt of her. I remembered the feel of her warm, wet arms around me as she spoke, trying to convince me that it was okay to stand down. Even then, the idea didn't sit right. "I can't turn my back on this, Neela. Your father made sure of that a long time ago. He made me indifferent to my own people and responsible for yours. He made me fight for them. Kill for them. Care for them. And now you expect me to walk away like none of it ever happened, while you give everything that I bled for—everything your mother died for—over to the enemy?"

"If you challenge him, Draken will kill you."

"Then he kills me. It's been a long time coming anyway."

"No. I won't have it. I couldn't bear losing you."

"But that's just it, Neela. You could bear it fine, because what you're feeling is nothing but a byproduct of the spell I used to heal you. And when it's gone, you'll go back to your royal protocols and your icy disregard. And I'll go back to being just another slave for you to scold." I hopped over the wrecked door and out into the cave.

"Wait," she called after me. "Ian, please…I love you."

My insides sunk. "No, you don't. You *can't*," I said, backing away. "You're just a dream."

FIFTY FIVE

Something was in the wine.

It had only taken a few sips to realize I should call for help. Then about one second to realize it wouldn't do any good. The old library where Liel had brought me to wait for the ambassador was an out of the way chamber in a lesser-used corridor. For anyone to hear me they would have had to be passing right by. And the way things were going lately, the only person passing by would have been the one who wanted me unconscious in the first place. So I hadn't bothered.

Coming to now, in hindsight, I should have spent that second stretching out on the floor in front of the fire. Passing out in the chair as I did, had left my backside numb and my neck feeling twisted like a washerwoman's laundry.

Rubbing at the ache, I got up. I was facing a wall with a row of tall windows. When I'd first entered the room, I'd thrown open all six curtains. Morning sun had filled the ransacked room, making clear the degree of loss to the most extensive library in all of Rella. Now, as moonlight streamed across the floor instead, something else was clear. I'd been set up.

I was guessing the lone figure leaning against the frame of the open door had something to do with it. Watching me, standing beyond the range of the fire, in a persistent spot of darkness, the definite masculine shape pushed off the threshold and left the shadows. Fire and candlelight converged on him, and the sight bolstered my spirits.

I knew him. *At least I used to*, I thought, my optimism swiftly dwindling as I worked out what his presence meant.

The Malaq Roarke sauntering toward me wasn't here as my friend. He was here as Draken's Ambassador. And damn did he look the part.

In place of his normal distinctive, fitted attire was a more billowing, embroidered silk tunic and breeches, both in the deep gray and red of his father's land. His cloak had been swapped out for a sleek, black waistcoat. He'd forsaken Natalia, too. In her place, two short, thick swords hung from his belt. They were ugly, functional weapons compared to her style and beauty. The coral ring that identified his claim to Rella (the one I'd spelled for him) was hidden under the studded gray gloves that covered his hands and forearms. His hair was uncombed, his goatee neglected, and he was flaunting the beginnings of a beard.

It was odd to see him this way. Yet, I understood his need to infiltrate and blend, and I didn't look twice at the serpent clasp fastened to the collar of his coat. It wasn't even the most flagrant example of his Langorian lineage and loyalty that put me off—though I was having trouble looking at the coin-sized, circular symbol burned into the left side his face. What I really couldn't stomach, was how easily Malaq wore it.

"Troy." Reaching me, he slapped a firm hand on my arm. "It's good to see you."

"Same here," I said, though with less enthusiasm.

As he took a step back, Malaq's smile was reserved. His sharp, gray eyes held their usual shroud of nothing. "Sorry for the accommodations."

"Then I do have you to thank for my nap," I said, not surprised.

His smile twitched, making the serpent on his face jump. "Let's talk."

At a sound, we both turned to watch Liel enter the library. A tray in his hands, the boy gripped the edges tightly, making the contents shake as he walked. Crossing to the only erect table in the room, Liel placed the tray down. His blatant avoidance of my eyes was downright uncomfortable as he filled two mugs from a tall, slender bottle, then left without a word.

I stared at the door as Liel closed it behind him. "Is he angry with me?"

"With you? No." Malaq pointed at the mugs. "Shall we?"

Returning to my chair, I threw myself down in it. "I think I'll let you drink first."

He frowned a little. "You must know this was for your own good. Any attempt to prevent Neela's marriage will only make the situation worse. For all of us."

"Not if it works."

The frown passed into his voice. "You really have no idea what it takes to govern, do you? What it takes to be responsible for the daily welfare of thousands?"

"Apparently, it takes drugs and deception." I took one of the cups and sniffed it. "*Coura*," I said, pleasantly surprised. "You know this stuff used to be hard to find, especially in Rella. Now you guys invade and suddenly it's everywhere."

Malaq grabbed the remaining cup and drank half, as if to prove it was clean.

"Drugging me doesn't really do much for our friendship," I told him plainly.

"I could have had you thrown you in a cell."

"And I could have knocked you out cold before we got there. But we've had this conversation before, haven't we?"

Wiping a hand over the hair on his face, Malaq made a weary, resigned sound. "Forgive my ill temper." He pulled over a chair and sat down. "I haven't slept in days."

"You should try whatever you slipped me. It'll put you right out."

"What will it take for you to let this go? A formal apology?"

"How about an explanation?" I tipped the *coura* and took in a mouthful, enjoying the burn. "Why don't you start with that brand on your face? I didn't think you'd be joining the family so soon."

"I had to take the mark and pledge myself. Refusing would not have gone well."

"You've been to Darkhorne?"

"A thoroughly dismal place," he said with a shudder. He leaned closer, as if someone might hear. "Draken is building an army."

"When isn't Draken building an army?"

"This one is different. It's all Shinree. Handpicked. Sorted by the strength of their abilities. It's remarkable what that man, Reth, can employ as a weapon. At the moment, he has only a handful capable of any real damage. But that will change."

"What do you know of him?"

"Reth?" Malaq crossed his legs and brushed the dust from his boot. "I know you're his son."

"Have you seen him? Recently?"

"Unfortunately, I have. And I assure you, Troy, I find little family resemblance."

"Then he is alive?"

Malaq looked up from his grooming. "Yes."

The air left my body. I sunk deeper into my chair. "I had him, Malaq. I beat him. He was dying. But...so was she." I tossed back the mug and drained it. "I should have cut the bastard's head off. I should have made sure he was dead."

"Saving Neela is no small feat."

I sensed more. "But?"

"You can't believe sleeping with her was a good idea. And that night in the Faernore, what you did to save Jarryd was entirely ill-conceived." Malaq's lips pursed. "You're too close to all this, Ian."

"I thought you'd be happy I'd left my hermit ways behind."

"I'd be happy if you stopped being an ass. Stopped making rash decisions and attachments that could get you killed."

"Jarryd was dying," I said tightly. "If you'd seen him, you would have done everything in your power to save his life. My power just happens to be a little different than yours."

Swearing under his breath, Malaq sucked an impolitely large amount of *coura* into his mouth. When he was done, he refilled the cup and drained it again. Glancing around, pretending to be interested in the few remaining books lining the shelves, he shifted in his chair, fidgeting with the armrest.

His right leg started bouncing.

"You're nervous," I said.

"Me?" he laughed. "I'm never nervous."

"I know." I leaned over and clamped a hand on his leg. "Which makes me nervous," I said, letting him go. "Start talking."

Malaq looked away. Then back again. "It's Jarryd."

His grim tone turned my blood cold. "He's not dead. I would have felt that."

"No. He's not dead. Draken wants him kept alive."

"Goddamn it." I rubbed the anguish from my face. "Where is he?"

"Darkhorne."

"That's why he's blocking me. Pain overwhelms the link." I swallowed the lump building in my throat. "He's trying to spare me."

"It could be Reth. He said he'd found a way to interfere with your connection."

I started to ask how, but that wasn't what I wanted to know. "What the hell happened?"

"It appears the eldring were given specific targets. General Aldous, being one of them, was killed immediately. Jarryd, they were careful to apprehend with minimal harm. My brother has one of those Shinree that makes doors, and—"

"Jarryd's capture was planned?" I held Malaq's stare. "Did you know?"

Indignation set his jaw. Fighting it, Malaq emptied more drink into his cup. He set the bottle down deliberately. "I didn't."

"Have you seen him?"

"I made a request. It was denied." He took a quick drink. "I heard him, though."

Slamming my mug down on the table, I stood.

Malaq bolted out of his chair. "Where are you going?"

"Where do you think?"

"Langor? Really, Ian?" Malaq's laugh was short and irritated. "Do you think Draken is going to make it that easy?"

"I don't want easy, Malaq. I want blood. I want to torture and dismember every Langorian between here and Darkhorne until Jarryd is free."

"Then you'd be killing innocent men for no reason."

"They're Langorians. They're far from innocent."

"Look," he said, jaw grinding, "I'm as scared for Jarryd as you are. I've toured my brother's dungeon. I know what goes on there."

"Then you know I will bring all of Langor down around me to get him out."

"No, if you plunge the realm into chaos, it will shut itself off again. There will be no hope for peace." Malaq stepped closer. "I can't let you do that."

"Get out of my way."

"We can negotiate. There are proper channels for this sort of thing."

"Fuck you and your fucking proper channels. While you spend months or years lobbying for his release, making deals with fat noblemen in back alleys, Jarryd will be chained to a wall. They'll beat him until he's pissing blood every goddamn day. Just how long do you think he'll last?"

Solemnness steeled his jaw. "Jarryd's got you in him. He'll last."

"Don't pull that bullshit on me, Malaq. Now, move."

"Ian..."

I called to the shard. It warmed against my throat, glowing as bright and eager as the look in my eyes. "I won't ask again."

"So this is what it comes to? This is your answer?" Malaq shook his head in disgust. "This is always your goddamn answer," he said, his voice turning into a snarl. "You stubborn son of a bitch. What the hell is wrong with you?" I didn't answer fast enough, and he charged me. Balling my shirt into his fists, Malaq rushed us both backwards into the shelves. "Think about what you're doing! You can't solve everything with blood and magic!"

"I have to," I shouted back, "that's all I'm made of!"

With another hard shove, Malaq threw himself off me. He put some space between us, retrieved his drink, and scowled at me over the rim.

I scowled back. "They took him because of me."

"I know, Ian. Just give me a chance. Give me some time. I'll do everything I can to get Jarryd back. I swear," he said, and I believed him. Malaq meant his vow to me, as much as I'd meant mine to Neela when I swore to save her sister.

I'd given her my word. Now I understood why it wasn't good enough.

Malaq rubbed his eyes. He sighed in surrender. "Draken wants a meeting with you. Neela refused to allow it, but...there's a chance he'll trade."

I reached up and closed my fist around the black stone. "I can't give him this."

"It's more than that now. He wants you to fix whatever you did to the crown."

"What's wrong with it?"

"It has no power." Malaq gave me a funny look. "You didn't know?"

"Why would I? I channeled it and put it back. If something's wrong ask Sienn or my father. From what I hear, they had it last."

A trace of worry tensed his features. "Reth thinks it was you. He told Draken you could repair it. That's part of the reason he agreed to Neela's request to spare you."

"Draken trusted my father? Gods, he should know better than that." I moved for the door. "I'm guessing Neela is gone. How long ago did she leave?"

"Right after you passed out." Guilt leached some of the color from his skin. "We couldn't have you slaughtering her escort."

"What route did she take?"

There was regret in him, but he still said, "I can't."

"I know I'm a shitty friend, Malaq. But you really don't want me as an enemy." My stare tightened. "Think about that while you draw me a map."

Malaq's curses followed me out of the library and down the hall. I yelled a few times for Liel until he popped out from around a corner. He slunk toward me, head hanging like a child waiting to be scolded. "My Lord," he said timidly. "I'm sorry. I didn't want to deceive you."

"Never mind that now," I said, brisk but kind. "With General Aldous dead, who are you pledged to?"

"I took an oath to Queen Neela, but," he sounded lost, "she surrendered her reign. Perhaps the new Regent will ask for me if I make myself useful. Or maybe I should go home."

I put a hand under Liel's chin, demanding his eyes. "Swear yourself to me."

Beneath the hair, I caught a glimpse of his forehead scrunching. "To you?"

"I need help, Liel. And right now you're the only one I come close to trusting."

A shy smile crept over the confusion. "I'm honored, My Lord, but—"

"I have to leave."

"Then you'll want your horse. I found her outside. I've been taking care of her."

"Thank you. But I need you to look after something else for me while I'm gone."

"Gone for how long?"

"I don't know." I talked over his protest. "This is where your vow comes in. If you want to serve the Regent, I understand. If you want to go home then go. Do what you like with your life, Liel. But what I'm about to ask of you must stay between us. No one can ever know. Especially if I don't come back. Do you understand?"

He nodded vigorously. "What can I do?"

"I need a stone. Do you know where the healer's chamber is?"

"Yes, My Lord. Only he isn't there. The Queen said he was taken by the Langorians weeks ago."

"I figured that. But I'm betting they didn't give him time to pack."

FIFTY SIX

I was three days past Rella's western border and two from the edge of Langorian territory, in the middle of a vast desert wasteland. Around me were the bare, rocky hills and arid valleys that had once been a part of the Shinree Empire. As far as the eye could see and beyond had been lush, fertile lands and a great gleaming city.

More recently, the region had been a well-used battlefield. Year after year, waves of men would roll up over the peeks and down into the hollows, rushing toward a victory that was always just out of reach. A victory both sides had coveted for so long, their soldiers had forgotten what they were dying for.

I ended that with the Crown of Stones. I created an empty, desolate expanse that after ten years nature still didn't know how to heal. And it was just as I'd left it. Even the bodies were still here, buried underground. Their numbers had been too great to bring home. Instead, wagons full of Shinree slaves had been shipped in to dispose of the remains. Numbed by the *Kayn'l*, incapable of grieving the enormous loss of life, the slaves hadn't cared that they were dumping the remains of Rella's finest soldiers to rest for all eternity in giant mass graves with their enemies.

I was thinking the soldiers cared though, which was why they were haunting me. Why their invisible bones were underfoot, shattering and crumbling with each fall of Kya's hooves. Why their corpses, transparent, decaying specters, were shimmering in and out of existence across the barren land.

Ghostly scavenger birds hopped on tiny feet, picking hungrily at empty eye sockets and gaping mouths, tearing at shriveled skin as it baked in the blistering afternoon sun.

Illusion, I told myself. Then, more emphatically: "Reth."

I dug my heels into Kya's side with an abrupt kick. Her hooves, sliding in the loose dirt, found purchase, and we sped up the steep grade in a sudden rush of hot wind and crunching bones. The momentum she built wanted to carry us down the other side, but when we reached the top, I had to rein her in with a rude yank.

"Sorry, girl." Moving Kya brusquely away from the edge, I retrieved the spyglass from my pack and jumped down amid the phantom bodies. Lying on the hot sand beside them was damn unnerving. With effort, I kept my focus straight ahead and trained my sights on the valley below.

We were up high. With no landmarks, I couldn't be certain. But judging by the hills and the rock formations, I was looking at the exact place where I discovered the Crown of Stones. It was also where Jillyan of Langor had undertaken her excavation of the empire in an attempt to break the spell on her brother. I hadn't expected the work to be still ongoing. Or that the site would be so huge.

The entire valley floor was peppered with open trenches and crisscrossed by an intricate system of tunnels. Inside the shafts, sunlight stretched down to gleam off exposed sections of ancient stone roads, walls, and other pieces of Shinree history long forgotten. Fractured columns, toppled statues and buildings, all protruded proudly up from great chasms in the sand.

Portions of the area had been plowed flat to make way for more modern roads. Occupied by slaves, soldiers, and oxen hauling carts, the roads looped around the ruins and trenches, passing by an assortment of tents and makeshift buildings. Large wooden pens were scattered about the outskirts of the camp. One was directly below me. It looked to be constructed as a corral for animals. At the moment, it was full of people. Hundreds of Rellan, Kaelish, and Shinree prisoners were crowded inside, huddling together on the ground, roasting in the heat; because there was no roof, no shade, and no room for them to do much else. They certainly couldn't escape. The sides of the fence were too tall to climb. Just in case anyone thought to try, the tops of the posts had been sharpened to fine points. Lashed to several of the posts were the bodies of what I assumed were uncooperative prisoners. None were moving.

As a bonus deterrent, guards were everywhere. More than twenty surrounded the nearest pen. Five lurked at the edge of each ditch, overseeing the slaves. Two stood at attention at every tent. Even more watched over the larger pavilions.

It wasn't ideal, but if that were all I had to contend with, I could manage. What tipped the odds completely in the wrong direction was the army spread around the base of the dunes. About half the soldiers were decked out in shining mail and crisp leather. The rest wore uniforms that were old, tattered, and caked with mud. Their weapons, showing signs of age and battle, were discolored with rust and blood. Yet, despite the poor condition of their arms and attire, they stood at attention, immobile, tall and proud—which was interesting since they were most definitely dead.

This time I wasn't looking at flashing transparent specters. The scores of deceased soldiers defending the parched plain below were solid, if not whole. Missing limbs, jaws, and other significant pieces, clumps of putrefied skin clung to their visible bones. Skulls were cracked. Chests were caved. Dry, vacant eyes dangled from fractured sockets. Moldy, twisted fingers gripped axes, swords, and clubs. On some of the uniforms, spots of crimson and gray were visible between the grime. On others, it was blue and black.

They were the soldiers that died here. They were the men I killed with the Crown of Stones. They were my victims. And my father had brought them back.

Evidently, he was expecting me.

Closing the spyglass I slid away from the edge. I didn't want to wait. With Jarryd in prison and Neela about to be married, every second counted. Yet, I had my doubts that bargaining with Draken was going to work like I'd hoped. My only alternative was to hold off until nightfall and sneak in. At least then I had a shot of getting Neela out.

I swung up into the saddle. I was about to turn Kya around when I heard the army marching. They only took a handful of steps. Then each and every one pivoted in my direction. Without hesitation, collectively, they directed their weapons to the crest of the mountain and aimed them on my precise position.

They must have seen me. Or, the ghosts were a boundary spell, and I'd triggered it. Regardless, instinct was shouting for me to run like hell. I had a chance of getting away. The valley floor and a whole mountainside stood between us. But knowing my father, it might as well have been spitting distance. And with the work he'd put into my welcome, he wasn't about to let me escape. Not when I had something he wanted.

My first plan, and now my second, of no use, I steered Kya to the edge of the sandy ridge and headed down. The sharp drop forced me to keep it slow. As I drew closer to the valley, the prisoners in the pen took notice. The bulk of them stared in silence with starved, sunken eyes. Some rushed to the fence and called for help. As word of my presence spread through the crowd, they called me by name.

More voices joined the chorus. Kya's hooves hit level ground and scrawny arms stretched through the posts, reaching for me. Bodies pushed and shoved against each other, wailing and screaming, begging to be heard.

Their pleas went through me like a bitter wind. Their curses, as I kept going, hurt more so. But I couldn't help them. Casting here, without so much as a single blade of grass within fifty miles for my spells to draw from, would leave the prisoners as dead as their captors.

I picked the closest road and held Kya to a leisurely unthreatening pace as I traversed the camp. No one stopped me. I kept my weapons sheathed, though I was itching to draw them. Looking around, I was in awe. Langorians in civilian dress (something I'd rarely seen) worked diligently, brushing dust away from great slabs of stone. Others assembled broken statues and pottery with great care. Slaves hauled buckets of dirt and sand up out of the gaping holes. They gave me barely a disinterested glance as I went by. They had no grasp of the significance of what they were doing. I envied them, anyway. Touching the walls our ancestors once touched, walking on the same pieces of road they once traveled. I would have relished the opportunity to uncover such ancient sites, to dig for bits of a life that seemed so incredibly foreign.

Reaching the middle of the camp, soldiers, both dead and alive, approached me from all sides. They herded me in a strange, silent procession to the rear of the site. It was less busy here. There was only one large pavilion sitting at the base of a tall dune. The center post boasted a red flag with a gold and gray snake in the shape of a circle. The same emblem was sewn into the wall of the tent and burned into the faces of the Langorians guarding the opening. Well-armored and alive, their bulky garb was in sharp contrast to the female Shinree exiting the tent. Wearing a thin wrapping of pale green over her breasts and a matching swathe for a skirt, without thought or expression, she held the flap open and waited.

She would stand there all day if those were her orders, but it only took a moment for her master, King Draken, to appear in the doorway.

Pausing, surveying us all in smug silence without ever actually looking at a single one of us, Draken seemed even more majestic than usual. Remarkably clean-shaven, the King's glossy silver tunic gleamed in the blazing sun. A lavish cloak of leather and fur rested on his broad shoulders, fastened shut with the famed serpent clasp. Fake or not, the pin was blindingly shiny in comparison to the lackluster stone circlet resting on his head.

The Crown of Stones had definitely seen better days.

Draken stepped aside, and a woman emerged. It took a moment for her identity to register. Her blood-red gown was crafted with far too little material to be fit for a Queen.

Sheer, almost to the point of being nonexistent, the skirt of Neela's dress was split into strategically placed strips of gossamer layers that hung to her ankles. The bodice had no sleeves, only a set of gold chains that extended down from the shoulders to cuff at the wrists. Large rubies—tantalizing against dark skin—studded a neckline that laid bare a good half of Neela's breasts and kept going, all the way to the gold chain girdle about her waist.

Her hair, even more elaborate, was gathered high atop her head and contained in a casing of leather a hands-width tall. The restrictive binding stood straight up, forcing the bulk of her curls to burst out from the top and fall back down, surrounding her face and shoulders like a dark erupting volcano.

By Rellan standards, her appearance was scandalous and disgraceful. It was also incredibly erotic. I couldn't take my eyes off her. I was still gawking when Draken leaned down to whisper in Neela's ear.

Jealously, I followed his hand. It glided across the rubies adorning her fingers and up over the golden bracelets on her wrists. *No*, I thought, *not bracelets*.

My heart jumped as I looked closer. *They're serpents.*

Understanding their significance, I stared in dread at the snakes wrapped around Neela's wrists. Then Draken brushed a curl back from her downcast eyes, and my horrified gaze transferred to the branding on the left side of her face.

I was too late.

The imprint was barely a few hours old, but Draken's claim was evident. No one could dispute Neela's new title as Queen of Langor or her status as Draken's wife.

I swung a leg over the saddle. As I slid down off Kya's back, Draken's smooth voice glided like silk across the sand. "I knew you would come, Troy. Your endless pursuit of martyrdom never fails to entertain."

"Consider it a wedding present."

"Ha!" he laughed. "I have a present for you as well." Draken tossed something small through the air. Catching it, I folded my hand closed over a jade archer's ring. "It might be a bit bloody," he grimaced apologetically. "My men tend to get overzealous."

"It's fine." I reached behind me and slipped Jarryd's ring down inside one of the packs on my saddle. "You can scrub it clean…after you let him go."

Snickering, Draken tugged Neela closer. "I can see why you like this Shinree, my love. He's so confident." His tone darkened. "It's a shame it won't last."

"Threats. Intimidation. Abduction." I forced a thin smile. "You have all the foundations of a happy marriage, Draken. I wish you luck."

"How thoughtful—considering Shinree don't believe in luck."

"You'll need something if you don't want to end up with a blade in your chest like your father did."

"To the contrary, Troy. My wife is most accommodating. She knows exactly what's required to safeguard the lives of her people." Gently, Draken placed a hand on Neela's stomach. "Already there could be a child growing inside her. And when he is born, there shall be another. One for Langor's throne. One for Rella's. Both of them mine. None of them yours." He stared down his long nose at me. "Don't worry. Our union was very unlike the dreams. There was no blood, no forcing of any kind. Neela's screams were those of pure pleasure. Isn't that right, my love?" Grinning, Draken eyed her with a lewd sneer. "Shall we show him? Here? Now?"

Faintly, Neela answered. "If you wish, My Lord."

"Oh, I do." Draken slid his hands unceremoniously inside the bodice of her dress. Glancing at me with mocking eyes, he pushed the material aside, putting her on display. "Beautiful, isn't she?"

I grabbed the sword at my hip. "She's your wife. Show some fucking respect."

"Or you'll what? You're powerless here, Troy. Impotent. I, however, am nothing of the kind." To prove his advantage, a dozen decomposing soldiers edged up behind me. "I have dominion over this land." Kneeling down, Draken took the divided hem of Neela's dress in his hands. He parted the fabric up to her knees. "And over her."

My hand clutched my sword tighter. "Let her go."

He raised the dress higher, to her thighs, and I squeezed the grip so hard my hand ached.

Higher still, and the muscles burned up my arm.

There was no doubt about it. The sight and smell of the dead, with bits of mud and flesh hanging off their bones, disturbed me far less than Neela's quiet allowance of Draken's touch. Her indifference, her submission, was killing me. Standing, exposed, in a camp full of leering men, she was calm and poised, not moving or protesting, letting Draken do as he pleased to her—while I was screaming inside.

Draken pulled Neela close. He tossed me a sly grin and buried his face between her legs.

"Goddamn you!" I drew both swords, and the dead closed in around me. The living guards pulled their weapons, aiming them at Neela's back. She was unaware of the danger. As Draken continued to devour her, Neela's eyes had fallen closed.

I told myself it was from revulsion that she shut them, not pleasure.

After a long, tense moment, Draken lifted his head. Resting his cheek against her small swath of hair, he looked at me through the rotting leg bones of his underlings and licked his lips. "This goes straight through you. Doesn't it?"

I was in too much pain to lie. "Yes."

"Can you still feel her beneath you?" Draken brushed his lips against her dark skin. "Encasing you? Soft...warm." His fingers dug into her legs. "Can you still hear her? I can make you hear her." He pressed harder and Neela gasped.

"You're insane," I said, shaking.

"I am. But you made me this way. You and your magic and your crown." Draken planted a gentle kiss on Neela's thigh. Standing, he let her dress fall back into place. "You robbed me of ten years, Troy." Tugging on the flimsy fabric of her bodice, he covered her breasts. "Ten years," he said again. Abruptly, he locked fuming eyes on me. "I have to take it out on someone."

"Then take it out on me."

"Oh, but I am," Draken laughed heartily. "I most certainly am. And best of all…" He slapped Neela across the face. "You're wide awake." He hit her again, and she fell.

This is the last place I should forget what I am, I thought desperately, as Draken kicked her. *The last place I should lose control.*

But as Neela's frightened eyes looked up at me, it was already done.

FIFTY SEVEN

The howl that burst from my throat wasn't in the least bit belonging to a man. Laced with wrath, fueled by aggression, driven by need; the world had become obsolete. There was only my target. The living corpses between us were unimportant. The crushing odds against me were of no consequence. I rushed straight for Draken, into the line of Langorian dead, and I had not a single thought to strategy or safety. No notion of anything but the raw vengeance that traveled down my arms and into my swords.

But with the familiar weight of steel in my hands, instinct and reflexes kicked in.

I evaded with intuition, swung with experience and purpose. The instruments of my fury bit smoothly into necks and shoulders. They cut across exposed veins and ruptured bloated, liquefied organs. Slashed through broken rib cages and dangling cords of muscle; chopping off rotting limbs with impudence.

I struck blow after blow to the scantily skinned frames and delighted in the way their bones fractured on impact. Kneecaps shattered with one kick. Spines snapped with ease. Heads toppled and turned to dust beneath my boots.

All around me the dead died again.

Dying twice wasn't enough, though. Moments after I put them down, whatever was left got right back up. The only remedy for their condition (and my situation) was magic.

But there was a storm in me. If I cast to save myself, or even for the strength to keep fighting, I wasn't sure I could stop. I could feel it simmering—how badly I wanted to kill, to annihilate anyone that dared oppose me. And without the Crown of Stones or Sienn's abilities, I couldn't bring them back. Not Neela or the prisoners. I'd wake up as I had ten years before, the lone survivor.

So I pressed forward. Intent on nothing but gaining ground, I fell swiftly into an unconscious pattern of swinging, dodging, thrusting, and lunging. I barely detected my ears ringing with the constant clash of metal. The trembling ache in my arms was a distant notion as I ducked and rolled, striking out at a sea of legs on my way back up.

Standing, I turned sagging toothless jaws to powder. I tore into moldy throats and hollowed out stomachs. As ghastly hands grabbed at me, I hacked away their dead limbs and threw off the pieces. I didn't flinch at the taste of rot in my mouth or the vile, viscous things running down the blades and onto my hands. And it didn't have a damn thing to do with bravery or nerve; I didn't have anything close to a level head. I simply had no chance to notice. No time to acknowledge that each breath brought pain to my lungs or that my overworked muscles quaked with every move. I just kept going.

Because there were as many behind me as there were in front.

I didn't even know where Neela was anymore.

I spun around, straining to see through the flood of shields, blades, and bodies, but I couldn't catch so much as a glimpse of her crimson dress.

The army seemed to mushroom further; a never-ending flux of mindless cadavers.

The truth hit me hard: *I have no hope of winning. No hope of reaching her.*

If I couldn't reach her, I couldn't avenge her.

Protect me, I thought. *That's what she said. No matter the cost.*

A part of me knew her words weren't real, that this Neela never said them. But the thought of letting her down, of failing her—of watching her die again—unhinged me.

I couldn't avoid it anymore.

I opened the gates and embraced the obsidian the crown had left behind inside me. I soaked up the auras at my wrist; every drop of every stone. Then

I reached further, taking what was sprinkled about the camp, embedded in goblets, saddles, and swords, adorning trinkets and garments. I felt more, buried under miles of rock and dirt, unseen and untouched for centuries, and I invited it in. I absorbed until I couldn't breathe. Until swirling, bright auras were bursting from my hands and shooting off the ends of my swords in great colorful streams that rendered all who stood in its current to dust.

Magic surged like everlasting lightening through my veins. And I gladly turned it on my enemies.

They bore down on me in groups and died as such. A glancing blow sheared torsos in half. At full force, whole bodies exploded into fragments of bone and ash. I slayed whatever was in my path, without thought or design, and in minutes, a heavy cloud of remains hung thick and gray in the air around me. Entrenched in it, I didn't see the soldier until his sword edge ripped across my back.

In that first instant, there was no pain. Then, deep and burning, it spread like a lava flow running downhill; spilling over my shoulders, emptying into my arms.

It sunk lower, into my veins, coursing through them, setting my blood afire.

Crying out, I lost my grip on the magic. My spells came to an abrupt end, and the horde piled in. Their oncoming blows were vicious and nonstop. Pain became constant. I struggled to block my opponent's attacks, but the shock of impact was adding up faster than I could recoup.

A weapon was knocked from my hand, and I was down to one.

There were too many. They were in too tight.

A blade cut into my right leg.

Another split open my left side.

Invisible flames licked both wounds, and I went down.

On one knee, leaning heavily on my remaining sword, covered in gore, and laboring to slow my breathing into something that didn't hurt; I tried to reach the stones. I told myself to get up, to keep swinging, to push through the pain and keep fighting. But an inferno was raging inside me. My wild, desperate strikes had no hope of hitting anything. My magic, if any was left in me, wasn't responding. Neither were my limbs.

It's over, I thought. *I've come full circle.* Fate was delivering me into Death's hands. Bringing me back to where I should have died all along.

I wasn't that surprised. Ansel used to say you can only outrun a debt for so long before it bit you in the ass. Mine had crawled out of its grave and kicked me in the teeth.

Done, I collapsed. Taking it for surrender, the resurrected soldiers walked away. As they returned to their posts, Draken's laughter penetrated the echo of battle in my head. As usual, the irritating sound pissed me off. Yet, knowing what he'd done, he had a right to it. "My Lord," I said, raspy and trembling. "You are a tricky bastard."

Draken approached through the scattering crowd. "Was that a compliment?"

"You earned it. You and my father. Resurrecting the dead, scores of innocent prisoners to keep me from casting—tainting your soldier's weapons with *Kayn'l.*"

"Ah, so you know what's been done to you. I trust it's working well?"

"Certainly hurts like hell." I flinched as the scalding pain dug further inside. "Must be kind of a hollow victory, though. Seeing as you had to cheat to beat me."

Draken drew back and punched me so hard I tumbled over backwards. "Now I can beat you whenever I please." He waited for me to pick my face up out of the sand then asked, amiably, as if we were having a pleasant chat over a mug of ale, "Do you know what *Kayn'l* does to a normal man?"

Splayed out in the dirt, I glared at him. "Am I supposed to?"

"Nothing," he said. "It does nothing."

"Thank the gods," I breathed in exaggerated relief. "Now I can die in peace."

Draken's grin didn't bode well. "Not quite," he promised. "What about a normal man bound to a Shinree? What would *Kayn'l* do to him?" He tapped me with his boot. "Focus, Troy."

I couldn't. All of a sudden his voice was bouncing and the sand was undulating in waves. Everything had a rolling glow around it. "You better talk faster," I said, rubbing at the shadows moving across my eyes. "Or I'm going to black out before you spit out anything close to important."

"If, for instance," he said impatiently, "I were to take *Kayn'l*, it would render my connection to Reth inactive. Once the drug was purged from my body, the link would mend itself. But if I remained on it indefinitely, his absence would begin to feel permanent, as if he was dead—as if half my soul had died inside me." Draken ran a thoughtful hand over his chin. "Of course the ensuing mental injury is only a rumor. No one knows what the loss of a joined soul would do. The type of bonding we've taken part in hasn't been done in centuries. Still, such prolonged isolation would undoubtedly have a profound effect. Not true insanity like I knew, but an internal blackness. A pain so acute it would change a person. Harden them. Burrow emptiness in so deep it might never go away." Draken made a concerned face. "Slightly tragic, don't you think?"

I struggled to sit up. "You're giving Jarryd *Kayn'l*."

"Glad to see you're following along. Though, as a prisoner of war, that drug is the least of his worries...unless you secure his release. Perhaps, by offering me something in exchange?"

My reply was a pain-filled, angry laugh. It wasn't for Draken. It was more of a self-directed hostility for how I'd stupidly followed every step my father had laid out for me. I'd done exactly as he predicted, right from the beginning.

Almost.

With an unsteady hand, I reached for the stone around my neck. I gave it a sharp tug, and the cord broke. I hesitated briefly. Then I flung the black shard down in the sand between us.

Draken stared at it. His eyes lifted to mine. "No clever comment? No crude jest?"

"I'm all out. But if you come a little closer I'll shove it up your ass."

Grinning, his gaze dropped back to the shard. I half expected a spot of drool to form in the corner of his mouth. *If he were Shinree he'd look a little less excited,* I thought. But being merely a greedy man, Draken had no clue the stone he was coveting was the wrong one. The piece of the crown he wanted so badly was in Kabri. By now, it was at the bottom of the sea, or smashed into a thousand pieces. My instructions for Liel were to destroy it if he could, keep it safe if he couldn't. I didn't really care what he did with it, as long as no other living soul knew where it was.

It was a decent plan. At least, it had been. If I'd kept my cool instead of losing it over Neela, I might have managed to strike a deal with Draken. Now that I'd fucked everything up, all I could hope was that I'd bleed out before my father realized what I'd done.

"Let them go," I said. It was futile at this point, but I still tried. "Release Neela and Jarryd, and you can have me and the piece that completes the crown."

"I already have you. And them." Draken scooped up the obsidian so fast sand sprayed us both. "And now I have the stone." He clenched it tight in his grip. "I hope you enjoy pain, Troy, because I have waited so long to personally cut that flip tongue from your mouth."

"Yet you won't. You'll go on like you have been, holing up in Darkhorne, hiding under Reth's skirt."

"Better than you, hiding behind the truth. Your soul is as black as those streaks in your hair. Just like your father."

Bent, weak and trembling, I shouted at him. "I am not my father! If I could drain Jem Reth's blood out of me, I would do so right now."

"What a lovely idea. But it's not your father's blood that concerns me."

I opened my mouth to reply—and toppled over.

Suddenly, the sun was too bright. My eyes were too heavy.

"Fetch our guest a drink," Draken said, glancing over his shoulder. "Until recently, Troy," he said, looking back at me, "I had no idea you were such a prize. The gods themselves must have guided Jem's seed the night he lay down with V'loria. Or your people's loins are simply more finicky than we thought."

"What the hell are you talking about?"

"Blood, I believe."

Neela interrupted. A metal jug in her hand, she sat down and lifted my head onto her lap. The sour wine she offered turned my stomach, but I was so parched, as she put the jug to my mouth, I pulled in great gulps.

Gently, her hand smoothed the hair off my forehead. "Forgive me," she said.

There was way too much guilt in her voice.

Swallowing, I looked at her. It was on her face too.

I pushed the wine away. "You wanted me to follow you. You led me here," I said, louder as it started to make sense. "You led me to *him*."

"I had no choice."

"Like hell you didn't."

"The cost of harboring you was a hundred Rellan lives a day. I couldn't...." her voice cracking, Neela shrugged regretfully. "After the cave, when I woke up in the castle, there was a dispatch from Draken insisting on your confinement. He made the consequences quite clear. I wanted them to take you when you were still unconscious. It would have been easier that way. But Draken maintained you must give up the stone freely. He said we had to find your," her lips trembled, "breaking point." Neela tried to shake off her distress. "I had to get you out of Kabri. Malaq would never have let me turn you over."

Relief dulled the pain. "Malaq isn't a part of this?"

"My cousin truly believed he could keep you safe in Kabri. But I've felt what's inside you, Ian. I knew you couldn't let me go." Neela dipped her head down to rest against mine. "Life will be different for you now. But Draken has promised you will be well cared for." I choked on my amusement, and her head bolted up. "My husband will honor our agreement, Ian. He signed an accord."

I full out laughed then, until the pain was such that I couldn't breathe.

Dismayed, Neela said again, adamantly, "He signed an accord."

"Great," I gasped. "Then I have nothing to worry about."

As doubt clouded her eyes, Draken reached down and yanked Neela to her feet. "Hands off the new slave, love." He removed the crown from his head and gave it to her. "Go," he said, shoving her away. "Take this inside and wait for me."

Neela didn't argue. She walked off and didn't look back, and I found a kind of twisted comfort in the ignorance that was coming. *At least I won't know. Draken can do what he likes with her. He can destroy the world, and I won't have to know. I won't have to care what he does.*

Or what I've done.

"They kept the truth from you," Draken said, hovering. "It's what they do. Raynan, Aylagar, my wife. They were all terrified of what knowledge would make you become. Of what would happen if you found out how long and deep the betrayal ran. But there's no harm now. What anger you can manage will fade with the *Kayn'l.*" Studying me, his eyes flashed. "Do you know what your mother's greatest flaw was?"

I winced through a shrug. "Bad taste in men?"

"Trust," he sneered. "V'loria believed every lie the Rellans told her. She thought she was a simple village girl with a family. She believed herself a healer because she was raised by a healer. She was trained as one. Told her name designated her as one. The poor woman never sought to be anything more."

"My mother was… She…" my thoughts flew away. I tried to gather them back. "She had a sister." The details escaped me. My awareness kept pausing and starting.

"Your mother had no siblings. V'loria was given to that family to bring up as their own. I have no doubt they were well compensated. Seeing as they were caring for an erudite."

"What? No…" I struggled to speak, to keep up, but I was like grains of sand on a beach, helpless to fight the waves as they swept up and out, carrying pieces of me away.

"When your father found the records of V'loria's birth and discovered her true lineage, how the Rellans had covered it up, the lies they spun…it all made sense then. The uproar her pregnancy created, the reason the Arcana's let you live—your correlation to the crown. But it was quite a blow. All that power he wasted when he killed her. Then he realized what it meant for you. He realized what you are."

"I'm…" I couldn't say it. "I can't be."

"Sure you can," Draken smiled hungrily. "An erudite line trumps all others, so breeding with them only ends one way. Yet, it appears, the few erudite babes born since the empire fell were all female. A male child, such as you, is rare and valuable indeed."

I shoved the words out. "No. I carry a soldier's blood. That's what I am. That's all I am."

"The crown is turning your father into something quite frightening, Troy, but not you. An erudite was its creator. It recognizes that distinction in you. That's why Reth sent his pretty pale witch to you in Kael. He whipped up an allurement spell, something to make Sienn believe you two were fated. He was hoping nature would take its course."

"Why?"

"Why would Reth care if you fucked her?" Draken bent down and cuffed me in the head. "Pay attention! He was hoping to create that which hadn't existed in over five hundred years. A child with limitless magical potential. A child of two erudite. Your child, Troy," he said, hitting me again. "Yours and Sienn's." He backed off. "But you couldn't even do that right." Draken dangled the obsidian shard in my face. "You're going to tell your father how to fix the Crown of Stones. And I wouldn't disappoint him. He's not too happy with you right now." With a jerk of his head, he said, "Take him. Before he passes out and pisses himself on my doorstep."

Soldiers surrounded me. They pried the sword from my hand, picked up my feet, and dragged me away. The dry ground seemed to rush by forever. Sun burned in my open wounds. Dust piled up in my throat and eyes. My head, bouncing on the ground, was pounding by the time we stopped.

Abruptly, my captors jerked me up straight. They slammed my back against a fence post, shoved a fist in my stomach, and I was back on the ground.

A bucket of water in my face later, they were tying me to the post. I didn't fight it. I was grateful for the ropes to hold me up because I couldn't. Everything around me was distorted and blurry. The shouting in the pen behind me sounded miles away. One of the prisoners, a small child, pushed his head through the fence and stared at me. Smudge-faced and skinny, his vacant eyes were somber. He watched the soldiers tear open my shirt and press a thick, black paste into the wound on my side. I screamed, and his expression went unchanged.

They pressed in more. Blood bubbled out with the pressure. It mixed with the *Kayn'l* and streaked black over my skin.

"Disgraceful," a man said.

Blinking, I looked at him. Standing off to the side, his white angry gaze peered out from inside the hood of his cloak. His hands protruded from the garment's long sleeves. His flesh was a murky blend of twisted color that was in no way natural.

I shrunk when he came near me.

Grabbing a handful of hair, he yanked my head up. "Idiots," he scolded, glancing behind him. "I wanted him coherent." Whipping back around to me, the man's hood fell off. He was bald underneath and his head, face, and neck were mottled in a swirling chaos of ugly, muddy hues. They were like his hands, only worse. "Who am I?" he said. I pulled away and he struck me. "Don't do that! Look at me!"

I did. "What do you want?"

"Not this. Never this. But you brought us here, son. You destroyed us both. You took something from me when you took the crown's power. You weakened my spells." The painted man made a wide, sweeping gesture at the army. "Look at them! Rancid, festering…I couldn't even resurrect them properly." His colorless eyes tensed. "Fix it. Repair the crown, L'tarian. I *need* that power back."

"Go away."

"You and I—we lost everything. Neela is with Draken. Sienn betrayed us equally. Without the Crown of Stones, creating a new empire will be most difficult. And you, my only son, have fallen to the level of common breeding stock." He stared at me, enraged. Then his fury died with a sigh. "Maybe it's for the best. To truly appreciate freedom you must know what it's like to live without it. After all, slavery is the ultimate magic-price." He leaned close and shouted at me. "What is your name? Who is Neela Arcana? Do you know what happened here? How many people you killed?"

Panic woke me up. "I killed someone?"

"That's right," he said smoothly. "You're a murderer. You've been found guilty and will be punished for your crimes. Only through pain will you atone and earn the gods' forgiveness." The colors on his face seemed to run together as he grinned. Resting my head back on the pole, he spoke to one of the soldiers. "I want a guard on watch at all times. And get rid of his horse. Send it into the desert. Something will eat it."

He answered, "Yes, Lord Reth," and moved off. Another stayed behind. He handed the one called Reth a wooden grip with a silver chain. I followed the chain back to where it wrapped around the neck of a tall, thin woman in a filthy dress. Strands of bedraggled white hair hung about her dirty face. Matted clumps stuck wet and red to a large bloody gash on the side of her head.

Her eyes, like his, also lacked color. There was an unfocused quality about them. But when they looked at me, I had the urge to touch her.

482

"I'm sorry," she said to me, slow and trembling. "I wouldn't have hurt you. I just couldn't let you kill him. And now… I didn't know he was this far gone. I didn't think he would…" she drew a rough breath. "I'm sorry. Gods, Ian, I am so sorry."

"Sienn," Reth barked. "I said you could see him, not talk."

I whispered the name he called her. "Sienn." Reth looked startled, but it seemed to make the woman feel better; hopeful, almost. "It's alright," I told her. "I killed someone. I deserve to be punished for my crime."

"No." Teary-eyed, Sienn shook her head. The hope I saw in her, vanished. "Don't listen to him, Ian. Don't believe him. He lies—he fucking lies!"

"Enough!" Reth tugged sharply on the chain and led Sienn off.

Fighting him, reaching back to me, she cried, "I'll find a way out of this, Ian. I swear. No matter how lost you feel, just hold on. Promise me, you will hold on!"

"I promise," I said, but I didn't know what it meant. I didn't understand why the woman cared. I didn't know her. I had no idea who Ian was, or why he should be so lost.

None of her words made sense.

Yet, something made me follow Sienn's pale, desperate gaze until I couldn't see it anymore. And when she was gone, I closed my eyes and saw hers in the dark.

They were sad, compelling, beautiful eyes. I didn't want to let them go.

But as hard as I tried, I couldn't hold onto them.

I couldn't hold onto me.

EPILOGUE

A hand struck my face. "Wake up."

It came at me again, and I grabbed it. It was soft and small. *A woman.*

I let her go. I spent a moment coughing the dust from my lungs. "I felt that," I said, clearing my throat, "when you slapped me. Why is it strange that I felt that?"

"Can you stand?" she said. "We don't have much time."

I shoved the hair out of my face and sat up. Rocks and dirt covered me. I pushed the debris away and squinted at her through the haze. It was so thick I could barely see her. "What happened?"

"The mine collapsed."

I looked around. There was nothing but dust and shadows. "Was anyone hurt?"

"Yes." Grunting, she helped me to my feet. "This way."

We moved into a tunnel. It was low and tight. A faint glow lit the distance.

"I don't understand," I said. "Where are the guards?"

"Dead. But more are coming."

"Wait." I stopped. "You don't belong here. Who are you?"

"That doesn't matter. Just keep going. We'll be out soon."

"I can't leave. I'm not supposed to. This is where I live."

"Here?" she snapped, spinning around. "In these rocks? These caves?"

"I…?"

She rushed toward me. Strands of long white hair blew back from her face. Her eyes were swirling with a dozen different colors. "Do you know what goes on in this place? What they've done to you? What they made you do?"

I couldn't grasp why she was upset. "No."

"You will. And when the drug is gone, you'll wish you could forget."

"How long have I been here?"

She hesitated. "Too long."

"Then my sentence is over? I've paid for my crimes? Reth says—"

"Jem Reth says a lot of things. Few of them are true." The woman drew a frustrated breath. "You aren't here because you broke the law. You're here because you're a threat to him, and to Draken."

"King Draken? I know him. He asks me questions. He gets mad when I don't answer."

"Yes. He does." Her head fell slightly. She made an odd sound.

"Are you crying?" I raised a hand to her cheek.

"Don't," she hissed, pulling away.

"I'm sorry. I don't know why I did that."

"We have a man in the prison. He's been adjusting your dose of *Kayn'l.* You're having moments of…sporadic clarity," she said kindly. "I can't explain right now."

I heard footsteps. "The guards are coming. I should go find them."

"Those aren't guards. They're with me. And they're risking their lives to get you out of here. So you need to move."

"You have the wrong man. Why would anyone take risks for me? I'm just a—"

"What, Ian? A slave? A soldier? A magic user?" Her breathy voice turned ominous. "You have no idea what's inside you."

I clenched my scarred, calloused hands shut. Blood dripped from fresh cuts across my knuckles. "This is all that's inside me."

"With this," she said, squeezing my hands, "you could build an empire."

Her eyes, I thought. I couldn't stop staring at them. Even as she let me go and her gaze wandered, I tried to get it back. "Who are you?" I asked again.

"Sienn," she said, quiet and reluctant. "I was here too, for a time. I know what you're going through. And I know you don't believe me, but…"

"Are they true? These things you're saying about me?"

"Yes. Outside these walls, people are counting on you, Ian. They need you. They care about you. This isn't where you belong."

Muffled shouts escaped the gloom behind me. The sounds of approach in front grew louder. From the same direction, only closer, sparks of colored light glinted off the walls. Growing steadily brighter, they followed the natural arch of the tunnel, flickering and pulsing to form what resembled a door.

Sienn stepped toward it anxiously. Then she paused and turned back. "I asked you once to join me. You had a dozen different reasons for saying no. But things have changed. And the *Kayn'l* has wiped you clean. There's nothing to sway your decision. No magic, no love, or suspicion. No guilt or responsibility. This time you choose by instinct alone." Sienn held out her hand. "Come with me, Ian. Take back your life. Free the Shinree. Give us a home."

Home, I thought.

The word pulled at me. Suddenly it was all wrong; this place, me.

I felt aimless. Adrift.

Unnerved, I looked at her. "I don't know where home is."

"Neither do I," she said sadly. "But I know it isn't here."

"You're right. It isn't." I took Sienn's hand, and I stopped drifting.

Made in the USA
San Bernardino, CA
10 August 2016